The Real People
Book Ten

D1491055

CHEROKEE DRAGON

*Also by Robert J. Conley*

The Rattlesnake Band and Other Stories
Back to Malachi
The Actor
The Witch of Goingsnake and Other Stories
Wilder and Wilder
Killing Time
Colfax
Quitting Time
The Saga of Henry Starr
Go-Ahead Rider
Ned Christie's War
Strange Company
Border Line
The Long Trail North
Nickajack
Mountain Windsong
Crazy Snake


*The Real People*

The Way of the Priests
The Dark Way
The White Path
The Way South
The Long Way Home
The Dark Island
The War Trail North
The Peace Chief
War Woman
Cherokee Dragon

# CHEROKEE DRAGON

A Novel of the Real People

Robert J. Conley

UNIVERSITY OF OKLAHOMA PRESS
*Norman*

Library of Congress Cataloging-in-Publication Data

Conley, Robert J.
    Cherokee Dragon : a novel of the Real People / Robert J. Conley.
        p.    cm.
    ISBN 978-0-8061-3370-6 (paper)
    1. Dragging Canoe, d. 1792 — Fiction.    2. Cherokee Indians —
Kings and rulers — Fiction.    3. Cherokee Indians — Fiction.
I. Title.

PS3553.O494 C47 2001
813'.54 — dc21

                                                    2001027567

The paper in this book meets the guidelines for permanence and
durability of the Committee on Production Guidelines for Book
Longevity of the Council on Library Resources, Inc. ∞

Copyright © 2000 by Robert J. Conley. Published by the University
of Oklahoma Press, Norman, Publishing Division of the University,
by arrangement with St. Martin's Press, LLC. All rights reserved.
Manufactured in the U.S.A. First printing of the Red River Books
edition, 2001.

# CHEROKEE DRAGON

# Introductory Note

One of the great figures in Cherokee history, Dragging Canoe (Tsiyu Gansini) has been sometimes maligned by historians and otherwise relegated to near obscurity in scholarly journals. One likely reason for that is that Dragging Canoe rose to prominence during the American Revolution and, because of the circumstances of the time, was set against the rebellious colonies during that turbulent period. Patriotism, it would seem, has demanded over the years that all enemies of the revolution be deemed—by historians of the United States—monsters, madmen, or at the least, villains. Perhaps. Yet Tecumseh, who grew out of the same grand scheme that was developed by Dragging Canoe and who also fought with the British against the United States, has not been dealt with thus.

Perhaps the fact that the Cherokees, in the minds of so many people, are regarded highly as a "civilized" Indian tribe has something to do with Americans' not wanting to acknowledge the greatness of Dragging Canoe. His cousin Nancy Ward is seen as a friend of the white Americans and a proponent of progress. Since Dragging Canoe and she did not agree, he must be seen, I suppose, as her opposite.

Whatever the reason, Dragging Canoe certainly deserves a place in history and in our hearts and minds alongside other great Native leaders who defended their soil and their ways of life by resisting the encroachment of foreigners on their land. Because of that, I have long felt the need for a new treatment of the life and career of Dragging Canoe in a popular format. In following such a course, even having exhausted the resources for information, I found it necessary to use a considerable amount of imagination to fill in some gaps. Such is always the case with historical fiction, but I hope that where I have done that, the depiction is true to the times and to the people. Such has been my intention.

There may be some who will quarrel with the characterizations I have given certain historical figures. My only defense is that I gave the characters such qualities as the historical record indicated to me. My particular point of view and bias is decidedly and unashamedly Cherokee and, more specifically, pro Dragging Canoe and the Chickamaugan movement.

Dragging Canoe was certainly on target when he predicted that there was a danger that some day nothing would be left of Native People but their "names imperfectly recorded." The evidence of his startling foresight is in the historical records, where history has left us with such names as Moytoy, Amouskossittee, Attacullaculla, Cotetoy, Cunecote, Totaiahoi, and many others, equally un-Cherokee in appearance and unpronounceable to a Cherokee speaker. Where close examination of these names, or research, or the help of fluent speakers of the Cherokee language has allowed me to arrive at the probable original from which these atrocities were arrived, I have used that probable original name in my text. For example, I have used 'Ma'dohi rather than Moytoy, Ada-gal'kala rather than Attacullaculla, and so on. Explanations are provided in the glossary following the text. Where I have been unable to untangle an incorrectly recorded name, I have used the corrupt form and made a note of it in the glossary.

In my search for the proper form of names as well as in examining the history and the lives of the people involved in this story, I have relied heavily on the following texts: *History of the Cherokee Indians* by Emmet Starr; *The Cherokees* by Grace Steele Woodward; *The Dividing Paths* by Tom Hartley; *Historical Sketch of the Cherokee* by James Mooney; "Notable Persons in Cherokee History: Attakullakulla" by James C. Kelly, "The Battle of Lookout Mountain: An Eyewitness Account" by George Christian, edited by E. Raymond Evans, "The Counsel of Caleb Starr" by Jim Stokely, all in *Journal of Cherokee Studies*. Volume

III, No. 1; "Notable Persons in Cherokee History: Dragging Canoe" by E. Raymond Evans, in *Journal of Cherokee Studies.* Volume II, No. 1; *Weaving New Worlds* by Sarah H. Hill; *The Southern Indians* by R. S. Cotterill; *When Shall They Rest* by Peter Collier; "Oconostota" by James C. Kelly in *Journal of Cherokee Studies.* Volume III, No. 4; "Notable Persons in Cherokee History: Bob Benge" by E. Raymond Evans, in *Journal of Cherokee Studies.* Volume I, No. 2; *Heart of the Eagle: Dragging Canoe and the Emergence of the Chickamauga Confederacy* by Brent Yanusdi Cox; *John Ross: Cherokee Chief* by Gary E. Moulton; *Adair's History of the American Indians* edited by Samuel Cole Williams; *History of the Indian Tribes of the United States* by Henry Schoolcraft; *Treaties and Agreements of the Five Civilized Tribes* by the Institute for the Development of Indian Law.

For cultural and ethnological information, *Myths of the Cherokee and Sacred Formulas of the Cherokee* by James Mooney; *The Swimmer Manuscript: Cherokee Sacred Formulas and Medicinal Prescriptions* by James Mooney; *Cherokee Dance and Drama* by Frank G. Speck and Leonard Broom in collaboration with Will West Long; *Fire and the Spirits* by Rennard Strickland; *A Law of Blood* by John Phillip Reid; *The Cherokee Perspective* by Laurence French and Jim Hornbuckle; *The Southeastern Indians* by Charles Hudson.

For language, *Cherokee-English Dictionary* by Durbin Feeling, edited by William Pulte; *Dictionary of the Cherokee Language* compiled by J. T. Alexander; *How to Talk Trash in Cherokee* by Don Grooms and John Oocumma; and Mooney's glossary for *Myths.*

In addition, I am greatly in debt to my good friends Tom Belt, Gregg Howard, and Tommy Wildcat for their valuable assistance with the Cherokee language, and to Earnie Frost, Wilma Mankiller, Brent Cox, Chad Smith, Murv Jacob, and others for fascinating and useful discussions on Cherokee history and culture. There are probably others I should have named here, and for any such lapses of memory, I sincerely apologize.

And of course and always to my lovely wife, Guwisti, for gracefully putting up with the life of a writer.

Robert J. Conley
Tahlequah

PART ONE

# Genesis

# 1

*1737*
*at Tanaɘe in the Overhillɘ of the Cherokee Nation*
*(in what iɘ now Tenneɘɘee)*

Ada-gal'kala sat in the townhouse at Tanase. He sat quietly and alone and smoked ancient tobacco from a short-stemmed clay pipe. Other men from time to time tried to engage him in casual conversation, but to no avail. His mind was elsewhere. He was generally recognized as the second man in the Cherokee Nation, and he longed to rise to the highest position. 'Ma'dohi had been named "Emperor of the Cherokees" by the English, and many of the other Cherokees had casually accepted that designation. They, of course, did not recognize "Moytoy," as the English stupidly called him, as "emperor" in the English sense of that word, did not even fully understand what the English meant by the word, but they did seem sometimes to act as if the man were the "Principal Chief" of all the chiefs of the whole nation. Even that was a new concept to the Cherokees, who had existed for as long as anyone could remember in autonomous towns, each with its own two chiefs—the war chief and the peace chief. Now, because of the English, they were beginning to act as if 'Ma'dohi really was the "Principal Chief" over all of the Cherokee Nation. Ada-gal'kala wanted that distinction for himself.

And because of that strong desire, he thought about other things, things that would help him rise to the eminence he so desired. He thought about the British with their colonies so close to the Cherokees and their constant demand for more land, and he thought about their rivals the French. He considered ways of dealing with both nations of invaders that would work out to his own benefit. And then there were the Spaniards. They too might prove to be useful one day. He considered all these things.

But his mind was also somewhat occupied with the more immediate reality that, at just that moment, his wife Ni-on-e was involved with her clanswomen, giving birth. He hoped that she would have a son. Given the new circumstances of the Cherokees, a son would be more useful to him than would a daughter, for if Ada-gal'kala should achieve his goal of becoming the next "emperor," then a son would be there in later years to succeed him in that exalted position, a position that, Ada-gal'kala was certain, would become more and more important as time passed.

All this, of course, was contrary to ancient Cherokee practices and beliefs, he knew, but he also knew that things were changing. Cherokee women were not quite so powerful as they had once been, and the practice of passing things down through the mothers was being constantly violated. The women complained about the loss of their old prerogatives, but it seemed that there was not much they could do about it. The outside influence of the British was just too strong. Some Cherokee women had actually married white men, usually marriages sanctioned by their fathers to solidify trade relationships with the colonies, and their children were carrying the surnames of their fathers, the traders. This was in direct conflict with the old practices dictated by the Cherokee matrilineal clan system, a system in which descent was traced strictly through female lines.

Not only was the idea of central government developing and being accepted, not only were the towns slowly but surely giving up their autonomy, and the women watching their own authority gradually erode, but the influence of the English had brought other changes as well, changes to almost every aspect of Cherokee life.

Hunters now hunted for hides for the trade business, and women spent much of their time in the preparation of the hides. Hunting had become a commercial pursuit, a small industry involving both men and women. Because of its intensity, game was getting scarce, and hunters had to move out farther and farther all the time in search of their prey. Many trade items had all but killed off traditional occupations. Steel pots were replacing traditional clay pottery. English weapons were replacing traditional weaponry. Many of the craftspeople were no longer engaged in their traditional crafts. And the people were allowing all of these things to happen. Perhaps it simply didn't mean much to them one way or the other. Perhaps the changes had all been so gradual that they didn't really seem to have any effect on their daily lives. Only the women complained, and only some of the women, some of the time. As for the "emperor," let the English call him what they will. Let 'Ma'dohi puff up his chest and strut around his town.

Ada-gal'kala knew all this, and he also felt certain that he could take advantage of these changes for his own good. It would take patience and diplomacy, but he had those two qualities in abundance. He had watched the Englishmen closely for some years now, and he had learned their language. Along with six other young Cherokee men, he had actually traveled across the great water all the way to England seven years ago, in the year the white men called 1730, and he had met the great King George II, face-to-face. In those days Ada-gal'kala had been known as Uku-unega, the White Owl, and the English, in their famous inability or stubborn refusal to speak properly the words of the Cherokee language, had called him "Owen Nakan" and given him the title of "captain." He had been presented to the king as Captain Owen Nakan.

And he and the others with him had signed a paper with the King's men while they were there. The English had called the paper the Articles of Agreement, and with the words on the paper, the Cherokees had promised to trade only with the English. They had also promised that should the English and the French get themselves into a war, the Cherokees would fight on the side of the

English. Of course, they had known that they could speak only for themselves, not for all of the Cherokees. Just a year ago, when the French emissaries had come to the Cherokees seeking an alliance similar to the Articles, Ada-gal'kala had remembered his trip to England. He had remembered signing the Articles, and he would have nothing to do with the Frenchmen. He had urged other Cherokees to ignore them as well.

And this in spite of the fact that two years back, when the funny little white man, Christian Priber, had come to live with them, Ada-gal'kala, along with others, had befriended him. Priber, who called himself the secretary to the "Emperor Moytoy," was helping Ada-gal'kala with his English and his French and was even teaching him to read and write some. The English were afraid of Priber and hated him. They called him a German and a Jesuit, but they believed him to be an agent of the French, and Priber had indeed introduced Ada-gal'kala and others to various Frenchmen from their fort, which they called Toulouse, in the heart of the country of the Ani-Gusa, the Muskogee People, the people the English were calling Creeks, the near neighbors and sometime enemies of the Cherokees. On reflection, Ada-gal'kala thought that perhaps Priber was working for the French, but what did he care? French, English, what did it matter? They were all foreigners and invaders, and as far as Ada-gal'kala was concerned, were to be called friends only when such a relationship would benefit the Cherokees—or when it would be to his own personal benefit.

Ada-gal'kala called Priber friend and used Priber for his own benefit, but the great War Chief, Ogan'sdo', on the other hand, the old friend and sometime rival of Ada-gal'kala, had, it seemed, fallen completely under the spell of Priber. It didn't matter to Ogan'sdo' that Priber was proposing a new form of government for the Cherokees and that he was pressing for an alliance with the French. Ogan'sdo' could see nothing but good in the man. He seemed to stand in awe of the funny little man and his powers, which included putting words on paper to be read later. He had learned the Cherokee language, and he could write words in

French or English or Cherokee. Any time that Ada-gal'kala went to visit Priber, Ogan'sdo' was jealous. Ada-gal'kala could tell.

And Ada-gal'kala had learned a great deal from Priber, too, to add to the knowledge he had gained on his trip to England. He had become quite knowledgeable about both the French and the English, and so he was certain that there was no man other than himself in the entire Cherokee Nation better equipped to deal with the white invaders or to lead the new government, whatever form it might take. He was in a very good position, indeed, one from which he and his family should profit well.

He well knew that there were those Cherokees around who were suspicious of his motives, but he had no fear of them, for they also knew that they needed him to talk to the English for them. They were incapable of doing it for themselves. Those jealous and suspicious ones said of his name, which translated into English as "the Leaning Wood," that it meant there was no telling which way he would lean on any given issue, that he might lean one way one day and the other way the next. The English took his name very differently. They called him "the Little Carpenter" because they said that he was so skilled in crafting a bargain. He liked that interpretation.

In the *osi*, the small, dome-shaped winter house that stood beside the larger *gahl'jodi*, or main dwelling, owned by Ni-on-e, the wife of Ada-gal'kala was on her hands and knees, her legs spread wide. Four old women of her clan were in there with her. Outside, an old man stood and chanted toward the east.

"Hey, you little man," he said, "come down out of there in a hurry. Right now. An ugly old woman is coming to get you. Come out and get your bow and your arrows. Now. *Yu.*"

He walked a quarter of the way around the *osi*, stopped, facing the north, and repeated the charm. He walked another quarter and spoke to the west. Then he moved to the south and recited the formula once more. He moved back to the place from which he had begun and prepared himself to circle the *osi* once more, this time preparing to call out to a little girl, but before he could begin, an old woman poked her head out of the *osi.*

"It's done," she said. "It's a ballsticks."

The old man turned and walked toward the townhouse. The old woman disappeared back into the *osi.* Inside, she was one of the four old women in attendance. Another one, just behind Ni-on-e, was holding the howling infant boy in a white cloth, while yet a third was busy tying and cutting the cord. That task accomplished, she busied herself cleaning the mother, who had already been helped into a position half sitting, half lying down on her back by one of the others. The woman with the baby bathed it and wrapped it in a fresh cloth, then sat down against the wall to hold it.

Ni-on-e smiled and looked at her son while the old woman bathed her. "Has someone gone to tell my husband?" she asked.

"The old man outside has gone," said one of the old women.

Ni-on-e leaned back to relax. She was relieved to have it over with and to see that she had given birth to a healthy boy. She had felt confident, for she had done everything that she was supposed to do to ensure success. Upon her first realization that she was with child, she had told her husband and her friends about it. Thereafter she had been taken to the water with every new moon to bathe and to pray.

The first time, she had gone with Ada-gal'kala, her mother, her mother's sister, and an old conjurer. Ada-gal'kala had given the conjurer two beads, a red one and a black one, and a length of white thread. He had laid these out on a piece of white calico the length of his arm. Then with everyone standing on the riverbank, facing the water, the old conjurer, with the red bead held between the thumb and index finger of his right hand, the black bead held similarly in his left, had recited his formula:

*"Ha,"* he said. "Now the white thread has come down. The soul of the small human being has been examined there where it is growing. Soon he will come and be born to her. He has been examined.

"Now from up above, you have caused the white threads to come down. His soul has been examined. Now it has come to rest on the white thread. His soul has been lifted up as far as the upper world.

"In the Seventh world above, the white seats have been let down and the white cloth has come to rest on them, and his soul has come to rest on the white thread. At the Seventh world, his soul will appear in all its splendor."

While he spoke, the beads had begun to quiver and then to move, seemingly of their own volition, first the black, and then the red. By the time he had finished, the red bead had become very active, dancing along the entire length of his right index finger. That had been the first sign of success. That had been Ni-on-e's first reassurance that all would be well.

The old conjurer had then strung the two beads on the white thread and dropped them back onto the white cloth. Then he had taken Ni-on-e and the others all into the water. When they came out again, Ada-gal'kala had folded the white cloth, enclosing the thread and the beads, picked up the bundle, and given it to the conjurer. The conjurer had taken it away with him. They had followed this same ritual at each new moon, Ada-gal'kala supplying new beads, thread, and cloth for each, and each time the red bead had danced between the thumb and index finger of the old man. Each time the ritual had predicted a successful birth.

And there had been more. Throughout the time of her pregnancy, Ni-on-e had from time to time drunk teas made of *ðawuhjila* to make it easy for the child to come out, of *walelu uh natsi luhgisði* to frighten the child and make it come out, of the roots of *ganuhgwa ðliski* and of the cones of *notsi*, both evergreens, to impart their qualities of long life and lasting good health.

She had been careful about the food she ate. She had eaten no *saloli*, for if she had, the child might want to go up instead of down, and it might lie in her womb bunched up like a squirrel. She did not eat *ðuhðisði*, lest her child die. She had eaten no *kubli*, for if she had, the child would likely develop the infant's disease they called *wanigisti*, or "something is eating them." *Atj'a* would have given her infant black spots on his face, so she had left that alone. The meat of *tsisðu* would have given it large eyes which would stay open

*9*

when it slept. *Tsisduh* because it runs backward would have caused the child to back up in the womb instead of coming out when it should. She had left all of these foods alone during the entire term of her pregnancy.

Nor had she eaten the flesh of any animal killed by gunshot or bowshot but only those caught in snares or clubbed. She had been very careful about all these things and about other kinds of things as well. She had allowed no woman in her bleeding time of month to come into her home and visit her. She had not lingered in or near any doorways. Every morning she had gone to the creek to bathe her hands, face, and feet in the clear, fresh running water. She had not combed her hair backward, nor worn a scarf around her neck or a belt around her waist. She had taken care not to look upon a corpse and not to attend any dances where masks were worn.

Ada-gal'kala too had been forced to observe certain restrictions. He had not attended any funerals. Like his wife, he had not worn any scarves around his neck or belts around his waist. He had gone in and out of doors quickly. When Ni-on-e had needed to go outside during the night, he had gone with her, and he had gone with her to the stream every morning.

Ni-on-e looked with pleasure on her healthy son, who was still yowling in the arms of the old woman, and she thought about all the precautions she and her husband had taken for those long months, and she thought that it had all been well worth while. She would have done more, much more, for such a healthy son.

Back at the townhouse, the old conjurer walked in and found Ada-gal'kala still waiting there patiently. "It's over," he said. "Your wife has given out with a baby boy. Go now and do what you must do." Ada-gal'kala thanked the old man, left the townhouse, and walked in a fast pace to the *osi* beside the house of his wife. He stood outside and called out, "I'm here." One of the four old women came out and handed him a small bundle in a white cloth. He knew that the bundle contained the placenta from the recent birth. He

10

thanked her, took it, and turned to walk away. He walked out of Tanase, looking back over his shoulder frequently to make sure that he was not being watched or followed. Safely out of town, he walked over two hills.

He stood for a moment looking around again to make sure that he was alone and unwatched. Then he knelt and scooped out a hole in the ground. He placed the small bundle down in the hole and covered it. "I'll have another one two years from now," he said in a whisper. Then he went back to town by a different route.

Back at the *osi* one of the old women gave the new little human being a name, but it was mostly called *usdi* by everyone around. When it grew larger, it would be called *'chooch'*. Some day, when he had grown even more and when he had developed his own distinctive personality or done something of note, he would be given yet another name, one which he would carry with him for the rest of his life.

# 2

*1738*

The *usdi* was but one year old when his father's sister, Tame Doe, gave birth to a little girl. They called the new girl child Nanyehi. Tame Doe and her husband had observed all the same precautions as had Ni-on-e and Ada-gal'kala, and their new little girl was healthy and strong. That same year a terrible disease struck the Cherokee settlements. The conjurers and doctors had never seen this disease before. It was something new and frightening, something that they had no experience of and therefore no cure for. The people stricken by this dread disease became feverish and frequently vomited. Horrible pustular eruptions developed on their faces and bodies. Not knowing what else to do, the doctors prescribed plunges in the cold streams for their patients. When that failed, they put them in the small *osis* and gave them sweat baths. The treatments did no good, and the awful pestilence spread rapidly from town to town, and many people suffered, and many died.

At last James Adair and other white men living among them, mostly traders, identified the scourge as smallpox, a disease brought into Charlestown with the black slaves and then spread in the Cherokee country by infected trade goods. Even so, the doctors proclaimed that the horror had been sent among them because of the misbehavior of many of the young people who had become sexually promiscuous. Since their promiscuous activities had been engaged in mostly at night, the doctors had made them lie on the ground at night and had poured cold water on them. This too had failed.

Some patients were then given sweat baths and taken immediately to the nearest river or stream and plunged into the cold water where they died at once. The people began to lose faith in their doctors and conjurers, and the doctors and conjurers, completely at a loss and no longer held in esteem by the people, decided that they must have been stripped of their powers. They smashed the pots that held their herbs and the pots in which they boiled their medicines. They broke or burned their wands and hoops and feathers, all their professional paraphernalia, and many of them cut their own throats in shame and despair.

Many of the people, now horribly scarred by the terrible disease, looking into mirrors at their disfigured faces, threw themselves off mountainsides, or shot or stabbed themselves. Some even flung themselves into flames, screaming and filling the air with the pungent odor of burning flesh.

Ada-gal'kala hurried up to Ni-on-e's house. He did not bother going inside or even poking his head in the door. He stood outside and called his wife by name. She answered him, but her voice was weak. "Bring the *usdi*," he said, "and come with me." She stepped out the door with her child in her arms.

"He's not well," she said, and her face was drawn with worry and pain.

"Come on," said Ada-gal'kala. He took her by the arm and started to walk, but she held back.

"Where?" she asked. "Where are we going?"

"We're going away from here," he said. "Somewhere away from this white man's disease."

"Let me pack some things," she said.

"No," said Ada-gal'kala. "The smallpox is on everything here. Leave it all. Come on now. Maybe we can save our lives. If we stay here, we'll all die."

Still she hesitated. "Look around us," Ada-gal'kala said. "They're sick and dying everywhere. This place is not safe."

And so, with no food, with no extra clothing or blankets, they walked out of town. They walked for several days, Ada-gal'kala hunting along the way for their food, he and his wife both looking for edible plants and gathering them. At last, he decided that they had gotten far enough away from the pestilence, and he had gathered a few skins from the game he had killed. He selected a place high in the mountains, a place flat enough for comfort and near some fresh, cold running water, and he and Ni-on-e built themselves a rude house. They built a small fire and burned their blankets and clothes. Ni-on-e started all over with the skins that her husband had provided, and he hunted more and brought home more game for fresh meat and for skins.

The horror lasted for a year, and by the time it came to an end, the population of the Cherokee people had been cut in half. They said that they'd had six thousand fighting men before, and when the smallpox had run its course, 2,590 were left alive.

Ada-gal'kala survived it, as did his wife and son. His sister and her daughter also survived. Back home at last, they found that things had changed tremendously. Many of their friends and relatives were gone. Houses had been burned. The two *usdis* too saw the terrible effects around them, heard the weeping and wailing, witnessed death by disease and by suicide. They were possibly young enough to forget, had they been allowed to, but they would hear the awful tales throughout the years as they were growing up, and so they would never actually forget. And the boy, now called Chooch, had other, more painful and more constant reminders, for the disease had stricken him, and though he had survived it, it had left him marked for life.

Ada-gal'kala's old rival Agan'stat' also had suffered the smallpox and somehow survived. He too was left with a scarred and pitted face, a horrible reminder of his pain and anguish, and it turned him all the more against the English, for it had been their trade goods, had it not, that had brought the pestilence among them? He even believed, and voiced his beliefs out loud, that the English had done it on purpose in a devious and sinister attempt to wipe out all the Cherokees.

## 1740

With the great horror at last behind them, the Cherokees got back into their normal routines as much as possible. Little 'Chooch', with his now pockmarked face, was given *distayuh* tea to make him strong, and the root of *ani-waniski* to chew, rub on his lips, and swallow to make him eloquent in speech. He was scratched with the *kanuga* on his back from his shoulders to his heels to make him fleet of foot, and as soon as he was old enough to walk around on his own, he was given his freedom. He could go anywhere and try to do anything that came into his mind. He learned the dances by watching the men and women dance. He watched men make bows and arrows, and soon he was making his own little versions and shooting his little arrows at anything that moved. He watched the men playing the *gatayusti* game and the big teams contesting against one another in *anetsodi,* the ball play, the little brother of war. He learned these things by watching and by trying them for himself, and he was good at everything he tried. One day he told his mother, "When I grow up, I'll be a great man."

The Englishmen had marked out a trade route from their town of Charlestown into the heart of the Cherokee country, and more and more English traders were coming into their midst. 'Chooch' was fascinated by the goods the traders brought: guns and shot, steel knives and steel tomahawks, brightly colored cloth and paint, tightly coiled springs, mirrors, and the strong drink called rum that many of the men used to drink themselves into a stupor or make them act crazy.

He didn't understand everything that was being said, but he did get the idea that one reason the English were working so hard to befriend the Cherokees was that they were afraid that the French would become their friends and allies, and if that were to happen, the English believed, the Cherokees would become their enemies. The French and the English hated one another, it seemed, and the English were afraid that the French would talk the Cherokees into killing Englishmen. That was as much as he understood of the things the men and women were talking about.

## 1741

He was four years old when he heard that just recently the funny little white man Priber had been on his way to Fort Toulouse to visit with the Frenchmen there, and along the way, some Englishmen had seized him and taken him as a prisoner to their own settlements in Georgia. Shortly after that someone came and said that the English claimed that Priber had become ill and died in their prison. Upon hearing that word, Agan'stat's pockmarked face darkened with anger, and he said, "They've killed him. He was my friend." And Agan'stat's had one more reason for hating the English.

It wasn't long after that when 'Chooch' heard that 'Ma'dohi had died. He had not been stricken by the smallpox, but he was old, and the terrible things happening around him might well have hastened his end. There might have been a scrambling for power among the most influential of the Cherokees, but, as they had done with 'Ma'-dohi, the British intervened. They made it clear to everyone that they intended to treat only with Ammouskossittee, the son of the dead "Emperor," just twenty-three years old and therefore still 'chooch' in the minds of many of the Cherokees. But as they had done in the case of "Moytoy," the Cherokees by and large accepted the appointment and let it go. It had no real effect on their daily lives.

Ada-gal'kala, however, quietly seethed over the decision. He knew that he should have had that position rather than this young upstart. It was foolish of the English, he told himself, not to recognize his influence with the people and his abilities. Or perhaps, he considered, they had recognized those things about him, and for that very reason had selected the weaker Ammouskossittee so that they might the more easily control him. Well, whatever their reason, he would keep his feelings to himself and bide his time. His time, he was sure, would come, sooner or later.

The British called the young Ammouskossittee the "Emperor of Tellico," Tellico being his place of residence. He was a weak leader, though, and therefore his uncle, Guhna-gadoga, the brother of the deceased 'Ma'dohi, advised him and really made all of his decisions for him. Guhna-gadoga, the Standing Turkey, called Old Hop by the English, became the real leader of the Cherokees. It was a lucky break for Old Hop, Ada-gal'kala thought. He would never have risen to a position above Ada-gal'kala on his own merits. He had done so only because the English had recognized his nephew as "emperor."

Ada-gal'kala's 'Chooch' was only four years old, and had a new baby brother, when his father left on a trip and was long overdue returning home. At last someone came and gave his mother the sad news that Ada-gal'kala had been captured by the Ottawas, a people from the far north. Ni-on-e mourned almost as if her husband had been slain. Seeing his mother's distress, 'Chooch' went to her side and put his arms around her neck. "Don't worry, Mother," he said. "It may be a long time, but Father will be back." Ni-on-e was puzzled by the certainty in her young son's voice and the serious look on his face. She wanted to believe him, but, after all, he was only a child. She went to see the old conjurer in town.

"I know why you have come to see me," the old man said. "You're worried about your man."

"They said that he was taken by the Ottawas," she said.

"I know," the old man said. "Let me see what I can see."

The old man went into his house and was gone for quite some time. Ni-on-e sat quietly and patiently waiting for him, but inside, she was anxious. She wondered what the old man would say. She

17

could hear him talking there inside his house, and she recalled that people said of him that he had little people living with him. Sometimes they helped him. Other times they played tricks on him, hid his things from him, and he would fuss with them. She thought that his voice sounded angry, as if he were indeed fussing with someone, but she couldn't understand the words he was saying. Now and then there was a noise as if the old man had angrily turned something over. Finally he came back out of the house, and he was carrying a small bundle, something wrapped up inside a small soft skin.

He sat down across his tiny fire from Ni-on-e, and slowly and carefully unwrapped the thing that he had brought. Then she saw that what he had was a bright and shiny crystal. *Ulunsuti*, she thought, and she felt a slight chill. She had heard of the powerful crystal that came from between the eyes of the great Uk'ten', but she had never before actually seen one, had never knowingly been close to one. *Ulunsuti*, she had heard, was so powerful that even its owner had to move it to a new hiding place from time to time, not to keep someone else from finding and stealing it, but to keep it confused regarding its own whereabouts so that it would not escape from him. He also was compelled to take it out occasionally and feed it by rubbing it over with fresh blood. The old man held the crystal between the tips of his thumb and forefinger, and to the eyes of Ni-on-e it seemed to glow, even burn. He held it close to his eyes and gazed intently into its depths for a long time. "Ahh," he said. "Umm."

At last he wrapped it back up carefully, and he stood and took the precious and frightening bundle back into his house. She heard him speak sharply to — someone. Then he came out again and sat down where he had been before.

"Ada-gal'kala," he said, "is alive and well. I saw him in the crystal. I saw him standing up in front of a crowd of people as if he were making a speech to them, and they were all listening carefully and showing him respect. He'll come back to you, but it will be a long time."

Ni-on-e felt a great sense of relief. She wondered how long it would be, but at least she knew that her husband had not been killed, and that he would indeed return to her. She would wait patiently, as patiently as she could. But she also wondered about her young son. Could it be possible that at his age, and without the long years of training of the old conjurer, he could accurately see the same things? She wondered.

'Chooch' continued to grow and to learn and to develop his skills. By the time he was eleven years old, he could throw the stone disc and toss the spear after it with as much accuracy as most men. He had made himself a bow and a set of arrows as good as those most men had, and he could hit almost anything he shot at. He was equally good with the blowgun, but already he was scorning it as a child's weapon. He was good with his ballsticks, too, but the men, of course, would not allow him to take part in the ball play with them. Men were sometimes killed during the ball play, often injured. He played ball with the other boys, but he longed to play with the men.

When his mother visited Echota, or when Tame Doe visited Tanase, he would play with his cousin Nanyehi, and she played the same games as he. She also had a small bow and small arrows, and she could shoot them almost as accurately as he could shoot his. Both children had small blowguns made from river cane and darts made from the thorns of a honey locust tree tufted with the down of bull thistle. Playing one day at the edge of Echota, Nanyehi touched her cousin and whispered. "*Ni,* 'Chooch'," she said. "Over there."

He looked and saw there where she indicated two fat field mice nibbling at the wall behind the house of one of the residents there. The children looked at one another and nodded. Each fitted a dart into one end of a blowgun. Almost together, they put their blow-guns to their mouths. They took deep breaths and puffed out their cheeks, and then they each expelled their breath in a sudden *poof,* sending the darts flying hard and fast, and each one hit its mark. Nanyehi's prey was killed immediately. The other, when hit, jumped straight up in the air, flipped over and landed on its back.

It lay there kicking for a bit and then expired. The children looked at one another and smiled, then ran to examine their fallen prey the more closely.

"When I grow up," said 'Chooch', "I'll kill the enemies of our people just as easily as that."

"I will, too," Nanyehi said.

"You'll be at home being someone's mother," he said.

"No I won't," she said. "I'll be out there the same as you."

"Well," he said, "I can run faster than you."

"No you can't," she said.

He propped his blowgun against the wall of the house just beside where the dead mice lay, and he said, "Let's go, then."

She put her blowgun there beside his. "Where?"

"We'll race to the townhouse," he said.

They stood side by side, ready to run. "Now," he said, and they started. He ran as hard as he could, but she was right there beside him. He put everything he had into his running. He sucked in deep breaths as his feet slapped again and again against the ground. He ran until he thought that he was no longer even touching the ground. He was running over it but not on it, and still she was right there beside him. At last, out of breath, they ran together into the side of the townhouse, and they looked at one another, and they laughed.

# 3

Life wasn't really much different for 'Chooch' without his father around. Ada-gal'kala had always left him pretty much alone anyway. His mother's brother was much closer to 'Chooch' than was his father, and that was as it should be, as it had always been with the Cherokees. They hunted together and played games together. Uncle explained things to him, like how things got to be the way they were. He told him stories, like the story about how the world was made and the one about the first man and first woman, and the one that tells why the Cherokees have to work for a living.

"A long time ago," Uncle said, "there was nothing down here but water. The whole world was covered with water. Down underneath in the Underworld the Uk'ten' lived, along with other creatures that we don't see so much anymore, and up on top of the Sky Vault all of the original forms of life lived. The original man and woman, the original deer, the original eagle—all of them. Those two worlds were set against each other, so the pressure was great here on the water. It was rumbling and roiling all the time.

"But it got crowded up there on top of the great Sky Vault. You know it's like a bowl turned upside down over this world, and it's made out of rock. But it got crowded up there, and the animals talked it over, and some of them decided to come on down here. So they did. But they found out that it was all water. They didn't have anyplace they could even sit down. They talked it over and decided that maybe there was something underneath the water, and the duck said, 'I'll dive down there and find out. If there's anything there, I'll bring it up.'

"So he dived into the water, and he was gone a long time. The others started worrying about him, but finally he came back, all out of breath. When he caught his breath, he said, 'I didn't find anything down there.'

"Well, the others weren't ready to give it up, and the otter said that he'd try it, so he went down and was gone a long time, and he came back just like the duck did. He hadn't found anything, either. They were about to give it all up and go back up on top of the Sky Vault, when the little water beetle said that he'd like to try. They laughed at him. 'If the duck and the otter couldn't find anything,' one of them said, 'what makes you think that you can?'

"But the little beetle was determined, and so they waited while he went under the water. He was gone longer than either the duck or the otter had been. He was gone longer than both of them put together. The animals decided that he must have drowned down there, and they were getting ready to leave, when he finally came back up, and he brought some mud up with him.

"Then they spread the mud out on top of the water to make this world, but it was too wet to stand on, so the great buzzard flew way down low over it flapping his wings to dry it out. When his huge wings came down, the wind they caused made valleys, and when they went up, they sucked mountains up out of the mud. After a while it was dry, and the animals had a world down here to live on.

"The first man was called Kanati. He was also known as the Great Hunter. His wife was Selu. And they had a son. They never had to worry about anything, because when they wanted something to eat, Selu would just go out to their store house and go inside. When she came back, she'd have a basket full of corn or beans. Kanati would go out into the woods and just be gone a short while, but he always came back with fresh-killed game, a deer or a buffalo, whatever he wanted to have for his next meal.

"Their little boy went out playing one day down by the river, and from their house they could hear him having fun. But Kanati said, 'I hear two voices.' When the boy came home later, Kanati said, 'I could hear two voices while you were out. Who were you playing with?' And the boy said, 'My friend.'

"So the next day, when the boy went out to play, Kanati and Selu followed him. They hid in the woods and watched, and shortly another little boy came out of hiding. This boy looked wild. His hair was all a mess. He didn't have any clothes, and he was dirty. They called him the Wild Boy. The two adults slipped back home to talk it over. When their son came home that night, Kanati said, "Tomorrow when you go out to play, I want you to get your friend to wrestle with you. Get him down and hold him. Then I'll come out of the woods and catch him and bring him home. We won't hurt him. We just want to clean him up and give him some clothes and provide a home for him.'

"So the next day, Kanati's son did what he'd been told to do, and Kanati ran out of the woods and took hold of the Wild Boy, but the Wild Boy kicked and screamed. Selu was there watching. 'We won't hurt you,' she said. 'We just want you to come home with us.'

" 'You don't want me,' the Wild Boy said. 'You threw me away.'

Then Selu knew that the Wild Boy had grown from the blood out of the river where she had been washing their meat before she cooked it. 'You're my son,' she said, 'and this is your father. The boy you've been playing with is your brother.'

"They took the Wild Boy home and cleaned him up and dressed him, and the two boys became very close. But the Wild Boy was always getting himself and his brother into mischief. One day he said, 'Where does our father go to get meat?' His brother said that he didn't know. 'I've always been told not to follow him,' he said. 'Let's find out,' said the Wild Boy.

"The next time Kanati went out to hunt, the boys followed him through the woods. They watched as he approached a cave with a big boulder blocking its entrance. Kanati rolled the boulder out of the way, and a deer came running out. Quickly, he rolled the boulder back into place and shot the deer. The boys watched with wide eyes. They kept quiet until Kanati had loaded up his kill and headed for home. Then Wild Boy said, 'Let's take a look in there.'

"It took all their strength, but finally they managed to roll the boulder aside, and then all of a sudden all kinds of animals came running out of the cave: deer, buffalo, elk, raccoons, squirrels—all kinds of animals. The boys were caught by surprise. They couldn't roll the boulder back in place. The deer knocked them down and everyone who came after the deer ran over them. When the animals were at last all out of the cave, the boys sat up stunned. They were dirty, and they were bruised all over.

"When Kanati got home, he found out that the boys were gone, and he suspected that they had followed him, so he left his deer at the house with Selu, and he went back to the cave. He found the boys sitting there in the dirt, all beat up, and he saw the boulder where they had rolled it away from the entrance to the cave. He knew then what they had done, and he was very angry. He didn't say anything to them, though. Instead, he just walked into the cave and found a big jar sitting there with a lid on it, and he kicked the jar over. All kinds of insects came swarming out of the jar.

"Kanati just left the cave and started walking home again. He left the boys sitting there, and bees came buzzing out of the cave, and they swarmed all over the two naughty boys, stinging them all over. The boys screamed and kicked. They slapped at the bees and rolled over and over in the dirt. Then the hornets came and the mosquitoes. Before it was over, both boys were covered all over their bodies with big red bumps.

"You might think the boys learned their lesson from that, but they didn't. The Wild Boy was watching Selu one day when she went into the store house. She came out with a big basket full of corn and beans. When she went back into the main house, he looked inside the store house, and it was empty. 'How does our mother get all that food?' he asked his brother, but the other boy didn't know. 'Let's find out,' the Wild Boy said.

"The next time Selu went to the store house, the two boys waited until she was inside, and they ran up to the store house and found a chink in the wall where they could peek through. They watched as Selu sat down on the floor and put her empty basket between her legs. She raised an arm and rubbed herself under there, and the basket filled up with beans. She raised her other arm and rubbed herself, and corn piled up on top of the beans in the basket. She stood up, picked up her basket, and started back for the main house. The boys ran and hid.

" 'Did you see that?' the Wild Boy said. 'Yes,' said his brother. 'Our mother is a witch,' the Wild Boy said. 'We have to kill her.' They got their axes and waited for her to come out the door, but when she stepped out and saw them, she knew what was in their minds. 'I won't try to stop you,' she said, 'but before you kill me, listen to what I have to say. After I'm dead, drag my body seven times across the field there in front of the house. You'll have fresh corn to eat every morning.'

"So the boys killed her with their axes, and then they dragged her body four times across the field, and the Wild Boy said, 'I think that's enough. I'm tired.' Because they didn't do what she told them to do, we now have to wait for the corn to grow.

"When Kanati came home and found out what his boys had done, he was very sad. They thought that he'd be angry with them, the way he had been at the cave, but he wasn't. He just walked away and left them alone there at the house. He went back to the Darkening Land on top of the Sky Vault, and there he found Selu waiting for him. The two bad boys followed them up there, though, and now Kanati is Thunder and the boys are his sons, the Thunder Boys. Sometimes we call them the Little Thunders."

Chooch thought that it had been awfully bad of the boys to kill their own mother. (It was even hard for him to imagine such a thing—he loved his mother and knew that he could never do anything like that.) And the bad boys had made it so hard for the people to get their food, either hunting or growing, but then he thought that he was going to be a great hunter, and he knew that his mother and the other women grew fine food in their gardens, and there was always plenty to eat. He guessed that the Cherokees had learned to live with the world the way the boys had made it. The songs of the Stone Man had helped, too. Uncle had told him that tale as well.

"It was back in the early times," Uncle had said. "All the people were out hunting one day, and one man went up on top of a high hill to take a look around. He saw a river down there on the other side, and across the river an old man was walking along a ridge. The old man carried a long stick, but it looked like the stick was made out of rock. Now and then the old man would stop and point his stick around, then bring it back and sniff the end he had pointed. At last he pointed in the direction of the hunter, and when he sniffed the end of his stick, he changed the direction of his walk. He started walking toward the hunter. When he got to the river's edge, he threw his stick, and it became a bridge. The old man walked across the bridge, turned and picked it up again, and as he did, it became his stick once more. He walked toward the hunters' camp.

"The hunter watching from the hilltop became very much frightened, and he ran back to tell the others what he had just seen. After he had told his tale, a wise old man among them said, 'I know who that is. He's called Nuhyunawi because his skin is made of solid rock. He wanders these hills looking for hunters to kill and eat.'

" 'Let's run away,' one said.

" 'He'll just follow us,' said the wise man. 'His stick is like a dog. It will find us, and he'll just keep following us.'

" 'Then let's kill him before he can kill any of us,' said another.

" 'That's not easy to do,' said the wise man, 'because of his skin. But there is a way.'

" 'Then tell us quickly before he gets here,' they said.

"So the wise man told them that the Stone Man could not stand

26

the sight of a woman in her bleeding time of the month. 'We need to find seven such women,' he said. So they asked all of the women in their group, and they found seven. The wise man walked with the seven women out onto the road the way he knew that the Stone Man would be coming. He left them at different places along the way, and he told them, 'As soon as I leave you here, take off your dress.' He left them, and they undressed.

"Pretty soon, the Stone Man came along, and he saw the first woman standing there beside the road. He looked away and covered his eyes. 'Ugh,' he said. 'You're in a bad way.' By and by he came to the second one. He groaned out loud and hurried on. Then he came to the third one, and he started to gag and stagger. When he saw the fourth one, he fell down on his knees. At the sight of the fifth one, he fell forward, and he started crawling on all fours like a baby. The sixth one laid him even lower, and when he arrived where the seventh one was standing, he was just barely dragging himself over the ground. When he saw her, he rolled over on his back. He was too weak to go on.

"The people came running out then, and the wise man had them drive seven sourwood stakes through the body of the Stone Man and pin him to the ground. Then he had them gather sticks and logs and pile them all over the Stone Man, and when the Sun crawled out from under the western edge of the Sky Vault, they set the sticks on fire.

"Nuhyunawi began to talk. He told them about all the plants and what medicine each plant could provide for them, and this talk lasted until the middle of the night. Then he started to sing, and he sang all of the hunting songs. By the time the Sun was crawling out from under the eastern edge of the Sky Vault to start a new day, the flames had died out, and the voice had stopped singing.

"The wise man had the people rake the ashes away, and there he found a large *woði* stone and a bright *Uluhnðuti.* Then he lined all the people up, and he took up the *woði.* He painted the face and breast of each person there, and while he painted, the person prayed, and whatever he prayed for while being painted, he received."

'Chooch' thought that the people had been fortunate indeed to have been in the path of the Stone Man and to have had the wise man among them when the Stone Man came along.

## 1748

Then one day, everyone in town was astonished when Ada-gal'kala came riding up on a fine white horse with a French saddle. Ada-gal'kala was dressed in beautiful clothing, a combination of native buckskins and European trade goods. He was handsome, and he rode with his head held high, arrogant and proud. He rode as if he were coming home in triumph, not as if he had just escaped from captivity, and he had the appearance and bearing of a very important visiting dignitary from another nation.

Ni-on-e wanted to run to him and embrace him and take him home to hold him close and to talk to him in private, but she knew that she would have to wait. The people of the town would gather in the council house to hear what Ada-gal'kala had to tell them about his seven-year absence. He must have had some wonderful adventures to tell them about. He must have seen many things and many people that most of them had never seen and probably would never see. Everyone was anxious, but they fed him first, and then they all gathered in the townhouse to hear his tale.

'Chooch', now eleven years old, squeezed himself into the crowded townhouse and watched his father and listened, fascinated, to what he had to say. When Ada-gal'kala stood up before the crowd a sudden hush came over the smoke-filled room. He straightened himself up, stood his tallest, which was not very tall, and puffed out his chest. He was wearing fine moccasins, decorated with the dyed quills of porcupines, fine leggings of buckskin, and a bright red, embroidered breechcloth. The designs on his clothing were not Cherokee, so the people, having heard of his capture long ago, assumed that they were Ottawa. His arms and chest were covered by a white shirt with full sleeves and lace cuffs and collar, and he had draped over one shoulder a beautiful red blanket. His *giðhla*, or scalp lock, was adorned with a bright feather, and he wore multiple necklaces of beads around his neck.

"My friends and relatives," he said, "it's good to see all of you here. My heart is glad that I am back home at last after my long enforced absence. When I left home seven long years ago on a mission that should have taken but a few days, I was surprised and set upon by a number of Ottawa warriors. They had ranged far south of their homelands, and they captured me and carried me with them back to their home in the north. At first I feared for my life, but I soon learned that my tongue was my best weapon. It was my diplomacy that kept me alive.

"The trip back to their homeland was long and tiring, and all along the way I was made to perform menial chores, building their fires and cooking their meals, fetching water for them and the like, but I did all those things without complaining, and by the time we had reached their home, my captors were all treating me more like a visiting friend than a prisoner.

"Soon I was liked and respected by all of the Ottawas. I was still their captive and was not free to leave the town in which they kept me, but as long as I did not try to escape, I was free to roam the town at will. I met all of their head men and befriended them. To my thinking, the greatest of them all was a man they call Pontiac. He's a man younger than myself, but he's a very capable leader of his people. Even he came to me for advice in dealing with the white men. But the Ottawas have the French to deal with where we have the English. I was thankful that I had met the French at Toulouse, and that I had learned about them from Priber while he was here with us.

"I met with many of the Frenchmen and learned to speak their tongue easily, for, you may recall, I had begun learning it some years ago from Priber, and I found them to be more honest and dependable than are the English. When I got to know them better, I was not surprised that the Ottawas call them their friends. I served my captors well. I even fought with them against their enemies a few times, and after seven years, Pontiac himself told me that I was free to go. He even gave me a fine horse and saddle, as you saw when I rode in, and provided me with an escort all the way to the frontiers of our country.

"And now, my friends, I would like it very much if you would allow me to go home now with my wife and children. I've been away from them for such a long time that I'm not sure that my sons will even know me."

'Chooch' ran through the crowd to find his mother and stand by her side. He took hold of her arm to get her attention, for she was looking toward her husband, who was being greeted and congratulated by almost everyone. At last Ni-on-e glanced at her son. "I told you, Mother," he said. "I told you he'd come home."

# 4

Ada-gal'kala was not surprised to learn, on his return home, that the Cherokees were at war once again with their neighbors and old enemies the Ani-Gusa. Some things never seemed to change. He was a little surprised, though, to hear that white men from the Virginia colony had found their way across the mountains in the Cherokee country. They had even named the way, calling it the Cumberland Gap, and there were settlers from Virginia moving out onto Cherokee land.

He was astonished to see how much his two sons had grown in his long absence. The younger one, still called Usdi, tagged along after 'Chooch' as much as 'Chooch' would allow. Ada-gal'kala thought that it was about time for 'Chooch' to get himself another name, for the little one was almost too old to be Usdi. He should be 'Chooch' pretty soon.

When he had still not been home long, news was brought of a Creek raid to a nearby Cherokee town. Ada-gal'kala and some friends decided they would retaliate.

They were headed for the water's edge, where their war boats awaited them, those long and heavy dugouts the white men called canoes, a word they had picked up from some other Indians. They would get into the boats and head for the enemy town. They were a war party, and they had prepared themselves by dancing, fasting, and sleeping on ashes in the townhouse away from women for four days and nights. They were ready for the fight.

But Ada-gal'kala happened to look back over his shoulder, and back there behind them was his young son running along after the men. The boy carried his own bow and a few arrows. A war club dangled at his side.

"'Chooch', where do you think you're going?" Ada-gal'kala asked, his voice loud and demanding.

"We're going to fight our enemies," the boy said.

The proud father smiled then and dropped to one knee in front of the boy.

"We're going," he said, "but you have to stay home with your mother. You're not yet old enough to go on a trip like this."

The boy held his bow out in front of him. "But I'm ready," he said. "I want to go with you. I want to fight."

Some of the other men chuckled at the bravery of the lad. The father put a hand on his son's shoulder.

"Not this time," he said. "Not yet. You go back home to your mother now. One of these days, you'll go out to fight, and it will be soon enough. This time, 'Chooch', you're needed at home. Someone has to watch things while we're away. Now go on back."

Ada-gal'kala stood and turned back toward the river. As he walked away, the boy's face flushed and hot tears welled up in his eyes, but he fought to hold them back. He let the men walk on for a short while, and then he started following them again. A few more steps, and his father glanced back and saw him still there, still following along.

"Go home, I said," he called, his voice now stern, almost angry.

The boy stopped and stood still, and the men moved on. Again, the boy followed along, the expression on his round, scarred young face determined, his eyes almost vanished into dark slits above his round cheeks. He was not used to taking orders, especially not from this father who had left him for seven long years. Ada-gal'kala turned back once more. He shouted this time, and now his voice was angry indeed.

"Go home," he said. "Do you hear me? Go on."

This time he did not turn away. He stood watching, waiting to be obeyed, and so the boy had no choice. He had to turn around and head back toward the town. He walked slowly, though, his head hanging, dejected. He looked back to see his father still standing there, still watching him, looking stern. He walked on. After a few more steps, he looked back again. His father and the other men were walking on toward the river and not looking at him any more. Quickly, he ran into the woods at the edge of the path and turned around to make his way once again after the men, toward the river. He would not give up. He fought his way through tangled brush and bramble that clawed and scratched at his skin.

At the water's edge, the men all took hold of one large dugout and started to lift it to their shoulders in order to carry it toward the water, but just as he was about to lift, Ada-gal'kala glanced up to see his son once more coming up behind them. He decided then that shouting was no longer the right tactic. He would use his famous diplomacy on his own young son. Secretly he was proud of the boy, but he knew that he could not allow him to join the men on this potentially dangerous mission. He would have to try yet another approach.

"Still coming, are you, 'Chooch'?" he asked.

"Yes," said the boy, a pout on his hard-set face.

"Determined to fight?"

"Yes."

"All right, then," said Ada-gal'kala, "if you're that determined, I won't try any more to stop you. Put your boat into the water, and follow us."

'Chooch' anxiously grabbed hold of the bow of the next war boat. He could barely lift one end. He wondered what his father had meant. Several big men were carrying the other boat. How could he carry this one all alone? But his father had said that he could go along with them if he put his own boat into the water. He moved in front of the boat, his back to the water, and grabbed hold of it with both hands. Then he pulled with all his might.

Ada-gal'kala and the other men then heaved their own craft up off the ground and walked toward the water with it. That would be the end of it, Ada-gal'kala thought. But just as he was stepping into the water, he heard one of his companions call out in astonishment.

"*Ni,*" said the man. "Look." The father and all the others turned their heads to see what it was the man wanted them to look at, and then the man finished his statement. *"Tsiyu gansini."* And from that day forth, 'Chooch', the boy, had a new name, Tsiyu Gansini, He's Dragging the Canoe.

# 5

Ammouskossittee was dead. He had only reached the age of twenty-eight years. He had never become an effectual leader. He had not even been a strong man. As a result of his untimely death, Guhna-gadoga, with whom the English had been forced to deal anyway, assumed the leadership role over the Cherokees. Ada-gal'kala could see that the idea of a central government for the Cherokee Nation would very soon become a reality. The man the English knew as "Emperor," now Guhna-gadoga, was, in effect, a Principal Chief, a chief of chiefs over all the war chiefs and peace chiefs of the various Cherokee towns. The English, this time, had accepted the man who had, in effect, been chosen by the Cherokee people, rather than one of their own selection. Ada-gal'kala fancied that only he could see what was happening. He was the only one who could see the gradual evolution of the English-appointed Cherokee "emperor" into a Principal Chief of the Cherokees, and still, secretly, he aspired to that role for himself and later for his oldest son.

Dragging Canoe, now sixteen years old, for the first time went out alone to hunt. He remembered all the things his uncle had taught him. He had fasted, and he had gone to water, for killing was not a thing to be undertaken lightly. He recalled his uncle's story about the way in which disease had come into the world, and how the Cherokees had gotten medicine.

"A long time ago," his uncle had told him, "when the world was still new, everyone got along pretty well together, the people and all the other animals. But then things got a little too crowded, and about that same time, people invented bows and arrows, knives, blowguns, spears, and hooks to catch fish with. They started killing more and more animals. They killed them so easily with their new weapons, and they killed so many, that the animals got worried. The bears decided to have a council, and they met in their council house at Kuwahi. The old white bear chief was in charge, and he listened to everyone who wanted to say something.

" 'They killed my best friend,' said one.

" 'They stuff their bellies with our flesh,' said another.

" 'It's not even fair anymore,' another one said. 'They have bows and arrows and other weapons. We have only our claws.'

" 'What do they make their bows out of?' one asked.

" 'The bows are made of wood,' said another. 'Then they make the string out of our own guts, and they use it to kill more of us.'

" 'They kill us with bows and arrows,' said yet another. 'Why don't we make bows and arrows and kill them?'

"The old white bear chief agreed, so someone carved out a bow, and one of the bears, in order to save all the rest, gave up his own life so they could have his guts for the string. Another made some arrows, and then the council met again. A bear stood up in front of the rest and fitted an arrow to the string. He pulled back the string, but when he let it go, his long claws caught the string, and the arrow flew off to one side and fell short.

" 'His claws were in the way,' someone said, so they cut his claws short, and he shot another arrow, and this one went straight to the mark. The bears all cheered, and they said they'd cut their claws

36

and make bows and arrows, but the white chief calmed them down.

" 'We need our long claws,' he said. 'We have to climb trees. One of our people has already sacrificed himself to these bows. Let's not lose anyone else.' They couldn't think of anything else to do, and so the council broke up without having accomplished anything.

"Then Awi Usdi, the chief of all the deer, called a council, and they discussed the problem. One of the deer there at the meeting came up with an idea. 'Why don't we make the hunters apologize when they kill one of us?' he suggested. The rest of the deer quickly agreed, but one of them asked, 'How can we make them do that?' Awi Usdi then said, 'Whenever a hunter kills a deer, I'll be right there at the side of our fallen brother, and as his spirit is leaving his body, I'll ask him if he heard the hunter's prayer of apology. If he did not, I'll strike the hunter with rheumatism.'

"The deer all liked that plan, and so the whole council approved it, and they immediately put it into practice. When the other animals heard about the deer's plan, they called their own councils, and each one came up with another horrible disease to inflict upon the casual, disrespectful hunter, and hunters began suffering from these afflictions. The suffering was so great that the plants took pity on men. They called their council, and each plant chose one of the new diseases and provided a cure for it.

"In the meantime, the people, having figured out where the diseases were coming from, began to be more respectful, and they devised the rituals and prayers we use today. Even so, in case a hunter has forgotten to do something the proper way, to be careful, on his way home, he should build four fires in his path behind him to throw the spirit chief of the dead animal off his track. And we do this always when we hunt, unless we're hunting for bear."

So Dragging Canoe knew what he must do, and he knew why he must do it. When he went out in the morning, he was still fasting, and he traveled all day without eating or drinking. He made his camp for the night beside a stream, and he waited there until the

Sun was just beginning to crawl under the western edge of the Sky Vault to disappear for the night. Then he went into the water again. He sang the deer-hunting song the people had learned from the Stone Man so long ago.

"Give me the wind," he said. "Give me the breeze. Oh, Great Hunter, Kanati. Give me the wind."

When he had finished his prayer, he came out of the water and went back into his camp. He cooked and ate his supper, rubbed his chest with ashes from the fire, and lay down to sleep for the night. He was up early and on the trail of the deer. By the time the Sun was directly overhead visiting her daughter's house, he had come to the site of an old abandoned town. Quietly, he made his way to the edge of the town, there where the gardens had been. He saw nothing there, so he settled down in the edge of the woods to watch and wait.

It was late afternoon when the big male deer stepped out of the woods and walked out onto the abandoned garden. It was clear and lush, and it made for good browsing. He looked around and stood listening for a moment. At last, convinced that there was no danger near, he lowered his head to eat. Dragging Canoe slowly and carefully nocked an arrow. He raised his bow, drawing back the string at the same time, and as he pulled it back, he said, very softly, "Instantly, the red tip of my arrow strikes you in the very center of your soul. Instantly. *Yu.*" And with the last syllable, he let go the string, and the arrow flew straight and true. The big stag jumped forward, then its front knees buckled, and it fell to the ground with a thud.

Dragging Canoe ran quickly to its side, drawing his knife as he ran. He knelt beside the body and quickly slit its throat. "My brother," he said, "I apologize for having to kill you, but my family needs the meat."

On his way home, his prize slung over his shoulders, he stopped four times, lay down his burden, turned around and built a small fire there in his path. Having done everything he could remember that he was supposed to do, he felt safe and secure carrying the carcass of the deer back home to his mother. And he was proud of his first big kill, his first hunt alone, like a man.


## *1754*

Dragging Canoe was seventeen years old when the messenger came down from the north asking for his father by name. The man was exhausted from his trip, and some held him up and helped him to the townhouse, while others ran to find Ada-gal'kala. They fed the man and let him rest a little, but they were all anxious to hear what he would have to say. At last he was ready to speak. He was an Ottawa, and he had been told by the great Pontiac himself to take his message directly to Ada-gal'kala.

"We are at war with the English," he told them. "The English sent their soldiers up into our country to drive out the French. They built themselves a fort, but the French, with our help, drove them out of there. The French took over the fort. They call it Fort Duquesne. But the English have not given up. They are at war with the French and want to drive the French clear out of the country. The French are our friends and allies, and so we are at war with the English, too.

"I was sent down here to tell you about all this, and to ask you to help us fight the English. There are Frenchmen here in your country, too, at a place they call Fort Toulouse. If you talk to them, they'll join you in the fight against the English here."

Agan'stat' stood up when the Ottawa was through talking.

"Our Ottawa friend has made a good talk," he said. "I think that we should join with the French and the Ottawas and fight the English. The English keep pressing into our country every day. They brought us the smallpox, which killed many of our people and left many of us scarred and ugly for life. They killed our friend Priber. They keep asking for more of our land. Already we've given them too much land. Let's give them no more. Instead, let's drive them off our land where they have already intruded. Why should we try to be friends with the English? Why should we not fight them?"

Ada-gal'kala remembered his trip to England. He remembered signing the agreement with the King's men. But he also recalled his seven years with Pontiac and the Ottawas, and he remembered with fondness the Frenchmen he had met while he was there. He stood up when Agan'stat' had finished with his talk. He did not speak at once. He stood there in front of everyone as if in deep thought.

"Let's consider this matter for a while," he said at last. "I have met Frenchmen in the north country and at Toulouse, and I have been to England. I know Englishmen, Frenchmen, and Ottawas. All of you know my experiences. But this is not a time to be rash. Why should Cherokees fight and die for white men, either French or English? And we have to remember that we get our trade goods from the English at Charlestown and at Williamsburg. Could the French supply us from Fort Toulouse as readily as do the English?"

Some of the people agreed with him, and others agreed with Agan'stat', wanting to go and attack the English right away. No decision was made. Dragging Canoe listened, and he puzzled over his father's words. Why did he not want to help his old friends the Ottawas in this war against the English? He couldn't tell. He knew, though, that his father and the war chief Agan'stat' were often at odds with one another. Maybe Ada-gal'kala needed no other reason to oppose the war than the fact that Agan'stat' was supporting the idea. He felt the scars on his own young face and thought of the words of Agan'stat'. He also considered the way in which some Cherokees interpreted his father's name—The Leaning Wood— and he wondered if they were right about him. He wondered.

It was not long before Agan'stat' made a trip to Fort Toulouse. He was surly when he left, and he told no one why he was going. He went off alone. His reason for going was his own business—his alone. When he returned, he defiantly put up on a pole outside his house a flag the Frenchmen had given him.

## *1755*

Then two English traders from Virginia, one called Nathaniel Gist, and the other Richard Pearis, came to see the Cherokees, but they came not to trade but to persuade. The Cherokees knew Gist and Pearis. They had traded with both men for some time. Both men had even married Cherokee women, and had fathered Cherokee children. Many of the Cherokees counted Gist and Pearis among their friends. Some actually called them brothers. They gathered there in the townhouse at Echota to hear what the traders had to say.

"We've come to you from Virginia," Gist told them. "Colonel Washington himself sent us to speak with you. He urges you to help us drive the French out of this country. He asks you to recall the promise you made to the King to fight only for the English. He promises you that if you fight with us against the French, the trade goods will continue to come to you from Virginia and from the Carolinas. You'll have many guns and plenty of ammunition supplied to you.

"And Colonel Washington does not want you to directly engage the French in battle, but instead to fight their allies, your own old enemies, the Shawnees."

Agan'stat', hearing that he would get more guns and ammunition to use against the Shawnees, chose to remain quiet. He did not want to admit that he had been wrong, or to seem to be changing his mind so easily. He did not want to appear as if he had let an Englishman sway his opinion, and so he did not want to openly call for war against the French in support of the English. But secretly he liked the bargain. Some others who had been undecided were swayed as well when they learned that they would be getting weapons to turn on their traditional enemies the Ani-Sawahoni. Even so, the final decision was still in doubt.

Richard Pearis moved to the front of the crowd, and he lifted his account book up high for all to see. "All of you here know what this book is," he said. "Many of your names are written down in here along with the amount of money you still owe me. This is my fortune. It's my livelihood. You make your livings with hunting and with your gardens. This book is my living. Now watch me — watch what I will do with this book."

Still holding the book up high for all to see, Pearis walked to the fire which burned in the center of the townhouse. With a flourish, he lowered his arm and dropped the book into the fire. He spread his arms wide. "The debts have vanished," he said, "consumed by the flames along with the book. I have done this to show the love we bear for you."

Everyone was silent for another moment, and then the people all began to murmur to one another. Finally Ada-gal'kala stood up to speak. He praised Pearis for his generous action, and he urged the Cherokees gathered there to agree to make a new treaty with Virginia — on certain conditions.

"We'll fight the Ani-Sawahoni for you," he said to Pearis and Gist, "if you will build forts in our country where your soldiers can stay and protect our women and children while our men are away fighting in your war."

"How many forts?" Gist asked.

They signed a new treaty with Virginia and gave up some more land to pay for the building of the forts. The treaty also promised more trade goods for the Cherokees. The English agreed to build three forts, but they were two years in getting the job done. At last they completed them. Fort Prince George was on the Savannah River near Keowee in the Lower Towns, and Fort Loudon near Big Island Town and Tuskegee in the Overhills, where the Little Tennessee River and the Tellico River came together. Both of these forts were built by South Carolinians, and Fort Loudon had as its second in command John Stuart, another trader, a Scot from Charlestown who was married to a Cherokee woman and was already a friend of Ada-gal'kala's. The Virginians, however, who had initiated the whole process, built their fort directly across the Little Tennessee River from Echota, but they did not bother to man it. They did not even give it a name.

Some of the people were just as glad of that, and Agan'stat' was one of those. He did not particularly like having the English forts so close to Cherokee towns. But Ada-gal'kala's argument had been a sound one. It was difficult to dispute. When the young men were away fighting the Shawnees, the old men, women, and children would be vulnerable to attack from any enemy who chose to take advantage of the situation. Agan'stat' kept his thoughts on the subject to himself.

While they were waiting for the forts to be built, they met the Creeks at a place called Taliwa. The Creeks had been at war with the Cherokees for longer than anyone could remember, and now, with the Cherokees recently allied with the English against the French, the allies of the Creeks, the war intensified. In spite of his personal feelings about the English forts, Agan'stat' thought that a bargain was a bargain, and he would not allow the young men to fight the Shawnees until the English had fulfilled their promise to build three forts in the Cherokee country, and so the young men were glad for the diversion with the Creeks. They were anxious to fight, eager to win honors for themselves.

Dragging Canoe, now eighteen years old, had volunteered for the fight, as had his younger brother, White Owl. Their cousin Longfellow, the older brother of Nanyehi, had gone with them, and so had Nanyehi's young husband, Kingfisher. Nanyehi had said that she would go along, too. Such a thing, though not common, was not unheard of, either, and there was nothing to stop her from doing what she wanted to do.

"You should stay home," Dragging Canoe had told her.

"I go where my husband goes," she had said.

Dragging Canoe had then turned toward Kingfisher. "You should make your wife stay at home," he said.

"You know that a man can't make his wife do anything against her wishes," Kingfisher had said. "If I dared to try such a thing, she might throw me out of her house."

"The white men who have Cherokee wives tell their wives what to do," Dragging Canoe had said.

"Just let a man try to tell me what to do," Nanyehi had said, "Cherokee or white. It doesn't matter to me. I'll pound him up one side and down the other."

Under the careful direction of Ostenaco, a War Chief selected by Agan'stat', the young men had prepared for war. Dragging Canoe had carved for himself a new wooden mask to wear in the dancing, a warrior's fierce face with a rattlesnake coiled on top of its head. This would be a sign to everyone that he had no fear. All the young men had fasted for four days. In the evenings they had danced *inaða iyuðti*, snakelike, and they had worn their masks. The women had danced with them, wearing the turtle-shell rattles strapped to their calves. Then the young men alone had danced the Brave Dance, carrying their war clubs, imitating the gobbling sound of the turkey, which was their war cry, and striking with their clubs as if bashing in the heads of their enemies. At night they had slept in the townhouse away from all women, and they had slept on a bed of ashes.

Nanyehi danced with the men, but she was not allowed to sleep in the townhouse with them. She slept alone in her *oði* on her own bed of ashes.

They were ready for a big fight when they met the Creeks there at Taliwa. Rushing down from the mountainside, gobbling like turkeys, the Cherokees attacked the Creeks in their own country, hitting the town at Taliwa. The surprised Creeks took a moment to react, and several fell to the deadly rifle fire of the Cherokees on the side of the mountain. Creek men came out of their houses with their own rifles and returned the Cherokee fire.

Kingfisher crouched behind a rock on the mountainside, Nanyehi preparing his rifle balls for him by gnawing them with her teeth. He had dropped three of the enemy before a Creek ball tore into his forehead, killing him instantly. Nanyehi was horrified, but she refused to let that give her pause. She was also filled with rage directed at her husband's killers. She took up his rifle, reloaded it, and fired it at the Creeks. She killed one, reloaded, then killed another.

A little higher up the mountainside, Dragging Canoe's younger brother, White Owl, watched her in wonder and with pride. "Brother," he called out, and Dragging Canoe looked toward him from where he crouched. "Look at our cousin," White Owl said, and he gestured toward her. Dragging Canoe looked and saw her as she fired the rifle again. Another Creek man dropped to the ground.

When they were out of ammunition, they laid their rifles aside, took up their war clubs, and raced down into the town to battle according to their own ancient ways. Nanyehi took up her fallen husband's war club and rushed out from behind the rock that had been her cover. "Kill. Kill. Kill," she shouted, and she rushed into the fray with the men. The fight was bloody, but it was soon over. All of the Creeks left in the town were dead. Many had run away. The Cherokees had won the fight. Dragging Canoe, White Owl, Ostenaco, and all the other Cherokee men were covered in the blood of their enemies. And there was as much blood on Nanyehi as on any of them.

Back home, victorious, the warriors were greeted with cheers, and a great feast was laid out for them. The young men danced the victory dance, and Dragging Canoe, who had told his girl cousin to stay at home, told the people what she had done there at Taliwa. "She fought as well as any man there," he told them. Agan'stat' and Ada-gal'kala conferred with each other and with their councilors. Then secretly they all conferred with the leading women of the seven clans. Four days later, in spite of her youth, they held the ceremony to declare Nanyehi to be Giga'hyuh, the Red Woman, the red signifying war and victory and success, the position being one of great honor and some privilege. After that the people sometimes called her the Beloved Woman, sometimes 'War Woman.'


### 1756


The forts had been built at last. It was time for the Cherokees to keep their end of the bargain, but Agan'stat', still not wanting to seem to be in charge of the military operation on behalf of the English, once again appointed Ostenaco, known also as the Mankiller of Tellico, who had distinguished himself at Taliwa, to lead one hundred warriors against the Shawnees, old enemies of the Cherokees and recent allies of the French. Many young men volunteered, anxious for yet another chance to earn the honors that could be gained only in war. Once again, one of the first to volunteer was Dragging Canoe, now nineteen years old.

It was *gola* the cold time of the year, the time of the eagle. It was not the traditional time of year for making war for the Cherokees, but Virginia had sent a man to command the expedition. His name was Andrew Lewis, and they called him "Major." He was nominally in command of the Virginia fort, still without a name, and the few Virginians under his command would go with the Cherokees to attack the Shawnees. The Virginia fort would remain unmanned. It was not the time for war for the Cherokees, but for the English it was the best time.

"If the Shawnees feel as you do about making war in the winter," Major Lewis said, addressing the warriors gathered there, "then they will be caught completely by surprise. They won't be expecting an attack from you. We'll kill as many as we can, but those who run away won't have any homes to come back to, for we'll burn the towns, and we'll burn the food supplies. If they escape us, they'll freeze and starve. It's the best time to attack."

Listening to Major Lewis, Dragging Canoe thought that everything about Cherokee life was changing because of these white men. He knew from listening to his father and other old people tell tales that a great many things had already changed. Much land had been given up to the English, more land with every treaty. Cherokees now depended on trade goods from the English in order to survive. They had to have the guns and ammunition, for their enemies had them. Men and women were wearing more and more clothing made from cloth of English manufacture. Therefore hunting patterns had changed.

They were keeping horses and cattle and hogs. The ancient canebrakes were disappearing because of the numerous domestic animals, horses, cattle, and hogs—white man's animals. More and more warriors were going into battle with the steel trade tomahawks and abandoning their traditional war clubs. Traditional male and female roles were slowly and insidiously changing. Watching the families of the Cherokee women who had married white men, other Cherokee men wanted to be the heads of their own households, and Cherokee women were fighting back to hold on to their own traditional status.

It was the male time of year in the month of *Unoluhðani.* Cold, the month called January by the Englishmen. It was the wrong time to be going to war, according to Cherokee beliefs, but the Cherokees were going. They had made an agreement to fight the Shawnees for the English, and so they would fight a white man's war in the way of the white man, according to the white man's beliefs. Dragging Canoe accepted all of that as another sign of the changing times, but while thinking about moving north at this time of year, he recalled the story of the Ice Man that his uncle had told him.


"Once a long time ago," Uncle had said, "the people were burning the woods the way they do when their fire caught a poplar tree. The poplar tree just kept burning, even after the fire all around it had gone out. The fire moved down to the roots of the tree, and it burned a great hole in the ground. The people became frightened. They were afraid that the fire would burn up the whole earth.

"What will we do?" one cried.

"I know of a man far to the north,' another said. 'He lives in a house of ice. He can put out the fire.'

"Let's send someone to bring him here,' they said, and they all agreed. So they sent messengers north, and they found the ice house easily enough. Inside the house was a little man with long hair that dragged on the ground. It was plaited into two braids. The messengers told him why they had come looking for him. 'I can help you,' he said, and he unwrapped his braids and gathered all his loose hair into one hand. Then he slapped it like a whip against the palm of his other hand.

"The messengers felt a cold wind blow against their cheeks. Then the little man slapped his hand with his hair again, and it started to rain. He slapped a third time, and the rain turned into sleet. He slapped yet a fourth time, and the air was filled with large, hard hail stones. But it seemed to the messengers that all this had come from the ends of the little man's hair.

"Then the little man sent the messengers away. He told them to go back home, but he said that he would be with them the next day. When they got back, they found the rest of their people still gathered around the burning hole, still worried about the fate of the world. The next day, a cold wind came out of the north, but the wind fanned the flames, and they burned hotter. Then a light rain began to fall. The rain fell harder, and then it changed to sleet, and from sleet to hail, and the fire at last went out, and smoke and steam rose up hissing from the black hole.

"The storm was ferocious by this time. The people ran home, frightened for their lives, and the wind blew the ice into their homes. It put out all their fires. It froze all the water. The people were very much afraid that it would kill all of them, but at last it grew weary and died out. The people came out of their homes again, and they went to the place where the fire had been. There was nothing there but a great lake."

Dragging Canoe considered the tale that told of the possible fury of a winter storm, and the ages-old Cherokee practice of staying home during such times. Even so, he headed north with the others toward the Shawnee settlements on the Ohio River with Major Lewis in command. Richard Pearis, a man the Cherokees knew well, a trader from South Carolina, went with them to serve as interpreter. Pearis had a Cherokee wife and had learned the language. He also had a young son who was called George Pearis. The Pearises served as one of many examples of the changing Cherokee family. It was turned upside down. The man was the head of the house. His children carried his name.

The Cherokee family was a clan in which descent was traced strictly through the female line, and children belonged to their mothers. This English family was upside down to the Cherokee mind, yet it was slowly encroaching, working its way into Cherokee society. The Pearis family was only one. There were the Doughertys, the Stuarts, the Gists, and many more. It seemed to Dragging Canoe that there were more every day. He accepted it. There was nothing more he could do, for it was happening all around him. And so he was going to war with the Englishmen, carrying English weapons, under the command of an English major in the coldest time of the year.

Some of the men traveled on horseback. Others traveled by boat. They would rendezvous at certain predetermined sites along the way. The men in the big Cherokee war canoes made good time. At the first two meeting places, they waited for the horsemen to arrive, then camped with them, and they all talked among themselves about the coming fight. But the next day, farther north, nearing the Shawnee settlements, they came into a frozen river.

"Break through," Lewis shouted, and almost as soon as he had roared the command, the canoe in which he was riding hit the ice, and it was much thicker, much more solid than he had thought it would be. Lewis and the others in the boat were thrown into the icy water. There was shouting and splashing and the sounds of the heavy canoes hitting the ice. Other boats overturned. Men swam as hard as they could, desperate to get to dry land and to get out of the freezing water.

Dragging Canoe shouted orders to the other men in his boat, coming up just behind Lewis's, and they managed to turn it just as it hit the ice. The side of the boat bashed into an ice floe, but the boat did not capsize. They managed to row it to shore. As he was getting up on land, Dragging Canoe looked out into the water. Three of the big boats had overturned. Men struggled to get to land. As they dragged themselves up and out of the water, one at a time, dripping and shivering, Dragging Canoe, with the help of Pearis, who had been in the same boat with him, quickly gathered up some sticks of wood and kindled a fire. The cold and wet men gathered around it. Trembling, they huddled as closely to the fire as they could get. Others contributed more and larger sticks, and the fire soon roared.

Lewis pulled off his wet coat and backed himself up to the fire. "As soon as we get ourselves dry," he said, his voice quavering along with his shivers, "we'll all head home."

"We haven't met the Shawnees yet," Dragging Canoe protested.

"And we won't," said Lewis. "Not this trip. One of the boats we lost was carrying all our supplies. Food and ammunition. Bloody damn."

The Englishmen, all except Pearis, took their horses and headed back for their Virginia settlements. The Cherokees, including Ostenaco and those others who had come on horseback, and Dragging Canoe and others on foot, started back toward their own homes. Pearis stayed with them. Before leaving the edge of the river, Dragging Canoe checked the boat in which he had been riding and found that, though it had not capsized, the collision with the ice had damaged it. Pearis looked into it and found a jug of rum he had secreted there. He retrieved it, tucking it under his coat. Considering the damage to the canoe, Dragging Canoe and Pearis decided that they would go on foot with the others. It was a long and cold way home, and they had no supplies. They had even lost most of their guns and ammunition in the river. Only Dragging Canoe, Pearis, the few other men who had been in the boat with them, and the men who had come on horseback had rifles and dry powder. In addition, Dragging Canoe carried a steel trade tomahawk and a steel knife.

It was a disappointing end to a campaign that had begun so boastfully. A white man's campaign, he thought. A winter war. He was hungry, and he knew that the others were, too. They traveled all the rest of that day without eating. Then they camped for the night. Pearis sat alone and drank from his jug.

One of the men killed and butchered his horse, and they all ate of it. They slept that night beside small, scattered fires, and in the morning they all woke up hungry and cold. Toward the middle of the day one man spotted a lone deer and killed it. They stopped to butcher the deer and cook and eat it, but it was a small one. There was not enough meat to go around, so they killed another horse.

"We'll all be on foot soon," Dragging Canoe said.

"It's better than starving," Pearis said.

The next few days proved the truth of Dragging Canoe's prediction, for all the horses had been slaughtered for food. The Cherokees were all tired and hungry and cold. Dragging Canoe was thinking that it had been a big mistake to agree to go along with those Virginia Englishmen. They were once again moving through land that those English considered to be part of Virginia, thought of as their own, and soon, Dragging Canoe knew, they would come across scattered farms of the white settlers. Perhaps they would be able to get some supplies from those farmers.

They had just emerged from a heavily wooded area into an open plain, and up ahead a few horses ran loose. "Look," said one of the men.

"Go easy," said Ostenaco. "Don't frighten them off." He was thinking that it would be good to ride again, and the horses would get them home much more quickly than would walking.

But one of the men had no patience. Instead of moving slowly toward the horses, he dropped to one knee, took aim, and fired, killing one of the beasts. The others ran away frightened. The man ran toward his kill, pulling his knife as he ran. Others followed him. They butchered the animal, built fires, and cooked it right there. They made the meat go around as far as it could, and they still wanted more, but the other horses had disappeared. They put out the fires and started walking again. Pearis left behind him an empty jug.

It was early evening when they came across the farmhouse. They watched for a while from a safe distance. There didn't seem to be anyone around. They moved in closer. Chickens strutted and clucked around the yard. "Let me approach them," Pearis said, and he went up to the house alone. As he moved into the yard, he yelled out, "Hello, the house." No one answered. He walked on up to the door and pounded on it hard. There was still no answer. He turned to face the Cherokees again. "No one's home," he shouted.

They ran in and began grabbing squawking chickens. Men and

chickens ran in all directions. When they had at last killed and eaten them all, they found the eggs and ate them. Then they went into the house to see what else they could find to eat. "When these folks get home," Pearis said, helping himself to a jug he found in a cabinet, "I hope they ain't hungry."

"Or thirsty," Dragging Canoe added. Pearis looked at him and grinned.

They sat around their small fires again that night, Pearis sipping on his newly acquired jug. Dragging Canoe sat beside the same fire. "I don't think anyone's hungry tonight," Pearis said.

"Except maybe those white people whose food we ate," Dragging Canoe said.

"Look at it this way," Pearis said, "the sons of bitches owed it to you."

"How do you figure that, Pearis?" Dragging Canoe asked.

"They're Virginians, ain't they?" said Pearis. "It was Virginia that begged you to go on this campaign. We wouldn't be in this mess at all if it hadn't been for Virginia. Their worthless major and his men ran home and left us when the going got tough. We got to survive and get home somehow, don't we?"

Dragging Canoe chuckled. Pearis offered him the jug.

"No, thank you, Pearis," Dragging Canoe said. "If we were at home, I'd drink your rum with you, but I want to wake up in the morning with a clear head. We still have a ways to travel and food to get along the way."

The path they traveled went down into a valley between high hills. They had moved into the natural hallway when the shooting started. They had been taken completely by surprise. Those not killed by the initial volley ran for hiding places. Those with rifles looked for someone to shoot back at. Soon both sides were pinned down with no clear shots at anyone on either side. Pearis waited for a quiet moment, and then he shouted, "Who are you?"

"Virginians, by God," came the reply.

"I'm an Englishman," Pearis called. "You're making a mistake."

"You're the one making a mistake," came the voice from the proud Virginian, "traveling with thieving redskins. Come out with your hands up and walk this way. We won't kill you."

Dragging Canoe, crouched behind a small boulder near to Pearis, gave the South Carolina trader a look. "I don't trust him," Pearis said. "I'll stick with you." He waited a moment, then added, "But what are you going to do?"

"We'll wait for dark," said Dragging Canoe. "Then we'll move out of here."

Early the next morning, the Cherokees, with Richard Pearis, went back to the bloody pass. They moved in cautiously until they were sure the Virginians had gone. Down on the trail they found the bodies of twenty-three of their comrades. They had all been scalped.

"So these were our allies," Dragging Canoe said. "Virginians."

"They'll take the scalps in for bounty," Pearis said. "Virginia pays for the scalps of enemy Indians, and they can't tell one Indian scalp from another."

"The Virginians will be paid for this," said Dragging Canoe. "I'll pay them myself."

# 6

Back in the Overhills Cherokee country, Dragging Canoe and Richard Pearis arrived at Tamatly not far from the new South Carolina fort named Loudon. The others had dropped off at their own towns or at roads that would lead them home. Word of the abortive military mission had already spread throughout the country. They found themselves a good meal at the home of some of Dragging Canoe's clan sisters. Then, having thanked the cooks kindly, Pearis stood up and patted his belly. "Well," he said, "I'll be moving on to the fort. What about you?"

"I'll stay here, Pearis," Dragging Canoe said. "I want to find my father and have a talk with him."

"I can get more rum at the fort," Pearis said.

Dragging Canoe laughed. "Get drunk, Pearis," he said. "After what we went through together, you deserve it."

"Come along with me," said Pearis. "You went through it, too. You deserve as much."

"No," Dragging Canoe said. "You go ahead. I'll see you later."

Pearis shrugged and went on alone toward the fort. Dragging Canoe stood for a moment watching Pearis. He smiled. For an Englishman, he thought, Pearis was all right. He wandered the streets of Tamatly, looking to see who he could see. He spoke to people he met, talked briefly with a few, and asked after his father.

Finally, he found Ada-gal'kala at the townhouse. As they greeted one another, Dragging Canoe looked down at his father. He had long since outgrown the older man. Then they sat down side by side on one of the benches there. He told his father the details of the abortive Virginia expedition and about the surprise attack of the Virginians on the Cherokees, about the twenty-three killed there in the mountain pass. "I mean to get some young men to go with me and pay back those Virginians," he said.

"They haven't lived up to the bargain they made with us," said the old man. "The Virginia fort is still standing empty. Empty of soldiers. Some Cherokees have moved in there with their families and built new houses for themselves inside its walls."

"I owe the Virginians for twenty-three Cherokee lives," Dragging Canoe said.

No further explanation was called for. Both men knew, of course, that for the Cherokees, balance was everything. All things in nature were balanced: summer with winter, day with night, male with female. The rituals and ceremonies the Cherokees practiced were all designed to help this world maintain its own precarious balance between the two opposed worlds, the one above and the one below. And a life must be balanced with a life.

"Wait," said Ada-gal'kala. "There are other ways to deal with this matter. Diplomatic ways."

"I know nothing of diplomacy," Dragging Canoe said. "I only know to pay for a life with a life."

"Wait yet a while," his father said. "We need the English trade goods. Especially we need their guns and ammunition to help us in our fight with the Ani-Tsiksa. We ought to remain on friendly terms with the English if we can. Let me try my way first. I'll talk to John Stuart. If it doesn't work, then you can try your way."

Dragging Canoe reluctantly agreed. Ada-gal'kala was not only his father, he was also one of the most highly respected men in the Cherokee Nation. So he agreed, but he didn't like it. He wanted to tell his father that he hadn't been there, he hadn't watched the twenty-three Cherokees fall and die under the cowardly Virginia ambush. He had not been there when they packed the scalped bodies home over such a long distance, when they had to tell the wives and mothers what had happened to their young men.

They had gone out to fight the Shawnees at the request of Virginia and under the leadership of Virginia, and Virginia had handled the whole thing badly. Then Virginians had killed Cherokees. It was a supreme insult, one that would be cowardly and shameful not to avenge. And, then and always, there was the matter of balance. Dragging Canoe did not like this diplomacy. Yet his father was Ada-gal'kala, and Ada-gal'kala had spoken. That did not compel Dragging Canoe to obey. Nothing could compel a Cherokee. It did persuade him, though. For now he would keep his further thoughts to himself. He would hold his tongue.

"Did you hear about your cousin's new husband?" Ada-gal'kala said, changing the subject.

"No," said Dragging Canoe. "Which cousin?"

"Nanyehi," said his father.

"Ah," said Dragging Canoe. "I had wondered when she would marry again. Who is the man?"

"She's married a white man," Ada-gal'kala said. "The trader Bryan Ward. Now she calls herself Nancy Ward."

"So she's following the ways of the white man," Dragging Canoe said. "Will their children then be called Ward?"

"I'm sure they will be," Ada-gal'kala said. "It's always that way when our women marry white men."

"I never thought that she, of all our people, would follow the ways of the *ani-yonega*." Dragging Canoe said. Ada-gal'kala gave a casual shrug. "Everything changes," he said. He thought wryly about how he himself was playing the role of father to his son Dragging Canoe in the way of the English. According to the ancient practices of the Cherokees, he was usurping the role of Ni-on-e's brother, for the mother's brother was traditionally the teacher, advisor, and disciplinarian to her son. Perhaps, he thought, my son has not realized that fact concerning our relationship.

"And you," he said, "have you never followed the ways of the English?"

Dragging Canoe's face burned. He knew that his father was making reference to the recent winter campaign that had cost twenty-three Cherokee lives. There were other things, too. He knew it, but he did not want to think about it anymore.

Dragging Canoe was on the *gatayusti* playing field in front of the Tamatly townhouse. He was balancing a stone disc in his left hand and holding a spear in his right. He watched intently as another player made his toss. The spear stuck in the ground about a hand's width from where the disc quit rolling and fell over. It was going to be a hard toss to beat, but Dragging Canoe had bet his best rifle, powder horn, and shot pouch against a fine white stallion. It was his turn to toss, and he stepped up to the line.

Everyone was watching. Standing over against the town house, Ada-gal'kala and his friend John Stuart, the red-haired Scot who was second in command at Fort Loudon, watched, too, although they appeared to be in deep, serious conversation.

Dragging Canoe looked out over the field, judging how far his roll of the disc would last and, therefore, just where he would have to aim the spear. He hefted the disc, drew back his left hand, raised his right with the spear over his shoulder, and ran. After a few strides he slung the disc with a powerful underhand swing and let it fly. Before it had even hit the ground to start its roll, he gave the spear a mighty toss. He hopped a few times on his left foot and watched the stone roll, the spear make its arc.

The stone at last began to wobble, and the spear point drove itself into the ground just ahead. The stone wobbled on a little. It looked as if it would fall over to its side short of the mark, but it wobbled on until it touched the spear, then fell over. Cries of approval rose up from the crowd gathered there. Dragging Canoe walked over to where his opponent stood with the reins of the white horse in his hand. "He's yours," the man said, and he handed the reins to Dragging Canoe.

Turning to lead his prize away, Dragging Canoe found his path blocked by a young woman. She was about as tall as his father, and she was slender. She was dressed in the new fashion, wearing a blue cloth skirt and a white blouse obtained from the English traders. Her feet were bare, and her long black hair hung down over her shoulders, reaching almost to her waist.

"*'Siyo,*" she said.

"Hello."

"I am called Guque," she said.

"Well, Little Quail," said Dragging Canoe. "I am Tsiyu Gansini."

"I know," she said.

"Do you live here in Tamatly?" he asked her.

"No," she said. "I live at Malaquo. I'm here with my parents visiting. You played the game well, and you won a beautiful horse."

"Would you like to ride on him?" he asked her. "I have another. I'll go get it, and we can ride together."

They rode out of Tamatly and down the road. They rode for a while without speaking to one another, enjoying the speed at which they moved, the motion beneath them and the wind in their faces. Then Dragging Canoe turned his mount off the road, and she followed him. They stopped beside the river and dismounted. The two horses lowered their heads to drink from the fresh, cool water. Dragging Canoe sat on a fallen log, and Guque sat beside him.

"That was pleasant," she said. "Thank you for letting me be the first to ride your new horse."

"How was he?" Dragging Canoe asked her.

"He's a good horse," she said. "You made a good bet."

"Why did you come to meet me back there?" he said suddenly.

She blushed and looked away. "You went north with the Virginians," she said.

He waited for her to say more, but she was silent. "Yes," he said. "I did. So?"

"My brother went, too," she said. "Did you know him? He was called Bark—from Malaquo."

Dragging Canoe looked down at the ground as a dark expression crossed his face. "I knew him," he said.

"He was one of those who did not make it back home," she said.

"One of twenty-three," said Dragging Canoe.

"Someone said that you would pay the Virginians for those lives," she said.

"I would have gone already," he said, "but my father asked me to wait until he had tried his way—diplomacy. I promised I'd wait, but I did not promise that I wouldn't go. I mean to go and pay the Virginians."

"I'm glad to hear you say that," she said. "I want them to be paid."

"Is that why you came to talk to me?" he asked.

"Yes," she said.

"Well," he said, "we can go back to town now." He thought about the horrible smallpox pits on his face, and he thought that he should have known that no woman would want to talk to him just for his own sake, just to get to know him better. He stood up, and she looked up at him.

"I'm glad that we talked and rode together, though," she said. "Will I see you again?"

"You'll hear when I've paid the Virginians," he said.

"I know," she said. "I'd still like to see more of you."

Dragging Canoe thought much about Guque after that. She was a beautiful young woman. No woman had ever paid much attention to him before. He had always thought that it was because of his scars. The smallpox, he thought, had disfigured his face and made him undesirable to women. But Guque seemed to find him attractive. He told himself that she only wanted to make sure that he killed enough Englishmen to make up for the death of her brother. She wasn't really interested in him for any other reason. But the way she had looked at him caused him to hope—in spite of himself.

Ada-gal'kala walked through the gate into the South Carolina fort, Fort Loudon. No one attempted to stop him. He was a big man among the Cherokees, and all of the soldiers knew him on sight. Some spoke to him, some actually saluted. He acknowledged them briskly as he passed them by. Then he saw the Scot, John Stuart, second in command at the fort, walking across the way. Stuart was holding his hat in one hand, and with his other hand he was pushing his unruly red hair back from his forehead.

"Hey, Bushyhead," Ada-gal'kala called out.

Stuart looked toward the sound and spotted its source. He grinned and put the hat on his head. He counted many of the Cherokees as friends, especially since he had married the beautiful Susannah Emory, a mixed-blood member of the Cherokee Long Hair Clan.

"Ah," he said, "Carpenter, my friend, welcome."

The two men met and embraced. Then Ada-gal'kala stepped back.

"Is Susannah well?" Ada-gal'kala asked.

"Yes," said Stuart. "And all of your family?"

"They're well," said Ada-gal'kala, "but my oldest son is impatient."

"Is there a problem, my friend?" asked Stuart.

"Bushyhead," said Ada-gal'kala, "there are some things I must speak with you about."

"Let's go into my office," Stuart said, and he led the way to a small cabin. The two men went in, and Stuart shut the door.

"Sit down," he said. "How may I help?"

"As you know, it was I who stopped the young men from falling on the Virginians," Ada-gal'kala said. "My own son wanted to ride out immediately and kill some of them, enough to pay for the Cherokees they killed. You know me. I always prefer to play the role of the diplomat. I try to avoid the spilling of blood." He paused in his oration to let the impact of his words soak in. "But the Virginians have killed some of our young men, and our young men are impatient."

"My friend," said Stuart, "we should go to Captain Demere to speak of these things. His influence with Virginia is greater than mine."

Stuart led Ada-gal'kala over to the office of the commander of the fort, and he quickly gained an audience there. Ada-gal'kala was dressed in his finest, and he was holding himself stiff and straight, as if the meeting with Demere were a formal matter of state. He repeated the concerns he had already expressed to his friend Stuart. Demere harrumphed and shot a quick glance at Stuart. Then he looked back at Ada-gal'kala.

"But Governor Dinwiddie did send you Virginia's formal apology," Demere said, "did he not?"

"May I kill your brother," said Ada-gal'kala, "and then apologize? And will you then take my hand again and call me friend?"

"He sent presents for the families of the slain men," Demere added. "Did he not send enough?"

"How much would I have to pay you for the life of your brother or of your son?" said the old diplomat.

"I understand your feelings, Little Carpenter, but —"

"Demere," said Ada-gal'kala, "our quarrel is with Virginia, not with you and South Carolina. I come to you as a friend to tell you that many of my young men do not recognize, as do I, the difference between the two. In their eyes, you are all English, and the Virginians have turned the hearts of the young men against you all — all English. South Carolina may suffer because of what Virginia did. I hope that is not the case, but I fear for your safety, and that is why I came to you."

"My friend," said Demere, "we must do all we can to maintain the peace. There are young men on both sides who would like nothing more than to go to war. It's up to the wiser heads, yours and mine, to prevent that."

"Why will not the English punish white men who kill Cherokees?" Ada-gal'kala asked. "If a Cherokee kills a white man, do not the white men want that Cherokee to pay for what he did?"

Demere harrumphed again. "It would be very difficult to get Virginia to arrest and try the men responsible for the deaths of those Cherokees," he said. "It may not even be possible to determine who those men were. You'll have to content yourselves with apologies and presents. You must keep your young men at peace."

"That grows more difficult each day," said Ada-gal'kala. "While my son and others are waiting for a proper response from Virginia, some English officers at Fort Prince George went into the town of Keowee. The young men were all out fighting the Chickasaws. These bad officers took advantage of their absence and abused some Cherokee women there. The young men are very angry about that. I don't know if I can hold them back much longer."

And he did not. It was early morning when Dragging Canoe and his followers moved quietly up to the settler's cabin in Virginia. Smoke was rising from the chimney in the cabin. No one was outside. The others were anxious to attack. "Wait," he said. "Wait for them to come outside." He was afraid that some of the young men would lose their patience and attack the cabin anyway, but they waited with him. Soon a man and a boy, not quite a man, came outside. The cabin door stood open. Dragging Canoe gobbled like a big male turkey, and the others joined him, and as they gobbled, they ran toward the cabin.

The man and boy turned to race for the door, but two of the Cherokees stopped long enough to aim and fire their long rifles. The two whites dropped in their tracks. There was a scream from inside the cabin. Dragging Canoe stopped running and watched as some of the young men ran inside brandishing their clubs. He waited a while to let the young men finish the slaughter. Then he called them together again.

"Let's go," he said. "There are more settlers up the river."

They found two more cabins and attacked them with much the same results, and the tally was up to ten. Then they met two riders on the road. When the white men saw them, they turned their horses to make a run for it. "Use your rifles," Dragging Canoe said. Several of the men, including Dragging Canoe himself, raised their rifles and fired. Both white men fell from their saddles. "The first to get to them take their scalps," Dragging Canoe said, and the young men raced ahead. Twelve, Dragging Canoe said to himself. Eleven to go.

They moved farther along the road, the river running just to their right. Dragging Canoe knew that more Virginia cabins were ahead. Then they saw a boat coming down the river. Five white men were in the boat. "Take them," he said. They rode their horses to the edge of the water, where some of the young men dismounted and started wading into the river. Others rode their horses into the water. Still others sat in their saddles and lifted their rifles to fire.

Two of the white men fell to the rifle fire. By then two Cherokees had managed to swim to the boat. They grabbed the sides of the boat and attempted to overturn it. One white man lifted his rifle to smash at the fingers of the attackers. A rifle ball from shore tore into his shoulder. Then the two Cherokees in the water pulled hard together, and the boat overturned. The wounded man fell into the water between them. The two Cherokees reached for his head and shoulders and shoved him under the water. The other two white men had jumped out the other side as their boat capsized.

One of the horsemen had reached the boat on horseback, and he raised a pistol and fired, hitting one of the white men in the head. The other was swimming as fast as he could for the other side. A rifleman on shore took careful aim and fired. The man screamed. He flailed at the water for a moment, then relaxed. In a few more minutes, the Cherokees had dragged all five bodies to shore in order to take their scalps.

Seventeen, Dragging Canoe counted. Six more will do it.

On down the road they found a man alone plowing a field. A little beyond that, there was a cabin. There were four white people there. They took them and moved on. The final victim was a lone traveler. After killing him, the young men wanted to continue, but Dragging Canoe told them he was going back to Tamatly. "I came to cover the twenty-three Cherokees killed by Virginians," he said. "We've done that. Do as you please, but I'm going home." The others muttered among themselves for a bit, then at last decided to return with Dragging Canoe. After all, he had organized the raid. He was the leader. They would not go on without him.

Dragging Canoe and the others returned to Tamatly singing a song, and the people in town heard them coming and ran out to meet them. The returning men were painted all red from their faces to their feet, and some of them were carrying a long pole. The pole had been freshly cut and its bark stripped. It too was painted red, and from the pole, twenty-three red-painted scalps dangled.

Once inside Tamatly, they danced the victory dance, and the young men boasted of the number of white men they had killed. Nor were they ashamed to admit that some of their victims had been women and children. Dragging Canoe told his father that it was over. "We killed twenty-three," he said. "The Virginians have been paid back for what they did." Ada-gal'kala nodded his solemn agreement. He was not pleased, but there was nothing he could say. It was all right and proper, all according to the old ways. Then Dragging Canoe eagerly searched the crowd that was gathered around the dance ground until he at last saw Guque. He noticed that she was alone, and he went to stand beside her.

"You're not dancing," she said.

"No," he said. "I did what I set out to do."

"Yes," she said. "I heard, and I'm glad for what you did. Will you dance the next round?"

"Yes," he said. "I will." And he danced two rounds of the victory dance, and she watched him the whole time he danced, and then he left the dance and went back once more to her side. "Walk with me," he said, and she did, and his heart thrilled. There in the darkness by the light of the fire, she looked even more lovely than he recalled.

They walked together out of town and down to a nearby creek bank. There only the moon and the stars gave light to an otherwise dark night, and that little light was almost blocked out by the thick canopy of trees that hung over their heads. They stood for a while in silence, listening to the night sounds, the water rippling by, the songs of night birds, the leaves rustling gently in the slight breeze. Then Guque turned to face Dragging Canoe. She looked up at him, admiring his strong features, his broad and thick chest. She smiled, and she slipped out of her doeskin dress.

Dragging Canoe's breath was almost taken away from him at the sight of her shapely body. He looked her up and down, and slowly he reached out a hand and touched her. He slid his hand down from her shoulder to rest on one breast. Her skin was smooth to the touch, and the feel of it sent a thrill unlike any he had ever known racing through his own body. He stepped back from her to remove his own clothing, the leggings and breechcloth and the mocassins. Then he waded into the water to rinse the red paint from his face and body.

Stepping out of the water, clean and naked, he pulled her close to him with both arms and held her tight against him. He pressed his face into the angle between her neck and shoulder, and he breathed deeply, taking in the odor of her body and of her hair. She bent her knees to sit down on the ground, and as she did, she pulled on his shoulders, pulling him after her, and soon they were lying together in ecstasy there by the bank of the clear running spring.

"Mother," said Dragging Canoe, "I want this woman for my wife."

"Does she like you for a husband?" asked Ni-on-e.

"Yes," Dragging Canoe said. "We've talked about it already. I know that she wants me as I want her. I wouldn't even mention it to you otherwise."

"Then," his mother said, "it's time for me to talk to the women of her clan."

"You'll like her, Mother," he said. *Wado.*

The wedding was arranged by the women of the two clans. It was a simple, traditional wedding ceremony. It was just enough ceremony to let all the people in Big Island Town know that the two were becoming husband and wife. The people gathered around to watch as Dragging Canoe and Guque met in the center of town. She handed him a basket of corn. He handed her a haunch of venison. They turned to stand shoulder to shoulder, and an old man of her clan threw a blanket over both of them. They walked together to her house and went inside, and it was done.

So Dragging Canoe moved to Big Island Town, the home of his new wife, and there he moved into her house to live among her people. He became acquainted with the members of her family and settled into the proper relationship with each. He did not speak to his new mother-in-law, nor she to him. He treated his new brothers-in-law as if they had been best friends forever. He teased with his wife's sisters, and they teased him back. And he was pleased with his new family. They were good people, all of them, and they were also pleasant company.

Guque was as good as a wife can be. She was a good cook, and she had a pleasant disposition. She was obviously devoted to her husband, and they never quarreled. She did not nag at him as some wives did their husbands. And she was a wonderful lover. She and Dragging Canoe had great moments of ecstasy together. They should have been happy, but something was wrong. Dragging Canoe was not as content as he felt he should be. There was a restlessness in him, and it was something he could not define.

Maybe, he sometimes thought, he was feeling guilty for living such a life of ease and pleasure. He told himself that the times were troubled. It seemed to Dragging Canoe that Cherokee life was changing every day. "Everything changes," his father had said, but Dragging Canoe thought that they were changing too much and too fast, and he thought that the changes were not all good. The most troubling thing of all to Dragging Canoe was the knowledge that the Cherokees could no longer earn a living off their own land.

The white people had taken too much of it away from them and were wanting more all the time. The animals that once had been so plentiful had been thinned out severely with overhunting. And now, he admitted ruefully to himself, even if they could drive all the whites out of the land, they would not, for they could no longer live without them. They needed their trade goods in order to survive.

As if all that were not troublesome enough, he had heard that some young men from other Cherokee towns, inspired, it seemed, by his own recent work in Virginia, had gone out on their own to raid the whites, not only in Virginia, but also in the Carolinas. His own raid had been made in retaliation, to pay back the Virginians, twenty-three whites for twenty-three murdered Cherokees. These new raids could mean only trouble. He knew that. He could almost see it coming. It would be the Englishmen's turn to pay back the Cherokees. But if any Englishmen attacked Cherokees, he knew that he would have to join in the fight and help to defend his own people and his own land.

Were all of these troubles, these changes, the cause of his unrest? He couldn't be sure. He thought that they must have something to do with it, but there was more. There was a vague and distant feeling. There was a childhood memory in which he stood beside his mother, looked up at her, and said, "I'll be a great man." And there was a question that kept pricking at his brain. "If you think that you're to be a great man, then shouldn't you be doing something about these troubles?" But in response to the nagging question, all he could say to himself was, "What is there to be done? What can I do?" And so there remained the sense of guilt, the unease.

## 1759

Ada-gal'kala made a journey from Tamatly to the new home of his son in Malaquo, the Big Island Town. There was something he needed to talk about with his son. He went to the home of Guque and found the small family eating from a large pot of venison stew out in front of the house. Guque welcomed her father-in-law and gave him a bowl from which to eat. The little boy, about two years old, ran around naked, stopping beside his mother with his mouth opened wide when he wanted a bite to eat. For a while, they sat and ate, almost in silence, Ada-gal'kala remembering his own family when Dragging Canoe, not yet named, was the size of this little one. He chuckled to himself, for the *usdi* was an image of its father at that age. It was a young Dragging Canoe, he thought. At last Guque excused herself, took the little one, and went into the house, leaving father and son alone.

"You should stop fighting the English," Ada-gal'kala said. "Some of our important men have gone to Charlestown to make a peace."

"I know," said Dragging Canoe. "Sinawa, from this town, went along with them."

"I don't think that you need to kill any more Englishmen," Ada-gal'kala said. "You've paid them for what the Virginians did. You've done so much that you've become the war chief of this town. You're becoming a great man, my son, but a great man needs to know when to fight and when to make peace. We need to save our young men for the war with the Ani-Tsiksa. We need to make our peace with the English in order to be able to trade with them again. We need guns and ammunition. It's best to make peace."

"Maybe," said Dragging Canoe. "I killed only enough to cover the bodies of Cherokees killed by Virginians. Those young men who continue to raid in Virginia are not my young men. But if Virginians should come here seeking their revenge, what am I to do?"

Dragging Canoe filled a pipe with tobacco and lit it with a stick from the fire. He puffed to get the tobacco burning well, then he handed the pipe to his father. Ada-gal'kala took the pipe and smoked. He waited for his son's response. Dragging Canoe was a grown man and had achieved some status in Big Island Town. He had to be approached just as any other important man. Ada-gal'kala had to give him the respect of his office. He knew that. He handed the pipe back to Dragging Canoe.

"Wait for the news from Charlestown," said Ada-gal'kala. "Then we'll see."

"We'll wait to hear what happened in Charlestown," the young man said. "Will you stay with us until then?"

"No. I can't stay here," said the Little Carpenter. "The delegation will be returning to Echota in just a few days. I have to be there to meet them and hear what they have to say. Will you go with me?"

"Yes," said his son. "I'll go along."

"I had some news from up north," Ada-gal'kala said. "My friend Pontiac and his Ottawas have once more gone to war against the English in their country."

"It seems that the English are unable to keep the peace with anyone," Dragging Canoe said. "Do you think they can keep it with us?"

Ada-gal'kala shrugged. "We'll have to wait and find out," he said. "But if they cannot, let it be them and not us who fail to keep it."

Dragging Canoe put his pipe away. "I too have news," he said.

"Yes?" said his father.

"Guque is carrying another little one."

The older man smiled. "So I will be grandfather again," he said. "I hope that it's another ballsticks." He let out a long and weary sigh. "It would be good," he said, "if they could grow up in peaceful times."

"And then they would have no way in which to earn the honors brought by war," Dragging Canoe said. "No way to improve their status among the people."

"There are other skills," said his father.

Dragging Canoe made no response to that last statement. He knew how the old man had meant it. It was a way of boasting about his own reputation as a diplomat, but at the same time it had been an indirect way of telling his son to stop being a troublemaker and settle down to a peaceful life. It was like a sting, for Dragging Canoe did not believe that he had caused the late trouble. He had merely reacted to it in the only way a Cherokee was supposed to react to such things. He had not started the fighting and killing. He had acted only to balance things out for the Cherokees who had been killed by the Virginians. It really wasn't fair of his father, he thought, to chastise him for such action.

Ada-gal'kala and Dragging Canoe traveled together to Echota, and they waited there for four days before the delegation at last came back. Each Cherokee town had sent someone to the peace meeting in Charlestown. Sinawa had been the Big Island Town representative. It had been an important meeting, designed to bring about a peaceful settlement to the conflict between the Cherokees and the English colonies, particularly Virginia, the conflict that had begun as a result of the botched campaign against the Shawnees. Everyone met in the Echota townhouse to hear what the delegates would have to say. After a few words from Guhna-gadoga, Sinawa stood up to speak.

"Governor Lyttleton," Sinawa said, "wants us to give him every Cherokee who has killed a white man. He means to kill them all to even things up. Until we do that, he says there will be war. And, of course, there will be no more trade goods from Virginia."

Kittegunsta, a resident of the town, stood up. "At Fort Loudon, Demere said the same thing to us who live here at Echota," he said. "He told us that we have to deliver up to him all Cherokees who have killed Englishmen, so that the Englishmen can kill them. If we fail to do that, he said, the English will make war on us until we are wiped out."

Ada-gal'kala jaws tightened. He wasn't surprised at Lyttleton, but Demere had said that, too? And after he had pretended to be a friend? A part of him wanted to call for an attack on Fort Loudon to wipe out Demere and all of the soldiers there, all except Bushy-head, of course. Demere was not only deceitful, he was also a fool, for Fort Loudon was in the heart of the Cherokee country. Demere and his soldiers were surrounded and outnumbered. Who did Demere think he was? Did he believe that the Cherokees were so afraid of the English? He held back his anger, reminded himself of his role as diplomat and peacemaker, and stood up to speak.

"I think that the English," he said, "Demere and Lyttleton, have failed to understand the situation. I think that we should give them one more chance to listen to reason and avoid a bloody war that will cost the lives of many Cherokees and many whites."

Dragging Canoe sat in silence and listened. Had the decision been his to make, he would have called for continued war against the English. But he kept his silence. He would let his father talk. Ada-gal'kala was one of the two most respected and therefore most powerful men of the Cherokees. Let us see, Dragging Canoe said to himself, what he will suggest.

When the meeting was over, the persuasive words of Ada-gal'kala had won the debate. The decision had been made to send one more Cherokee delegation to Charlestown. Ogan'sdo' himself had volunteered to go along this time. The rest of the delegation was made up of other important men. Ada-gal'kala had thought that he too should go along. After all, they were sending their most important men, and he was one of them. He was also known to be a great diplomat.

"I think that you should stay here," Ogan'sdo' had said.

Ada-gal'kala at first thought that his old rival wanted to keep all the credit for the success of this peace mission to himself, that he wanted to claim his place as the most powerful man of the Cherokees. It was a way of keeping Ada-gal'kala away from important negotiations, where he might stand out as a very important man in Cherokee affairs. Before he could protest, however, Ogan'sdo' continued.

"We can't afford to have all the most important men of our people in the hands of the English at one time," he said. "We know the English can't be trusted. Stay here and be safe. Our people will need your services again, maybe very soon."

Guhna-gadoga then spoke. "Ogan'sdo' is correct in this," he said. "I think that you should stay here."

Thirty-two men were at last selected for the important mission. Ogan'sdo' would head the list. Tsinohe, Tsisanah, Tsisdu, Conasoratah, Katactoi, Kealharufteke, the Mankiller of Cowee, Nicholehe, Ukah, Ousanatah, Ousanoletah, Ousonaletak, Quarrasatahe, Sannaoeste, Skaleloske, Tahli-tihi, Totaiahoi, Whoa-tihi, Woyi, and Killianka were among the rest. Dragging Canoe thought about the words of Ogan'sdo' concerning the treachery of the English. He thought about his own recent experience in dealing with Virginia. He worried for the safety of this peace delegation. He wondered about the wisdom of his father.

They met in Charlestown, the English officials seated behind long tables they had set up for themselves in a courtyard, the thirty-two Cherokees standing in a group facing them. Crowds of curious English colonists, men, women, and children, were all around gaping to see the wild Indians. Ogan'sdo' could not help noticing that the Cherokees had been surrounded. Governor Lyttleton pompously

read off the names of twenty-two Cherokee men. "We have identified these warriors," he said, "as being the murderers of Englishmen,
and we demand that you capture them and deliver them into our
hands for proper execution."

Ogan'sdo' stepped forward.

"You're making a hard talk," he said. "How can we deliver these
men up to you when we cannot even understand your pitiful
attempts at pronouncing their names? We do not know what men
you are accusing. Those names you called out—they don't even
sound like anything in our language. Besides, we have our own
demands to make of you. But I did not think to begin this meeting
with demands. We should talk to one another in good faith. Tell me
what is bothering you and what you want of me, and then listen to
me while I tell you the same. We did not kill any Englishmen until
the Virginians had killed twenty-three of our young men—young
men who had gone to fight the Shawnees at the request of Virginia."

"There is nothing to discuss," said Lyttleton, "beyond what I
have already said."

"Then we have wasted our time coming to see you," Ogan'sdo'
said. "We'll go back home."

As Ogan'sdo' and the other Cherokees turned to leave, Lyttleton stood up and waved an arm, and soldiers with rifles appeared
from out of the crowd on all sides to surround the Cherokees.
Ogan'sdo' looked around at them. They had been ready. It was a
well-laid trap. There was nothing he could do. Lyttleton must
have planned it that way from the beginning, he thought. Ah,
well, he had long known that the English were no good. They had
no sense of honor. He could think of no lower form of treachery
than to capture men who had come to talk of peace under a white
flag. He could think of no lower form of life than an Englishman.

"You're all my prisoners," Lyttleton said. Then to an officer who
stood behind him, he added, "Get the men ready to ride and have
my horse brought around to me."

Lyttleton rode pompously at the head of an army of 1,400 men,
and behind his army his prisoners, the Cherokee delegation,

walked. His announced destination was Fort Prince George, adjacent to the Cherokee town of Keowee. It would be a good place, he said, in which to have the Cherokee murderers delivered up to him. Ogan'sdo' and the others were sullen. Ogan'sdo' remembered his own words of caution to Ada-gal'kala. "They can't be trusted." He was glad that he had managed to talk his old rival into staying behind, for one of them had to be free. He wondered what plans Lyttleton had in mind for him and his companions, and he wondered what kind of diplomacy Ada-gal'kala might be able to apply to the situation.

When word of what Lyttleton had done reached him, Ada-gal'kala traveled alone to Fort Prince George. Some cautioned him to stay away, lest he be thrown in with the other prisoners. He had confidence in his abilities as a diplomat, though. He knew that he could talk to the English and get at least part of what he wanted out of them. At the fort he was admitted into an office where Governor Lyttleton waited. The pompous little man puffed himself up behind a desk and frowned sternly at Ada-gal'kala.

"Well," he said, "Little Carpenter, is it? I've been told that you can be trusted, but I'm not at all sure that I accept that notion. However, they say also that you're a very important man in your nation. So let's hear what you've come to say."

"Our head men came to you to talk of peace," Ada-gal'kala said. "It's not good that you made them captive under such a circumstance. There are rules to govern the way in which nations deal with one another, even in time of war. I've come to ask you to release those men. Then we can talk of peace once again. I've already told our young men not to fight while we're talking peace. But when you put our head men in prison, the young men became very angry. They want to fight now. It's not easy for me to hold them back while our head men are in your prison."

"You can hold them back or not," said Lyttleton. "It doesn't matter to me a jot. I brought an army of over a thousand soldiers with me from Charlestown, all well armed and ready for action. If your young men want to fight, we'll give them a fight they won't forget—those of them who survive. You tell them that. I've been warned about you. They say that you're a crafty one. Well, don't try to be sly with me, old fox. Just tell your young men what I've said. That's all. Tell them that if they want a fight, I'll deliver them one they'll never forget."

"They don't want to fight," Ada-gal'kala said, "but they want our head men released."

"I want the murderers you're protecting," Lyttleton roared. "Give me the murderers, and I'll release your peace delegation. But not before. You have their names. Bring the guilty ones here to me, and bring them at once."

"You have Ogan'sdo' in your prison," said the Little Carpenter. "He's our head War Chief, and he's the only man in the nation who can accomplish what you want. Release him and two others with him, and give them time to find these men you want and bring them in. It can't be done in a day. They live in different towns. Some several days' journey from here."

Lyttleton scratched his forehead just under the front edge of his powdered wig. "All right," he said. "I'll release three men. You name them. But I'll hold the rest as hostage until you bring the murderers to me. And you must agree for all Cherokees that any Frenchmen found in your country will either be captured and turned over to me or killed outright. Agreed?"

"Agreed," said Ada-gal'kala. "We have no love for the French."

Ada-gal'kala was not at all pleased with the result of his efforts. So the Cherokees would not be allowed to stay out of this fight between the French and the English. That was one problem. The more immediate one was how to secure the release of the hostages without actually turning over twenty-two Cherokees to be killed by the ugly Lyttleton. At least, he told himself, he had secured the release of Ogan'sdo'. Ogan'sdo' and two more.

So Ogan'sdo' walked out of the prison. Woyi and Killianka followed him out. They assured the others that they would work hard to get them out as soon as they could. They were being held in very uncomfortable surroundings, a small room with scarcely enough space for six men. Now with the three released, there were still twenty-nine Cherokees crammed into the tiny room. It was hot, and the men had no room in which to sit down. They stood shoulder to shoulder. They rubbed their perspiration on one another. The air was stale and almost too thick to breathe. Ogan'sdo' was furious at the treachery of the English, and he let Ada-gal'kala know just how he felt.

"He has twenty-nine of our leading men in his prison," said Ada-gal'kala, "and he has more than one thousand soldiers. What can we do except produce the men he asks for?"

"We can tell him that the men he wants have all run away," said Ogan'sdo'. "We can say that we're trying to find them. That will give us some time, and in that time, maybe we can find a way to deal with this treacherous Englishman."

"Maybe," Ada-gal'kala agreed.

"I'd like to kill all the Englishmen," Ogan'sdo' said.

"Just now," said Ada-gal'kala, "that wouldn't be wise. They have our people in there as hostages. We have to think of them first. We have to try to get them out of there safely."

"I know," said Ogan'sdo', "I know, but I'd still like to kill all the Englishmen."

Lieutenant Coytmore, the commander of Fort Prince George, stepped into the office that Governor Lyttleton had appropriated for himself. "You sent for me, Governor?" he said.

"Yes," said Lyttleton. "The damnable savages have had ample time to bring the murderers in. I'm fast losing my patience, I can tell you that. Do you have someone trustworthy you can send with a message to the Carpenter?"

"We have some Cherokees working for us here in the fort, sir," said Coytmore. "We can send one of them out with a message. I trust them."

"Fetch one of them here to me," Lyttleton said. "I don't trust a damned mother's son of them, but I suppose that will have to do. It will serve."

When Coytmore returned to the office a little while later, he was still alone. His face was ashen, and he was short of breath from hurrying.

"Well?" said Lyttleton. "What's the matter, man? Where's the savage?" Then he noticed the pale expression of dread on the lieutenant's face. "For God's sake, what's wrong with you, man?" he said.

"Sir," said Coytmore, "the Cherokees here in the fort—they've all come down with the smallpox. God. It'll spread like wildfire among these Indians."

"Are you certain that it's the smallpox?" Lyttleton asked, his eyes opening wide.

"There's no doubt," said Coytmore. "I've seen it before. Two of the soldiers are showing signs, too."

"Great God Almighty in heaven above," said Lyttleton, breaking out in an almost instant sweat. "I can't stay here. This place will become a death's house. Gather my soldiers and get them ready to ride. Quickly. Well, hurry it up, man."

And Governor Lyttleton rode with his army out of the fort and onto the road that would take him back to Charlestown, fleeing from the smallpox and having accomplished nothing more than the arrest of the peace delegation that had come to Charlestown to talk with him. He left Coytmore with his small force in charge of Fort Prince George, abandoning them to face the spreading epidemic and the rising anger of the Cherokees as best they could. From a shaded spot at the edge of the woods Ada-gal'kala and Ogan'sdo' watched the arrogant, puffy-faced Englishman ride away at the head of his army, bouncing up and down uncomfortably in his saddle. They watched as the powdered wig slipped off the back of his head in the breeze. Lyttleton slapped at it but missed. He didn't stop to pick it up.

"He's riding fast," said Ada-gal'kala. "He rode out from under his own hair."

"If he doesn't slow down," said Ogan'sdo', "he'll kill all their horses before they get home."

"He's running from the smallpox, I think," Ada-gal'kala said.

"It's something that his own people brought here," said Ogan'sdo'. "It would be good if it caught him and carried him away from us for good. He's a bad man, even for an Englishman."

They watched until the last of Lyttleton's soldiers had disappeared down the road. Ogan'sdo' stepped out. "I think I'll go and collect Lyttleton's scalp," he said. Ada-gal'kala laughed as his old rival walked out to the side of the road to pick up the powdered wig.

## 1760

Again the Cherokees watched friends and relatives succumb to the horrible disease that had been brought to them by the English. Those who had lived through it before and had therefore become immune to its ravages recalled the horror they had gone through years before while watching others around them suffer and die. Everyone felt helpless and hopeless in the face of this dread invisible and silent killer. Watching their children suffer and die, parents could do nothing but weep. As before, the traditional medicine people were helpless, their herbs and potions and charms all useless in the face of this enemy brought from across the waters.

Ogan'sdo' rubbed his own rough face and remembered the earlier horror. As he watched the new suffering around him, his rage against the English grew until he could contain it no longer. His friends were still crowded into the tiny room inside the fort, and his people were dying all around from the horrible smallpox. He gathered around him all the healthy young men he could find. Dragging Canoe was among them. Ada-gal'kala tried to talk them out of going to the fort in their angry mood, but it was no use. He gave up the argument in a short while, telling himself that, really, he couldn't blame them.

It was *gola* again, but this time Ogan'sdo' needed no Englishman to urge him to action. This was not the traditional, formalized war of the Cherokees. This was something new, a thing of the white men.

78

And Ogan'sdo' accepted it for what it was. To fight the English, he must fight the way they fight. He would fight in winter. He would lie and cheat. He would kill or take captives under a white flag. The English had drawn up the rules. Now he would play by them.

He led the young men to the Savannah River, just across from the gate to Fort Prince George. The men hid themselves behind the trees and bushes that grew along the riverbank. Ogan'sdo' stepped out in full view and stood there, seemingly alone. A Cherokee woman walked up to the gate and called out. A soldier appeared to see what it was she wanted. She gestured across the river to where Ogan'sdo' stood waiting. She told the soldier that he was waiting to see Coytmore. He wanted to talk. Then the soldier went back inside, and the woman ran away. Ogan'sdo' waited.

Soon Coytmore appeared outside the wall. He looked across the river and saw Ogan'sdo' standing there alone, a bridle hanging down from his right hand.

"Hello, there," he called. "You want to see me? Come on across."

Ogan'sdo' raised his arm and swung the bridle around his head as a signal, and the young men looked out from behind the trees and bushes and aimed their rifles and fired. Almost as soon as he realized what was about to happen, Coytmore felt a sharp, hot pain in his chest. He looked down at the black hole there, and then he felt another, and then another. He jerked, staggered, crumpled, and fell.

"Close the gate," someone inside the fort shouted. "Bolt it. They've killed the commander."

"Man your posts. Prepare for an attack."

Soldiers ran to the parapets along the wall and looked out, but they saw no Indians. No attack was in progress. Looking over the edge of the wall, though, they could see the bloody body of their commander lying there in front of the gate.

"What's going on?" one asked.

"What're the savages up to out there?" said another.

"Nothing. They're not doing nothing."

"They just murdered Coytmore, is all."

"Come on," a soldier shouted. "Let's kill the hostages."

Outraged soldiers with small axes, knives, clubs, pistols, anything they could quickly grab up for weapons, ran to the small room where the twenty-nine prisoners waited hungry, sweltering, tired from trying to sleep on their feet leaning against one another, lungs starving for fresh air, and completely ignorant of what had just transpired. The soldiers jerked open the door and shoved their way madly into the already overcrowded room. Some killed Cherokees in the room, some grabbed hold of prisoners and dragged them outside where they would have more room in which to swing their clubs. Unarmed Cherokee prisoners were shot at close range, in the chest, in the head. Some were stabbed numerous times. Others had their heads bashed in.

Frenzied white men slipped and fell in the blood that ran thick from the victims, and even when the Cherokee prisoners had all been killed, soldiers continued to hack and slash and batter the bodies until their horrible excess exhausted them, and they fell to the floor to rest and regain their strength.

Word of the senseless slaughter soon reached the Cherokees outside and spread quickly to nearby Cherokee towns. Now Adagal'kala knew that there was no longer any reason to talk of peace. No one would listen, neither English nor Cherokee. Some of the young men continued to besiege Fort Prince George. Others laid siege to Fort Loudon over at the junction of the Tellico and Little Tennessee Rivers. Ogan'sdo' led yet others to the outlying South Carolina settlements. Dragging Canoe went with those. A full-scale war was in progress.

They burned several houses and killed all the white men they could find. On their way home, they came across another cabin, but it seemed deserted. "They heard that we were coming and ran away," one of the men said. "It could be a trap," Ogan'sdo' said. "Check it carefully." Dragging Canoe and a young man named Standing Deer ran to the house. Standing Deer shoved the door open and jumped inside. In another moment, he came out again. "There's no one here," he said.

Ogan'sdo' and the others then started walking toward the house. "We'll sleep in it tonight," Ogan'sdo' said, "and we'll burn it in the morning." They were gathered up there at the house when the white men came out of the woods and started shooting. "Inside," Ogan'sdo' shouted. Dragging Canoe was the last one to go through the door. There were already men at the windows with their rifles, looking for targets.

"The white men are hidden behind trees," one of them said.

"We're trapped in here," said another.

"If we go out," said Standing Deer, "they'll shoot us down — one at a time."

"Stay calm," said Ogan'sdo'. "We'll wait and see what happens."

They waited, some watching out the windows for a chance to shoot at someone. Now and then a Cherokee fired at a white man in the woods, and occasionally a white man fired at the house. No one was hit on either side.

"Don't shoot at them," said Ogan'sdo', "unless you're sure of your shot. If we run out of ammunition, we'll really be trapped in here."

They waited some more, and then a white man came running out of the woods, carrying a flaming torch in his hand. A Cherokee at the window fired a rifle shot, but he missed. The man kept running. "Get him," someone shouted, and the next shot staggered the man, but he swung his arm and tossed the torch high. A second shot from the cabin tore into his chest, and he fell forward to lie still, but the torch landed with a thud on the cabin's roof.

The Cherokees in the cabin looked toward the roof. Then they looked at one another. "Soon the whole cabin will be ablaze," said one.

"They mean to either burn us to death in here or to shoot us as we run out the door," said Ogan'sdo'. "Either way, our chances are slim."

"I won't stay in here to burn," Dragging Canoe said. "Even if they shoot me, maybe I can get one or two before I die."

The flames were already licking their way inside on the underside of the roof as Dragging Canoe stepped to the door.

"Wait," said Standing Deer. Dragging Canoe hesitated to see what the young man would say.

"If we go out the door one at time or one after the other," said Standing Deer, "they'll shoot us down one at a time."

"If we stay inside," another said, "we'll all die in the flames."

"But if one goes out alone," Standing Deer said, "and runs alone, maybe they'll all shoot at him, and then their guns will all be empty, and the others can get out safely."

"The one who runs out to draw their fire will surely be killed," said Ogan'sdo'.

"Yes," said Standing Deer.

"Who would do such a thing?" Ogan'sdo' asked.

"I will," said Standing Deer, and he stepped in front of Dragging Canoe, pulled open the door and ran. The others crowded the doorway and the windows to watch, as Standing Deer ran across the clearing toward the trees. A shot sounded from the woods. Standing Deer ran toward his left, then right. A second shot sounded. He kept dodging. A third shot tore into his side. He bent over but kept running. A fourth shot hit his thigh. He kept running, though with a limp. The shots came fast after that, for the target was slower, easier to hit. The Cherokees in the cabin were astonished at how many rifle balls hit Standing Deer before he fell. And when at last he fell, Ogan'sdo' shouted, "Let's go."

They ran out of the cabin and toward the woods where the white men were hiding. There were no shots from the woods, for the guns of the white men were all empty. Some of them rushed to reload. Others braced themselves for the Cherokee onslaught. Some turned and ran through the woods hoping to escape.

Dragging Canoe saw a white man jamming a ramrod down into the barrel of his rifle. He paused and raised his own rifle, taking careful aim, and fired. Sparks flew and powder burned, and the lead ball sped through the barrel and found its way to the white man's chest. Dragging Canoe dropped his rifle and pulled out his war club as he ran.

In the woods they cracked the skulls of all they could find, and when they were done, they took the scalps. They picked up the body of the fallen Standing Deer to take home for an honorable burial, and just before they left the scene, they looked back once more to see the abandoned settler's cabin engulfed in flames.

# 8

Keowee was nearly abandoned when the large force of 1,600 British soldiers under the command of Archibald Montgomery descended upon it. The smallpox was upon Keowee, and many of the healthy people had left for that reason. Many of the young men had left with Ogan'sdo' and Dragging Canoe to harass the outlying South Carolina settlements. Others, having heard of Montgomery's approach, simply ran into the mountains for safety.

The soldiers rode hard into the defenseless town, killing anyone they came across, but their victims were mostly sick with the smallpox, and it's likely they stayed in the town deliberately to be killed. While some soldiers shot or hacked down the unresisting Cherokees, others ran from house to house with torches, setting the town ablaze. Still others trampled the fields, destroying the crops with their horses' hooves. The mangled fields were then put to the torch, as were the orchards at the edge of town.

In the midst of the flames and the carnage, an officer rode up beside Montgomery. His head tilted back, his eyes looking up to the tops of the mountains, he said, "Look, sir." Montgomery looked, and there he saw the inhabitants of Keowee who had escaped before his arrival. They were standing high up on the green mountainside and calmly watching the destructive events below, watching their homes and their fields and orchards, their entire food supply, vanish before their eyes in smoke.

"Will we go after them, sir?" the officer asked.

"There's no way we can get up there," said Montgomery. "The cowardly bastards. We'll just let them starve."

Leaving Keowee nothing but ashes, Montgomery proceeded to the other Cherokee Lower Towns: Estatoe, Dak'siuweya, Qualatchee, Conasatchee, with much the same results. Montgomery and his men were feeling puffed up and bold. The Cherokees were not resisting. They were obviously no match for the proud British regulars. "Cowards," Montgomery said. His greatest worry was that his men would grow weary from the march before he had done the amount of damage he hoped to do. With the Lower Towns all effectively destroyed, their surviving populations homeless in the mountains, Montgomery led his troops toward the Middle Towns.

The way led them along narrow trails through mountain passes. They moved more slowly than before. The air thinned and cooled, and the whole world around them seemed damp and lush. The Englishmen found it difficult to breathe. Squirrels chattered angrily as they clattered by, and jays and magpies scolded from branches high up in the trees. When they found the room to do so along the way, they stopped and rested to regain their strength. It didn't seem to work, though, for when they were called upon to resume their march, they were still weary. They had left the ruins of the Lower Towns exhilarated by their own violence, thirsting for more blood and devastation. But the mountain trails wore them down. They were bedraggled, and they were bored with inactivity. They began to grumble and complain.

They moved on along the narrow trail, with mountains rising high on both sides, covered with thick green growth, blocking out the sunlight and blanketing everything with dark cool shadow. From his maps and his guides, Montgomery knew that not far ahead was a small town called Echoe. It would not take much time to destroy, and it would get the men in the proper mood again. They would move more cheerily along on the way to the next town, Cowee, having wiped out the smaller town. He was anxious to be shooting and hacking and burning again.

Then the eerie call of a male turkey cut through the damp air, and it sent a chill through Montgomery's body. He had not yet recovered from the start when a rifle shot sounded, and behind him a soldier called out in pain. Montgomery shouted orders to dismount and line up to return fire. Other shots sounded from above, from both sides, and other soldiers dropped, killed or wounded. The English soldiers fired up into the mountains, into the thick greenery from which the deadly shots were coming, but they found few targets. The enemy was well hidden. The British shots were haphazard and desperate. Most of their lead was wasted. The Cherokee shooters were too well blended into the darkly forested mountainside.

There was a sudden pause in the shooting, and Montgomery had a hope that the Cherokees had perhaps run out of ammunition. Then a voice called out from somewhere up above.

"Goddamned Englishmen."

And another. "Are you shooting your guns, or are you just farting at us?"

Montgomery turned to the scout who stood near him. "They speak English?" he said.

"Some have learned it," said the scout.

"Obviously only the vilest kind of English," said Montgomery. "Filthy savages."

"Assholes," came a cry from above. "Rusty assholes."

"They learn what they hear from the white men around them," said the scout.

"Montgomery," came a voice from above. "Poke your rifle barrel up your ass and blow it out your mouth."

Then there was another volley from the mountainsides, and more English soldiers fell. Captain Morrison of the Royal Scots fell, and the colonial militiamen behind him turned and ran, fleeing back down the mountain trail by which they had come. Men screamed and shouted, and some fired random shots up the side of the mountain. Frightened horses stamped and nickered and whinnied. Montgomery finally managed to rally his remaining troops and urge them forward. They raced ahead in disarray and found the small town of

Echoe completely abandoned. They also found it a safe haven, at least temporarily, for it was out of range of the snipers on the mountain. Montgomery waited anxiously, but the Cherokees did not bother attacking the English in Echoe. In fact, they seemed to have gone away. Montgomery waited a day, then ordered a hasty retreat.

By the time Dragging Canoe returned to the home of his wife at Big Island Town, the dreaded smallpox had at last run its course. Along with Ogan'sdo' and others, Dragging Canoe had done considerable damage to the frontier settlements of South Carolina. Those frontiersmen who had escaped their wrath had fled toward the colonies for safety. And he also found on his return that the invading English forces, after having destroyed the Lower Towns, had been driven from the Cherokee country.

But things had changed. Besides the destroyed Lower Towns, there had been lives lost, many lives. People had been killed by the English soldiers, but not so many. Many had been killed, though, by the smallpox. And when he went at last to the house of his wife there in Malaquo, he found the biggest change of all, the most devastating change for him. He found that Guque, his wife, the mother of his son, had been carried away by the horrible disfiguring scourge of the white man, the smallpox.

But Dragging Canoe did not mourn. For the death of Guque was but one of many deaths. Dragging Canoe's life was given over to fighting in response to the unnecessary deaths of Cherokees. He had no time for mourning. Let others mourn. He would fight. Did the death of Guque not hurt him? Would he not miss her? Of course it did and he would. But he would not mourn. If he once gave in to mourning, his life would be one long wailing. He could not afford it. He had his work to do, and besides, this one small death, though it came very close to him, was not an individual death at all. It was but a part of the larger death, the big death against which he fought.

The boy had been taken to be raised by Guque's sister, and her oldest surviving brother would teach him the ways of a man. That was the traditional way. His child had as many mothers as his wife and her sisters combined. If one was lost, there was another waiting to take over. So Dragging Canoe was alone. He considered his new position in life. He realized that he had been put in this new position for a reason, and the only reason he could see was that the Cherokee people were in a very precarious situation, and needed someone to help them. There were white people all around them, and white settlers were crowding more and more onto Cherokee land.

The traditional Cherokee hunting grounds already had been thinned of their animal populations by overhunting, a result partly of Cherokees hunting for purposes of trade with the English and partly by the hunting of frontier whites. It was a dangerous time, one in which, looking forward, it was easy to imagine the coming end of the Cherokees. Dragging Canoe could see that unhappy event approaching rapidly, unless the Cherokees, with the right leadership, dealt with the pressures very carefully, very quickly, and very decisively.

They would have to stop giving up land to whites. They would have to draw the line somewhere and hold it. In order to do this, they would have to stop fighting other Indians. They would have to cooperate with other Indians in holding the line against the land-greedy whites. That would not be an easy task. The Cherokees had fought against the Creeks, the Choctaws, the Chickasaws, the Shawnees, and from the north country, the Senecas and other northern Iroquois people for as long as any Cherokee could remember. To make this plan work, Cherokees would have to be convinced first, then the other tribes. It would not be easy.

But alone, bereft of his tiny family, in the midst of the recent devastation, Dragging Canoe saw a new role for himself. He felt as if he had been given a new and important assignment. It was not a life he had chosen for himself. It was one that had been thrust upon him, and having recognized it, he swore a solemn oath that the rest of his life would be devoted to fulfilling this new role, to accomplishing the task that had been assigned him. He would carry the banner for the consolidation of all the tribes of Native People in the land. The goal would be one of a vast union of Indians from north to south, and they would be united for the purpose of holding the line against any further westward movement of whites. There would be no more land cessions to the whites. No more whites would be allowed to move onto Indian land. Not Cherokee land, nor Creek, nor Shawnee. All together, united, they would hold the line.

Someone was needed, and he, it seemed, had been chosen for that role. It might even be better that he was now alone with no family to worry about. His family was now the entire Cherokee people. He could no longer worry about just one or two. He had to constantly think of them all. That was his destiny. He recalled his childish claim that one day he would be a great man. He had wondered about that from time to time over the years. It had not been an idle childish boast. It had been almost as if he had heard a voice telling him what his future would hold. Now, it seemed, the time had come for him to fulfill that predicted role.

When Dragging Canoe returned from the fighting on the frontiers and went back to Big Island Town, Ogan'sdo' made his own way back to Fort Loudon where other Cherokees still besieged the now desperate English soldiers inside the fort. Captain Demere's only hope had been Montgomery, but now Montgomery had fled. Things were looking bleak for the soldiers. They had already killed and butchered horses and dogs, as the food being brought in at night by the Cherokee wives of some of the soldiers was not sufficient for all the men in the fort.

It was early morning, just before sunrise, when Susannah and Ghigooie slipped out of the fort and made their way across the ford of the Tellico, holding high their skirts as they waded through the low waters. Stepping out of the water on the other side, they were startled to find Ogan'sdo' himself standing in their path, his arms across his chest, a stern look on his face.

"You came from the fort just now," he said.

"Yes," said Susannah. "You don't have to tell us that. We know where we've been."

"And what were you doing in there?" Ogan'sdo' asked. "Were you giving comfort to the enemy?"

"I was giving more than comfort," Susannah said. "I took food to my husband."

"John Stuart, the white man," Ogan'sdo' said.

"John Stuart is my husband," Susannah said.

"And mine is William Shorey," Ghigooie said. "You know him well. He's not a soldier. He's an interpreter."

"We're at war with these Englishmen," Ogan'sdo' said. "All of them. They've wiped out all the Lower Towns and killed and driven out our people. They would be doing the same thing to the Middle Towns had not the Raven of Estatoe driven them out. And they sent the smallpox to us. My own face is a testament to that. Then they sent it again. Many of our people are dead because of that. Many more disfigured. Many with grotesque faces like mine."

"Our husbands did not do any of those things," Susannah said.

"They're English," he said.

"They're the fathers of Cherokee children," said Susannah.

"They're the brothers of killers of Cherokee children," Ogan'sdo' said angrily.

"Do you want to call a council to see whether or not the people will all agree that we women have a right to feed and comfort our husbands, the fathers of our children?" said Ghigooie.

Ogan'sdo' seethed, but he knew that he could do nothing but fuss. Cherokees, both men and women, had always had a tremendous range of personal freedom. Despite the English notion of "emperors," no one among the Cherokees had any real power or authority over anyone else, nothing beyond the power of persuasion. While he stood there scowling, three more Cherokee women slipped out of the gate across the river. He wondered how many more might be inside the fort at that very moment as he stood there watching. In disgust, Ogan'sdo' turned and stalked away.

Dragging Canoe joined his father and Ogan'sdo' at the siege of Fort Loudon. They sat together around a small fire. "Father," Dragging Canoe said, "when I got back to my wife's house from the fighting, I found that while I was gone, the smallpox had taken my wife away."

The three men sat for a long moment in silence, and Dragging Canoe thought that in the flickering firelight he could see a dampness in his father's eyes. "Your mother too is gone," the old man said. "The last time, when you were little, we survived it, you and me — and your mother. This time it has hurt us both. It has taken away our women."

"I'm sorry for the loss of your women," Ogan'sdo' said. "And if there were time for such things, I would grieve with you for your loss. But just now, the way things are, this sad news only feeds my hatred for the English. I no longer want to balance things between us and the English. I want to kill as many English as I can, for as long as I live."

"What will we do about those in the fort?" Dragging Canoe asked, grateful to the old war chief for having changed the subject.

"I thought we could starve them out," Ogan'sdo' said, "but some of our women have husbands in there, Englishmen, and they are taking them food at night."

"Have you talked to these women?" Dragging Canoe asked.

"Yes," said Ogan'sdo', "but they only scream at me. They scream about their rights as Cherokee women. What can I say?"

"There is nothing you can say," Ada-gal'kala interjected, "when a Cherokee woman has made up her mind. Besides, they're only keeping the promises they made to feed them when they married those men. And they're asserting their rights, as you said." He chuckled.

"What's funny?" Dragging Canoe asked.

"Do you remember the time," Ada-gal'kala said, "that old 'Ma'-dohi drank too much of the English rum, and he made water right in the middle of the floor of his wife's house? His old wife was so mad at him, she picked up a stick and beat on him until he fell down in his own puddle of pee, and then she beat on him some more. He yelled and screamed, and she just kept beating on him. Finally he could stand it no more, so he rolled over to let her beat on his other side."

All three men laughed at the image of the old man being beaten by his angry wife, and when their laughter at last subsided, Ogan'sdo' said, "And this was the man the English called our emperor." At that they laughed some more.

Just then Susannah Stuart came walking over to their fire. The men suddenly became very quiet, waiting to see what she would have to say. She tossed her head in a gesture of pride and defiance.

"I've just come from the fort," she said.

"I'm not surprised to hear that," said Ogan'sdo'. "What were you doing there? Did you feed your Englishman? And after he had eaten, did you spread your legs for his pleasure?"

"And if I did," she said, "it's my business and none of yours."

"Ha," Ogan'sdo' said.

"I have a message for you," she said, ignoring the war chief's comments, "from Captain Demere."

"Go on then," Ogan'sdo' said. "What does he want?"

"If you'll agree to certain terms," she said, "Captain Demere is prepared to surrender and give up the fort."

Ogan'sdo' started to speak, but a quick gesture from Ada-gal'kala stopped him. "What are his terms?" the diplomat asked.

"Captain Demere says he will abandon the fort and its stores of ammunition to you," she said, "if you will promise him safe passage out of our country. Send some men along with them to ensure that they get safely away, and allow them to take with them only their personal guns and powder and ball—enough for hunting along the way."

"That's all?" Ada-gal'kala asked.

"Those are his terms," Susannah said. "I think they're reasonable. So do the rest of the women."

"We'll talk about it," Ogan'sdo' said. "We'll let you know."

Susannah turned to walk away, but Ada-gal'kala stopped her. "Susannah," he said, "how is my friend, your husband?"

Ogan'sdo' sneered at his diplomatic rival.

"He's well," Susannah said. "He's holding up."

"I'm glad," Ada-gal'kala said.

"And yet you're with these others," she said, "trying to starve him."

"I don't like this war, Susannah," said Ada-gal'kala, "any more than you do."

Susannah turned abruptly and walked away, leaving the men alone, and Ogan'sdo' said, "Well. What do you think, diplomat?"

"I think we've won," said Ada-gal'kala. "Demere is willing to give up the fort and all his ammunition."

"Almost all," said Dragging Canoe.

"Montgomery has retreated," Ogan'sdo' said, "and now Demere is willing to surrender. Yes. We've won."

"We've won two battles," said Dragging Canoe, "but there will be more."

"And we can win more," said Ogan'sdo', "with all the guns and ammunition inside the fort."

"Let's go talk with Guhna-gadoga and the others," said Ada-gal'kala. "We can't make this decision without them."

"But not with the women," Ogan'sdo' said. "Not this time. They've already talked and made up their minds anyway, and we know what they think."

Demere drew up a paper stating the terms, and he read it out loud for all to hear, but the Cherokees were suspicious. Remembering what Lyttleton had done, they did not trust Demere or any Englishman to be a man of his word. Ada-gal'kala could read some of the paper, because of the lessons he'd had from Priber, but he couldn't read enough. It had been too long, and he was out of practice. Besides, he had only just begun to learn when the English had taken Priber away. He thought for a moment, then drew Stuart aside. "Bushyhead," he said, "do the words say what Demere told us they say?"

"Yes," said Stuart. "They do."

Ada-gal'kala, Ogan'sdo', Guhna-gadoga, and others signed the paper, so the bargain was made. The Cherokees went back outside the fort, leaving the soldiers to pack their bags and load their horses. Leaving most of their weapons inside the fort, and led by their commander, Captain Demere, the nearly two hundred English soldiers marched single file out of Fort Loudon, leaving all behind them in the hands of the Cherokees. They moved out with their heads hanging low, dejected and defeated. Ogan'sdo', Dragging Canoe, Guhna-gadoga, and others walked along with them as they moved into the forest pathway headed back toward the South Carolina settlements and eventually Charlestown.

They walked for a day, hunted without incident, camped and ate their fill and slept the night. In the morning, Demere noticed that about half the Cherokee escort had vanished during the night, including Ogan'sdo' and Guhna-gadoga. They resumed their march, and the second day passed much like the first. On the third morning, Demere found that he and his men had been completely abandoned by the Cherokees. Ah, well, he thought, they were two days' march away from the trouble. They had made a bargain. Likely they were safe enough, but something was bothering him. He called Stuart over to his side.

"Your friends promised us safe conduct," he said, "and now they've abandoned us."

"We're safe enough now," Stuart said. "Unless they discover what you've done at the fort. Then nothing can save us. We'd better move quickly."

Arriving back at Fort Loudon, Ogan'sdo', Ada-gal'kala, and Guhna-gadoga were ready to relax and enjoy their latest triumph. But they hadn't had time even to sit down before they were confronted by angry Cherokees. Almost as soon as the last soldier had walked out of the fort, Cherokees had run inside to see what had been left behind for them.

"*Ni,*" said one. "Come with us and see what we found in there."

He and some others took hold of the three chiefs and practically dragged them inside the fort. They took them across the courtyard and showed them a place where a hole had been dug in the ground to reveal ten bags of powder and considerable shot. "We found it buried there," he said. "The white men tried to hide it from us, but we could tell that someone had just dug there, so we checked."

"Come with me," another said, and he led them back outside to a place beside the river. He showed them cannon, rifles, powder, and shot that had been thrown into the river to be ruined. "They promised to leave this stuff for us," he said. "Well, they left it all right. Ha."

Dragging Canoe's face burned with rage, but it was not his place to make any decisions. His father and the old war chief Ogan'sdo' were there, as was the Principal Chief, Guhna-gadoga. They were his elders. They had more experience, and they were in positions of authority. They had been at the siege longer than had he. He watched, listened, and waited.

"Demere lied to us," said Ada-gal'kala. "He made a bargain, and then he cheated us."

"All of you who feel as I do," Ogan'sdo' shouted, "follow me."

He knew that Demere and the soldiers were traveling slowly. They were on foot. They were tired, and they were taking plenty of time to hunt along the way. He also knew a quicker way through the woods to catch up to them and even get ahead of them. That was his plan. He ran, and others, including Dragging Canoe, Guhna-gadoga, and even Ada-gal'kala, followed him. They ran all the way, sustained by their anger and their sense of outrage. They ran until they were well ahead of the soldiers, and then they hid along both sides of the trail and waited.

Demere was the first to fall, several Cherokee rifle balls striking him in various parts of his body. The Cherokees continued firing until their rifles had all been discharged. Other Englishmen fell dead along the trail. Then Ogan'sdo' rushed out of the woods, followed by the rest. Gobbling like male turkeys, they rushed the remaining soldiers, many of whom dropped to their knees in a desperate gesture of surrender. Some had fallen to the ground as if they had been killed. When it became clear to Ogan'sdo' that the soldiers were no longer resisting, but were in fact trying to surrender, he called a halt to the slaughter. Then he found the body of Demere, and he knelt beside it. He scooped up a clump of dirt and shoved it into the gaping mouth of the dead Englishman.

"You wanted Cherokee land," he said. "Take some."

Ada-gal'kala looked around frantically until at last he saw John Stuart, apparently unharmed. He was pleased to see that Bushyhead was among the survivors. William Shorey was alive, too. He hoped that the other husbands of Cherokee women were unharmed. It would mean less trouble when they returned with the captives.

"How many are killed?" Ogan'sdo' asked.

"Twenty-nine," said Guhna-gadoga.

They turned the one hundred and seventy prisoners around and started them marching back toward Fort Loudon, and some of the Cherokee men began to claim prisoners. Ada-gal'kala found his way quickly to the side of John Stuart.

"This is my prisoner," he announced, and no one saw fit to challenge his claim. They walked along for a distance, and Ada-gal'kala took Stuart by the arm, pulling him off the trail and into the woods. "Come with me, Bushyhead," he said. He glanced at his son as he led his captive off the path. "We're going hunting," he said. Dragging Canoe knew what his father was doing. He was getting Bushyhead to safety, afraid that some of the young men might give in to a killing frenzy at any time along the way.

The two men sat together at a small fire in the woods that night, Ada-gal'kala and Bushyhead. They cooked themselves a meal from a deer they had killed earlier in the day. They ate in silence. They had spoken but little all that day. At last, their evening meal finished, Ada-gal'kala spoke.

"Bushyhead," he said, "we did not break our word. Demere is the one who broke the bargain."

"I know," said Bushyhead. "I tried to stop him from hiding and destroying the weapons and ammunition. He wouldn't listen to me."

"There was nothing I could do, either," said Ada-gal'kala,

"when the young men found out about Demere's treachery. They were very angry, and so was Ogan'sdo'."

"Well," Bushyhead said, "I can't blame them, but this will mean trouble. You know that."

"Yes," said Ada-gal'kala. "I know."

"I'll do everything I can," said Bushyhead, "in Williamsburg and in Charlestown. I'll tell them what really happened, and I'll talk for peace."

"And I'll do the same among my people," Ada-gal'kala said. "Whatever happens, Bushyhead, we two must always be friends."

Bushyhead reached across the flames to grasp Ada-gal'kala firmly by the hand. "We shall, Carpenter," he said. "We shall always remain friends."

They walked in the woods for several days, hunting along the way, until Ada-gal'kala at last had brought Stuart to the safety of a settlement in Virginia. "I'll leave you here, Bushyhead," he said. "You're out of danger now." The two men embraced. "I won't forget this, my friend," said Stuart, "for as long as I live."


### *June 1761*


Colonel Grant rode out from Fort Prince George with an army of 2,600 men. Among them were Chickasaws and Catawbas, long-time enemies of the Cherokees. The English had taken the fall and winter to prepare for their massive retaliation against the Cherokees, their revenge for the humiliating defeats of Montgomery and Fort Loudon. Ada-gal'kala had sent word that he would like to talk, but he had been refused, in spite of the fact that he had rescued John Stuart and taken him safely into Virginia.

The Cherokees knew that Grant was coming, so they abandoned their towns ahead of him and moved on farther into the mountains, going from town to town and carried the warning. "The English are coming," they would say, and they would join with the people of the town they had just warned and hurry along to yet another town. So Grant and his force found one abandoned town after another, and they burned them all, and they destroyed the crops and the stores. Soon fifteen Cherokee Middle Towns were reduced to ashes. Like the Lower Towns, the Middle Towns were no more.

So vigorously had Grant and his men done their duty, they found that they needed a rest, and they retired to Fort Prince George to feed and rest their animals and themselves, to clean themselves, their clothes, and their weapons and supplies, to check and replenish supplies, and to allow Grant and his staff the time to make plans for more vigorous action.

Always the diplomat, Ada-gal'kala traveled to Fort Prince George to try once more to meet with Colonel Grant. He went into the fort under a flag of truce and was admitted to parley. He was not taken into an office, however, nor offered a seat. Grant met him in the courtyard and faced him with a stern look.

"I've heard of you," he said. "They call you the Little Carpenter. Is that right?"

"The English call me by that name," said Ada-gal'kala. "And you are Grant."

"I'm Colonel Grant," the Englishman said. "I'm in command here."

"Yes," said Ada-gal'kala. "I've heard of you, too."

"And what have you heard, Little Carpenter?" the colonel asked.

"I've heard that you burn people's homes and gardens," the Carpenter said, "and you leave women and children to starve in the mountains. I've heard that you attack towns when the young fighting men are away from home."

"Why have you come here?" said Grant. "Did you come to trade insults and accusations? What do you want?"

"You've destroyed fifteen of our towns," Ada-gal'kala said. "Many of our people are without homes and food. We want this war to stop. I came here to talk to you of peace."

"There will be no peace," said Grant. "Not until your people have suffered enough to make up for what you did to Montgomery and to Fort Loudon. When I feel you've been punished enough, then there will be peace, and not before. When you go back to your people, tell them that. Tell them that we are engaged in total war. Tell them that it will not stop. It will not stop until I am ready for it to stop."

# 9

When Ogan'sdo' and the rest heard of the way Grant had treated Ada-gal'kala, they gathered at Echoe Pass, where they had surprised and defeated Montgomery, and they waited. Grant did not want to talk of peace. All right, they would give him war. What had he called it? Total war. They would give him that. Grant rode out again, ready to fight. He knew where the Cherokees had fought Montgomery. He was prepared to meet them there.

"Watch the slopes," he said. "They're up there, waiting for us. Keep your eyes open and watch carefully." Francis Marion and his rangers rode with Grant, as did other provincial troops, as well as Chickasaws and Catawbas. They would not line up to be killed as had Montgomery's regulars. They rode into the pass slowly, each man tense and ready, his head lifted slightly to watch for the Cherokees on the mountainsides. Then, "Up there," a ranger shouted.

From his vantage point high up on the slope, Ogan'sdo' fired the first shot, and down below a ranger fell. Then the firing was fast and furious from both sides. Some of the rangers and their Indian allies ran into the thicket on the sides of the trail. They took cover there and looked for targets up above. Some attempted to climb the steep mountainsides seeking their prey. But the steepness and the thickness of the lush growth was too much for most of them to negotiate. When they were successful climbing, they were unable to keep a careful watch up above. Dragging Canoe shot a Catawba who was coming up toward him.

The climbing stopped, and the fight became one of shooting back and forth from behind trees and rocks and brush. No one on either side wanted to show himself. Now and then a rifle ball found its mark. From time to time the firing stopped as men reloaded their weapons. Sometimes it was sporadic. At other times it was heavy. The air was filled with the odor of burned powder, and heavy smoke drifted across the pass. Now and then a rifle report was followed by an anguished cry. At last, their ammunition almost gone, the Cherokees began to slip away. Eleven Englishmen lay dead in the pass. Sixty or so were wounded. From high on the mountainside, Dragging Canoe watched as Grant and his men rode into Echoe. He saw them take the wounded into the townhouse. He watched as they burned all the other houses to the ground, as they destroyed the gardens and the store houses.

Down below young Francis Marion and others had been ordered into the cornfields with their swords to hack and slash the stately stalks. It seemed to Marion a shameful thing to do, and then he saw between the rows the tiny footprints of children, and he was sick at heart, and he was ashamed of his own actions, but he was a soldier, and he continued the hateful work, thinking all the while that little children would ask their parents who had done this dirty deed. "The white people," the parents would answer. "The Christians. They did it."

Three months had passed since the fight at Echoe Pass, and Grant had continued to lay waste to Cherokee towns. People were starving. At last, Ada-gal'kala had led a delegation of twenty important Cherokee men to Fort Prince George where Grant was headquartered and once again taking his ease. They had approached the fort under a flag of truce and were admitted. They had talked with Grant of surrender, and they had agreed on all terms so far. But Grant wasn't finished. It was too easy. He had to get one final thrust in to satisfy his sense of power over a vanquished enemy, one final thrust of the sword followed by a vicious twist.

"There is just one more thing," said Grant. "A small thing. You will deliver into my hands four Cherokee men to be put to death in front of my army."

Ada-gal'kala was astonished and horrified. "We cannot do that," he said. "We agreed to all your other terms. Why do you ask such a thing? Four men? Just any men? Men, perhaps, who have not done anything? What would their mothers and wives and children say to me?"

"It's either that or kill them yourselves and bring me the scalps," Grant said. "I'll give you twelve days. Four men or four fresh scalps."

"I cannot agree to that," Ada-gal'kala said. "I will not sign a paper with you. I'll go to Charlestown and talk with Governor Bull."

Grant shrugged. "Do as you wish," he said. "Until we have a treaty signed, I'll continue to do my duty as I see it."

Governor Bull received Ada-gal'kala warmly, gripping and pumping his hand. "Little Carpenter," he said, "I'm glad to see you. As you've always been a good friend to the English, I take you by the hand, and not only you, but those with you as well, as a pledge of their security while under my protection." After a period of exchanging pleasantries, the governor had a formal meeting declared. Ada-gal'kala presented him with a long belt of wampum.

"I come to you as a messenger from the whole Cherokee Nation," he said, "and I hope that we can live together like brothers. As to what has happened, I believe that it was ordered by the Great Father above, as are all things. We are of a different color than the white people, but one God is the Father of all. As the Great King said to me when I visited him in England, I hope that the path will never be crooked but straight and open for all to pass."

Satisfactory terms were agreed upon, and a treaty was signed. There would be peace once again between the Cherokees and

North Carolina, in spite of Grant. Governor Bull then had Ada-gal'kala dine with him. At the table, Ada-gal'kala said to Bull, "I hope that John Stuart can be made the chief white man in our Nation. All the Indians love him, and if he's there, there will never be any uneasiness."

"That appointment is beyond my authority to make," said the governor, "but my words will be listened to. I'll see what can be done."

Ada-gal'kala started his journey back home greatly satisfied at the results of his meeting with Bull. His faith in his own abilities was restored. The people would be safe once again in their own homes. He also marveled at the differences in Englishmen. Some, like Grant, were vicious and brutal, coldhearted and without honor. Others were good men. John Stuart was a good man. So, it seemed, was Governor Bull.

Two months later, Guhna-gadoga and others met with Colonel Stephens at the Virginia fort on the Holston River. Peace had been established with North Carolina, but there was still Virginia to deal with. Terms were agreed upon, and a treaty was signed. Then Guhna-gadoga stood up again to face Stephens. "There is one more thing I would beg of you," he said. "I want Virginia to send a man to stay with us. If we were to have a Virginian living with us, then all my people would be convinced that you mean well."

"I would fear for the safety of any Virginian in your midst," Stephens said, "because of the late hostilities. I trust you and believe you, of course, but there are hotheaded young men among the Cherokees, just as there are among the whites. I would not ask any man to comply with your wish."

A young lieutenant standing to one side stepped forward just then. "Colonel Stephens," he said.

"What is it, Lieutenant Timberlake?"

"I'd like to volunteer to go back with the Cherokees and stay with them, sir," he said. "The mission is very much to my liking."

Timberlake stayed for six months with Guhna-gadoga, Ostenaco, and others in the Overhills Towns. Then, feeling that his mission had been accomplished, for there had been no more trouble between the Cherokees and Virginia, he decided to return to Williamsburg. Ostenaco, Guhna-shote, and Pouting Pigeon made the trip with him. While visiting in Williamsburg, Ostenaco saw a portrait of King George III, the new King, hanging on a wall.

"Long have I wished to see the King my Father," he said. "This is his likeness, but I am determined to see him myself. I am now near the sea, and I will not depart until I have obtained my desires. I should also like to find out for myself whether or not Ada-gal'kala told us lies about England."

And so, on the 15th of May, 1762, Timberlake and the three Cherokee chiefs boarded a ship leaving Williamsburg. William Shorey, homesick for England, went along as interpreter. They were headed for England.

Dragging Canoe met with his father in Tamatly. There were many things on his mind. Guhna-gadoga had just died, and the English were recognizing his son, Ukah Ulah, as the new "emperor."

"They seem to believe that this office should pass from father to son," Ada-gal'kala said, "the way they do with their kings."

"Let the English think what they will," said Dragging Canoe. "We'll do what we've always done. All Cherokees know that you are the most powerful man in our nation. They'll listen to you, not to this so-called 'emperor.' "

"Um," Ada-gal'kala mused. "Perhaps you place too much importance on my status. Many listen to Ogan'sdo'."

"Your voice is stronger than his," said the son. "But we need both voices now. It's a dangerous time. We lost our Lower Towns and our Middle Towns to war, and now we've lost even more land to the peace. We gave up land to Virginia and to South Carolina. The white men are moving closer and closer to us all the time. They almost have us surrounded now. And they'll come back for more."

"We have an important friend now in Bushyhead," said Ada-gal'kala. "The English have a new king across the waters, and this new king has made Bushyhead an important man over here. He's my friend, and he's in charge of all of us Indians in the south. If any of the English treat us wrong, I can go to Bushyhead. He'll make them behave properly toward us."

"Stuart is a good man," Dragging Canoe agreed, "but he's just one man. The English from South Carolina and from Virginia have no respect for authority—not even their own."

"The Virginians have been quiet since they sent Timberlake into our country," Ada-gal'kala said.

"But Timberlake is gone now," said Dragging Canoe.

Ada-gal'kala chuckled. "Yes," he said. "He's gone to England, and he's taken William Shorey, Ostenaco, Guhna-shote, and Pouting Pigeon with him. They say that Ostenaco wants to find out if I told lies about England. I think he's just jealous because I met the King. You just wait. When he gets back, he'll tell everyone that I only met with the old King, the King that is dead, and he has met the new King."

### 1763
#### Augusta, Georgia

Representatives from all the southern Indian tribes were there, responding to a call from John Stuart, the newly appointed British Superintendent for Southern Indian Affairs. Ada-gal'kala, Ogan'sdo', Dragging Canoe, and others were there representing the Cherokees. Ada-gal'kala was puffed up with pride. After all, it had been he who had suggested the appointment of Bushyhead to this high office.

"My friends," said Stuart, declaiming loudly before the entire assembly, "the long war with France is over, and victory belongs to England. I have called you all here so that I could explain to you all at one time the new situation in which we now live. England has won its war with France, and by treaty with France, all of this land now belongs to the King of England, and you are all, we are all, under the jurisdiction of the British Crown. You are now secure in your lands, for the King has issued a royal proclamation establishing the boundary line between the colonies and the land of the Indians. No white man will be allowed to go into your lands to settle. Only the white men who are licensed to trade will be allowed to go onto your land."

When the big meeting at last broke up, Ada-gal'kala' and Dragging Canoe were summoned to a special meeting with the new Superintendent. Approaching Stuart's office, the old diplomat was still puffed up. Dragging Canoe spoke to his father in the Cherokee language. "I did not know that the French had the right to sell our lands to the English," he said.

"We won't speak of that in front of Bushyhead," said Ada-gal'kala. "Not just now. But the boundary line is good."

"If it holds," Dragging Canoe said.

They were ushered into Stuart's office, and Stuart jumped up from behind his desk, rushing around to hug Ada-gal'kala warmly. "My good friend," he said. "It gives me great pleasure to see you again."

"Bushyhead, I and all the Cherokees," Ada-gal'kala said, "are greatly pleased to see you in such an important position."

Stuart stepped back and turned his gaze on Dragging Canoe. "And it's good to see you, too," he said. "The son of my good friend."

"Bushyhead," said Ada-gal'kala, "the Virginians sent a man named Timberlake to stay with us. I thought that things would be better for us with an Englishman living among us. But Timberlake took Ostenaco and some others and went to England to see the King. Now if any English abuse us, we have no one to complain to except Pearis, Ward, and other traders who live with us, but they have small voices back in the colonies."

"I've already made arrangements, my friend," said Stuart, "to send two of my own representatives to stay with you. They're Alexander Cameron and John McDonald, my own countrymen and newly appointed deputy commissioners of Indian affairs. They will report directly to me and will keep me well informed of the way things are going with you. They're both good men. You may consider them your good friends, as I am your friend. You may speak to them as you would to me."

"When will they come to our country?" the Carpenter asked.

"It will take some time to get them here," said Stuart, "but I've sent for them already."

"It will be none too soon," said Dragging Canoe, "for lawless whites are crowding onto our lands every day. If your government fails to make them behave, then we'll have to take matters into our own hands."

"Carpenter," Stuart said, "I hope that you can keep your hot-blooded son and the other young men quiet until I can get my assistants among you."

"I will try, Bushyhead," said Ada-gal'kala, "but you know how things are with us."

"Yes," said Stuart. He paused a moment, looking thoughtful. Then, "I've heard that your head man has died," he said.

"Yes," said Ada-gal'kala. "Ukah Ulah is no longer with us."

"You're the real leader of your people anyway," Stuart said. "Some of us have recognized that for some time now. There are many chiefs among the Cherokees, but you are the principal one among them all. As British Superintendent of Southern Indian Affairs, I intend to recognize you as the Principal Chief of all of the chiefs of the Cherokee Nation, and I mean to see that even the King is so informed. As Principal Chief, you must do everything in your power to keep your young men at peace. And I ask you to do it in the name of our friendship, as well."

The door opened, and an aide came into the room with a silver tray, carrying a pot and three cups. He poured each cup full of coffee and passed the cups around. Then he placed the tray with the pot on a side table, stood at attention, and looked at Stuart. "Thank you," Stuart said. "That will be all for now." The aide left the room, closing the door behind him. Stuart sipped his coffee. He put the cup down on his desk and looked again at his old friend, the new Principal Chief of the Cherokee Nation. "You mentioned Timberlake's trip back to England," he said. "Have you any further word on that topic?"

"We heard that Shorey died on that trip," Ada-gal'kala said.

"I'm sorry to hear that," said Stuart, "for his own sake and for that of his wife."

"Timberlake stayed in England," Dragging Canoe said. "They told us that he was out of money and couldn't pay his own way back."

"And the chiefs?" Stuart asked. "Have they returned home safely?"

"They're safe at home," Dragging Canoe said.

"But they represented us poorly from what we've heard," said Ada-gal'kala. "We heard that they were drunk all the time. It would have been better had they not gone. I saw Ostenaco after he came back home, and I said to him, 'Well, did I lie to you about England?' He didn't want to talk to me about it."

At last, Ada-gal'kala, at the age of fifty-six, had achieved his most desired goal. He was recognized not only by a majority of his own people, but by the English as well, as the Principal Chief of the Cherokee Nation. He liked that new designation. It was better than the foolish English title "Emperor." He was pleased with himself and with his office, and he thought that his son, Dragging Canoe, would now surely succeed him some day in that office. It was the English way.

Both Dragging Canoe and his father left the meeting with Bushyhead feeling very good, although Dragging Canoe was still a bit skeptical. The Englishman in charge of Southern Indian affairs for the English king was their good friend. He was a man with a Cherokee wife and children, and he was sending his own chosen men to stay with them. They felt at last that peace might really be established between their two peoples. They felt that the horrors of war might really be behind them at last, and the women and children would be safe again in their own homes, and the corn would grow unmolested in the fields. Bushyhead, they were convinced, would make the illegal settlers leave Cherokee land, and his men would make the traders who were in their midst behave better.

And Ada-gal'kala felt good for himself, for now he was indeed the Principal Chief of the Cherokee Nation. His own people had long recognized him as an important man. The recognition of the English was all that was needed, and now he had that. He had cultivated Bushyhead's friendship over the years. He had saved Bushyhead's life after the Fort Loudon incident. He had suggested that Bushyhead be appointed Superintendent, and it had all worked out. Now, due to his diplomatic skills, he had reached his own personal goal at last.

## 1766

Dragging Canoe liked Cameron almost at once. He was himself twenty-nine, and thought that the Scot was probably a few years younger than he. Cameron was a handsome, well-dressed young man with a determined face. Almost as soon as the party started on its journey back to the Cherokee country, Cameron displayed a sincere interest in the Cherokee language, asking Dragging Canoe how to name things, and asking for the word to be repeated several times until he could get the pronunciation right.

"What beast am I riding on?" he asked.

*"Sogwili,"* said Dragging Canoe.

"Would you repeat that please?"

And Dragging Canoe repeated the word until Cameron remembered it and said it correctly.

"And upon what am I sitting?" Cameron asked.

*"Uk,"* said Dragging Canoe, and he laughed.

*"Uk?"* said Cameron.

Dragging Canoe raised himself up out of his saddle and patted his own buttocks. *"Uk,"* he said. "It's what you're sitting on."

"Oh," said Cameron, and he too laughed. "All right then. *Uk.* Now," he said, patting the saddle, "what is this?"

*"Gayahulo,"* said Dragging Canoe.

"What is your name?"

"Tsiyu Gansini."

*"Tsiyu,"* said Cameron. "Canoe?"

"Yes," said Dragging Canoe.

"And *gansini?* Dragging?"

"Yes. It means 'he is dragging it.' "

"Tsiyu gansini," said Cameron. "He is dragging it—the canoe. Dragging Canoe."

"That's right," said Dragging Canoe.

"And your father's name," said Cameron, "Ada-gal'kala, it means 'the Little Carpenter'?"

"That's what the English call him," said Dragging Canoe, "but the name means 'wood that's leaning.' "

*"Ada* is wood?" asked Cameron.

"Yes," said Dragging Canoe.

Dragging Canoe and Cameron left the others and rode ahead to hunt, and their hunt was successful. Along the way, Cameron learned to say *awi* for "deer," *tsisdu* for "rabbit," *tsisqua* for "bird," and he learned the important syllable *ya,* for he learned that *tsisqua-ya,* translated as "the real bird," was the Cherokees' name for the little sparrow. And he learned that *yunwi* is "person," *ani-yunwi* is "people," and *ani-yunwi-ya* is "Real People."

"That is our proper name," said Dragging Canoe. " 'Cherokee' is not even our own word. It has no meaning for us. The English learned it from other Indians, and so we get called 'Cherokee,' but we are *Ani-yunwi-ya.* Sometimes we say *Ani-Kituwagi.*"

*"Ani-Kituwagi,"* Cameron repeated. "And what does that mean?"

"Kituwah People," said Dragging Canoe. "All of us are from the ancient town of Kituwah, for it was the first Cherokee town, the town from which all other towns grew. We are all people from Kituwah."

"And what does 'Kituwah' mean?" Cameron asked.

"No one knows," Dragging Canoe answered. "It's a very old and very sacred name."

*"Ani-yunwi-ya,"* said Cameron. *"Ani-Kituwagi. Tsalagi.* Cherokee."

Dragging Canoe and Cameron kept the party supplied with meat, and Cameron made a good start on his command of the

Cherokee language. He learned other things, too. They were hunting in the woods one day when Cameron came across a steel trade knife lying in the grass. He bent to pick it up.

"Look what I've found," he said.

"It belongs to the Little People," said Dragging Canoe. "Tell them that you're taking it, or they may throw stones at us."

Cameron looked questioningly at Dragging Canoe for a moment. He stood holding the knife. Then he said, "Little People, I'm taking this knife. All right?"

Dragging Canoe took some tobacco from a pouch at his side and placed it on the ground where the knife had been.

"It's all right now," he said. "Let's go on."

They walked on a ways, and then Cameron said, "Tell me about these Little People. How little are they?"

"Oh," said Dragging Canoe, "about up to your knee."

"Are they Indians?" Cameron asked.

"They look like us," Dragging Canoe said, "but their hair reaches all the way to the ground. They like to sing and dance, but if you hear them, don't go looking for them. They don't like to be disturbed at their home. If you come on them, they'll make you confused, and you'll lose your way."

"Are they unfriendly, then?" said Cameron.

"Only if you bother them," said Dragging Canoe. "They take care of lost children, and sometimes they help our doctors."

It was on this same trip that Cameron came upon a rattlesnake, and he raised his war ax as if to strike it, but Dragging Canoe stopped him. He stepped around in front of the Scot and said, "Ujonati, let's you and I not meet each other again this summer." And then he led Cameron around the snake and out of its way. In a little while, they stopped to rest, and Dragging Canoe told Cameron this tale.

"One time," he said, "oh, I guess it was a long time ago, there was a hunter out alone, and he suddenly found himself surrounded by rattlesnakes. They were on all sides of him, and they were all standing up tall, the way rattlesnakes sometimes do. Have you ever seen it? They can stand up straight and tall like walking sticks. But one stood taller than all the rest, and he stood just in front of the hunter and looked at him. He was their chief. He said, 'Your wife just killed my brother there outside of her house. When you go home to her, tell her to go outside for water, and I'll kill her.'

"The hunter went on home, and he thought about what the rattlesnake had said. At last he said to his wife, 'I want some water.' She picked up a gourd and handed it to him. He took a sip and handed it back to her. 'No,' he said, 'I want some fresh water.'

"His wife took the gourd and went outside, and there the chief rattlesnake was waiting, and it bit her, and she died. The hunter went outside and found her there, and the rattlesnake chief was still there. The snake told the man, 'We're satisfied now. From now on, when you meet one of us, say these words, and we won't bother you.'"

"And those were the words you said a while ago?" Cameron asked.

Dragging Canoe nodded. "Yes," he said. "Those were the words."

They crossed out of the country of the Creeks into Cherokee country, and McDonald dropped off there at Chickamauga Creek. He would build a home and store there for the benefit of the Creeks to his immediate south and to any Cherokees in the southern reaches of their country. Dragging Canoe had not spent much time around McDonald on the trip, but he thought that McDonald was a nice enough young man. But he was a very young man. Dragging Canoe figured that McDonald couldn't be more than twenty years old. They left McDonald with some Cherokees there near Chickamauga Creek, and Cameron went on with Dragging Canoe. When they at last arrived at Echota in the Cherokee Overhills, Dragging Canoe introduced Cameron to everyone he met as "Scotchie," his brother.

Dragging Canoe was less than a day's walk from his own home when he saw the white settler hard at work on a log house. He stood and watched for a while. The four walls were already up, and the man was ready to work on his roof. He was in front of the house splitting a rail. To one side of the house a woman was cooking over an open fire. There were two horses, and there was a cow. Back behind the house a wagon stood. Dragging Canoe walked on down close to the settler. The man saw him and looked up from his work. "Hello," he said.

Dragging Canoe nodded. "Why are you building here?" he asked.

"Got to build somewhere," the man said.

"But this is my land," said Dragging Canoe. "Why are you here?"

"You a Cherokee?" the man asked.

"Yes," said Dragging Canoe.

"Well, I'm from Virginia," the man said. "There's peace between your people and mine now, so I figured it was safe enough out here. I found me a nice spot. No one was using it, so I'm building my home here."

"I think you should go somewhere else," said Dragging Canoe.

"It's too late now," the man said. "I've got too much work done here to leave it now. Besides, I like it here."

Cameron sat in his study in the fine home he had built for himself and his new Cherokee wife on the land the Cherokees had given him at the urging of Ada-gal'kala and Dragging Canoe. He was writing a letter to Stuart. "No nation," he wrote, "was ever infested with such a set of villains and horse thieves. A trader will invent and tell a thousand lies, and he is indefatigable in stirring up trouble against all other white persons he judges his rivals in trade."

A light rap on his door caused him to pause and look up from his work.

"Yes?" he said.

The door opened only slightly, and his wife peeked into the room.

"Tsiyu Gansini is here," she said.

Cameron stood up quickly. "Oh," he said, "please show him in."

Dragging Canoe walked into the study, and Cameron met him with an embrace. "Come in and sit down, brother," he said.

"Scotchie," said Dragging Canoe, taking a chair, "how are things going with you?"

"I'm well," said Cameron, "and my wife is now carrying a little one."

Dragging Canoe smiled. "That's good," he said. "You can raise it here among us where it will learn to be a Cherokee, and you can teach it all the things it will need to know to get along with the whites."

The door opened again, and Cameron's wife came in carrying a tray. She gave Dragging Canoe a bowl of *kanohena* and another to her husband. There were also coffee and cups on the tray. She put the tray down on a table and left the room. Dragging Canoe sipped the hominy drink, the drink that was traditionally served to visitors.

"It's good," he said.

They drank their *kanohena* and then coffee and made more small talk.

"So," said Cameron, "how are things going in Big Island Town?"

Dragging Canoe thought for a moment before answering. The expression on his face grew serious, almost somber. "Not well," he said. "The traders lie and cheat. They start fights. Some Cherokees drink their rum and get crazy, and they fight. Our young men are idle, and so they drink and fight with these white troublemakers."

Cameron sighed a heavy sigh. "It's the same in all the towns," he said. "Pearis and Ward and the other decent traders can't keep the rest in line. There are too many of them. Just before you came, I was writing a letter to Stuart about this very problem."

Dragging Canoe stood up and walked across the room. He turned again to face his adopted brother. "Scotchie," he said, "can you teach me to read English words? And to write them?"

Richard Pearis was in front of his house and trading post dealing with Wahya, a Cherokee hunter, for his skins. A small fire burned off to Pearis's right. Pearis and Wahya had argued for a time, but they finally made a bargain. Just then Harman Doaks walked up and watched. He held a jug at his side in his left hand. Pearis could tell that Doaks had already consumed a good deal of the jug's contents.

"Hey, Wolf," said Doaks. "That all he's giving you for them skins? Hell, boy, I can do better than that. Pick up them skins and come on over to my place. I'll even toss in a good long drink of this here rum."

Doaks held out the jug as if to entice Wahya away from Pearis.

"The deal's already made," Pearis said. "Go your way."

"I'll go my way where I want to go," said Doaks, "and the deal ain't been made till he picks up them goods and walks away. What do you say, Wolf? Have a drink?"

"I made my bargain with Pearis," said Wahya.

"It ain't too late to change your mind," Doaks said. "You ain't seen what I got."

"The last time I drank your rum," Wahya said, "I went home with nothing, and my head hurt all the next day."

Doaks laughed. "Ah, you just got to get used to it," he said. "Come on."

He reached down and took hold of Wahya by an arm and tried to pull him to his feet. Pearis jumped up and jerked Doaks's arm away. "Move along, Doaks," he said. "You're not wanted here."

Doaks dropped his jug and took a wild swing at Pearis, but Pearis ducked it neatly. He came up and drove a fist into Doaks's midsection, and Doaks doubled over with a loud expulsion of breath. Pearis grabbed him by the shoulders, whirled him around and shoved. Doaks fell back, landing on his rear end in the fire. He yowled, jumped up, and slapped at the seat of his britches. Pearis picked up the jug and slopped some of its contents on Doaks's hind end. Doaks howled some more and ran. Pearis threw the jug after him. Wahya and the other Cherokees around laughed hard as Doaks disappeared around another house.

Ada-gal'kala was amazed at the growth each time he paid a visit to Charlestown. There were more and more people, more and more buildings. More coaches ran the streets pulled by more horses and driven by more black slaves. It always made him recall his visit to England and the thousands and thousands of people he saw over there. They could keep sending people across the waters for years, he thought, and never empty out their island country. It also came to him that if they sent enough and keep building, one day this country would look like England. That thought depressed him, but he pushed it to the back of his mind. He had business, and he had to keep his mind on that.

He found his way, amid stares from the whites along the way, to the fine home of John Stuart, where he was admitted by a black servant dressed in fine clothes, and soon thereafter greeted warmly by Susannah. She took him directly to Stuart's office.

"John," she said, "look who's come to see you."

Stuart got up from his work and moved quickly to embrace his old friend.

"Welcome," he said.

Susannah called them into another room for food and drink, and when they had finished, Stuart excused himself and their guest, and the two men returned to the office. "Now, my friend," he said, "what has brought you all this way?"

"There are four towns of white men on our land," said Ada-gal'kala, "along the Watauga River."

Stuart took on a look of concern and leaned his head on a hand. "I had heard of that," he said. "I was waiting for confirmation. Now that you've brought it, I'll have to see what I can do to get them removed."

"Bushyhead," said Ada-gal'kala, "I don't like it that these white people think they can move onto my land without even asking my permission. But I've seen their towns. There are families there, men with their wives and children. I feel pity for the women and children especially. I don't like to see them without homes."

"Well," said Stuart, "what do you propose we do about them, then?"

"I don't want to sell my land, but we could give them a lease, could we not?" said the chief. "They could pay us for the lease each year."

Stuart marveled at the shrewdness of his old friend. He had certainly picked up on all the ways of the white man and was quick to take advantage of them for the benefit of his own people — or for his own benefit, he thought. Ah well, the Little Carpenter was the most influential man among the Cherokees, and his continued good will was vital to British interests. And he was a personal friend.

"I think perhaps we could negotiate such a lease," he said. "I'll send my brother, Henry, back with you to talk to the settlers on the Watauga. Have you heard the news of your old friend Pontiac?"

"I've heard that he was killed," said Ada-gal'kala, "by the English."

"Yes," said Bushyhead. "I wish that we could have made peace with him, as with you."

"We need more goods," said the Carpenter, quickly changing the unpleasant subject. "The Chickasaws gave us a drubbing not long ago, and it was because we had but little ammunition."

"I'll see to it that more is sent with you on your return," the Superintendent said.

## PART TWO

# Emergence

# 10

*1775*

Dragging Canoe stood back and apart from the boisterous crowd gathered along the river there at the Watauga settlements. He stood with his arms crossed over his chest, flanked by his friends Willinawa and the Terrapin. His own brothers, White Owl, Badger, and Whiteman Killer, were also there with him, as was his son, now grown and known as Young Dragging Canoe. They made a formidable-looking group, their chests bare, their body tattoos proudly displayed. Each man's head was shaved, a feather or two tied in the loose flowing topknot that they called *giðhla*, and each face wore a stern expression. The seven men calmly and boldly surveyed the scene there.

Dragging Canoe knew that his father had signed a lease with these whites. Even so, he could not bring himself to think of them as anything but squatters. After all, they had built their towns before the signing of the lease. And now the lease had at last expired. Dragging Canoe wanted the squatters moved out, but he knew that the old men, the recognized leaders of his nation, his own father among them, had already promised to sell the land to the white men. One of the front men for the company of land speculators had been the famous Daniel Boone, although Boone was not present on this day. Everyone else was, though, it seemed.

It was a lively and raucous crowd gathered there at Sycamore Shoals. Actually, there were two crowds, separated from each other by some distance. There were Cherokees from Echota and Malaquo and other nearby towns, men, women, and children. All ages were represented. They lounged along the edge of the Watauga River, cooking, eating, gossiping, the children running and playing, all waiting patiently for whatever was about to happen there. A small and crude log cabin stood alone close by, and a little farther away, a cluster of cabins, homes of the whites who were already known as the Wataugans, those people who had simply moved onto these Cherokee lands and built their homes, not asking permission of anyone, then later acquiring their lease from Ada-gal'kala.

At the cabins, settlers stood in small clusters and gawked at the Indians over by the river, waiting, like the Cherokees, to see what would happen. One among them sawed at a fiddle, sending out harsh, rasping tones through the early spring air. They had been gathered there like that for three days. Many of the Cherokees had been drinking the white man's rum. Many of the whites were also drunk and rowdy.

Ada-gal'kala, now sixty-eight years old, was there, and so were the old war chiefs Ogan'sdo' and Sawanooga, also known as the Raven. They had not yet seen Dragging Canoe and his companions. They were waiting there, in the company of other old men, their contemporaries, to meet with the white men Richard Henderson and Nathaniel Hart to finalize the deal they had previously made. Still rankled by a recent Cherokee defeat in battle at the hands of some Chickasaws, the old chiefs looked greedily at the nearby log cabin, which they knew was to be nearly filled with the weapons, guns, and ammunition that the white men were prepared to pay for the Cherokee land.

"Let's go examine the trade goods," Ogan'sdo' suggested to Ada-gal'kala, and the two old rivals went together into the cabin, where they were astonished at the number of rifles and the vast amount of powder and shot. There were also shirts and bolts of cloth and other typical trade goods. "I hadn't known it would be so much," Ada-gal'kala said. They already knew they would sign the papers, for when they had met privately before with Boone, and with Henderson and Hart, the two white men who called their company the Transylvania Land Company, they had all already agreed on the terms of the sale. "Let's go out and meet them," Ogan'sdo' said, and they went back outside.

But before Henderson and Hart arrived, Dragging Canoe appeared with Willinawa and the Terrapin and the others. As the old men stepped out of the cabin full of goods, their eyes still sparkling from the sight, they saw Dragging Canoe and the angry young men standing there, waiting to confront them, hard, determined, and accusing looks on their faces.

Ada-gal'kala at first started at the sight, then straightened himself up, composing himself inwardly at the same time, and walked boldly over to face his son. The son now towered over the father and was an imposing figure. Over six feet tall and of stout but lithe stature, Dragging Canoe at thirty-eight was still a handsome man, marred only by the facial scars left him by the horrible smallpox. He wore buckskin leggings, a breechcloth, and moccasins. Copper bands adorned his wrists and forearms, and a copper celt lay on his chest, suspended by a rawhide thong around his neck.

"Why are you staring at your own father in that hard way?" the old man asked.

"Because I believe you've come here to sell our land to these white men," Dragging Canoe answered.

"And you," said the father. "Why are you here?"

Dragging Canoe glanced over his shoulder, and with a sweeping gesture of his left arm, indicated the Cherokee people along the river's edge. "Many of our people are here," he said. "They're interested in what you plan to do here, I think. And so am I."

"You're not with them," his father said, and he repeated his earlier question. "Why are you here?"

"We've come here to stop you, my friends and my brothers and

I," Dragging Canoe said. "What you propose to do is foolish and it's wrong."

The old man sighed as he recognized the strong look of determination on the face of his son, for he had seen it many times over the years. The boy who had wanted to go to war so badly that he had earned the name he still carried with him had grown up to become the Head Warrior of Big Island Town. He had distinguished himself many times in battle. He had expressed his opinion too on many occasions, but never before had he actually openly stated his intention to oppose his father, the Principal Chief of the nation.

"This bargain has already been made," the old man said. "There is nothing you and your young men can do here now. Henderson and Hart will be here soon, and we'll sign the paper. Don't cause trouble for us now. Sign the paper with us. The cabin there is full of guns and powder and shot. And some other things. Blankets. Cloth. Right there. Go look at it. You'll have your share, too."

"If I were to have more guns and ammunition," said Willinawa, who was standing just behind and to the right of Dragging Canoe, "I'd use them to kill these white people who are calling themselves Wataugans."

"We want no war with the white men," Ada-gal'kala said.

"What are your guns and ammunition for, then?" asked Dragging Canoe. "To shoot squirrels with?"

"Have you forgotten the fight at Old Fields so soon?" said Ada-gal'kala, raising his voice in sudden irritation. "Have you forgotten so soon our humiliating defeat at the hands of the Ani-Tsiksa? That would never have happened if we'd had these weapons then."

"We should not turn these weapons on the Chickasaws," Dragging Canoe said. "We should go to the Chickasaws and extend our hand in friendship. We should not fight any Indians. All Indians should unite and keep the white men from moving any farther west. We all have a common enemy, one who will not stop taking our land unless we unite and stop him together."

"You're a dreamer," said Ada-gal'kala. "We've fought too long with the Chickasaws, the Creeks, and others. You will never be able to make friends with them all. Sign this treaty with us and forget your hopeless schemes."

Dragging Canoe stepped up close to his father and looked down into his red and watery eyes for just a brief instant. "Father," he said, "all my life you've taught me that the Real People never sell their lands. The bones of our ancestors lie buried in this land. The land is our mother and nourishes us all. The God over all gave this land to us to use."

"The Shawnees still claim part of this," the old man said in a near-whisper. He gave a shrug. "Maybe we're selling their land to these foolish white men."

"If the Shawnees think that any of this land is theirs, then let them make good their claim against us in a ballplay if they dare," Dragging Canoe said. "But don't sell the land to white men, especially these whites—these Wataugans—who have moved in here under our noses without even bothering to ask our permission, without even notifying us of their intentions. Their presence here is an insult. Do you not feel the sting of the insult? Has your skin grown so thick in your old age? We should have driven them out long ago, but you gave them a lease instead. Well, the lease has expired. Let them get out."

"The Wataugans are asking us now," said Ada-gal'kala, "and they're offering to pay a good price. A very good price." He paused and took a deep breath, and then he added, "And I want it. Besides, they've been here so long now that we've gotten used to it. We've not been using this land since they moved in. Why fight over it now?"

"The land these squatters are on is but a little of the land you propose to sell," Dragging Canoe said. "Whole nations have melted away in our presence like balls of snow before the sun and have scarcely left their names behind except as imperfectly recorded by their enemies and destroyers." He paused and looked around him. A crowd had gathered, with Cherokees on one side and whites on the other. He turned to face the whites, and he continued.

"It was once hoped that your people would not be willing to

travel beyond the mountains," he said, "so far from the ocean on which your commerce was carried and your connections maintained with the nations of Europe. But now that hope has vanished. You have passed the mountains and settled on Cherokee lands. And now you wish to have your usurpations sanctioned by the confirmation of a treaty.

"When that should be obtained, the same encroaching spirit will lead you onto other lands of the Cherokees. New cessions will be applied for, and finally the country that the Cherokees and our forefathers have so long occupied will be called for, and a small remnant of this nation, once so great and formidable, will be compelled to seek a retreat in some far-distant wilderness.

"Even there we will dwell but a short space of time before we will again behold the advancing banners of the same greedy host, who, not being able to point out any further retreat for the miserable Cherokees, will then proclaim the extinction of the whole race."

Ogan'sdo', who had kept quiet during this entire exchange between father and son, now stepped up beside his old friend and sometime rival and looked sternly at Dragging Canoe. "We've made this bargain," he said. "It's done. Get that in your head. You're only stirring up trouble here now. And you, young man, should show more respect for your elders. Not only are we older than you, you're standing here arguing in front of all these people, Cherokees and white people alike, with the two men who have been the leading men in our nation for longer than you've been walking on this earth. And one of them is your own father. You should be ashamed of yourself, Chooch."

Dragging Canoe's brow knit, and his face flushed an almost deep purple. He turned sharply and stalked away, followed closely by Terrapin and Willinawa. His brothers and Young Dragging Canoe stayed behind to see what would happen there at Sycamore Shoals. A short distance away, seven saddled horses grazed contentedly. Dragging Canoe, Willinawa, and the Terrapin mounted three of them and rode quickly away. The two old men watched them go.

"I'm afraid that he'll cause trouble for us, that son of yours," Ogan'sdo' said at last.

"He's always been trouble," said Ada-gal'kala. "Look. Who's that coming?"

Ogan'sdo' turned to look toward the Watauga settlement with Ada-gal'kala. Two riders were approaching, moving between the settlers' cabins. The old men strained their eyes, and when the riders were about halfway between them and the cabins, Ogan'sdo' said, "Ah. It's Richard Pearis. Our interpreter. And Vann is with him."

"Good," said Ada-gal'kala. "Then Hart and Henderson should be here soon."

Pearis and Vann rode up and dismounted, leaving their horses to graze with trailing reins. Pearis walked over hurriedly to the two old chiefs. "*Siyo*, Pearis," said Ada-gal'kala. "*Siyo.*" said Ogan'sdo'. Pearis returned their greetings almost brusquely and got right down to business.

"My old friends," Pearis said, "what you're about to do with these white men is not only unwise, it's illegal. I think you should turn around right now and go home before you've done something we'll all regret later."

"You sound like my hot-tempered son," said Ada-gal'kala.

"Dragging Canoe is a bright young man," said John Vann, who stood a little behind Pearis. "You should think more about what he had to say."

"We made a promise to these men," Ogan'sdo' said.

"But King George has drawn the line," Pearis argued. "This is Indian territory, and these Wataugans are here illegally."

"This land doesn't belong to King George," said Ogan'sdo'. "He says that he got it from the French. It never belonged to the French. It belongs to us, and if we choose to sell it, that's our business."

"Ada-gal'kala," Pearis said, "do you remember the Articles of Agreement you signed in 1730? You promised to sell land to no one but the King. Henderson and Hart do not represent the King. They have formed a private land company."

"Maybe I signed that thing you're talking about," said Adagal'kala. "When did you say it was?"

"The year was 1730," Vann said.

"I don't know your white man's calendar. Let's see now," said the old chief. "That would be how many years ago now?"

"About forty-five years," Pearis said.

"Hmm," the chief muttered. "No. I don't remember that far back. I'm getting old. Maybe I signed it, but if I did, I couldn't read the white man's words. I still can't. I didn't know what I signed. They probably lied to me about what it said. I don't remember agreeing to such a thing as what you tell me I signed. Besides, the English sign treaties with us promising to leave us alone forever, and then they come back for a new treaty. Nothing lasts forever."

"You signed it," Pearis said. "You signed it in England in front of the King." He turned in frustration to Ogan'sdo'. "You know about the Articles, don't you?"

"I don't know," said Ogan'sdo'. "Besides, Pearis, what are you so concerned about? You're an Englishman."

"I care about this because I am an Englishman," said Pearis, "a loyal Englishman, loyal to my King, and these other Englishmen are about to break the King's law. Deliberately. They know what they're doing, and they don't care. These men are rebels, not loyal to the King. The next thing you know, they'll be trying to talk you into fighting against the King's soldiers. Will you do that, too? And I care further because I have a Cherokee wife and child. You know that. You're selling my child's inheritance here today. Don't do it. I beg of you."

"They're coming now," said Ogan'sdo', and Pearis glanced back toward the settlement to see Henderson and Hart and a driver approaching in a wagon drawn by a team of horses. Two riders on horseback followed them.

"Can't you see that your own best interests lie with the King?" Pearis said, now nearly desperate to get through to the old men before it was too late. "The King has drawn the line. He wants to keep the whites off your land."

"We'll sell them this land," said Ada-gal'kala, "and then they'll have enough. They'll stay off our land then."

"It's three hundred square miles," Vann said, almost shouting.

"You're too late, Pearis, and you, Vann," said Ogan'sdo'. The wagon drew to a halt just behind Pearis, and the driver and the two land speculators climbed down. The two riders stayed in their saddles. Pearis noticed that they were armed. Richard Henderson smiled broadly and stepped toward Pearis, holding out his hand. "Hello, Pearis," he said. Pearis ignored the hand and the greeting.

"I protest this meeting," he said. "Where's Cameron? Where's McDonald?"

"Mr. Stuart was notified," Nathaniel Hart said. "If he failed to send his deputies, that's not our fault."

"I don't believe that he was notified," said Pearis.

"I'm not going to take that personally," said Henderson. "Come on, now. Let's all have a friendly drink together." He walked toward the rear of the wagon and broke open a keg of rum. He dipped out tin cups full for everyone there, and the two old chiefs drank greedily. Pearis frowned, but he accepted a cup of rum. He had never been one to turn that down. Hell, he told himself, I tried.

Dragging Canoe sat beside the river, a deep frown on his brow. He watched the cold, clear water flow swiftly by, and he wished that Long Man, the river, would talk to him and give him some sound advice. He tried to imagine what was in the minds of the old men, in the mind of his own father, to be doing this crazy thing. The whites were all around, and they were pressing ever closer. Couldn't the old fools see that? Couldn't they see that one day soon they would be surrounded by the whites? What would happen then? He watched the water flow by as if he were distracted. His companions paced behind him, impatient, wondering how long he would sit there and just stare like that.

"What are we going to do?" asked Willinawa, suddenly out of patience.

"What can we do?" Dragging Canoe answered. "I tried to talk

to them. They wouldn't listen to me. They've made up their minds. They've already made the bargain."

"It's a fool's bargain," said Willinawa.

"It's a traitor's bargain. They'll sell our country," said Terrapin.

"Where is Cameron?" Dragging Canoe said aloud but not really to anyone but himself. He thought of Scotchie. He knew Scotchie's mind, knew that Scotchie would not let such a thing as this proceed. Not only was Scotchie's heart against it, but Scotchie's chief, Bushyhead, was also against it, as was their King. The King did not want his subjects, the colonists, moving out onto Indian land. Dragging Canoe knew that.

"I don't know where Cameron is," said Willinawa, "or that other deputy, either—that McDonald. Why do we need them? What are we going to do?"

"There's nothing to be done," Dragging Canoe said sharply. "The old men have already done it."

Terrapin and Willinawa looked at one another. Dragging Canoe had not moved. He still sat staring into the running water. Willinawa said, "Let's go back and see what happens." Terrapin stared at Dragging Canoe's back for another moment, then said, "Let's go." They mounted their horses and rode away.

Sitting silent and alone, Dragging Canoe watched the water roll by. He recalled his resolve to live only for his people. He had fought since then, yes, but under the direction of Ogan'sdo'. He had met with the English, but he had been an observer to the diplomatic dealings of his father. What had he actually done more than any other Cherokee in those years? Nothing, he told himself. He had done nothing to fulfill the goal and the role he had recognized as having been set for him years ago. Well, he thought, this must be the time. This must be the time, but there was nothing he could do. The great men of the nation had spoken.

And then he saw before him there in the running water, as clear as the clear water itself, as clearly as if he had turned to look at Willinawa or Terrapin a moment or two earlier, the form of a distant, circling eagle. It must be a reflection from high above in the sky, he thought. The eagle circled from east to north to west to south and continued in that same direction, the direction in which the Cherokees danced. It continued circling, and then to his astonishment, Dragging Canoe saw the waters begin to stir, to circle with the eagle, and the eagle was swirling the waters, and Dragging Canoe was looking into a deep whirlpool.

And then he saw, coming out of the vortex, the figure of a man, but he knew at once that it was more than a man, for it had the appearance of a Real Man, yet his eyes were sharp, and a light seemed to emanate from them. Dragging Canoe saw that the man was wearing around his neck a rattlesnake and around each wrist a copperhead, and he held in his right hand what appeared to be a spear or a staff, but it was not a spear or a staff. It was a bolt of lightning. And running down both sides of his chest were streaks of lightning. Dragging Canoe at once knew that somehow he was face-to-face with the First Man, the Great Hunter, Kanati, the one they addressed in ritual and ceremony as the Red Man, but in ordinary speech as the White Man for fear of saying his real name in an improper context.

And Dragging Canoe was afraid. He did not know what to do. He did not know what to say. But the Great Hunter spoke to him and said, "Why have you run away? Why have you turned your back on your own people in their time of need?" Dragging Canoe answered, "I went to the place and talked, but the old men had already made up their minds. They told me to go away." Lightning bolts shot from the eyes of the Great Hunter and a great clap of thunder sounded all around them. "Who told you to go away?" the Thunder said. "My father and the other old men," said Dragging Canoe. And the Great Hunter said, "Are their words more powerful than mine?" Dragging Canoe said, "No. They are not." The Great Hunter looked at Dragging Canoe, and Dragging Canoe thought that the eyes were looking clear into his soul, and he was afraid that lightning bolts would shoot out of them again. But they did not. "Tsiyu Gansini," said the Great Hunter, "you are about to see things that no man has seen," and then the Great Hunter reached forth to take hold of Dragging Canoe, and Dragging

Canoe was drawn into the vortex with him, and he was afraid, for he was swirling in the swift waters, spinning with the whirlpool in the direction of the flight of the eagle, in the direction of the dances, and they spun around the wide circle seven times, and then they stopped, and they were at the eastern point of the circle. The two of them were standing side by side, and they were looking across a great plain, and dark, heavy clouds were rolling low and fast across the plain.

And Dragging Canoe saw that the plain was a circle, and it was floating on the water. And across the plain from east to west a line was drawn, and another was drawn from north to south. And there where the two lines crossed, in the center of the circle, in *ayehli*, a town was built, and he knew that the town was the home of the Cherokees where they lived in the center of the world. And the dark clouds continued to move over the circle or the plain both low and fast.

And out of the waters to the east came a great beast. He was like the *ukitena* for he was like a giant snake, but there were great antlers on his head and behind his head a pair of giant wings, but he was floating on top of the water, floating on his belly. And he reached the edge of the circle, which was the edge of the great plain and the edge of the world, and he opened his mouth wide, and horsemen came riding out of his mouth and rode onto the land. And there were more than Dragging Canoe could count. They kept coming out of the mouth of the beast. More and more of them. And wherever they rode, chaos reigned over the land.

And some of the horsemen rode the edge of the circle, but they rode not from east to north but from east to south, and then they gathered up there in that arc from east to south and they rode toward the center, and when they arrived close to the center, they spread themselves out, and they rode around it and closed it in. And behind them the land was in flames. All was in ruins.

And then as the horsemen rode smaller and smaller circles around the center, Dragging Canoe felt himself pulled again, and again he found himself spinning around and around the edges of the eddy, and he was moving faster and faster, and then he stopped again, and he was at the bottom of the waters, and he looked up, and he saw the spiral opening wider and wider above him, and it looked as if it would reach into the heavens, even up to the Seventh Height on top of the Great Sky Vault.

And from up there near the Seventh Height a tiny form appeared. And it was moving fast, almost as fast as the lightning strikes, and it sped straight down, and as it drew closer, Dragging Canoe could make out its form, and he could see that it was *Tinuwa*, the peregrine falcon, and it was preparing to strike. He looked down again, and there below on the floor of the vortex, he saw the horsemen still circling the center, still closing in, and then the falcon struck, and it struck with such force that many of the horsemen were killed at once by the impact of the blow of the falcon.

The falcon rose again, and it struck again, and again and again, and then tiny birds flew at it and tormented it, causing it to fly this way and that until at last it flew up high once more, higher than the tiny birds could fly, and it made another dive, as fast and as hard as it could dive, and it struck the earth with a powerful impact, and then it lay still. And chaos and madness ruled over all the circle of the earth.

And Dragging Canoe felt himself falling slowly backward until he was lying on his back, but he was floating, and then he started to spin again. This time he was rising toward the top of the vortex, and the world turned black, and when the light returned to him, he was sitting there beside the river as before. As before, the waters were running past him, and he saw nothing in the waters but the image of an eagle circling high in the sky.

He sat still for a moment contemplating all that he had seen, wondering if he had actually seen those things. The image of the eagle was no longer in the water in front of him. He leaned back and looked up into the sky, and there he saw it. The eagle was up there soaring easily high above. He wondered how long he had been sitting there beside the water, how much time had passed while he had been taken to . . . wherever he had been taken. He could not tell if only a few moments had passed or a few days. It seemed as if time had been suspended.

He stood up with sudden new resolve and moved with long strides back to his still saddled, unconcerned, grazing horse. Dragging Canoe picked up the reins and put his hands on the saddle horn. Then he hesitated. He stood for a moment looking across the back of his horse, drinking in the lush landscape around him. Then he jumped quickly onto its back and lashed it into a run. He had no idea if anyone would still be at the gathering at Sycamore Shoals, for he had no idea how long he had been away. But he would find out.

Soon he was back at the gathering place, and he saw that the crowds were still there. He rode fast up close to the wagon where his father and Ogan'sdo' and the two white men of the Transylvania Company were still standing, and he jerked his horse to a quick stop, scattering dirt and pebbles, causing the men there to step back. It was a rude gesture, and Dragging Canoe had meant it to be so. A table was set up beside the wagon by this time, papers laid out on it with rocks at their corners holding them down to keep them from blowing away in the light breeze that rustled the leaves of the trees. Dragging Canoe could see at once that the old men were already drunk on the white man's rum. As he dismounted, Richard Pearis, Willinawa, Terrapin, and some of the others noticed right away the marks around his eyes symbolic of the deadly falcon. Pearis walked unsteadily toward him.

"I tried to stop them," Pearis said.

"They've signed it already?" asked Dragging Canoe.

"It's all signed and sealed," said Pearis, his speech slightly slurred. "It's done. Over and done." He made a wide sweeping gesture with his right arm. "All your land between the Kentucky and Tennessee rivers," he said. "Between the Ohio River and the Cumberland Divide. Gone. All gone."

"Why was my brother Scotchie not here?" Dragging Canoe asked.

"Cameron was not notified of the meeting," said Pearis. "I don't believe he knows a thing about this."

"No," said Dragging Canoe. "You must be right about that. If Scotchie knew, he'd be here. And this paper would not have been signed."

"Ah, well," said Pearis, "when Cameron and Stuart hear about this, they'll most likely nullify the whole damned business anyway. It's all against the law, you know. It's against the King's law."

"It's worse than that," said Dragging Canoe. "It's against my law."

In spite of the prevailing drunkenness, the dramatic return of Dragging Canoe together with his new fierce countenance had cast a sudden pallor over the meeting, and everyone was quiet and looking in his direction, waiting to see what he would do. Henderson and Hart glanced nervously at their two armed guards. The guards touched the weapons at their sides. The entire crowd had become quiet and tense. Dragging Canoe took a menacing step toward the Transylvania Company partners. Then, looking directly at Henderson, staring defiantly and threateningly into his eyes, he pointed and spoke out in a loud and clear voice.

"You've bought a fair land, white man," he said, "but there's a black cloud hanging over it. You'll find its settlement dark and bloody. I, Dragging Canoe, promise you that."

Dragging Canoe rode south at the head of eighty armed warriors. He had heard that his brother Scotchie was coming to Echota with ammunition for the Cherokees, sent by Bushyhead, and he wanted to make sure that Scotchie and his pack train reached the Cherokee country safely. When he at last came upon them near the white settlement of Mobile, he found them at rest. Instructing his followers to form a guard around the resting camp of the white men, Dragging Canoe rode in to see Scotchie. The Scot recognized him at once and ran to meet him. Dragging Canoe slid off his horse's back, and Scotchie rushed to give him a warm embrace. Then stepping back, he smiled.

" *'Siyo*, Brother," said Dragging Canoe.

"I'm glad to see you," Scotchie said, "but what brings you here, and with such a force?"

"I heard that you were coming," Dragging Canoe said, "and I didn't want anything to happen to you."

"To me," Scotchie said, "or to your ammunition?"

"Not to either one," Dragging Canoe said with a smile.

"Come with me," said Scotchie. "There's someone I want you to meet."

The two men walked together to where another white man sat beside a small fire sipping from a tin cup. As they approached, he stood up to face them.

"Brother," said Scotchie to Dragging Canoe, "this is Henry Stuart, the brother of Bushyhead."

Dragging Canoe and Stuart shook hands, but Dragging Canoe gave Scotchie a puzzled look. "Where is Bushyhead?" he asked.

"He's not well, I'm afraid," Scotchie said.

"And he's gone to Florida for his safety," Henry Stuart added.

"What do you mean?" Dragging Canoe asked.

"He had to flee from Charlestown," Henry said.

"He's not safe at his own home in Charlestown?" Dragging Canoe asked, a questioning look on his face.

"No, he's not," said Henry. "Far from it. He fled Charlestown for his life."

"How is it that Bushyhead is not safe in Charlestown?" Dragging Canoe asked, puzzled by the strange news. "He's the King's man, is he not? An important man."

"A lot has happened, Brother," said Scotchie. "Sit down here, and we'll tell you all about it."

Henry Stuart offered both Dragging Canoe and Cameron a cup of tea. They accepted, and he set about preparing it. All three men sat on a log by the small campfire.

"I thought that Bushyhead would come with you," Dragging Canoe said to Scotchie, "to tell those Wataugans to get off my land."

"He meant to," Scotchie answered. "He was going to, but as I told you, he became ill."

"And then he had to get up from his sickbed and flee for his life down into Florida," Henry Stuart said. "That's why he sent me along in his place."

"All right," said Dragging Canoe. "Will you then tell the Wataugans to get off my land? The white people have almost surrounded us. They've left us with only a little spot of land to stand on. I believe that they want to destroy our whole nation."

"Well," said Henry Stuart, casually poking at the fire, "you Cherokees did sell the land to Henderson —"

"I had no part of that bargain," Dragging Canoe snapped. "It was a bad bargain. After the division of the goods, one young man showed me an English shirt and said that it was all he got for all that land. That sale was made by some of the old men, men too old to hunt or fight. As for me, I have my young men around me, and they mean to have their land."

Stuart looked up as if to respond, but Cameron silenced him with a gesture. Stuart poured a cup of tea and held the cup out toward Dragging Canoe. Cameron took it and handed it to his adopted brother. Then Stuart poured another cup for Cameron. At last Cameron spoke.

"Brother," he said, "we hope you won't attack the Wataugans, not just yet. Bushyhead himself sent us with this message for you. We know that the Henderson deal was a bad deal. It was against our own laws. The Governor of North Carolina has issued a warrant for the arrest of Henderson and others of his company. So has the Governor of Virginia."

Dragging Canoe nodded slowly. "Virginia also wrote a letter to the old men," he said, "telling them that what they did was a bad thing."

"Yes," said Scotchie, "well, from what I hear, Henderson and some of his followers ran away to avoid arrest. Bushyhead was ready to move against the illegal settlers, the Wataugans, and he would have done so but for two unfortunate occurrences. First, as we told you, he fell ill. He should have gone to bed and stayed there in his home at Charlestown, but something else happened. Something very bad.

"Many of the colonists are now involved in open and armed rebellion against the King, and Charlestown has fallen into their hands. For that reason, Bushyhead had to get out of Charlestown. The king's men are yet firmly in control in north Florida, and that's where he has gone. Well, the Wataugans, of course, most of them, have joined the revolution. They know that the King's law requires them to move off your land, and they don't want to move, so they've joined with the other rebels. They've declared themselves independent from Great Britain and say that the King's law means nothing to them."

"You say all that," Dragging Canoe said, interrupting, "and yet you tell me that you don't want me to fight the Wataugans?"

"I said not yet," Cameron insisted. "The time will come. I'm bringing this ammunition to you so you'll be ready when the time is right."

"My brother, Bushyhead, is afraid that if you and your people start killing Englishmen," Stuart injected into the discussion, "you won't be able to tell a rebel from a loyalist."

Dragging Canoe shot a questioning glance at Cameron, and Cameron explained further. "Not all the colonists are rebels," he said. "There are some who are still with us. Some who remain loyal to the King."

"Not the Wataugans," said Dragging Canoe.

"Even some of them are loyal," said Stuart.

"They're breaking the King's law by staying on my land," Dragging Canoe insisted. "If they break the King's law, they're not loyal to the King."

"Nevertheless," said Stuart, "my brother wants you to wait."

Dragging Canoe stood up and paced away from the fire, his back to the two white men. He thought that he didn't like this brother of Bushyhead. That didn't matter, though. Not just then. There were more important matters to deal with. He stood a moment in thought, then turned to face them again. "Our trade goods come from Charlestown," he said.

"They won't any more," Stuart said.

"This pack train has been sent from Florida," Cameron said.

"Bushyhead wanted us to get to you as soon as possible in order to assure you that we will continue to supply your needs with goods from Florida."

Dragging Canoe nodded solemnly. "Now I know why so many more settlers have been moving in with the Wataugans," he said. "There's no English law left to stop them. All the more reason for me and my young men to attack them and drive them out. The Wataugans are all rebels. Why should we wait?"

Henry Stuart cleared his throat suggestively. "My brother, the Superintendent," he said, "has asked me to say to you that he would like you to be armed and ready and await the arrival of regular British forces with whom you will coordinate your efforts. An attack on the rebels by you just now would be premature. In the meantime, I will send letters to the Watauga settlements and attempt to convince the settlers to pull back peacefully. That is what my brother asked me to tell you and what he asked me to do."

Dragging Canoe looked at Cameron. "What do you say, Scotchie?" he asked.

"My brother, I ask you to take the advice of Bushyhead," Cameron said.

Dragging Canoe sat back down on the log and heaved a sigh. "Then we'll wait," he said. "And for now, we'll get you and your people and our goods safely into Echota. Are you ready to travel now?"

"Yes," said Cameron. "We were just about ready to go when you arrived. Henry, would you get the men started?"

"Of course," said Henry.

As Henry Stuart walked away, Cameron spoke to Dragging Canoe in a low voice. "Bushyhead is right," he said. "It's not the right time to attack the Wataugans. It's too early."

Dragging Canoe put a hand reassuringly on Cameron's shoulder. "I said we'll wait, Scotchie," he said, "but we won't wait for long. Remember that."

They rode back toward the Cherokee country with Dragging Canoe's men riding point, along both flanks, and taking up the rear. Dragging Canoe rode alongside Cameron. He was relaxed, for he knew that the outriders were watching out for their safety, and he trusted his men. The sky was clear, and the air was crisp. The leaves on some of the trees were already beginning to change color.

"Scotchie," said Dragging Canoe. "Brother, I love this land as I love my mother. Perhaps I love it more than I love my mother, for this land is mother to us all, to all of the Cherokee People. The bones of all my grandmothers and grandfathers lie buried in this earth. The flesh of all my ancestors nourishes the land. And the bodies of my wife and mother, carried away by the smallpox. My people have fought and died to protect this land for generations, for longer than anyone knows. I can't bear to think of anyone selling this land.

"It's a beautiful land. I love to look at it. It gives me pleasure and peace. How can the old men think of selling it? For guns? What's happened to them, Scotchie? They used to think and feel as I do. They were my teachers."

"Perhaps it's a matter of age," Cameron suggested.

"I don't think so," Dragging Canoe said. "I'll never be that old."

"One of those old men is your own father," Cameron said.

"I'm ashamed of my father," said Dragging Canoe. "How would you feel if your father tried to sell your mother to a stranger?"

"You're not being fair," said Cameron. "I accept your metaphor, but really, it's not the same thing."

"Then you don't understand me," Dragging Canoe said. "Not really. Not even you, for it is the same thing. It's exactly the same thing. And I'm not going to allow it to happen. Not while I live."

"Perhaps," said Cameron, "I don't quite understand your feelings for this land, my brother, but I can assure you of one thing. The King doesn't want the land sold to the colonists either. I serve the King, and I'll stand by you, I and McDonald and Bushyhead and his brother Henry and all loyal Englishmen. When the time is right, we'll all fight those damned rebels. You can be sure of that."

"Well," Dragging Canoe said, "the right time won't come fast enough for me, but I'll try to be patient, for your sake and for that of Bushyhead."

"For the King," said Cameron.

"I don't know the King," Dragging Canoe said, "but I like the King's men. I'll wait yet a while before I kill the Wataugans."

# 11

Dragging Canoe came out of the big council meeting at Echota dissatisfied. Nothing had been accomplished, he thought. Willinawa, Terrapin, and some other young men spoke eloquently for war against the Wataugans, and to tell the truth, Dragging Canoe's heart was with them. He kept himself quiet, though. He could not just yet speak against his English friends and allies, Bushyhead and Scotchie. Scotchie spoke to the gathering and expressed to everyone present the words of caution sent down by Bushyhead. Ada-gal'kala and Agan'stat' both spoke for peace. Then Nancy Ward spoke in her capacity of Giga-hyuh, and many who were undecided listened hard to the words of the beloved War Woman.

Many Cherokee women, she told the people, had husbands among the whites. They had children. If the Cherokees were to go to war against the settlers, they would find themselves fighting their own families. She called on the Cherokee people to remember their ancient, honored traditions and listen to the voices of the women. She was eloquent and persuasive. Dragging Canoe remained silent, but he thought that a strange alliance had formed there at Echota in the townhouse: a peace faction made up of Scotchie, the old men, and Nancy Ward. And if something didn't happen soon, he was in danger of being thought to be one of them.

By his very silence, he would be thought to be opposed to going to war, and the young men would find themselves another leader. If that were to happen, he wouldn't blame them.

He himself did not like the waiting. He felt as if things were happening around him that he should be doing something about. The Wataugans were on his land. He should be driving them off. It seemed to him that the Cherokees were already surrounded by whites, and they had only a little of their once vast land holdings left. And now the once respected old men, the recognized leaders of the nation, were selling even more land to the whites. Now the Englishmen were about to fight among themselves. Some were calling themselves "Americans," but the others, the loyal ones, called them rebels. Those rebels, or Americans, were the ones who wanted the land, and they were the ones who were moving closer and closer to the Cherokees in large numbers. The white men who were friends to the Cherokees, those who called themselves "Loyalists," were but few in Cherokee country. The times were troublesome. It seemed as if the world were near its end.

Dragging Canoe was not quite sure why Scotchie and Bushyhead wanted him to wait, but he did understand that it had something to do with organizing a concerted effort of both British and Cherokee forces. Perhaps they were right about that, he thought. If they could gather a great force together, perhaps they could drive all the Americans back at once. But the real difficulty was in convincing Willinawa, Terrapin, his own brothers, and the other young men that Bushyhead had a good reason for asking them to wait. They were ready to fight, and if he failed to lead them, they would find someone else to do so. He was engaged in a delicate balancing act, and he knew it.

He understood the impatience of the young men, for he had the same feelings. Yet he trusted his English friends, and he wanted them to believe that they could trust him as well. He had told Scotchie that he would wait—but not for too long. He waited anxiously for word from Bushyhead to come through Scotchie or Bushyhead's brother Henry that would tell them the time had come. He longed for that day. It was as if he had an itch, and his hand was being kept from scratching it. His weapons were ready. He longed for action.

Bushyhead's assistants were not inactive, however, for Henry Stuart caused a letter to be sent to the Watauga settlements from Bushyhead and another from Ogan'sdo'. The letters urged the Wataugans to remove themselves from Cherokee land in order to avoid a bloody confrontation. Bushyhead's letter offered them land in northern Florida, if they would consent to move. All this took time, and time was hanging heavy for Dragging Canoe. Some of the young men were playing the *gatayusti* game there in front of the townhouse. He was standing there and watching. He did not play. He had not even bet on the outcome of the games. His mind was on the Wataugans and on the division that had formed among his own people: the war faction and the peace faction.

" *'Siyo,* Brother," someone said, a female voice. He looked over his shoulder to see Nancy Ward standing there. He nodded a greeting. She moved up to stand by his side. "I'm pleased that you did not speak for war in the council," she said.

"Make no mistake, Sister," said Dragging Canoe, "I want the war, but I promised Scotchie and Bushyhead that I'd wait. I warned them, though, that I would not wait for long."

"Did you hear my words at the meeting?" she asked.

"I heard them," he said.

"If you fight the Watauga settlers," she said, "some of our husbands and children may be killed."

"Then tell them to get out of the Watauga settlements," said Dragging Canoe. "Get them out of there before we attack. Besides, your own white man has left you, hasn't he? Ward's not even out there where he might be in danger."

"It doesn't matter where Ward is," Nancy said. "I have his children here with me."

"They're safe with you," he said. "They're not with the rebels."

"I speak for all the women," Nancy said. "Some of them have husbands and children there."

"Some of the women agree with me," Dragging Canoe answered her.

"It's not so simple as that anyway," she said. "If you kill white men anywhere, other whites will retaliate. We need to remain at peace. Our people have already seen too much war. The wars and the smallpox have carried away too many. The only safety for the Cherokees is in peace."

"They've surrounded us already," said Dragging Canoe, "and they press closer each day. They won't be satisfied until we've been wiped away as a nation. Where's the safety in that?"

"If my arguments won't persuade you," said Nancy, "then perhaps I can appeal to your sense of tradition, the time-honored tradition of listening to the voice of the women. Don't go to war without hearing the voice of the women's council."

Just then Scotchie walked up to join them.

" 'Siyo, Scotchie," said Nancy. "I'll be going now," she said to Dragging Canoe, "but think about what I've said."

She left the two men alone, and they stood there in silence for a moment.

"Brother," said Scotchie, "I have some bad news. I've heard that when the Wataugans received our letters, they made use of Bushyhead's letter to imitate his handwriting and his signature. They wrote another letter and made it seem as if Bushyhead had written it. They sent this letter to settlements in South Carolina and in Virginia and to other places. I don't know how many copies they sent out and where all the copies were sent. But the letter, the forgery they sent, called on all Loyalists to join the Cherokees in a fight against the Americans. They're trying to raise up all the rebels against us."

"The more reason we should strike now," said Dragging Canoe, "before they have time to strike us."

"Wait a little longer, Brother," said Scotchie. "I beg you."

There was much excitement at Echota, for everyone knew of the large delegation that was coming from the north. Headed by the

145

Shawnee, Cornstalk, the coming visitors included Shawnees, Delawares, Mohawks, Nancutas, and Ottawas. The people of Echota busied themselves preparing food for the visit, even though doing so strained their resources. Gardens were plucked clean, and men went out hunting. Runners kept the town posted regarding the progress of the northern delegation.

They knew too why the northerners were coming to visit. They had visited other nations of Indians along the way, and word of their mission had preceded them. They were allies of the King, and the British Loyalists up north had urged them to form an alliance of Indians to wipe out the American rebels. They were coming to Echota, which had come to be regarded as the Cherokee capital, to attempt to draw the Cherokees into their cause. Dragging Canoe kept quiet, but secretly he was elated by the news. There were others who were thinking as he was. That news was encouraging to him in two ways. First, it had the effect of confirming that his own plan was a good one. Others agreed with him, though they did not know yet how he was thinking. And then, and perhaps even more important, it meant that part of the grand work was already done. It would make his mission that much easier to accomplish. He was anxious for the arrival of the northern Indians.

The bustle at Echota somewhat covered over the deeper anxieties. These outsiders would be injecting themselves into an already divided community. They would be urging the Cherokees to go to war against the rebels. Quietly, Dragging Canoe, of course, hoped that they would succeed in convincing the peace faction of the wisdom of striking at the settlements. They had been sent by the English, and he hoped that fact would convince Scotchie as well that the time was right. He was most anxious for their arrival.

At last they came. For a day and a night after the arrival of the northern delegation, the people of Echota and visiting Cherokees from other towns feasted and danced, welcoming the visitors. Then the formalities began, and after speeches of welcome from Ada-gal'kala and others, the forum was turned over to Cornstalk.

The Shawnee drew himself up as he took his place before the large gathering of Cherokees. He wore leggings and moccasins, both decorated with dyed porcupine quills. His breechcloth was made of trade cloth, and he wore a white shirt of English manufacture. Its cuffs and collar were lace. Over that he had a British military red coat with epaulets on its shoulders. His hair was adorned with several beautifully colored feathers. A British saber dangled at his left side, strapped on around his waist by a shiny black British leather belt.

"Brothers," he said, and his voice was smooth and deep, "we have traveled a great distance to see you, and we've come on a mission of great importance to us all. The great King, our Father, needs our help. Some of his children have turned against him. They call themselves Americans, and they say that the King's law is nothing to them. They have taken up arms against the King's men, and they mean to drive the King's men into the waters. When they've done that, they mean to have our lands.

"The King, as you know, has drawn the line between his colonies and our land. He means to keep his white children on their own land and away from ours. He has asked our help in this great undertaking, and we have left our homes in the north to visit all the tribes of red people and make peace between us and an alliance against the rebellious Americans."

The young men grew more and more excited as they listened to the words of Cornstalk, and by the time he had finished his speech, many of them were already dancing and whooping. Dragging Canoe moved to the side of Scotchie, whose face showed a look of deep concern.

"It's time, Scotchie," he said. "I can wait no longer."

"Brother . . ." Scotchie began.

"These men have been sent by the King's men," Dragging Canoe said. "How can we not respond to their call? And look at the young men. They will have their war. They'll have it, Scotchie, no matter what you or I do or say."

"I'll send to Florida for more ammunition," Scotchie said.

The northern Indians all moved to the front of the assembly

again, and several took out and displayed long war belts. Cornstalk walked over to Ada-gal'kala where he was seated and held his belt out toward him. The old man bowed his head and did not move. The Shawnee then stepped over in front of Agan'stat' and held the belt out once more. Agan'stat', his eyes averted, pretended not to see. Looking for someone else of importance, Cornstalk turned toward the Giga-hyuh, and Nancy Ward gave him a look of scorn and turned away. Then Dragging Canoe suddenly moved to the front of the crowd and stepped boldly up to Cornstalk. Defiantly, he held out his hands, and Cornstalk gave him the belt.

The young men shouted their pleasure, and Doublehead, Bloody Fellow, and other young men followed Dragging Canoe's example and accepted war belts from the other northern Indians. The war dance then began in earnest. Henry Stuart, frightened and angry, sought out Cornstalk.

"You northern Indians," he said, "have come at a bad time. You've stirred up trouble here. You have proper white men to guide you, but these Cherokees do not. It's not time for them to go to war. They need the King's troops here to lead them."

"Those proper white men you mention," said Cornstalk, "are the very ones who sent us on this mission. This is the guidance they have given us."

Having overhead the brief conversation, Dragging Canoe stepped toward the two men and gave Stuart a hard look. "You've already done enough damage," he said. "It was your letters that started the trouble here. I don't want you to interfere any longer. For your brother's sake, I won't have you harmed, but stay out of our business."

Agan'stat' stepped up and put a hand on Stuart's shoulder. He drew him off to one side and whispered in his ear.

"I fear for your safety here," he said. "Get out and go home where you'll be all right."

Just at that time, Cameron, watching what had been going on, walked over to Dragging Canoe. "Brother," he said, "what's happening here?"

"Scotchie," said Dragging Canoe, "the time for waiting is over. I

148

.won't hear any more arguments, not even from you. The young men are ready to fight, and if I don't lead them someone else will. I have to go with them. For now, I'm going to tell the young men to make sure that none of the traders leave this town to carry warnings to the settlements."

Before Cameron could respond, Dragging Canoe turned and walked away. He found his brother White Owl and his friend Willinawa. "We have some work to do," he said. They took their weapons and left Echota. Soon they were riding along a road that wound its way to the Watauga settlements. Close in, they dismounted and left their horses beside the road. They walked to the nearest cabin.

Four white men were outside talking. Dragging Canoe could see the Wataugans' rifles propped against the side of the cabin. He motioned his companions to move slowly behind him, and he crept cautiously as far as the cover of the woods lasted. Then he stepped out into the open, close enough to the white men for a rifle shot. The others followed. They stood for a moment, rifles held at their sides. One of the white men looked out and saw them. He shouted something, and he and the others all went for their rifles.

One white man fired, his shot going wide. Dragging Canoe took careful aim and dropped the white man with his shot. He let his now useless rifle fall to the ground and, brandishing his trade tomahawk, ran toward the whites with a gobble. Another of the white men took careful aim at Dragging Canoe, but White Owl fired, and his ball struck the man in the jaw. The man screamed, dropped his rifle, and clutched at his face. The other two white men fired at Dragging Canoe, foolishly, for he was a running target. They discarded their empty rifles. One of them reached for the unfired weapon of his hurt companion, and Willinawa shot him in the chest. The man fell forward dead.

Dragging Canoe was suddenly upon them, and a swift blow of his tomahawk cut down one man. The last unhurt one of the bunch lunged at Dragging Canoe, but just then White Owl came up behind him and struck him in the head with his own steel tomahawk. Willinawa arrived last. He quickly dispatched the man who had been shot in the jaw. They could hear the sound of women screaming inside the house, and Willinawa made a move as if to go inside. Dragging Canoe stopped him.

"We have another purpose just now," he said, and he knelt to take a scalp from one of the fallen white men.

Back at Echota, the northern Indians were preparing to take their departure. It had taken Dragging Canoe and his two companions all night to make the trip to the Watauga settlement, attack the four white men, and return to Echota. They arrived just in time. Dragging Canoe walked up to Cornstalk. He held the four fresh scalps out for Cornstalk to take.

"This is our token that we are with you," he said. "Take these wherever you go as a sign that the Cherokees are with you. The Cherokees are fighting the Americans."

Stuart was gone, as were the northern Indians. The ammunition from Florida had been sent for by Cameron, and it was time to prepare properly for going to war. Dragging Canoe and all the young men painted themselves black. They fasted for four days and nights, and at night they danced the War Dance and the Brave Dance, and they wore their wooden masks with coiled rattlesnakes carved on top. They danced all night long, moving around the fire from east to north to west to south and back again to east. They made motions in the dance with their war clubs as if they were striking an enemy. Nancy Ward, the Giga-hyuh, watched the proceedings from a distance, her displeasure clearly showing on her face.

The ammunition from Florida arrived at long last, one hundred horseloads, and Dragging Canoe immediately confiscated it for the war effort. He made certain that Ogan'sdo', Ada-gal'kala, and their followers would not have any of it. Along with the ammunition came a message from Henry Stuart. Dragging Canoe could not read it perfectly, so he took it to Scotchie.

"I insist that you not attack the Watauga settlements prematurely," it said. "The British will attack Charlestown from the sea, and when that attack comes, it will be time for you to attack. If you fail to obey these orders, your supply of ammunition will cease."

"Little Stuart's too late," Dragging Canoe said. "The young men from other towns have already fallen on South Carolina settlements. The war has begun. We can't stop it now. Scotchie, I need to talk to all the traders. Can you get them together for me?"

The white men, all licensed traders except Cameron, gathered outside the townhouse to hear what Dragging Canoe had to say to them.

"As you all know by now," he told them, "we are going to war against the Americans. I want you all to know that this is not a war against all white men. We consider the whites just like ourselves. This war is only against the enemies of the King. If any of you choose to join us in this war, I'll be glad, but I'll not insist upon it. If you choose to stay behind, however, you will be expected to furnish my young men with ammunition and supplies from your stores."

When he had said all he had to say to the traders, he turned and went inside the townhouse where the Raven of Echota and Abram of Chilhowee waited for him. "The time has come," he said. "With the sun, we'll leave here. You, Abram, will lead your followers against the Watauga and Nolichucky River settlements. Raven, attack the settlers at Carter's Valley. I and my men will go to the Holston settlements near Long Island. Surprise them, and hit them hard. Do all the damage you can."

At the edge of Echota, at the trading yards, Nancy Ward stood in the shadows with three white men, the traders Isaac Thomas, Jarrett Williams, and William Fawling, and three saddled horses. "Go to Holston," she said, "and to Watauga. Sound the alarm from Wolf Hills to the west. Tell them all that Dragging Canoe is planning to strike them. His forces will be leaving here in the morning. Tell them to make themselves ready or to flee to safety. The choice is theirs, but tell them. Let them be prepared one way or the other."

The three men mounted their horses and rode off into the darkness, and Nancy Ward watched them go. She knew what would happen. Some of the settlers would stay, and they would be ready when the Cherokees arrived. The Cherokees would get a surprise. Likely some of them would be killed. The Giga-hyuh did not like to think about that, but she could think of no other way. She had tried to reason with her cousin, but he was stubborn.

She did not want him and his followers attacking the settlements. But since she could not stop him, she had chosen to send the warning. Let the settlers get out or be ready. She hoped to avoid an all-out war with the Americans. She had hoped the Cherokees could stay out of this fight. It was between King George's loyal men and the rebels. She did not see it as a Cherokee fight. The only thing she could think of to do was to send the warning. She hoped the Cherokees would be driven off without too many casualties, or better yet, that they would find only empty settlements.

In the fort on the Holston River in Tennessee, the frontiersmen had been warned of the approaching Cherokees. They prepared their weapons and were making ready to meet the coming attack. The white men argued with one another about the best way to meet the coming onslaught. Some wanted to stay inside the fort. Others, not wanting to allow the Cherokees to besiege them, thought it best to meet them in open battle. At last the proponents of meeting the enemy outside the walls won the argument, and they laid a careful plan.

Dragging Canoe and his party approached the fort at Holston. Their intent was to attack the fort, and if they could not break in, besiege it and starve the militiamen out, the way it had been done before so successfully at Fort Loudon. The approach to the fort was mostly open prairie, but there were wooded patches on both flanks. Leading his force, Dragging Canoe was moving between the two patches of woods on the wide prairie when he saw the militiamen coming at them from the fort. Firing and screaming, the two forces ran at each other.

Dragging Canoe's rifle dropped a militiaman. Other Cherokee

shots found their mark. Some of the white men too hit their targets, but the Cherokees were having the best of it. Suddenly, the whites turned and ran toward the fort.

"They're running," Dragging Canoe shouted. "After them. Get their scalps."

Whooping victoriously, the Cherokees raced after the fleeing enemy, when rifle shots came from the woods on both sides of them. Dragging Canoe was one of the first to fall. He felt the burning of a rifle ball tear through both his thighs, and he fell to the ground at once, helpless. He tried to get up, but it was no use. Then in the midst of the firing and yelling and screaming, he felt strong arms take hold of him and lift him up. Willinawa had him by his right arm, and his brother White Owl had him by his left. They started dragging him toward the rear, trying to get him to safety. Then White Owl was hit, once, twice, again.

Dragging Canoe was dropped, and Terrapin came up and took his arm. As his two friends hauled him to safety, he tried to look back to see what had become of his younger brother. When the Cherokees had at last reached safety, having carried their wounded along with them, he found that White Owl was still alive, though he had been hit by eleven rifle balls. They made a quick count and found that they had left thirteen dead on the field of battle.

"The *yonega* were waiting for us," Dragging Canoe said through clenched teeth. "They knew we were coming and laid a trap. Someone told them we were coming."

But there were only twelve dead on the battlefield. Sawga was not dead. He had been shot in the knee and could not retreat with the others. Knowing that he was alone, he dropped down into a large sinkhole to hide. He was not hidden, though, for a Wataugan named Moore saw him drop into the hole. Moore laid down his rifle, pulled out a knife, and jumped into the hole. Sawga tossed his war club at Moore, but Moore managed to duck out of the way. He moved toward Sawga, and Sawga pulled out his own knife. Moving quickly, Moore grabbed the blade of Sawga's knife and twisted, disarming Sawga and nearly cutting off his own thumb. Then he sank his own knife into Sawga's body, once, twice, again.

Just then fifteen-year-old Charles Young, standing at the edge of the sinkhole, stuck his rifle barrel down into the hole, almost touching the side of Sawga's head, and pulled the trigger. Two more bold Wataugans stepped up and fired their rifles into the body. There were, after all, thirteen dead Cherokees on the battlefield.

At about that same time, Old Abram and his force attacked Fort Caswell in Watauga. Many settlers, having been warned, were flocking to Caswell for protection. Many were still outside the fort, not expecting the Cherokees so soon, perhaps, or not expecting them to attack the fort. Three white men fell to Cherokee rifle balls, and the rest surrendered. There was one woman among them. Some started with the prisoners back toward Echota, while others stayed to lay siege to the fort.

In Carter's Valley, moving along the Clinch River toward Virginia, the Raven of Echota found only abandoned cabins, which he looted and burned. The settlers, having been warned, had all fled for their safety to the nearest fort. The Cherokees found no one to kill, no one to fight. They burned whatever they could find, anything and everything built by or grown by the white men. Standing in the glow of the flames that engulfed a cabin, the Raven turned toward his followers. "The Americans are cowards," he shouted. "They've all run away from us. They're afraid to fight us."

Some of Dragging Canoe's men were assigned to carry the wounded on hastily constructed litters back to Echota, some went to recover the bodies left on the battlefield, and the rest would continue their attack on the settlements. Dragging Canoe would not go back to Echota without having killed at least as many Americans as they had killed Cherokees. He could not. He insisted that he, on his litter, be carried along into further battle. The four bullet holes in his thighs, all made from one bullet, were stuffed with moss from the side of a tree trunk. They moved north toward the

Virginia settlements. They found isolated cabins, lone travelers and settlers who had not fled to the forts. They killed eighteen whites, and then they headed back for Echota. The dead Cherokees had been sufficiently covered by American dead. The entire campaign had taken two weeks.

Back at Echota, there was mourning for the Cherokee dead. But there was also rejoicing over the Cherokee victory. From her house, Nancy Ward heard the warriors returning. Picking up her white swan's wing, the symbol of her office, she left the house and went out to see if she could discover what had happened. She heard of the number killed on both sides, and she was glad that it had not been worse. Then she heard about the prisoners, but before she could get to them, she sensed the horrible odor of burning flesh. She hurried on, and she saw what was left of a man tied to a stake, flames consuming his body. Abram and others were rejoicing at the ghastly sight.

Tied to another stake but as yet unharmed was a white woman. Some had already piled up sticks at her feet, and one was moving toward her with a lighted faggot pulled from the other fire. Nancy Ward moved quickly and stood between the man with the flame and the helpless woman. "Stop," she said.

Old Abram stepped out of the crowd, a frightful scowl on his face.

"Why are you interfering?" he asked.

"I claim the ancient prerogative of my rank as Giga-hyuh," she said, raising the white wing. "I claim the life of this woman for my own. Untie her and give her to me."

Grudgingly, Abram nodded at one near him to do the bidding of the Giga-hyuh, and the woman was released. Trembling with fright, she stood still, not knowing what to do. Then the Giga-hyuh spoke to her in English.

"I'm Nancy Ward," she said, and she held out her hand toward the woman. "Come with me."

The frightened woman reached out a hand and Nancy Ward took it. She drew the woman closer to her and put an arm around her shoulder to comfort her. Then she started to walk away with her. The woman snuggled her head into Nancy Ward's shoulder. The Giga-hyuh held the swan's wing in her right hand. Her right arm went around the woman's shoulders, and the woman's face was sheltered by the wing.

"Don't be frightened," Nancy Ward said. "You're safe now. I'm taking you to my home. No one will harm you there."

"They burned young Mr. Moore," the woman said, her voice quavering. "They burned him alive. It was horrible."

"Don't think about it," said Nancy Ward. "Just think that you're safe now with me. What is your name?"

"Mrs. Bean," the woman said. "I'm Mrs. Bean."

"Is Mr. Bean safe?" Nancy Ward asked her.

"I think he is," said Mrs. Bean. "He was inside the fort. I was outside milking. That's how they got me. They came on us by surprise."

"I'm glad that your husband is safe," said Nancy Ward.

Mrs. Bean stumbled then and would have fallen had not the Giga-hyuh held her up. She stopped walking and steadied the white woman. "All right?" she said.

"Yes," said Mrs. Bean.

"Come on, then. Let's get on to my house," said Nancy Ward.

Dragging Canoe knew that the victory was a small one and was but temporary. He knew that the Americans would gather a large force to retaliate. He waited a little while as the people celebrated. He had to let them have that. Then he urged the young men to prepare for the coming attack. Scotchie sent to Florida for arms and ammunition and any reinforcements he could get from Bushyhead.

The Cherokee men made spears and arrows to supplement the rifles and powder and shot they had from the British. The conjurers made strong medicine for war and victory, and the young men fasted and prayed and danced. Dragging Canoe considered what the strategy of the Americans might be. All he had to go on was past experience. Recalling Montgomery and Grant, he knew that the American army would move through the Cherokee country seeking out towns to destroy. They would kill anyone they came across, men, women, children. They would destroy homes and crops and stored food. They would not concern themselves with seeking out the ones who had attacked the settlements. Any Cherokees would do.

The paths they would take would bring them first through the Lower Towns and the Middle Towns, once before destroyed but by this time rebuilt. He decided that the people in those towns should be warned. They should plan to abandon their towns and move for safety into the Overhills settlements. There Dragging Canoe could gather together all the young men who were willing to fight and be ready for the Americans.


### *July 1776*


Under orders from the Continental Congress, Colonel Andrew Williamson left South Carolina with 1,150 troops. Brigadier General Griffith Rutherford led 2,000 more from North Carolina. And Colonel William Christian rode at the head of 1,800 men from Virginia. Their orders were simple and direct: the complete destruction of the Cherokee Nation. Scotchie and Dragging Canoe with 2,000 Cherokees and British Tories rode to meet Williamson before he could reach the Cherokee towns.

Dragging Canoe and Scotchie, riding side by side at the head of their troops, saw Willinawa riding hard back toward them. He had gone ahead as a scout. Scotchie held up a hand to call a halt, as Willinawa came close and hauled back on the reins of his panting horse.

"The Americans are just ahead," Willinawa said.

Dragging Canoe looked around quickly. Thick woods were on both sides of them. He looked at Scotchie. "Let's move to both sides," he said, "and wait for them here."

Scotchie agreed, and the force was divided. Cherokees and Tories hid themselves in the woods and waited. Soon the South Carolina army came into view. In front were men on horseback.

Foot soldiers brought up the rear. Dragging Canoe waited for a sure shot. He took careful aim with his long rifle, drew back the hammer and pulled the trigger. Sparks flew from the struck flint and ignited the powder. There was a small explosion and a puff of acrid-smelling smoke. A man riding just beside Williamson jerked, then fell from his horse. The other Cherokees and Tories started firing, as Dragging Canoe started to reload his rifle.

"Take cover," Williamson shouted, and the American army scattered, horsemen riding hard for the trees, then dismounting and running for cover. The foot soldiers ran for their lives. The battle was on.

Christian halted his Virginia army before the front gate of the newly constructed Fort Patrick Henry in the midst of the Watauga settlements. From over the top of the wall, a Watauga settler hailed him.

"Thank God," the man called out. "We're desperate here." He looked down below and called out to someone down there. "Open the gate."

Christian led his troops inside the fort. The man on the wall had dropped down by then, and he ran to stand beside Christian's horse, looking up at the colonel. "You're a godsend," he said. "We've been waiting here expecting the savages to fall on us at any time. We couldn't have held them off alone."

Christian looked around, amazed at the number of people he saw inside the walls: men, women, and children. "Is your entire settlement gathered inside here?" he asked the man.

"The whole Watauga population is in here, sir," the man answered.

"My orders are to attack the Cherokees in their homes," Christian said.

"If you leave, you leave us defenseless," the Wataugan said. "I beg you to stay and protect us here. We have families."

Christian looked around, then looked back over his shoulder. "Dismount," he called.

Willinawa moved through the trees to come up beside Dragging Canoe. Scotchie was not far away, and he moved over to join the two Cherokees. There was a lull in the firing, and the quiet in the air was ominous. The only sound was the rustling of the leaves over their heads. Willinawa stopped close by Dragging Canoe and spoke low. "More Americans are coming," he said. "They're coming up behind these, riding in their tracks."

"How many, do you think?" Dragging Canoe asked.

"More than these here," Willinawa said.

"Are they close?" Scotchie asked.

"They should be here tomorrow sometime," said Willinawa.

"There are well over a thousand in this troop here," Scotchie said. "You say there are more than that? Maybe two thousand? As many as our own force?"

Willinawa nodded. "That many," he said.

"Our ammunition is low, Scotchie," said Dragging Canoe. "I think we should leave here after dark."

"We've held them at bay long enough," Scotchie said. "I agree. We'll withdraw tonight under cover of darkness. You go back to the Overhills and prepare for this invasion. I'm sure that's their goal. I'll go to Florida for more ammunition and, hopefully, for reinforcements."

"I'll go back through Echota," Dragging Canoe said, "and tell them there what to expect. Then I'll take my young men toward the Creek country."

"Where will I find you?" Scotchie asked.

"Chickamauga Creek," said Dragging Canoe. "There near the home of McDonald."

## PART THREE

# The Chickamaugans

# 12

Rutherford, with the addition of Williamson's South Carolina troops, rode to Fort Patrick Henry, where he assured the Watauga settlers that they were now perfectly safe. He added Christian's force to his own and, with nearly 5,000 men, followed the paths of Montgomery and Grant. The huge American force rode into the Lower Towns. Finding them mostly abandoned, they burned them and destroyed the crops. The few Cherokees they found along the way, they killed. Brass Town, Estatoe, Keowee, Seneca, Soconee, Sugar Town, Tomassee, Tugaloo, all were turned to black ash.

The long column was scattered along the trail. Six men rode together. Thousands were ahead of them and thousands behind. "I ain't seen one damned savage," one of them complained. "Just burned towns."

"Them up ahead is having all the fun, Sam," said another. "All we're doing is eating their dust and looking at the ashes they left behind."

"Hey, hold on there," said Sam. "We spoke too soon. Looky yonder."

The other five turned their heads to the right to see what Sam had seen. She'd have been easy to miss, for she was only a tiny rumpled lump in the tall weeds. An old Cherokee woman, she was sitting in the tall grass, bleeding from a wound in her shoulder. Her face was wrinkled, and her hair was white. The six riders urged their horses off the road and moved over to where the old woman sat.

"An old squaw," said one.

"Looks like somebody shot her," said another, "but only she ain't dead yet."

"She'll bleed to death soon enough," said another one. "Hell, she can't have much blood left in her. Look at her. She can't weigh more than eighty pounds."

"She looks to be about that old, too," said one. "And shot like that. She must be suffering."

Sam drew out the long sword at his side. "Well, I think we ought to alleviate suffering wherever we can. Don't you, boys?" He moved toward the old woman. She looked up at him and grinned.

"Am I all that you could find to kill?" she said, speaking in the Cherokee language. "You great soldiers. I'm an old woman ready for the grave. I'm not even worth killing. You pieces of dog shit."

Sam swung his sword, and the old woman sagged and said no more.

They rode forth toward the Middle Towns. Ahead of the Americans the Cherokee people fled to the Overhills, many going into the ancient peace town of Echota. Echota was crowded beyond its capacity, but people kept coming. Ogan'sdo' talked with Ada-gal'kala.

"We cannot hold up any longer against this American onslaught," he said. "This war was made by your son, but we must be the ones to beg for peace with the Americans."

"I agree with you," said Ada-gal'kala, "but I'm too old to travel. Let's ask Sawanooga to go to the Americans. He should tell them that we're beat. We want to make peace. We never wanted this war in the first place. It was my hot-blooded son and his followers. Tell them that Dragging Canoe does not represent the Cherokee Nation. He joined with Shawnees and Englishmen against our wishes. He and his followers are outlaws."

The people of the Middle and Valley Towns of the Cherokees fled to the Overhills as Rutherford and his army marched upon them.

164

Here the army found almost no one to kill. They destroyed homes and crops again and headed for the Overhills. A messenger from Sawanooga met them as they were moving through a mountain pass. He held a white flag. Rutherford halted his column and allowed the messenger to approach.

"I come from Echota," the messenger said. "From the head men of my nation."

"What is it you want to say?" Rutherford asked, sitting in his saddle and looking down at the Cherokee man.

"We want peace," the messenger said. "Dragging Canoe and his people do not represent the Cherokee Nation. Our Principal Chief is Ada-gal'kala. You know him as the Little Carpenter. He's a man of peace. Dragging Canoe and those others are outlaws, joined with Englishmen and Shawnees. It was not the Cherokee Nation that made war on you. I come to beg you at least to spare our ancient peace town, Echota. All of the people who want peace and are afraid have come into Echota. Our town chief, Sawanooga, begs you not to set the torch to our town."

"I'm going to Malaquo," Rutherford said. "I mean to destroy it and anyone there. That's Dragging Canoe's town, isn't it? After that, I'll consider your request."

Moving south toward Chickamauga Creek, Dragging Canoe was followed by several hundred men and many of their families. Along the way they were joined by others. They were a mixed group, comprised of full-blood Cherokees like Willinawa, Terrapin, Dragging Canoe's brothers Badger and White Owl, who had miraculously survived his wounds, and many more; mixed-blood Cherokees with names like Bob Benge, John Bowles, John Watts, and John Walker; and white men, Tories, like John Chisholm, Tom Tunbridge, Richard Pearis, and others. Many of these white men had Cherokee wives and children of mixed blood.

Angry refugees from the Lower and Middle Towns came to join them. These people had done their best to stay out of the war, yet the Americans had burned their homes and fields and left them destitute. Their friends and relatives had been killed. Filled with new hatred for the Americans, they had gone to join Dragging Canoe. The Americans had driven them to it.

All along the way, Dragging Canoe, Willinawa, Terrapin, Badger, Pumpkin Boy, Doublehead, and others led small raids against the cabins of lone settlers. Reaching Chickamauga Creek at last, they selected locations for their new towns. Dragging Canoe decided that they would build five of them along the creek not far from the home and trading post of McDonald.

Back in the Overhills, Rutherford, having thus far spared Echota, called a meeting with Ogan'sdo', Ada-gal'kala, and others. They met inside the townhouse at Echota. The people in the now dangerously overcrowded town were nervous and anxious. For all they knew, Rutherford might unleash his huge army on them at any moment. They prayed that the diplomatic powers of Ada-gal'kala had not diminished with his age.

"Your warriors are still killing innocent white people," Rutherford said. "Why should I stop destroying your country?"

"Dragging Canoe is no longer a part of this nation," said Ada-gal'kala.

"Is he not your son?" Rutherford asked.

"Yes," the old man admitted. "He is, but he no longer listens to my advice. He and his people have gone their own way, and we here have no control over them. You are fighting the British. The Shawnees are allies of the British, and my son has joined with the Shawnees. We have nothing to do with him. We have no control over him. He has moved his towns to Chickamauga Creek near the border with the Muscogees and the home of the Tory McDonald. No one here has ridden against your armies or your settlements. You are punishing the wrong people. We only want peace."

"By what authority do you speak these words to me?" Rutherford asked.

"I am the Principal Chief of the Cherokee Nation," Ada-gal'kala said.

"Will you then declare Dragging Canoe, your own son, to be an outlaw," Rutherford asked, "and will you promise to deliver into my hands Dragging Canoe, any of his followers, and any Tories you find in your midst? Especially Cameron and McDonald?"

Ada-gal'kala looked at Ogan'sdo', standing there beside him.

"Yes," said Ogan'sdo'. "If they dare to come back among us, we will take them captive and hold them for you. Or we will kill them."

"Then I will also place on their heads a bounty of one-hundred pounds," said Rutherford. "They shall be declared outlaws and not a part of the Cherokee Nation. There will be peace between you and me. In order to distinguish between our friends, the Cherokee Nation, and our enemies, Dragging Canoe and the others will be called Chickamaugans from here on out."

The word spread quickly, and soon a disgruntled former resident of one of the Lower Towns slipped away from Echota. He headed for Chickamauga Creek.

Dragging Canoe sat in front of his house in the newly built town of Chickamauga. It served as the headquarters of his new community. Other towns scattered along Chickamauga Creek were Settico, Keetoowah, and Talase. Not far away was the home of John McDonald. Dragging Canoe sat smoking and thinking of his next campaign. He wondered how his brother Scotchie was doing in Florida in his attempt to raise reinforcements and to get more ammunition. He was staring toward the creek when he saw Ellie Watts walking toward him with a stranger, an Indian man. He waited until they had come close to his house.

" *'Siyo, El-i,* " he said.

His visitors came closer, and Ellie said, " *'Siyo,* Tsiyu Gansini. I've brought someone who wants to meet you. He's called Long Dog. He's from Nottley in the Valley Towns."

"What brings you to me, Long Dog?" Dragging Canoe asked.

"The Americans burned my town," Long Dog said. "They killed my family. I didn't want this war until then. Now I want it. I came to ask if I can join you in this war."

"You're welcome, Long Dog," Dragging Canoe said.

"*Wado,*" Long Dog said. "And I brought you some news from Echota."

Dragging Canoe looked up at Long Dog for an instant. Then he looked back down at the ground and puffed his pipe. "What is this news from Echota?" he asked.

"The old men there have made peace with the American, Rutherford," Long Dog said. "They said you are no longer a Cherokee. They called you outlaw and promised to give you to the Americans if they ever get their hands on you. Then Rutherford said that he would give one hundred pounds for your head and one hundred more for the head of your brother Scotchie."

Dragging Canoe stood up. "I am not a Cherokee," he said, "nor are any people here with me Cherokees. We are Ani-yunwi-ya. We are the Real People. Those old men at Echota and the other Overhills Towns, those who are too old or too afraid to fight, those are the Cherokees. *Idi yunwi-ya*. We are the Real People."

That night when Dragging Canoe was about to go to sleep there on the ground in front of his house, Ellie Watts came again. He looked up at her. She stood in the dim light of the moon and stars, looking down at him.

"Ellie?" he said.

"You're alone?" she asked him.

"Yes," he said.

"May I stay with you tonight?" she said.

"You have no husband?" he asked her.

"He was killed in the Lower Towns by the Americans," she said. "I have no one."

Dragging Canoe stood up and took Ellie by the hand. He looked at her. She was light skinned and had light brown hair, but her features clearly bespoke her Cherokee heritage, showed that she was of mixed blood.

"I belong to all of the Real People," he said. "I can no longer belong to a woman."

"Just for tonight?" she said.

Still holding her hand, he led her inside his house.

〰〰〰

The next day, Dragging Canoe went to the home of McDonald, where he was welcomed and invited in.

"I want pen and paper," he said. "I want to write a letter to Scotchie."

"Come with me," McDonald said, and he led the way into a small study. He gave Dragging Canoe a chair behind a desk and placed pen and ink and paper before him. Dragging Canoe looked at them for a moment.

"Will you help me?" he asked. "Scotchie tried to teach me, but I can't always remember all the letters or how to spell the English words."

McDonald pulled another chair up to the desk and sat down beside Dragging Canoe.

"Scotchie," Dragging Canoe wrote, "I am glad you are where you are, for our great man —"

He stopped writing and looked at McDonald. "I don't know how to put Ogan'sdo's name into English letters," he said. McDonald spelled it out, and Dragging Canoe continued writing.

"Our great man Oconostota wanted to take your life as well as mine. While I live, you shall never be hurted, for I shall never forget your talks to us. The Americans offered at least one hundred pounds for you, and one hundred pounds for me, to have us killed. Let them bid up and offer what they will. It never disturbs me. My ears will always be open to hear your talks, and those of our Father, the King. I will mind no other. Let them come from where they will. My thoughts and my heart are for war as long as King George has one enemy in this country. Our hearts are straight to him and all his people."

Ogan'sdo', Ada-gal'kala, Sawanooga, Old Tassel, and other old men from Echota journeyed to Fort Patrick Henry to settle the terms of the peace and to negotiate and draw up new treaties with the Americans of Virginia and those of North Carolina. They brought with them the trader John McCormack to act as interpreter. McCormack's sixteen-year-old half-breed son, known as Big Bullet, accompanied his father. The two parties introduced themselves to each other all around and visited for a day. Each side assured the other that they only wanted peace. They slept that night, and the next morning, the body of Big Bullet was discovered. The young man had been stabbed to death in his sleep.

"They brought us here to kill us all," Sawanooga said. "Let's get out before they do it."

The Cherokees all withdrew, but Colonel Christian and some others rode after them. "I assure you," Christian said, "we know nothing about the unfortunate death of the young man. We feel very bad about it. We'll do all we can to discover his murderer. If we find him, he will be put to death. I beg you to return to our good talks."

Reluctantly, the Cherokees returned to the fort to continue the negotiations. Grief-stricken, McCormack begged to be replaced. Another trader, Joseph Vann, was named the new interpreter.

Dragging Canoe had received word of this meeting, and he led a small band back north into the settlements of the Wataugans. Within fifteen miles of Fort Patrick Henry, they attacked a small cluster of cabins.

At the negotiations, the Cherokees quickly discovered that the Americans wanted to talk about more than peace. As ever, they wanted more land. It came Ogan'sdo's time to speak. He stood up. "I am not such a good speaker," he said. "I want my brother Old Tassel to speak for me." The Americans agreed, and Old Tassel stood up. Not handsome, but a man of dignity with a stately demeanor, he stood in silence for a moment until he was sure he had the full attention of the American delegates.

"I'm surprised," he said, "that anytime we talk with our white brothers of peace, they want to talk about land. I think that you demand it because you know that we dare not refuse. But you have assured us that we will be treated fairly here, and so I feel I must refuse to give up this land that you want.

"On what do you base your claim to this land? What did you do to claim a conquest? You marched through our land. We have marched through as much of your land. We knew that you were coming, so we took our women and children to the safety of the woods. You killed a few scattered individuals and burned our towns.

"So I ask again, by what law or authority do you claim a right to our land? None, I say. Your laws extend not into our country, nor ever did. The laws of nature and the laws of nations are all against you.

"You've said much here about our lack of what you call civilization. You've suggested that we adopt your laws, your manners, your customs, your religion. Before we hear more talks or listen to you read more papers on these subjects, we would like to see the effects of these things in your own practices toward us.

"You ask, why do not the Indians till the ground and live as we do? We could as easily ask, why do not the white men hunt and live as we do? If any of our young men kill a cow or a hog for their food, you call it criminal, yet white men kill our deer and other game, sometimes just for the love of killing.

"The Great God of Nature has placed us in different situations. He has given you many advantages over us, but we are not your slaves. You have your lands, stocked with cows, hogs, and sheep. We have our land with buffalo, bear, and deer. Yours are tame and domestic. Ours are wild and require more space for grazing and art to hunt and kill them. You have the advantage in this. Even so, our animals are as much ours as yours are yours, and neither they nor our lands should be taken away from us without our consent and without compensation of equal value."

The American commissioners were still harrumphing and considering how to answer Old Tassel's speech, when to their great relief, a settler broke into the meeting unannounced. "The Chickamoggies hit us," he shouted. "They killed eight. Killed Robertson, Calvitt, Crockett, Crockett's wife, and all but two of their kids. They carried off two of the Crockett boys. Four more is hurt and like to die. Ran off our livestock. Burned the cabins."

Rutherford stood up from behind the long table at which he sat. "Where are they, man?" he said.

"Long gone," said the settler, still panting for breath. "They done their damage and left—filthy savages—headed south. I've run all of fifteen miles to tell you about it. They're long gone."

"How do you know it was Chickamaugans?" Rutherford asked the man. He looked at Ada-gal'kala as he waited for the man's answer. "Could it have been other Cherokees?"

"It was the Cherokee Dragon himself," the man said. "I think he left some of us alive just so we could tell it. Just before they rode off, he turned in his saddle and yelled back at us. 'I'm Dragon Canoe,' he said. 'Dragon Canoe. We're the Real People.' That's what he said. He was like the devil hisself riding on a big white horse. Dragon Canoe."

"The Cherokee Dragon," said Rutherford. "How appropriate a mistake this man has made."

Still sitting in his chair next to Rutherford, Christian said, "I call him the Savage Napoleon. That's what I call him."

"My son has done this thing," Ada-gal'kala said, "to show his contempt for what we are doing here. We beg you to remember that he and his followers are no longer Cherokee."

Back at Chickamauga, Dragging Canoe prepared to meet a large group of Cherokees who were coming from the former Lower and Middle Towns. Scouts had given him advance notice of their arrival, so he was ready for them. McDonald too came down from his house to see the new arrivals. When they at last came into Chickamauga, Dragging Canoe felt pity for them, for they were ragged and poor-looking. Some were nearly naked. They carried few belongings, and most of them were on foot. Dragging Canoe called for food, and the visitors were fed. At last it was time to talk.

"My friends," Dragging Canoe said, "what brought you to this condition, and why have you come to see me?"

One man stepped forward. He wore only leggings and a breechcloth. He was dirty and obviously weary. But there was anger underneath all the wretchedness.

"I'm called Striker," he said. "Our homes were in the Lower Towns and the Middle Towns. They've been destroyed twice, some of them three times, but we always rebuild. Now the old men at Echota have sold all of our land to the Americans. Now we have no place in which to rebuild our homes. They said they had to give up land to make a peace with the Americans, but their towns are all in the Overhills. Why did they give away our land?

"We've come to live with you and to fight with you if you'll have us."

"My friends," said Dragging Canoe, "you're welcome. All of you are welcome here with us, with the Real People."

And then, looking over the crowd of recent arrivals, Dragging Canoe spied a familiar face. It had been some time since he had seen her, but he was sure that he was looking at Ghigooie, the widow of the interpreter William Shorey. He walked into the crowd and approached her. "Ghigooie?" he said.

"Yes," she said. "I thank you for your hospitality."

"You're welcome here, of course," said Dragging Canoe. "It's been a long time since I've seen you. You're welcome with the others. Is this your daughter here with you?"

"Yes," she said. "This is Annie. Annie Shorey."

McDonald was standing nearby, and he noticed that Dragging Canoe had gone into the crowd and was talking with two women there. He looked at the younger woman and saw that she was beautiful. He stepped quickly to the side of Dragging Canoe and looked at the two Shorey women. "Hello," he said. "I'm John McDonald."

Dragging Canoe looked at McDonald and saw at once the way in which McDonald looked at Annie. He smiled a little. "McDonald," he said, "this is Ghigooie. Mrs. Shorey. You remember William Shorey, of course."

"Yes, of course," McDonald said. "It's a pleasure, Mrs. Shorey. I was terribly sorry to hear the news of your husband's death."

"Thank you, Mr. McDonald. It's an honor, sir," Ghigooie said. "May I present my daughter, Annie Shorey?"

McDonald looked into the big brown eyes of the daughter and held out his hand. "It's a great pleasure," he said, and his heart thrilled at the touch when Annie put her small hand in his.

In the weeks that followed, others came to join with Dragging Canoe. The people the frontier was beginning to know as the

Chickamaugans, or "Chickamoggies," became an even more mixed group. To the secessionist Cherokees and English Tories were added Shawnees, Creeks, and Chickasaws. Everyone who was tired of being pushed back or crowded by the land-greedy Americans, it seemed, moved to Chickamauga. There was no place else for them to go.

## 1777

Ellie helped Dragging Canoe dress in his best clothes. The scouts had come into Chickamauga to report that the pack train from Florida would arrive in town soon. They also brought word that Cameron was riding along with it. Dragging Canoe, like all of the Chickamaugans, was anxious for the arrival of the supplies. But he was also anxious to see Scotchie. He walked out of his house with a red blanket draped around one shoulder. He could see the pack animals in the distance. One rider broke away from the train and rode hard toward Chickamauga. As the rider came into closer view, Dragging Canoe could see that it was Scotchie. He walked to meet him, and at the edge of town, Scotchie reined in his mount. He quickly dismounted, and the two men embraced.

"Scotchie," said Dragging Canoe, "I'm glad to see you. I didn't know you were coming along with these supplies, but I hoped that you would."

"And I'm glad to see you, Brother," Scotchie said.

They walked together into the town, where Dragging Canoe introduced Scotchie to Guhna-geski, his newly appointed second in command, a sandy-haired, light-skinned man of mixed blood, also known as John Watts. "Scotchie is my brother," he told Guhna-geski, and to Scotchie he said, "You may talk to him just as you talk to me."

McDonald walked up then and exchanged warm greetings with Cameron. The pack train came on into town, and Dragging Canoe left Guhna-geski in charge of the unloading and distribution of the goods. Cameron also appointed a man from his command to take charge. McDonald, figuring that the two brothers would like to talk privately, went along with Guhna-geski. Then, an arm on the shoulder of Dragging Canoe, Cameron said, "We have much to speak of, Brother." They walked together to a place where they could talk alone, a place on the far edge of Chickamauga and down by the creek. There they found a large, flat rock to serve them as a bench, and they sat down. For a while they sat in silence, watching the clear waters of Chickamauga Creek rush past.

"It seems peaceful here," Cameron said. "It belies the reality of the situation around us."

"Yes," said Dragging Canoe, "but look more closely. Somewhere in that water, a big fish is eating a small fish. Somewhere in those woods, a snake is stealing the eggs from a bird's nest. A wolf is killing a young deer."

"Yes," said Scotchie, "and somewhere out there American forces are gathering to descend on you and me."

"They want all of this land, Scotchie," Dragging Canoe said. "They want to wipe the Real People out and have it all."

"I have reports from the Overhills," Scotchie said. "We have spies who bring us the news from time to time. Ogan'sdo', and not your father, is now recognized as the Principal Chief by the Americans."

"I'm not surprised at that news," said Dragging Canoe. "And it may be good news for the people in the Overhills. My father's useful years, it seems, passed long ago. But then, so have those of Ogan'sdo'. Perhaps it doesn't really matter."

In spite of his words, his face betrayed a deep sadness, and Scotchie could see it. "He was a great man in his time," Scotchie said.

"Yes," said Dragging Canoe. "In his time." He recalled the time he had watched in awe as his father returned from his long captivity with the Ottawas, when he had ridden back home in triumph and splendor. He remembered the day that Bushyhead had recognized him as the Principal Chief of the Cherokee Nation. And he recalled his father's oft-repeated words, "All things change."

"There's more news," said Scotchie, anxious to change the tone of the conversation. "The rebel army has made Gist a colonel. You remember Gist?"

"I remember him," said Dragging Canoe.

"Ogan'sdo' and the other old men have given Long Island to him for as long as he lives," Scotchie said.

"Let's hope that will not be long," Dragging Canoe said with a frown. "That's my island. It's not theirs to give away."

"The Virginians have appointed a man named Joseph Martin as commissioner to the Overhills, and North Carolina has named James Robertson as their commissioner. Robertson is living at the mouth of Big Creek in the Cumberland Valley. Martin is living on Great Island, presumably with the blessing of Gist, and he's married to Betsy Ward, the daughter of your cousin, Nancy."

"The Overhills Cherokees have fully embraced the Americans, it seems," Dragging Canoe said.

"For now," said Scotchie, "but they're almost destitute. All of our supplies, of course, are coming to you. The Americans have sent them nothing. To make matters worse for them, the Wataugans are moving farther onto their land. They're not satisfied with what they got from the last treaty. Some of the Overhills people are talking of joining with you."

"Some already have," Dragging Canoe said.

"Likely there will be more," said Scotchie.

There would be more, and they would come from farther away than either Dragging Canoe or Scotchie could imagine. It was in *Gogi,* the warm time of the year, when the large delegation of Shawnees came to Chickamauga to visit and to talk of the problems that both peoples faced. The Shawnees and the Cherokees had been bitter enemies for more than a hundred years, for longer than anyone there could remember. Dragging Canoe welcomed them as long-lost brothers. They were treated as honored guests.

"Brothers," he said to them, "we cannot forget the talk you brought to us some years ago, which was to take up the hatchet against the Virginians. We heard and listened to it with great attention, and before the time that was appointed to lift it, we took it up and struck the Virginians. Our nation was alone and surrounded by them. They were numerous and their hatchets were sharp. And after we had lost some of our best warriors, we were forced to leave our towns and corn to be burnt by them, and now we live in the grass, as you see us. But we are not yet conquered. And to convince you that we have not thrown away your talk, here are the four strands of wampums we received from you when you came before us as a messenger to our nation."

Dragging Canoe then presented the wampum strands to the Shawnee Warrior, the leader of the visiting Shawnees. The same belts he had received from the Shawnees before were being returned.

"We should put aside all our differences from the past," he said, "and be friends and brothers from this day forward. When you return to your own land, I will send a number of our young men back with you, to live with you and fight with you and to remind us all of our unity."

The Shawnee Warrior accepted the wampums and agreed with the words of Dragging Canoe.

"And when my young men go back home," he said, "as a pledge of our bargain, I will stay here with you, and I'll ask that some more of my people come back here to join me. From this day on, our fortunes are tied together."

"It's good," Dragging Canoe said. "You know, already there are some of your people here with us. It will be good to have more of you."

Ghigooie and her daughter Annie approached the home of John McDonald. They had been invited to dine with him. Before they reached the front door of the fine home, it was pulled open from the inside, and McDonald stepped into the doorway, a wide smile on his face.

"Welcome," he said. "Please come in. I have our supper all laid out."

"I hope we're not late," said Ghigooie.

"No," said McDonald. "Oh, no. You're just on time."

177

He led the way into his dining hall and seated his guests around a long table. The dishes had all been placed and the platters of food waited in the middle of the table.

"Mr. McDonald," Ghigooie said as she sat down, "you live here alone?"

"Yes," he said. "I do."

"You've prepared a fine meal for a man alone," she said.

"Oh," he said. "I suppose I could take credit for it, but I won't mislead you. I paid a woman from Chickamauga to prepare it. She's done a wonderful job of it, too, I believe."

As they ate, it was all McDonald could do to keep from staring at Annie. And she could tell. So could Ghigooie. Now and then Annie would glance up at McDonald, only to look quickly back down to her plate. McDonald knew already that he wanted this lovely young woman for his wife. He wondered, though, if he should say anything to her just yet. He wondered, too, if he should say something first to her mother. Annie was a creature of two different cultures. Which, he wondered, should he follow in pursuing her hand?

Dragging Canoe led men back to the Watauga settlements, and the Shawnee Warrior went with him. Willinawa led another group, and yet more were led by Doublehead, Bloody Fellow, Guhnageski, and others. The Wataugans never knew where they would strike next. Lone travelers on the road might be ambushed. A settler's cabin might be attacked here, another there. Bands of self-styled militiamen on their way to hunt for Indians were harrassed and driven away. No one, it seemed, was safe on the frontier, and the names "Savage Napoleon" and "Cherokee Dragon" were on the lips of all the settlers.

In his office in Richmond, Governor Patrick Henry drummed on his desk impatiently. The door opened and a young man poked his head in. "Colonel Evan Shelby is here, sir," he said.

"Well, show him in," said the governor. "He's late. I'm waiting."

Colonel Shelby stepped quickly into the office as the young man barely stepped aside in time. He stopped at attention in front of the governor's desk. "Sir," he said, "I made the best time I could, sir."

"Yes, well," said Henry, "have you raised the troop I asked for?"

"Yes, sir," said Shelby. "I have six hundred Virginians, all good fighting men."

"I want you to take those men," said Henry, "and go directly to Chickamauga and totally destroy that and every settlement near it that the offending Indians occupy. I mean all those who may be affiliated with the damnable Cherokee Dragon. The frontier won't be safe for decent people to raise their families in until those devils are exterminated. Do you understand?"

"Yes, sir," said Shelby.

Annie Shorey dipped a bucket into the cold waters of Chickamauga Creek. As she straightened to lift it, she was startled by a voice close behind her. "May I take that for you, Miss Shorey?" She looked quickly around to see John McDonald standing there. Recovering her composure, she said, "Thank you," and McDonald took the bucket. They walked slowly toward the Shorey house there in Chickamauga.

"Miss Shorey," McDonald said, "I want to ask you a question. Well, I want to ask a question of your mother — if that's appropriate — but first I want to ask you a question."

"What is it?" she said.

"I want to ask for your hand in marriage," he said. "Would you object?"

"I think you should ask my mother," she said. "And I think you should call me Annie."

"Oh, Annie," he said, "I believe you've just made me the happiest man in all the world. But what will your mother say, I wonder?"

"Let's go right now and find out," Annie said.

Dragging Canoe and his followers hid in the woods on the outskirts of a small Watauga settlement. The sun was just beginning to lighten the far eastern horizon with a tinge of pink along the distant treetops. The morning was being announced by the sounds of birdsong from the forest. Smoke began to rise from first one chimney, then another in the small settlement. One man came out of his cabin and moved to a woodpile to pick up an ax and start splitting firewood. A dog ran up to him, its tongue lapping out. The man ignored the dog. From another cabin a woman emerged, bucket in hand, going for water.

Dragging Canoe waited while the cluster of cabins came alive. They were not part of the original Watauga settlements, illegal enough in the mind of Dragging Canoe, but were rather some of the newest outreaches, settlements that went beyond even the bounds of the latest treaty. Three more men appeared and two more women. It was enough. Dragging Canoe gave the call of the male turkey, and he and others rushed out of the woods waving their war axes over their heads.

The settlers ran for the imagined safety of their cabins, but Chickamauga warriors caught several of them still outside. Other Chickamaugans stopped, took aim with their long rifles, and dropped some of the whites in their tracks. Arriving at the cabins, some of the attackers shoved their way into the settlers' homes before the frightened inhabitants could bar the doors. Some, grabbing pieces of burning firewood from inside the cabins, began to set fire to the dwellings. Dogs barked. Women and children screamed.

A band of heavily armed militiamen rode toward Chickamauga bent on revenge. There were fifty of them altogether, and they even imagined that they might be strong enough to destroy the Chickamauga towns. They rode in silence, their faces grim. Their leader called a halt when he saw his scout riding hard toward them. They waited for the scout to come in and halt his mount.

"There's a group of men riding toward us," the scout said. "I'd guess might near as many as what we got here."

"White men?" the leader asked.

"Yeah," the scout said. "They're white men, all right."

"Are they armed?"

"Yeah."

"Well," said the militia leader, "let's meet them and see if they want to join us. With a hundred men, we can sure wipe out the Chickamoggy towns."

They rode ahead slowly, and soon they saw the other group. The leader hailed them with a wave. A man in the front of the other mounted group waved back. They rode closer. The militia leader called out. "Hello, there," he said, "I'm Hoskins. Who are you?"

"Jones is my name," said the leader of the second group, but it was not Jones. It was Guhna-geski, also known as John Watts. Riding with Watts were John and Bob Benge, John Chisholm, Archibald Coody, James Colbert, George Fields, and other mixed-blood and white Chickamaugans. It was a carefully selected group. All of them were either white or could easily pass for white.

"We're headed for Chickamoggy," said Hoskins. "We aim to wipe out the Cherokee Dragon and everyone else at Chickamoggy and then burn the whole damned place down. You men want to join us? We'd take it kindly if you did."

"We'll join you," said Watts, "and gladly."

"Good," Hoskins shouted. "Let's go."

As Hoskins and his men rode forward, Watts and the others with him turned their horses to join the crowd, and as they did, each man paired off with one of the passing Americans. They rode along for a distance like that. Then, with no warning, John Watts pulled a pistol from his belt and reached over, almost touching the side of Hoskins's head with its muzzle, and he pulled the trigger. Blood and brains shot out the other side of Hoskins's head. His head bounced foolishly on his shoulders for a bit before the body went limp and sagged in the saddle. As he fired his pistol, Watts called out the shrill gobble of the male turkey, and shots sounded behind him. Each of the Chickamaugans killed the white man next to him, some with guns, some with knives or war clubs.

In almost no time, fifty white militiamen lay dead in the road. Watts and the others took their scalps, their weapons, and their horses. They left the bodies where they lay and rode back toward Chickamauga.

In Dragging Canoe's house at Chickamauga, Ellie was just waking up. Dragging Canoe and all the young men were away making war on the Americans. She was content. She knew that she likely had no future with Dragging Canoe. He was a man of war, and therefore the chances of his getting killed in battle were great. She also knew that she could never really have him, not all of him, for he belonged to the people, to the Real People. His life was not his to give her. He knew it, and she knew it. Still, she felt an intense attraction for him.

He was what he was, and she had gone to him because of what he was. Perhaps she would have loved him, given herself to him, even in different circumstances. He was an attractive man. He was a man with a forceful personality. Perhaps, even had the times been peaceful, she might have found him attractive. But she had never known peaceful times, and in these troubled times, he had emerged as the great leader, the one man that the Real People could count on, could believe in, and for those reasons, she loved him, and for those reasons she would give herself to him for however much time they might have together, or for however long he should want to have her around.

She was just waking up from a deep and peaceful sleep when she heard the sounds: barking dogs, then some shouting and the sound of rapidly approaching horses' hooves. She got quickly to her feet and threw a robe over her body. Ducking low, she went out of the house. Then she saw them. Yelling and screaming white men on horseback racing toward Chickamauga, some waving their long swords over their heads, and through the dust cloud stirred up by the pounding hooves of their horses, more men, foot soldiers running along behind them.

Other residents of Chickamauga came out of their houses. Women and children screamed. "Run for your lives," someone shouted. An old man stepped out his door just in time to be shot down by a Virginian's bullet. People ran for the creek. Others ran in the opposite direction, hoping to reach the security of the woods behind them before a soldier reached them. Ellie saw a child alone across the way, and she thought to run and grab it up and run for a hiding place with it, and just then a mounted Virginian rode up close and slashed at her with his sword. His vicious swipe almost took the head off her shoulders.

The attack was over almost as soon as it had begun. Some of the old men, women, and children had managed to flee for their lives. No Chickamauga residents were left alive in the town, and all of the houses were in flame. His excited horse stamping and turning and frothing at the bit, Colonel Shelby surveyed the scene of destruction. Governor Henry had called for total destruction. This seemed like a good start. There were at least ten more Chickamauga towns, Shelby knew. Maybe more. From what he had heard, more were being built all the time as more and more disaffected Indians joined with the Savage Napoleon and his renegade Cherokees and Tory friends. At least ten more towns, and then the home of the notorious Tory, McDonald.

Dragging Canoe stood in the ruins of Chickamauga. He looked at the spot where his house had been, the place where Ellie had been waiting for his return. McDonald stood beside him. The other men who had been away with Dragging Canoe when Shelby came were elsewhere around the one-time town site, looking at the ruins of their own homes or weeping for lost relatives and friends. The people who had run away from Shelby's attack had come back down into the cold ashes when they saw the approach of Dragging Canoe and the warriors. McDonald had been with them.

He told Dragging Canoe of the attack, told him of the devastation. He related how, once Shelby had ridden on, the people had come back down to take care of the dead. He told him what had happened to Ellie and the others who had been killed there, and explained that the same thing had happened to all of their eleven towns. The pattern was a familiar one to the Real People. The towns had been destroyed along with the crops and the food supplies.

"I'm glad that you escaped," Dragging Canoe said to McDonald, "before they reached your home."

"What will you do now?" McDonald asked.

"We'll build new towns," Dragging Canoe said. "We'll keep fighting. We'll fight until the King has no more enemies in this country or until we are all dead. Where is this Shelby now?"

"I don't know," McDonald said. "He did his dirty work here, and he rode away with all his troops. They left here riding east. That's all I know."

"If I can't find Shelby," said Dragging Canoe, "other Americans will pay for this. It's all the same big fight."

"I have more news," McDonald said. "Do you want to hear it now?"

"Yes," Dragging Canoe answered.

"Before Shelby came," said McDonald, "I had a letter from Scotchie. Bushyhead has died, and Scotchie has been temporarily appointed to his position, until a suitable permanent replacement can be found."

"I'm sorry that Bushyhead is gone," Dragging Canoe said. "He was our friend, but it's good that the King gave his place—even temporarily—to Scotchie."

"I've sent news of what happened here to Scotchie," McDonald said. "I've asked him to send supplies and more men."

Dragging Canoe put a hand on McDonald's shoulder, then turned and walked away to survey more of the damage. Then Annie Shorey came out of the crowd of now homeless Real People to stand beside McDonald. She took him by the hand.

"You may want to change your mind about me now, Annie," he said. "I've lost everything. I don't even have a home."

"We'll build us a new one together," she said.

Dragging Canoe did not waste much time in mourning. He sat alone for a while watching the waters of Chickamauga Creek flow by. He thought of the ones who had died in the towns there, the helpless ones who had been caught while he and the young men had been away. He thought about Ellie. But he did not mourn for those recently lost lives. His heart had mourned for all of his people and for their land long ago. It was the same mourning. There was no need to renew it. There was work to be done.

He decided they would build new towns, but they would not be built on the sites where the old towns had been, there where they had been destroyed. They would select new locations, more strategic locations, moving south along the Tennessee River down into the country of the Creeks. A number of Creeks were among them anyway, and the Creeks were sympathetic to his cause. He would build his own town, the headquarters for the Chickamaugas, on the north bank of the Tennessee River, just below the narrows, and he would call it Amagayunyi, "Running Water."

The people busied themselves with hewing logs and clearing space for houses and for fields. They build their homes in the new towns in the manner of frontier whites, small, single-room log houses with dirt floors and roofs covered over with split shingles. They built a cluster of homes for each of the five new towns. There was Running Water, Dragging Canoe's place of residence and headquarters for his entire Chickamauga movement. Before they were done, there were one hundred dwellings there. Turtle at Home, one of Dragging Canoe's younger brothers, lived in one of them. Diwali, called Bowl, Otter Lifter, and John Archie settled there. Almost a hundred Shawnees who had responded to the call of the Shawnee Warrior to join forces with the Chickamaugas lived there, as well as the Shawnee Warrior himself. Among them were three brothers known as Cheeseekau, Tenskwatawa, and Tecumseh.

Just across the river from Running Water, John Vann, Breath, and others built Nickajack, a town of about forty houses. A little farther south was Long Island Town. Lookout Mountain Town was several miles east of the river near the mountain from which it took its name. Owl's Son was prominent there. Moses Price, Glass, sometimes called Thomas, Doublehead, the conjurer Richard Justice, and others helped make up its population. Young

Dragging Canoe, known familiarly by this time as Young Canoe, had his home there. Crow Town, Kogayi, was on the north bank of the river, the farthest south of the five towns and the largest.

John McDonald, with the help of his new wife Annie, built his new home at Lookout Mountain. He was still very near the Chickamaugans, ready to receive messages or supplies from Cameron, and Annie was near her mother, who had settled in Running Water.

Finally, Tuskegee Island Town, the farthest away and the farthest north of the towns, was established by Bloody Fellow overlooking the entrance to the Suck, or the boiling pot, a dangerous whirlpool in the Tennessee River. Anyone coming down the river would be vulnerable to the Chickamaugans at places dangerous to pass even under the best of conditions. The only other approaches to the towns were through narrow mountain passes, difficult to negotiate and almost unknown to the white Americans. Richard Pearis settled there at Tuskegee Island Town to continue his trade and to be in safe company.

Dragging Canoe was pleased with the new towns. More and more people were joining with him all the time. More Cherokees came down from the Overhills, dissatisfied with the decisions made by the old men and outraged by the arrogant behavior of their nearby white neighbors. Creeks added their strength to his force. Although he had called for only five towns to be built, other towns built by his new allies sprang up around them. There was Creek Crossing, Will's Town, Doublehead's Town, and Creek Path.

Dragging Canoe stood before a huge gathering of almost all of the Chickamaugans there at Running Water. It had been a chore to feed them all, but it had been done. Willinawa and others called them together and quieted them down at last, so that they could all hear what Dragging Canoe had to say.

"My Brothers," he began, "I'm glad to have you all here in Running Water Town. I'm glad that we're all together here. We are together in all ways, for we are united in spirit in support of our just cause. We alone in the southern part of this country continue to fight to keep the Americans out of our land. We alone continue in our loyalty to King George.

"We are many people here today. Real People, Creeks, Chickasaws, Choctaws, Shawnees, Englishmen. But we are one in brotherhood, and we are one in our resistance to the greedy Americans. But we're not enough. We need all Indians in this country from south to north united in this effort to hold back the Americans. I call for some of you to journey to all the different tribes of red men and tell them about our cause and our purpose. I call for men to travel all over this country to help bring all the tribes together in this cause. All of us who work together in this cause, no matter where we come from or the color of our skin, all of us the Americans call Chickamaugans—we are the Real People."

And while he talked, no one listened more intently than the young Shawnee Tecumseh.

### 1780

Cotetoy was watching the Suck when he saw the boats coming, six of them, all filled with whites. He watched for a moment fascinated as the first two boats barely escaped the Suck and raced on down the river. Then, coming to his senses, he turned and ran toward the heart of Tuskegee Island Town, calling out as he ran, "Bloody Fellow. Bloody Fellow. There are whites in the river."

Bloody Fellow came out of his house, his face intense, just as Cotetoy came running up to him, panting for breath. "Where?" he said.

"Six boats," said Cotetoy. "Just passing by the Suck."

"Let's go," Bloody Fellow cried out, and a number of young men ran for their rifles or their clubs or other weapons. Bloody Fellow himself ducked quickly back into his cabin and came back out as quickly, rifle in hand. He ran toward the Suck, followed by at least a dozen men. By the time they reached the river, five boats had passed the Suck. The sixth was having problems getting around the deadly swirl. Cotetoy pointed to the first five boats.

"They're getting away," he shouted.

"Forget them," said Bloody Fellow. "Let's get this one."

The large dugout canoe had twenty-eight people in it. There were men, women, and children. Bloody Fellow took aim and fired. A white man yelled, grabbed his chest, and slumped over in the boat. The women screamed. The Chickamaugans ran for the water. Three of the white men in the boat, seeing them come, jumped out, leaving their companions behind. They tried to reach the opposite shore. One was caught by the Suck. He screamed as he was swirled around. Then he disappeared under the roiling waters. A Chickamaugans ran downstream from the Suck and jumped in to cross the river. He ran after the two cowards who had escaped to the other side. Others swarmed around the boat, some grabbing its sides to capsize it, others hacking with their war axes at the men inside the boat, still others clutching at the women to drag them out into the water.

Soon it was all over. Bloody Fellow had four prisoners, two men and two women. The rest were dead. They dragged the captives out of the bloody waters of Chickamauga Creek back to Tuskegee Island Town, and one of the wretched men was tied to a stake right away. The other would have been as well were it not for the intervention of Richard Pearis.

"I'll pay his ransom," he said to Bloody Fellow. "I'll give you a keg of rum for him."

"He's not worth a keg of rum," Bloody Fellow said, "but I'll take it."

Already firewood was being piled around the feet of the other white man. Pearis took hold of his captive and said, "Come on. I don't want to be around this." He led the man out of Tuskegee Island Town as fast as he could go, but it wasn't fast enough. On the outskirts of town, he heard the first of the screams. He felt sick, and he wanted a drink.

# 13

From the high vantage point of the porch of his new home, McDonald could see the long line of troops and pack animals well before they had reached Running Water Town. "Annie," he called out over his shoulder. "Annie, the reinforcements and supplies are arriving from Florida. I'm going down to meet them." Annie stepped out of the front door with her husband's hat and coat. She put the hat on his head and then held the coat up to help him put his arms in the sleeves.

"Put this on," she said.

"All right," he said, slipping his arms into place and allowing her to pull the garment up over his shoulders and straighten it. "Will you come along?" he asked her.

"No," she said. "I'm busy here. You go on."

McDonald kissed his wife on the cheek, then started walking down the hill briskly. There was really no reason for him to hurry, for he would be in the middle of Running Water Town well before the troops. As he walked between houses on toward the road that ran parallel to the Tennessee River, Dragging Canoe came walking to meet him.

"Did you see the supplies coming?" Dragging Canoe asked him.

"Yes, and reinforcements," said McDonald. "They should be here soon."

"Yes," Dragging Canoe agreed. They stood there together in

silence until the first of the long line rode into town, and an officer riding at the head of the troops stopped his mount just ahead of them. The man looked down at McDonald and gave a sharp salute. "Mr. McDonald, sir?" he said.

"Yes," said McDonald. "I'm John McDonald, and this is Dragging Canoe."

"I'm Lieutenant Baron, sir," the officer said, swinging a leg over his horse's back to dismount. As he did so, the soldier riding next to him did the same, and Baron handed the reins of his horse to the other soldier, then walked on over to stand before McDonald.

"It's a pleasure to meet you," he said. "Uh, both of you." Reaching inside his coat, Baron produced a paper, folded and sealed with wax. He held the paper out toward McDonald. "For you, sir," he said, "from the Superintendant."

"From Scotchie?" Dragging Canoe said.

McDonald broke the seal and unfolded the paper. He read in silence, then put a hand on Dragging Canoe's shoulder. Glancing at Baron, he said, "Excuse us a moment," and he turned away from the officer, Dragging Canoe turning with him. McDonald then led Dragging Canoe a few steps away from the others.

"It's not from Scotchie," said McDonald. "I'm sorry. It's from Colonel Thomas Browne, the new superintendant. I'm afraid there's bad news, my friend. Cameron — Scotchie — is dead."

Dragging Canoe looked away from McDonald. There was a long moment of silence, as he thought about the man he called Scotchie. He recalled the first time they met and the way they had taken to one another almost immediately. He recalled the way the man smiled and laughed. He thought about the ease with which they had conversed, almost as if they had known one another all their lives.

At last McDonald spoke again, breaking in on Dragging Canoe's thoughts. "I'm sorry," he said. "I know he was your friend."

"He was more than that," said Dragging Canoe. "He was my brother. I'll miss him."

"Yes, well, there's more," McDonald said.

"Tell me," said Dragging Canoe.

"Colonel Browne, Scotchie's replacement, is in Augusta," McDonald said, referring to the letter in his hand. "The Americans are headed for Augusta with a large force. They mean to take it away from the British. Browne needs our help."

"Then he shall have it," said Dragging Canoe. "These men and supplies came just in time. I'll have all my young men get ready."

"The Americans will reach Augusta before we can get there," McDonald said.

"Then Browne will have to hold out until we arrive," Dragging Canoe said, "but we'll hurry."

McDonald stepped back over to Lieutenant Baron. "Lieutenant," he said, "Browne needs our help immediately. Have your men dismount and rest while they can. As soon as we're ready here, we'll all be on the move again. To Augusta to meet an American attack."

"To Augusta?" Baron said. "We just came from there. Why didn't we just stay where we were?"

McDonald shrugged. "There's no explaining the way the administrative mind works, Lieutenant," he said. "Ours is but to obey. Have your men ready." He hurried back up the hill to arm himself and to tell his wife what was happening. Behind him in Running Water Town, all the Chickamauga fighting men were already moving about, gathering their weapons, saddling their horses, and making whatever other preparations necessary before leaving on the long but desperately important mission.

Dragging Canoe was ready before anyone else, except the regular soldiers who had only just ridden in. He mounted his favorite horse, a white mare, and he waited. He knew that McDonald would be riding back down the hill in a short time. He saw that other Chickamaugans were already mounting their horses. Sitting there waiting, he thought about the quickness with which they were going into a major battle, and he thought about the days when the Cherokees prepared themselves for four days, fasting, dancing, praying, before daring to go into war. Once again, he considered the profound changes brought about by the white men.

191

They were deep and permanent changes, and it was no longer even meaningful to ask if they were for good or for ill. It was too late for that.

Dragging Canoe and McDonald rode side by side at the head of a thousand men, a Chickamauga army made up of Real People, both full and mixed blood, Creeks, Choctaws, Chickasaws, Shawnees, British Tories. Baron, at the head of his British regulars, rode behind them. It was a long and hard ride. Knowing that Browne was desperate and counting on them, they drove themselves on, stopping but little for rest, and that more for the sake of the horses than of the men. Close to Augusta at last, they could hear the sound of distant gunfire and cannon shot. They hurried ahead. As they topped a rise, McDonald and Dragging Canoe could see the American army attacking down below. Beyond, the British had laid down a breastworks of barrels, crates, wagons, cotton bales, whatever they could find, and were firing from behind it. Behind the defending British army was the city of Augusta. Dragging Canoe looked at McDonald.

"Ready?" McDonald said.

"This is what we came for," said Dragging Canoe. "Let's kill Americans."

McDonald drew out his sword and glanced at Dragging Canoe. Dragging Canoe took a steel trade tomahawk loose from his belt, raised his right arm, and looked over his shoulder at the troops behind him, the largest command he had ever led into battle. Then he made a sweeping forward gesture with his arm and simultaneously sounded the call of the male turkey. He kicked his horse in the flanks, and McDonald did the same. Side by side they raced toward the rear of the attacking American forces, their strange army just behind them. As he rushed headlong toward the fray, Dragging Canoe's heart thrilled with excitement. The noise of the battle was such that almost before the Americans realized they were being set upon from behind, the Chickamaugans were among them. Those rebels who first caught on turned and fired at this new threat. They shouted in desperation to their comrades to turn with them to face the attack from the rear, but not many of them heard the shouts. The Chickamaugans killed a good many who were totally unaware of the danger coming up behind them.

Gobbling like a male turkey, Dragging Canoe felt a rifle ball whiz past his face as he fought his way into the violent crowd. Ignoring it, he forced his way farther into the suddenly confused crowd of rebels. He swung his weapon as he rode up beside one of the Americans, and he split the man's head with one blow. Blood and brains splattered his side and his thigh. He turned, looking for another enemy to kill.

When the Tory defenders of Augusta saw their attackers turning to face a surprise counterattack and realized that they now had reinforcements on their side, they began climbing over their own bulwark and rushing out upon the now turned backs of the Americans. Dragging Canoe found himself in the middle of the melee. There was fighting, screaming, and shouting around him on all sides. He lost sight of McDonald and of all the other Chickamaugans. He saw only the Americans, and he slashed at them, one after another, killing or crippling as many as he could as fast as he could. He fought in a frenzy, a frenzy of hatred for the men who would steal his land and destroy his nation. He fought desperately for the survival of everything he knew, everything he owned, everything he believed in.

The humid Georgia air was made even heavier and thicker with the sweet smell of blood and the acrid smell of gunpowder smoke. It was filled with the moans of the dying, the screams of the hurt, the cracking of gunshots, the stamping of horses' hooves, the clatter of steel weapons, the thumping and thudding of weapons against flesh, flesh against flesh, yelping, shrieking, hoorawing — all the sounds of boistrous, raucous battle. Indian war cries split the muggy air and mingled with the hoorays of the Tories and the desperate shouts and curses of the surprised and overwhelmed Americans. Soon the American commander called the retreat, and the Americans fled in total disorder, for most of them had not even heard the command. They were pursued by Chickamaugans, Tories, and British regulars. Stragglers were cut down with ease.

The battle was won, but fighting and killing continued, for the fighting fever had seized upon them, and it would not easily release its hold.

The relentless victors pursued the fleeing defeated, and when they caught those who lagged behind, they hacked them down mercilessly. They pursued them for miles, breaking into smaller groups and going in various directions, and when they came across lone cabins or clusters of cabins, they burned them to the ground. They spread the battle for Augusta out into the outlying settlements. Eventually, tired and spent from the chasing and the killing, they gave up their bloody pursuit and began dragging themselves wearily back to Augusta.

But McDonald and Dragging Canoe had not ridden out with the frenzied pursuers. Back at the battle site there at the edge of the city, McDonald saw Dragging Canoe calmly surveying the carnage. He picked his way over mangled corpses to stand beside his companion. "It's a good day, McDonald," Dragging Canoe said. "I've been swimming in an ocean of American blood."

"Yes," said McDonald. "A victorious day. Would you come with me? I think I see the new Superintendent over there near the bulwarks."

Stepping over, around, and sometimes on bodies, they walked toward the breastworks where a few men were standing looking out over the battlefield. All of them were dirty and bedraggled from the hard fighting. "Colonel Browne?" said McDonald. "Yes?" The man who turned to respond had obviously been in the heat of the battle along with all the others. He stood there in a torn and dirty shirt, spattered with blood and soot. Dragging Canoe liked the man for that. Not all of the English officials he had known would get into the thick of a battle alongside their soldiers. He recalled with an inward smirk the foolish fat Lyttleton running away from danger, puffing and sweating as he rode, his powdered wig flying off his head in the breeze. This one, this Browne, he thought, was all right.

"I'm your assistant, John McDonald," McDonald said, extending his hand.

"Yes, of course," said Browne, and he took hold of McDonald's hand and pumped it vigorously. "What a wondrously timely arrival, Mr. McDonald. I'm very pleased to meet you, and you couldn't have come at a better time, I promise you that. I don't think we could have held the buggers off much longer. In fact, I was very much afraid that we were lost."

"I'm pleased that we arrived in time to be of service," said McDonald. "Colonel Browne, sir, may I present Dragging Canoe," he added, turning and gesturing toward the Chickamauga chief standing there beside him. Browne's mouth gaped and his eyes opened wide. He looked as if he had just been introduced to King George. He held his hand out and waited for Dragging Canoe to take it.

"A great honor, sir," he said. "A great honor, indeed. It makes my heart glad to meet so great an ally of the King."

"All the King's men are my friends," Dragging Canoe said, as he studied Browne's appearance. He had ceased being surprised at the extreme youth of the Englishmen appointed to high office. This one, he was pleased to note, was handsome, straight and tall, lithe of limb, and of a pleasant disposition. A good man was needed to take Scotchie's place. Dragging Canoe decided that this one had been a good choice.

"The King is greatly in your debt, sir," Browne said, "as am I. As are all the loyal Englishmen in Augusta, indeed, in all of America. Had you not arrived when you did, we would surely have been overrun, and Augusta and all of us would have fallen into the hands of the rebels. Our lives wouldn't have been worth a cracker."

"Thank God we did arrive in time, sir," McDonald said.

The next morning, after a good night's sleep and a hearty breakfast, McDonald and Dragging Canoe met again with Colonel Browne. This time Browne looked every inch the official. He had bathed and put on a clean suit of clothes. At this desk in his office, he had tea served.

"Gentlemen, I have need to call on your services again," he said.

"Yes, sir?" McDonald said.

"Tell me what needs to be done," said Dragging Canoe, "and I and my young men will do it."

"I have a great need for you to keep the frontier militiamen west of the mountains occupied," Browne said. "It will mean a great deal to Lord Cornwallis and to our entire war effort if you can keep those vagabonds busy out there so they can't meddle elsewhere."

"Then that is what we will do," Dragging Canoe said. "We won't give them time to sit down and eat a meal in peace."

The Chickamaugans rode west of the mountains, and then they broke up into smaller bands. Redheaded Bob Benge and others found a band of militiamen camped around a fire preparing their noon meal. They gobbled, whipped their horses, and rode hard straight into the camp. Surprised and confused, militiamen ran for their weapons, but most were cut down before they could even lay hands upon them. Few shots were fired. The attackers used mostly their clubs and axes. Then, there in the middle of the bloody bodies, Benge and his troop sat down to eat the untouched meal. Benge sipped hot, steaming liquid from a tin cup.

"They made good coffee," he said.

The Shawnee Warrior and his Shawnee contingent came upon a lone cabin in a field at the edge of a wood. The settler there saw them coming and went quickly inside. He fired his rifle out a window, but missed his mark. The Shawnees swarmed over the house, set it afire, and waited for the inhabitants to come out. When the blaze began to overtake the cabin, the Shawnees backed away from it and watched. No one came out. They continued watching. They heard no screams, but the cabin was eventually reduced to ashes, and so, obviously, were its unfortunate inhabitants.

Dragging Canoe, McDonald, and others came across a surveying crew laying out a road. As they rushed into the camp, several men picked up rifles and fired. The Real People rushed hard upon them, swinging tomahawks and war clubs. Dragging Canoe jumped off his horse to tackle the man who had been sighting through his transit. They rolled on the ground struggling with one another until Dragging Canoe's knife blade slid between the man's ribs. Then Dragging Canoe stood up, took hold of the transit by its three long legs, and smashed it against the trunk of a tree.

"No white man will use this land stealer again," he said.

They continued to operate in small guerilla bands, harassing travelers, settlers in their homes, militiamen on the march or in their camps. Chickamaugans seemed to be everywhere, and no American felt safe west of the mountains. And so a man named John Sevier riding at the head of a band of American militia from Tennessee went into the Overhills to burn all the Cherokee towns there. Cherokees had been burning the white frontier settlements west of the mountains. He would kill some Cherokees and burn Cherokee towns. To Sevier, it mattered not that the Overhills Cherokees had nothing to do with the attacks west of the mountains, that they had not been involved in any fighting whatsoever. He saw no difference in the Overhills Cherokees and the Chickamaugans. In his mind, a Cherokee was a Cherokee, and the entire race should be exterminated.

His invasion was, of course, totally unexpected. In the Overhills, the Cherokees thought they were safe. They thought that everyone knew that Dragging Canoe had withdrawn from the Cherokee Nation, that he and his followers no longer even called themselves Cherokee. Dragging Canoe and his followers were outlaws. They were secessionists. The Cherokees in the Overhills were at peace. They were safe.

When Sevier's rowdy and undisciplined frontiersmen rode into the Overhills towns, the people were taken completely by surprise. Terrified children ran and screamed in fright. Frontiersmen rode alongside them as they screamed for their mothers and bashed in their heads or hacked them with their long blades. Sevier's men killed everyone they saw, man, woman, or child, young or old. It didn't matter to them. They devastated the Overhills Towns and left the entire area in ruins, and all of the people who survived were left destitute, their towns, fields, gardens, and orchards completely destroyed.

Ada-gal'kala lay on his deathbed. He knew it was that. He thought about the burned towns and the people who had been killed by Sevier on these latest raids, and he thought that, in the end, his diplomacy had failed him utterly, and Sevier had punished people who had done nothing wrong. Perhaps his powers had failed him because of his age. Perhaps his powers, like his body, were worn out and useless. Perhaps. He was old. In his seventies. And he had seen much in his long life. He recalled the time when, as the young Uku Unega, called Captain Owen Nakan, he had visited England. He recalled the crowded cities and the splendor he had seen there at the castle, and he recalled his meeting with the Great King.

Perhaps, he thought, his hotheaded son was right after all. Perhaps he himself should have held more closely to the English right up to the end. He had tried to keep the Cherokees out of this war, had tried to be friends with the rebelling Americans, and what had become of it? Sevier's raid. Death and destruction for the Cherokees. Ah, he thought, if I were young again, I could kill— But he was old and dying, and it was his son who was doing all the killing. And anyway, he had been the most important man among the Cherokees for a long, long time. He wondered what would become of the people in the future. He wondered, if he had his life to live over again, what he would do. Would he be the same diplomat he had been, or would he fight? He wondered. And then he drifted away into a deep and profound sleep, one from which he would not awaken again—not on this world.

Richard Pearis sat in his small cabin on a bench at a rough-hewn table drinking from a jug of rum. His "prisoner," the man he saved from a horrible fiery death, sat across the table from him. Pearis took a long swig of rum and shoved the jug toward the other man. "Have a drink, Samuel," he said. Samuel took a swig and gave the jug back to Pearis. "When are you going to get me out of here?" Samuel asked.

"Stop worrying," said Pearis. "You're safe enough here in my house."

"It's not right," said Samuel, "you, a white man, keeping me a prisoner here among these savages."

"I've kept you alive, haven't I?" Pearis said. He took another slug. "Besides, where would you go if I got you away from here? Huh? Where? Somewhere to squat illegally on Indian land? To join some rebel band and fight against the King? You're a prisoner of war, you bastard, so get used to the idea. Do you think I enjoy your bloody company? Well, I don't. I don't like you. I hate you, you and all your kind. Hell, man, I'd give you back to Bloody Fellow in a minute, but I don't like the smell of burning flesh."

"Give me another drink?" Samuel said.

"Go to hell," said Pearis.

"You're worse than a British soldier," Samuel said. "You're worse than a regular Tory. You've joined with a bunch of bloodthirsty savages is what you've done. Killing and scalping white people. There's nothing worse than a white man who runs with savages and kills his own kind. You're—"

"Shut up and have a drink," Pearis said, shoving the jug across the table. "I have a wife among these people," he said, but he was no longer talking to Samuel. He was musing aloud. "A wife and a child. My little George. But then, I have another wife in Charlestown. A lovely white woman but a nag. If I had to choose between the two—"

Samuel shoved the jug back, and Pearis stopped talking. He picked up the jug to drink. Just then there was a knock on the door. "Come in," Pearis shouted. The door opened and McDonald stepped in. He glanced briefly at Samuel, then looked at Pearis. "I have some news," he said. "It's not for his ears." Pearis got to his feet and followed McDonald outside. They walked a few steps away from the house, and McDonald spoke low in Pearis's ear. "It's over," he said. "Lord Cornwallis has surrendered, and all British troops have been ordered out of this country. I have to go now and break the news to Dragging Canoe. Will you go with me?"

"God," said Pearis. "None of us will be safe here. Yes. Yes, of course, I'll go with you." He stuck his head back inside his cabin. "Samuel," he said, "can you pack a horse?"

"Sure I can," Samuel said. "I ain't helpless."

"Then pack everything in here on my horse," Pearis said.

"Why should I?" Samuel grumbled. "I may be your prisoner, but I ain't your goddamned slave."

"You want to get out of here, don't you?" Pearis asked.

"You bet I do," Samuel said. "The sooner the better."

"Then pack my horse, you bloody bastard," said Pearis. "We're going on a trip."

Dragging Canoe sat in front of his Running Water house with Diwali, Doublehead, Bloody Fellow, John Watts, and others. They were gathered around a table, studying a map, and planning their next raids on the western frontiersmen. Dragging Canoe looked up to see McDonald and Pearis approaching side by side. He stood to greet the two white men.

"I'm glad you're here," he said. "Sit down and join us."

McDonald sat across from Dragging Canoe, but Pearis remained standing. Just then Dragging Canoe noticed the long faces the two Englishmen wore.

"I bring bad news," said McDonald. "Spain and France have joined with the Americans to drive the English from these shores. They've taken Pensacola as well as Augusta. Lord Cornwallis has surrendered at Yorktown, and a meeting is planned for Paris, France, where a treaty of peace will be signed. I've received orders from Colonel Browne to withdraw all British forces. I'm sorry, my friend. We've lost the support of the British Army."

Dragging Canoe stood and walked away from the others. He stood in silence with his back to the small group for a long moment. "I had not thought that the great King would ever surrender to these Americans," he said. "I had not thought that he would turn his back on us and leave us to fight on alone."

"What will you do now?" McDonald asked.

"We will keep fighting the Americans," Dragging Canoe said. "Without the King's men to help keep them away, they'll go after more of my land. There will be nothing to hold them back. Nothing but me. The King may have lost interest in this land, but I have not. It's my home. I live here. And this land is nourished with the blood and flesh of my ancestors. God gave me this land to live on, and I will not abandon it. I'll fight the Americans as long as I have strength enough to lift my arm." He paused for a brief moment, then looked at McDonald. "When will you leave?" he asked.

"I won't leave here," said McDonald. "I'll resign my position. My place is here with my wife and children—and with you, with the Real People. Nothing can change that now."

Dragging Canoe put his hands on McDonald's shoulders and smiled. Then he looked at Pearis. "And what about you?" he asked. "What will you do now?"

"I'm not a soldier," Pearis said, "and I'm getting out. It won't be safe around here for a man like me. I think I'll go to the Bahamas. There might be opportunities for a packhorseman over there. Anyway, it'll be safe from these rebel American bastards."

"You too have a wife and child here," McDonald said.

"Yes," said Pearis. "I know. I'll miss them, I suppose. But they'll be better off here without me." He didn't mention the other one— the white woman in Charlestown.

Dragging Canoe stepped over to take Pearis by the hand. "I'll miss you," he said. "We rode some trails together, you and I, good ones and bad ones. I'll miss you, but we'll have your son here with us to remember you by. And his children and grandchildren after him. You'll always be with us, Pearis. I hope you find peace, good fortune, and a long life there in the Bahamas."

McDonald stood also to take Pearis's hand. "Good luck to you, Richard," he said.

"No hard feelings?" Pearis asked.

"None," said McDonald. "Of course not. Each of us has to make his own choice."

"Look after George for me, will you?" said Pearis.

"I will, of course," McDonald said. "He's going to grow into a fine young man."

"I'd like to see that," said Pearis, "but I'm sure I won't be back. I hate these—Americans."

With that, Pearis turned and started walking back toward his cabin. He did not look back. Dragging Canoe and McDonald stood for a moment watching him go. Then, "Sit down," said Dragging Canoe, and they sat once again with the others.

"Without the English," said Bloody Fellow, "what will we do for supplies?"

"We'll steal them from the Americans," said Diwali.

"England is giving Florida back to Spain," McDonald said. "I think we should go to the Spanish."

"You said that Spain helped the Americans," Dragging Canoe said.

"They did," said McDonald, "but not out of any love for them, believe me. They did it for themselves—to get England out of their way. And you see, it worked. Now England is pulling out, and they have Florida back. The Americans will be looking toward Florida soon enough. You can believe that. And Spain knows it as well. I believe they'll help us, at least for as long as it's in their interests to do so."

Dragging Canoe stood up and spoke emphatically. "Good," he said. "Then we should take advantage of the time. We'll go to the Spanish. If they'll provide us with ammunition to fight the Americans, we'll be their friends—for a while, for so long as it's in our interests."

Then he thought, How like my father that sounded.

PART FOUR

# Standing Alone

# 14

Annie lay in the arms of her husband. It was a quiet night, belying the turmoil in their lives, the violence that raged all around them. "I'm glad you're staying here with us, John," she said.

"Did you think for a moment that I'd leave you?" he asked her. "You and our little Mollie?"

"Other white men leave their Cherokee wives and children," she said. "Some have white wives and children back in the colonies."

"Oh, sweet Annie, I have no other wife," McDonald said. "I want no other wife. You are the love of my life, and I mean to stay with you for the rest of my life. I have cast my lot with the Real People — with you and your people. I love you, Annie. I love you desperately. Nothing but death will ever take me away from you."

"I'm glad," she said. "I love you, too."

Alone, considering his new circumstances and his current plans, Dragging Canoe found himself thinking more and more about his father, the great diplomat, the "Little Carpenter." He smiled. Going to Spain was just what Ada-gal'kala would have done had he found himself in this same predicament. He would turn where he saw the advantage. Perhaps, after all, they were not so different one from the other. They had simply lived in different times. That was all.

Then he wondered how long it would all last, all this fighting. And did he really have a chance of winning the fight? As long as the British were involved, it had seemed possible. He had even thought it a certainly. Now it was more important than ever to have the different tribes all united in a common effort. His father had always said that all things change, but thinking back over the years, Dragging Canoe thought that the changes he had seen had all been for the worse. He could see only a pattern of loss: lost land, lost lives, lost ways. Perhaps the end would be the loss of it all. Well, if that were to be his fate, he would accept it, but he would fight right up to the end. He would never surrender to the Americans. He would never willingly give up his land or his freedom or his ways.

"Do not be afraid of the stupid Americanos," Governor Miro, the new Spanish governor of Florida, was saying. A short, pompous man with a thin, curled mustache, wearing a full dress military uniform, he was standing on a platform in the middle of a plaza with a large crowd of Indians around him. His voice was thin and high pitched, and when it rose to its highest level, Miro also rose up on his toes. "You, our brothers the red men, are not without friends. The Americans have no king, and they are nothing of themselves. They are like a man that is lost and wandering in the woods. If it had not been for the Spanish and French, the English would have subdued them long ago."

Dragging Canoe, in the crowd along with McDonald, Guhna-geski, the Shawnee Warrior, Young Canoe, and other Real People, thought that the Spanish and French should have stayed out of it then, and if the British had subdued the Americans, then everything would be all right. He did not like the little Spaniard, this man who talked out of both sides of his face, but for now he would keep his thoughts to himself. He had to live with the reality that England was gone, and he and his Chickamauga followers would have to carry on the war alone. He wanted the Spanish supplies, whatever the Spanish motivation. He thought wryly that perhaps he had learned a little diplomacy from his father after all.

"The King of Spain desires the friendship of all red nations," Miro went on, "and looks upon them as his brothers. No other nation except Spain can now supply your wants. Only Spain. In a short time the Spaniards expect to be at war with the Virginians, and we look upon the Indians as our allies to aid and assist us when called upon."

We will assist you, Dragging Canoe thought, when you fight our enemies, when your fight is our fight, and that is the only time we will assist you, for I believe that you would smile at me and then stab me in the back when I turned to walk away.

The small band of westering pioneers moved slowly through a narrow mountain gap, one man ahead of them on horseback, others walking. Two covered wagons pulled by oxen lumbered along, women on the seats handling the reins. Children's legs dangled out behind. The steep mountainsides around them were a deep, wet green, so dark in places they were almost black. The air was cool and crisp in the deep, dark shadow that encompassed them.

Suddenly shots rang out around them. The man on horseback fell out of his saddle, and the man walking beside the lead wagon jerked and fell forward on his face. The other men readied their weapons and looked for something to shoot at. Another shot from the thickness dropped another pioneer. Then the sound of angry male turkeys filled the air, and Chickamaugans came out of the tangle of green, rushing at the wagons, brandishing war clubs. It wasn't much of a fight. It was soon over. The men in the invading group were all dead. So was one woman. The other women and the children were captive. Young Canoe and the others took the scalps of the dead. The Spanish supplies were ample and good.

Dragging Canoe sat on the porch of McDonald's house sipping tea with the Englishman. Annie was inside doing the things that women do in their homes. "Look there," said McDonald. A small group of people were walking from Running Water toward McDonald's house. Soon they could see that Guhna-geski, along with Bloody Fellow, was leading them. The strangers looked ragged and weary. "Who could they be, I wonder?" McDonald said. "We'll see," said Dragging Canoe. The group, which included men and women, arrived at the porch, and Guhna-geski stepped forward.

" 'Siyo, Tsiyu Gansini," Guhna-geski said. " 'Siyo, McDonald." The two men returned the greetings, and Guhna-geski continued. "These people here with me," he said, "have just come from the Overhills. They want to speak with you."

Dragging Canoe stood up and walked to the edge of the porch. "Welcome. I'm Tsiyu Gansini. What is it you want of me?" he asked, and a man from the Overhills group stepped forward.

"We want to live here with you," he said. "Things are not good back in the Overhills."

"You know that we're fighting the Americans," Dragging Canoe said.

"We have not been fighting the Americans," said the other. "Still they burn our towns and crops. Still they kill us. Why should we stay there? Why should we not join with you? If you'll have us, we'll fight with you."

"You're all welcome here," said Dragging Canoe. "Tell me, what's the news from back there?"

"Ogan'sto' has died," the man said.

"He was old, and he had a good and useful life," said Dragging Canoe. "It was his time. Has a new chief been named?"

"Old Tassel is now the Principal Chief of the Cherokee Nation," said the man, "and Hanging Maw has been named War Chief."

Bloody Fellow scoffed aloud. "Do you think he'll go to war," he said, "this new war chief?"

"No," said the man from the Overhills. "I don't believe he will."

"No," said Bloody Fellow. "I don't either."

"I have more news," the man said.

"Tell me," said Dragging Canoe.

"The man who burned our towns, the one they call Little John Sevier," the man said, "claims to have made a new state. He named it Franklin, and he made himself its governor. Many of his people are moving onto our land along the Nolichucky River. Some are not more than a day's walk from Echota. Old Tassel has appealed to North Carolina and to Virginia, but it seems that Little John won't listen to North Carolina or Virginia. He makes his own law."

"Maybe he'll listen to me," said Bloody Fellow, almost in a rage. "I'll send him a letter. I'll tell him what will happen if he doesn't get out of there. Will you write it for me, McDonald?"

"Of course," McDonald said.

"There's yet more," the Overhills man said. "Old Tassel and the other leaders are planning to meet with the great men from all thirteen states at Hopewell to make a new treaty."

"Another treaty," Dragging Canoe repeated. He heaved a sigh. "Then they'll be giving away more land. There's hardly any left to give."

### November 18, 1785
### Hopewell

Old Tassel, Hanging Maw, thirty-six other chiefs, and a total of nine hundred and eighteen Cherokees met at Hopewell with United States Commissioners Benjamin Hawkins, Andrew Pickens, Joseph Martin, and Lachlan McIntosh. The Cherokees camped on the banks of the Keowee River. Abram of Chilhowee and Gritts were there from the Chickamauga towns. On the first day of the meeting, Commissioner Hawkins stood before them all and made a speech.

"Great Britain is no longer the sovereign in this land," he said. "The sovereign is now the Congress of the United States. This change is the result of the successful termination of the late revolution. We are meeting with you here to inform you of that change and to make sure that you fully understand it. Rest assured that the Congress wants no more of your land, nor does it want anything else that belongs to you. We are here to express our friendship and to listen to any grievances you may have. If you have such, express them freely. We intend for the conclusion of this meeting to be a treaty of perpetual peace and friendship between you and the United States."

When his turn to speak came, Old Tassel stood up and introduced to the commissioners Nancy Ward. "She is our Beloved Woman," he said. "Her words have always been wise, and she has always been a friend to the Americans. She has learned the ways of the white people, too. She can spin and weave, and she owns an inn and black slaves. I want you to listen to her words. I want her to speak here for us."

The white commissioners looked at one another, and Hawkins gave a shrug. "It's a bit unusual," said Pickens, "but I suppose it's all right."

"We'll listen to Mrs. Ward," said Hawkins.

Nancy Ward, now forty-seven years old, still tall and straight and stately in appearance, stood up to speak, and as she spoke, she carried a pipe and a pouch of tobacco to the table where the commissioners sat. "I have here," she said, "a pipe and a little tobacco to give to the commissioners to smoke in friendship. I have seen much trouble in the late war. I am now old, but hope yet to bear children who will grow up and people our nation, as we are now under the protection of Congress and have no more disturbances. The talk that I give you is from myself."

Old Tassel then stood and walked to the table where the commissioners were seated. He was carrying a large piece of rolled paper, and he spread the paper on the table. It was a map of the Cherokee country. "We've had good talks here today," he said, "but I want you to see this map. Our only grievance is that white people are moving onto our land. I want you to look at this map and see where our land is and see where your people have moved, and I want you to make things right between your people and mine."

The commissioners looked at the map and whispered in the ears of one another. Then Hawkins stood up and pointed to a place on the map while McIntosh produced a piece of paper from a portfolio. He laid the paper out on the table, turned so that Old Tassel could see it. "According to the paper that Commissioner McIntosh has there before him," Hawkins said, "you sold this land here to the Transylvania Company, represented by Misters Hart and Henderson."

Old Tassel, Hanging Maw, and Nancy Ward huddled together for a moment, speaking in low voices. Then Old Tassel turned again to the commissioners. "We had not thought that was a good bargain," he said. "They told us that it was against the King's law."

"The King's law means nothing here anymore," Hawkins said.

Old Tassel and the other two whispered together again, and then Old Tassel gave a casual shrug. "If you believe it was good," he said, "we will be content with it."

"I want to know if the Cherokee Dragon is here," said Pickens.

"Dragging Canoe is not here with us," Old Tassel said.

"How can we talk of peace," Pickens said, "if the man who has been making war on us is not here?"

"Dragging Canoe and his followers are no longer a part of the Cherokee Nation," Old Tassel said. "They've gone their own way for some time now, and we have no control over them. We've been punished for things that they did. We have not been at war with you, even though we're here asking for peace."

The commissioners mumbled to one another again, and at last Hawkins spoke for them all. "We consider Dragging Canoe and his Chickamaugans to be still Cherokee," he said. "If they remain at peace after we have concluded this treaty, his past will be forgiven. If, however, he takes up the hatchet again, he will be regarded as a renegade and an outlaw, and he will be hunted down and dealt with as such."

Ten days later, after much talking, the treaty was at last drawn up, and it was signed. Old Tassel, Hanging Maw, and thirty-five other Cherokee chiefs signed. For the Congress of the United States, the commissioners all signed. Everyone was satisfied. It was a good treaty. It gave "peace to all the Cherokees" and received "them into the favor and protection of the United States of America." It called for the Cherokees to turn over all prisoners taken in the late war, and it promised that the United States would do the same. It called for the Cherokees to acknowledge no sovereign other than the United States. It drew the boundary lines of the Cherokee Nation according to the map presented by Old Tassel, with the exception of the Transylvania purchase.

It stipulated that if any white person should settle on Cherokee land and refuse to move, the Cherokees could deal with him as they saw fit. It called for Congress to regulate trade with the Cherokees, and it gave the Cherokees the right to send a deputy to Congress. Finally, it promised perpetual peace and friendship between the United States and the Cherokee Nation. The treaty seemed to satisfy everyone.

Abram and Gritts hurried back to Running Water Town as fast as they could to report to Dragging Canoe following the breakup of the meeting.

"It's a good treaty," Abram said, and he went over all the terms for Dragging Canoe.

"It sounds good," Dragging Canoe said, "but I don't believe the Americans will keep their promises. We'll wait and see."

"Will we stop fighting?" Abram asked.

"Yes," said Dragging Canoe. "We'll stop fighting, unless we find white men on our land. The new treaty says that we can deal with them how we choose. Did you say that?"

"Yes," said Abram. "It says that they cannot move on to our land, and if they do, we can do what we want with them."

"Then if they leave us alone on our land," Dragging Canoe said, "that's all I ask. There will be peace."

Dragging Canoe contemplated his new situation. The old men of the Cherokee Nation had signed yet another treaty—this one with the new United States, and apparently the United States still considered him to be a part of that nation. There would be peace if he ceased his raids on the frontiersmen, and the Cherokee people would be all united once again. It all sounded almost too good to be true, and he knew that there were still illegal settlers on Cherokee land. But according to the treaty, as he understood its terms from Abram, those settlers would be told to move. If they refused, he could drive them out or kill them.

He had decided that it would be wise to wait a while and give the new country a chance to live up to its promises. He didn't really believe that they would. He did not trust them. Still, it was a new country, they had promised, and he thought that they should be given a chance to keep their promise. He called together all the other leaders of the Chickamaugans to tell them his thoughts. "Let's not make war for a while," he said. "Let's wait and see what happens with this new American treaty." And they all agreed. But quietly, he thought, What about John Sevier? The Americans say that he's an outlaw. What will they do about John Sevier? Will they arrest him and punish him under their laws?

## 1785

Ignoring all laws except those of John Sevier, settlers from the self-proclaimed state of Franklin again began moving farther onto Cherokee land. Some even moved dangerously close to the Chickamauga Towns of Dragging Canoe, and word soon reached him there. Guhna-geski called Dragging Canoe out of his house. As he stepped out, Dragging Canoe saw that Bloody Fellow was there with Guhna-geski and others.

"Dragging Canoe," said Guhna-geski, "Bloody Fellow saw whites moving close to us here."

"They're daring us to do something," said Bloody Fellow. "They not only moved across the line, they're just over there." He made a sweeping gesture with his right arm. "Building their homes."

"According to the treaty," Dragging Canoe said, "we can deal with them as we please. Is that not what the treaty says?"

And Abram and others who had been there when the treaty was signed agreed and assured him once again that those were the words in the treaty. "But these, I think," Abram added, "are Sevier's people. They don't believe that treaty binds them."

"They think they're above all law," said Dragging Canoe.

"Except the law of Little John Sevier," Guhna-geski said.

"Let's show them that they're not above our law," said Bloody Fellow.

"I'll talk to them first," Dragging Canoe said. "I'll tell them to move."

Charles Simpson and his wife had just finished their new cabin. With their teenaged son, Charles, Jr., they had moved out onto Cherokee land with the advice and blessing of John Sevier, whom they knew as Governor Sevier. They believed that they were living in the new state of Franklin. It was close to noon, and Mrs. Simpson, Edith, was in the cabin getting lunch ready. Smoke from the fire in her fireplace billowed out into the damp, rich atmosphere. Simpson and Charlie were outside. They were hard at work chopping at the trunk of a large oak tree. It was right in the middle of the cornfield that so far existed only in the mind of Charles Simpson. Once the big tree was down, its stump and roots would have to be pulled out. There were other trees too that would have to go. Simpson sank his ax blade deep into the flesh of the old tree, then drew it back ready for another swing.

"Paw," said Charlie.

Simpson hesitated in mid-swing. "What is it?" he said.

"Look, Paw," said the boy.

Simpson looked at his son, who stood still, staring off toward the river. He stepped up beside him and looked in the same direction the boy was looking. Eight Indians were walking toward them. "What'll we do, Paw?" Charlie asked.

"Stand still, boy," Simpson said. "If they was up to no good, they'd sneak up close and then run at us. I reckon they just want to talk." In spite of his own calm words, Simpson glanced nervously to his right where his long rifle leaned against a tree trunk. In another moment, the Indians were close enough to talk, and they stopped. One stepped out ahead of the others.

"I'm Dragging Canoe," he said, "and you're on my land."

The name struck terror into the heart of Simpson, but he was staunch. He was independent, and he knew his rights. He had worked hard to build his new home, and he meant to keep it.

"This is free land from the state of Franklin," he said. "I have a right to be here. I have Governor Sevier's word for that."

"I came to warn you," said Dragging Canoe. "This is my land. When I come back, if you're still here, I'll kill you."

"Now you listen to me, redskin," said Simpson. "I made my home here, and I ain't moving, not for no Cherokee Dragon or nobody. Now you take your braves there, and you get off my land. If you don't come back, I won't bother to report this to Governor Sevier."

Dragging Canoe turned and walked back to where the others waited for him. He turned his head and called back over his shoulder.

"One week," he said. "I'll be back."

Simpson hesitated but an instant. Then he made a lunge for his rifle. He grabbed it up, thumbed back the hammer and took aim. "Paw?" said the boy. Simpson pulled the trigger, and the man walking to Dragging Canoe's right dropped to the ground. It was a fool move. Simpson had no time to reload. Dragging Canoe and the others rushed him, war clubs ready. Dragging Canoe crushed the skull of Simpson, and another killed the boy. They raced on over to the cabin, where the shot had brought Mrs. Simpson out to see what was going on.

She stopped, a look of terror on her face. "Charles?" she cried out. "Charlie?"

One of the Chickamauga men ran toward her. She screamed and ran back into the house, slamming the door. The man pushed at the door, and he was soon joined by two others. Together they pushed the door open and rushed into the cabin. The woman turned to run, but one of the men grabbed her arm. Another lifted a steel tomahawk and split her skull. She fell dead instantly, dropping like a sack of grain. The man who had first touched her knelt to take her scalp, while the other two rushed around the house looking for anything of value. They found some powder and balls, some foodstuffs, some cloth and clothing. Taking it up, they all raced back outside. Dragging Canoe walked calmly into the cabin. He glanced at the dead woman there on the floor, then walked over to the fireplace where a nice fire was blazing away. A pot of beans hung over the fire. Dragging Canoe found the cold end of a burning piece of firewood. He took hold of it, looked around the room, and tossed it onto the bed. Then he went back outside where he and the others waited and watched until the cabin was engulfed in flames.

Some miles away at the site of another Franklinite's homestead, Bloody Fellow and eight more Chickamaugans approached another cabin. Two men in front of the cabin opened fire on them at first sight, and the Chickamaugans rushed upon them with war clubs. Soon that cabin too was in flames. Its inhabitants were all dead and scalped.

## 1787
### On the Tennessee River near Nickajack

They knew that it was coming down the river, a white man's boat, a flatboat with a deckhouse. They did not know how many white men would be on board. Four Chickamauga war canoes were loaded up at Nickajack, each containing ten to twelve men. James Vann rode in one. When they saw the boat coming, they paddled out to meet it. As they drew close, Vann could see one white man on board, and he was looking tense.

"Hello," Vann called out. "Where are you headed?"

"That's close enough," the man said. "There're too many of you."

"We're peaceful," Vann called, as the Chickamauga canoes drew closer all the time. "Look." He held his arms out to his sides to show that he was carrying no weapons. "We thought you might have something to trade. Are you trading?"

"I'm moving my family," the man said. "I'm not out to trade."

"Well," Vann said, "we have some things to trade. We'll show you what we have, and you might want to trade with us."

The canoes were by then touching the flatboat, and Watts and some others boarded the white man's boat. One Chickamauga was carrying a sword. The white man who had spoken stood at the

216

stern of the boat nervously shielding a boy of about fifteen. In the bow five other men and two more boys stood. By then the boat was crowded with Chickamaugans. In the stern of the boat, the man with the sword reached for the boy, and the white man shoved him back.

"This is my little boy," he said. "Don't touch him."

He looked around desperately for Vann, for someone to talk English to, but the boat was too crowded, and he could not see Vann. He did turn his head away from the Chickamaugan with the sword, though, and it was a fatal mistake. The Chickamaugan swung the sword, nearly severing the head of the white boatman, slinging blood over himself and the boy. The boy ran forward to the bow, hoping for the protection of the men there, and as he did some of the Chickamaugans broke into the deckhouse. Women screamed. Then the boy could see nothing because of the crowd and the flurry of activity.

He felt someone take hold of his arms from behind, and then some of the Chickamaugans began moving back into their own canoes. The one holding him pulled him into a canoe. He could see others going into the deckhouse. He could tell that they were looking for anything that they might want to take with them. The activity on the bow cleared, and he saw that the five men who had been there had all been killed. He looked around desperately, and he saw a canoe going down the river, away from the boat, and he could see that his mother, three sisters, and his little brother were being taken away.

The canoe he was in started moving back toward the shore, and then another was loaded and started after it. The boy twisted his neck and saw in the second canoe his older brother and his mother's black female slave. He felt some sense of relief at that sight. He was not totally alone. He worried about his mother and sisters. The canoe carrying them away was almost out of sight. He was afraid, but when they reached shore, he thought, he would ask his brother what they should do.

That plan was thwarted when his brother was taken away by some Indians in a different direction from where he was taken. He wasn't sure where the big white man came from, but all of a sudden, he was there, blocking the path. The boy stared at him, his mouth hanging open. The big man extended a hand. "Come with me," he said.

The big man led the boy through town, between some houses, and then out on a trail. They had walked maybe half a mile before the big man spoke again. "I'm Tom Tunbridge," he said. "What's your name?"

"Joseph Brown," the boy said. "They killed my father."

"You're lucky they didn't kill all of you," Tunbridge said.

"Where'd they take my mother and sisters?" Joseph asked.

"I don't know," Tunbridge answered. "The men who took them were Creeks."

"What about my brother?"

Just then some shots were fired. Tunbridge did not bother answering Joseph Brown's question. They walked on and eventually arrived at a small cabin. Tunbridge opened the door and walked in. Without bothering to look back, he said, "Come on." Joseph followed him inside. An old woman looked up from where she sat at the table. "I brought this boy," Tunbridge said. She looked at Joseph with a scowl on her face.

"He looks big enough to help me hoe corn," she said.

Then another woman came in. She hadn't knocked, hadn't even announced herself. She just barged in and started fussing in Cherokee. Joseph could not understand a word she was saying, of course, but he could tell that she was angry. When she finally left, he asked Tunbridge, "What was she so mad about?"

"She's mad at me," said Tunbridge, "for protecting you. She said they've killed all the other men. I told her that you're just a boy, and she said that you're old enough to run away and lead Americans back here to kill us."

Joseph thought about his older brother, and he recalled the shots he had heard. He felt like crying, but he did not want to let these people see his tears. And besides that, he couldn't yet quite believe that all this had happened.

"She said that her son's coming here to kill you," Tunbridge said. "Don't worry, though. I'll stand between you and him."

Tunbridge stayed in the doorway, his massive frame almost filling the space, and in a few minutes, sure enough, an Indian man appeared just outside. Joseph figured it to be the son of the angry old woman. " 'Siyo, Cotetoy," Tunbridge said. "What can I do for you?"

"Do you have a little white boy here?" Cotetoy asked.

"I do," Tunbridge said.

"I know how big this little boy is," Cotetoy said. "I mean to kill him."

"It's not right to kill women and children," said Tunbridge. "Go your way."

"This little boy will be a man soon," Cotetoy said, "and he'll guide an army back here to attack us and burn our towns."

"Well," Tunbridge said, "this little boy is a prisoner of Young Tom, my son, so if you want to argue the point, you'll have to talk to Young Tom."

Cotetoy then stepped up close to Tunbridge, the scowl on his face menacing. He looked Tunbridge directly in the eyes. "Are you now a friend of the Virginians?" he asked.

"No," Tunbridge snapped, and he stepped aside. "Take him and be damned."

Cotetoy stepped into the cabin, knife drawn, and approached Joseph. The old woman at the table stood up. "Don't kill him in my house," she said. Cotetoy took hold of Joseph's arm and dragged him outside where ten other Chickamauga men waited, all holding knives or war clubs. Cotetoy's old mother was there with them. The old woman inside the house had followed, and standing in the doorway, yelled, "Don't do it there, either. That's the path I use to carry water."

Cotetoy scoffed. "We'll take him to Running Water," he said, "and we'll have some fun with him there. Take off his clothes."

They stripped Joseph naked and started walking down the trail. Tunbridge yelled after them. "Young Tom will be seeing you," he said. They had not walked far down the trail when Cotetoy called a halt. They stopped, and the others all looked toward him. He stood a moment in deep thought.

"We can't kill this little boy," he said at last. "If I kill this little boy who belongs to Young Tom, then Young Tom will kill the black woman I took from the boat. My wife wants that black woman to wait on her."

Cotetoy's mother stepped up behind Joseph, pulled a knife from her belt, grabbed a handful of Joseph's hair and hacked it loose. "I'll have his hair at least," she said, and all the men laughed. Then Cotetoy took hold of Joseph and led him roughly back to Tunbridge's cabin.

"Tunbridge," he shouted at the door, "I brought back your son's little boy, I don't want to make your son mad at me. I love this little white boy. I'll come back later to make friends with him."

# 15

The Franklin settlement at Muscle Shoals was substantial, and the Chickamaugans approached it in large numbers. Dragging Canoe himself led them. Also with them were Bloody Fellow, Doublehead, John Watts, Bob Benge, McDonald, Young Canoe, Young Tom Tunbridge, and others. They moved in quietly to surround the entire settlement. Several cabins surrounded a small fort. A few of the cabins had been completed, but the rest, like the wall around the fort, were still under construction. The Chickamaugans crept in closer until they were at the edge of the surrounding woods. From somewhere inside the fort, a dog barked. The horizon to the east was showing a tinge of pink.

Dragging Canoe sounded the call of the male turkey, and dozens of other voices joined in as the Chickamaugans rushed out of the woods. Some charged the cabins and banged at the doors to try to break them open. Others ran straight to the walls of the fort. Some climbed the walls, and some battered at the gate, even though still others had found the gaps in the unfinished wall and had already run inside. Still others set fire to the wall. Cries of surprise and fear came from inside the cabins and inside the fort. Desperate shouted commands were called out, but the defenders were too disoriented to obey. Chickamaugans broke open the gate, and Dragging Canoe, Young Canoe, and others ran into the courtyard of the fort. They found some half-dressed settlers who had been trying to hold the gate. The Chickamaugans fell on them with their war clubs. From a small cabin inside the walls a settler took aim and fired. A Chickamauga next to Dragging Canoe clutched at a gaping hole in his chest and fell forward.

Dragging Canoe ran for the man who had fired the shot. The man grabbed his rifle, now useless except as a club, by the barrel and swung it at Dragging Canoe. Dragging Canoe ducked under the rifle and came up clutching the man's throat with his left hand. The man dropped his rifle and with both hands tried to pry loose the fingers that were choking him. He fell back against the wall of the cabin. Dragging Canoe raised high his steel tomahawk and brought it down hard and swiftly and split the man's skull.

He turned looking for another victim. He saw a rifle in the hands of a settler aimed at him, and he sprang to one side just as the rifle ball thudded into the log wall behind him. Then he saw Young Canoe come up behind the rifleman, grab him around the throat with one arm, and plunge a knife into the man's back with his other hand. He felt a quick moment of pride in his son. The world became a swirl of violent confusion and uncontrollable passion, a haze of smoke and blood, a cacophony of screams, rifle shots, crackling flames and thuds, and a beautiful stench of fresh blood, burnt powder, burning wood and burning flesh. Then it was over.

Joseph Brown, his head shaved except for a scalp lock, wearing a leather skirt that hung nearly to his knees and a shirt that hung down about the same length, was hoeing the corn. He was involved in his work and was almost at the end of a row before he happened to look up and see the young Indian lurking there. He could tell in an instant that the young man meant him no good. He held a war club. When Joseph saw him, the young man raised the club and moved toward Joseph. Joseph dropped his hoe, turned and ran as hard as he could back to the cabin of Tom Tunbridge. Close to the cabin door, the young man gave up his pursuit. Joseph went inside, gasping for breath.

Tunbridge and his old woman were seated at the table drinking coffee. "What's wrong?" the old woman asked.

"A boy just tried to kill me," Joseph said.

"A boy?" said Tunbridge.

"Well," said Joseph, "a young man, I guess. He was hiding at the end of the corn row, and when I got close to him, he came at me with a tomahawk."

"I guess you don't know his name," Tunbridge said.

"No," Joseph said. "In fact, I don't think I ever seen him before. I'll know him if I ever see him again, though."

Tunbridge stood up with a moan and walked over to the wall. He reached up and took a knife in a scabbard off a shelf. He walked over to Joseph and handed him the knife. "Carry this," he said. "Use it to defend yourself if you have to."

"Well, I don't understand," Joseph said.

"Don't understand what?" asked Tunbridge.

"Can these different men and boys just keep on trying to kill me and nobody do nothing about it?"

"Come over here and sit down," Tunbridge said. Joseph, carrying his new knife, moved to the table and sat across from old Tunbridge. "We're the Real People, Joseph," he said. "I know I'm a white man, but I've lived here a long time, and I've been adopted by a clan. We're the Real People. What does that make you?"

Joseph shrugged. "I don't know," he said. "I'm a white man."

"You're not a Real Person," said Tunbridge. "Our laws are only for Real People. It's against our law for one of us to kill another Real Person. There ain't no law against killing someone else, someone who's not a Real Person. You see?"

"Well, yeah," said Joseph. "I guess so."

"Suppose I come across some Real Person trying to kill you," Tunbridge explained further, "and in trying to stop him, I killed him. Well, it wouldn't have nothing to do with you or who you are or none of that. I'd have killed another Real Person, and that's all anyone would consider. His people, his clan, would come to kill me to set things right. If they couldn't find me or couldn't catch me, they'd kill someone else from my clan. They'd kill him in my place."

"The only thing that kept you alive that first day you was here, the only thing that kept old Cotetoy from killing you—it wasn't me, it was the thought that Young Tom would get even with him by killing his black slave. Now you carry that knife with you wherever you go, and I'll find another boy to go with you. A Real Person."

Joseph agreed. Of course, there was nothing else he could do.

It took him four months to get around to it, but Little John Sevier led his troops again into the peaceful Overhills Cherokee towns. He was determined to avenge the attack on the Muscle Shoals settlement, a place that had been under the command of his younger brother Valentine. Valentine had survived the attack, miraculously, but the Cherokee victory was a severe blow to the big ego of Little John Sevier. It was a blow against his state of Franklin, against his family, and against him personally. He would exact terrible revenge, and in his twisted mind, one Cherokee was still the same as another. It would always be so to Little Sevier. Besides, the Overhills towns were such easy targets, easy victories, for the innocent people there, not expecting any attacks, would be, as before, taken completely by surprise.

Like others before him, and like himself on his previous excursion into the Cherokee Overhills, Sevier burned several towns on his way to Echota, and he and his frontiersmen killed a few Cherokees, those too old or too weak to run for their lives, but before approaching Echota, he gave a surprising command. "We will not attack 'Chota," he said. "We will instead demand its surrender. I want those two old chiefs alive. You hear me? I want Old Tassel and I want Hanging Maw."

Echota gave them no resistance. A white flag flew in front of the townhouse, and Sevier rode boldly into the heart of the sacred town, leading his entire troop of Franklin militiamen. Old Tassel and Hanging Maw, side by side, stepped out to meet them. There were few other people in the town, the majority of the population having fled before the approaching invasion. "Why have you attacked our towns?" Old Tassel said. "We've done nothing to you."

"No," said Sevier, "you've done nothing. But your young men have murdered many of my people."

"Some young men have attacked settlers who were living illegally on our land," Hanging Maw said. "We have that right by treaty."

"The people who were killed were living on my land," Sevier said. "The sovereign state of Franklin. And lately your bloodthirsty warriors savagely attacked the new settlement of peaceful, God-fearing people at Muscle Shoals. My settlement. They totally destroyed it and killed many good and innocent white people. They killed Colonel Christian."

"It was not me or my people who did that," Old Tassel said. "It was Dragging Canoe and the Chickamaugans. They are no longer a part of this nation. They have among them some British who urge them to continue the late war, and we have no control of them. They are not my people that spilled the blood and spoiled the good talks. The people in my town here are not with Dragging Canoe. They will use you well whenever they see you. The men that did the murders are bad and no warriors. They live at the mouth of the Holston River. They have done the murders. My brother Colonel Christian was a good man and took care of everybody. I loved Colonel Christian and he loved me."

"You're a lying, treacherous old snake," Sevier said.

"I don't lie," Old Tassel protested. "We here in the Overhills are peaceful people."

"So you say," Sevier said. "Nevertheless, you're now my prisoners." He glanced quickly over at Major James Hubbard, sitting next to him. "Hubbard," he said, "I'm riding on to Hiwassee to burn it to the ground. Keep twenty men here with you and—take care of these—chiefs. Catch up with us at Hiwassee."

Sevier turned his mount and led the main part of his troop out of Echota. As the last horse rode out of town, Hubbard said, "Four of you—lay hold of them." Four men dismounted and quickly moved around behind the two old chiefs. Before they knew what was happening, each of the chiefs had a Franklinite holding each of his arms. They struggled, but in vain.

"What are you doing?" Old Tassel said.

Hubbard slowly dismounted. He walked around behind the old chiefs. He drew out of his belt a steel war ax, and he sank the blade deep into the skull of Hanging Maw. As the old man sagged in the arms of his captors, Hubbard tried in vain to pull the war ax loose. "Ah, shit," he said. He gave it up and stepped behind Old Tassel.

"We stayed here to meet with you and have a talk," said Old Tassel. "We could have run away. Instead we put up the white flag and waited here for you. What you're doing is bad."

Hubbard drew the pistol out of his belt and held it by the barrel. He brought the butt of the pistol down hard on Old Tassel's head. The old man moaned, and Hubbard hit him again. He struck again and again until the head was bashed in and the brains splattered out on himself and on the two men who were still holding up the lifeless body.

"So much for the Cherokee chiefs," he said. "Let's mount up and catch up with Sevier."

Leaving the bodies of the two chiefs lying on the ground in front of the few remaining astonished and horrified residents of Echota, Hubbard and the others raced their mounts out of town. Lashing their beasts, they reached the small town of Ustally, a few miles south, on the way to Hiwassee. It was there they caught up with Sevier. He and the rest of his Franklin militia were on a rise looking down onto the town. Hubbard's men fell in line, and Hubbard rode up beside Sevier.

"You caught up in good time, Mr. Hubbard," Sevier said. "The old chiefs?"

"Their brains are on the ground feeding flies," Hubbard said.

"Good," Sevier said. He nodded toward the town below. "We'll take this one out, too," he added. "It's right on the way."

Down in Ustally, a woman looked up to see the dreaded militiamen charging fast down the hill toward town. "White men are attacking," she shouted. Just then, Bob Benge, visiting Ustally at the home of his brother Martin, came running around a corner of the house to look. His red hair gleaming in the sun, Benge began shouting directions to the people. "Get out of town," he said. "Follow me into the woods." Five Cherokee men grabbed up their weapons and prepared to meet the attack, to slow down the militiamen while the others got into the safety of the woods. The rest of the people in town followed Benge.

When Sevier's men broke into the town, the five men fought hard and killed a few, but they were soon overcome. Some stragglers were then spotted by Sevier, and the Franklinites raced after them. One man leaned down from his horse and grabbed a small boy. The boy kicked and struggled, but the man held him fast. A woman just entering the thick woods was shot in the back and fell dead. From the woods, a few Cherokees fired back at the militiamen, slowing their pursuit, while at the same time other Franklinites raced through the town setting torches to the houses.

Soon the firing had stopped. Sevier, wild-eyed, his horse prancing, proudly surveyed the results of his vandalism. Every house in Ustally was in flames. He rode along the edge of the woods until he located a path wide enough for his horses. "This way," he shouted, and he led his men into the woods. The fleeing Cherokees were not on the path, he knew, but he estimated their direction of flight. He would catch up to them soon enough. Back behind him, the man with the Cherokee boy dropped the boy to the ground and raised his pistol. He fired a shot into the boy's head.

"That was just a child," an astonished companion said.

"Nits make lice," the killer said, and he rode gleefully after Sevier and the others.

Benge paused in his flight through the woods. His brother Martin stepped up beside him. "They're coming through the woods on the path," he said. "Some of the people behind us saw them and heard them. We should change our direction, or they'll catch up to us at the mouth of Valley River."

"That's an idea," Benge said. "Let them catch up to us there."

"What do you mean?" his brother asked.

"I'll take some fighting men on down to Valley River and wait for them there," Benge said. "We'll give them a surprise. You lead the others on in a safe direction."

Sevier held up his troops just before they were to ride on down to the river. "They'll be coming out down there," he said. "Scout it out, Mr. Hubbard. See if there's good cover for us to lay in ambush for them."

Twenty men followed Hubbard down to the water's edge. Some of them rode in one direction, some in the other. Hubbard sat still, studying the foliage on the other side of the river. A man rode up beside him. "Over there," Hubbard said. "There's good cover. We can crawl in there and wait. When the savages come along, it'll be like swatting flies. Ride back and tell Sevier."

Then from across the river, there was a flash and then a pop, and the man to whom Hubbard had been speaking howled in pain. Blood ran freely from a fresh hole in his right shoulder. Another shot sounded, and a man downriver from Hubbard dropped from his horse and splashed into the river and lay still. His blood colored the clear water around his body. Then the eerie sound of the turkey call seemed to come from all around. More shots were fired. Hubbard and the others turned their frightened and neighing horses and raced them back up the hill toward Sevier, running into one another, crowding one another off the road, knocking one another over. Hubbard himself was knocked out of his saddle, but scrambled to his feet and ran the rest of the way on foot.

"Ambush," he screamed. "Ambush."

"Retreat," Sevier called out, and turned his own mount around, but he was unable to lead his inglorious retreat, for those who had been behind him were already racing back toward the burned ruins of Ustally. Sevier chased his band of cowards back up the path through the woods.

Across the river from behind his protective brush, Bob Benge looked at the man next to him. "It seems Little John has no taste for fighting," he said, "when he's facing fighting men." He thought for a moment, studying the two loose horses that milled around on the other side of the river. "You and the others join Martin and the rest of the people," he said. "I'm taking a horse and going for help."

At Ustally, or what was left of it, Sevier at last managed to regain control of his undisciplined militia. Hubbard got himself rehorsed, and once again he sat beside his commanding officer in front of the ragged formation. "Let's ride," Sevier said.

"Where to?" Hubbard asked.

"On to Hiwassee, of course," Sevier answered. "We still have work to do."

Bob Benge rode hard. He wanted desperately to get someplace where he could raise a sufficient army to counter Sevier's attacking militia, but the only place he could do that was in the towns near Dragging Canoe. It was a long ride. Even if he could get there, raise the men, and return with them before Sevier was safely away, Sevier would have time to do serious damage to several more towns. Benge lashed viciously at his captured horse. He would ride it to death if need be.

The Chickamaugans had been relatively inactive since the big battle at Muscle Shoals. It was time to get out again and let the squatters know that they were still not wanted. Reports of new cabins and new settlements seemed to come every day. And so John Watts had raised four hundred men from the Chickamauga towns and was riding toward the illegal settlements. He was leading his army along at a leisurely pace. There was no sense in wearing out the horses before they'd even reached a place to fight. Then he saw a lone rider coming hard at them. He halted his column and waited. Soon Bob Benge rode up and jerked his horse to a stop.

"I'm glad to see you," Benge panted. "They're burning the Overhills towns."

"Who is it?" Watts asked. "Do you know?"

"No," said Benge. "I don't know for sure, but I think it's the damned Franklinites. Who else?"

"Little John Sevier," Watts said. "How many men?"

"Two hundred," said Benge. "Maybe more."

"Where are they now?"

"When I left," said Benge, "they were going back to Ustally, but they had already burned it. They probably went from there to Hiwassee. After that, who knows?"

Watts looked back over his shoulder. "Someone give Benge a fresh horse," he said. "We have to ride fast now."

Hubbard stood at the blazing edge of a vast field of corn, a torch in his hand. He looked up at Sevier, who was watching from his horse's back. "There must be a hundred acres here," he said. "This could take all day."

"Burn it all," Sevier said. Just then a rider came pounding up hard beside him.

"Colonel," he said, "there's four hundred Indians coming from the south."

"Four hundred?" Sevier said. "Are you sure?"

"Mounted and armed," the man said. "It's a goddamned army."

"Coming this way?" Sevier asked.

"Right at us," said the man.

"Mr. Hubbard," Sevier called out. "Get the men ready to ride. We're getting the hell out of here."

Riding ahead of the others as scout, Bob Benge saw the fleeing Franklinites. They were already too far ahead for pursuit. He watched them for a moment, then turned to ride back and report to Watts. When Watts saw him coming, and not hurrying, he led his troops on casually to meet with Benge. "Little John, or who-ever it was," said Benge, "must have seen us coming. He's showing us his ass. The coward."

The Overhills survivors moved south into lands claimed by Georgia, and they built new towns near Dragging Canoe. The new capital of the Cherokee Nation was established there, and they called it Ustanali, a natural barrier of rocks across a stream. They named Little Turkey the new Principal Chief of the Cherokee Nation, but Little Turkey and others of influence spent much of their time seeking the advice of Dragging Canoe. Dragging Canoe was pleased to have the Cherokee Nation back together again. He was glad to call all of the Cherokees Real People again at last. And he considered his new and powerful position among his people. Like his father before him, he had become one of the most important men in the Cherokee Nation. He had become, perhaps, the most important man among his people. With a keen sense of irony, he thought, This is what Little John Sevier has done for us.

He sat in front of his house smoking Sacred Tobacco in a clay pipe with a short river-cane stem. It was a still day, and the thick white smoke hovered around his head. The taste and the smell of the smoke were good, and though it was rising slowly, it would rise, and it would carry his thoughts to the spirits at the Seventh Height on the other side of the great Sky Vault, there where the one Great Spirit, the Apportioner, the God over all gods, resides.

The fire in the pipe bowl went out just before McDonald came walking up to his house. Dragging Canoe stood and took the Englishman by the hand. "Welcome, my friend," he said.

"I've come with news," McDonald said. "Some of our scouts have seen a large army of white militiamen coming at us from east of Lookout Mountain."

"Then there is but one way they can get to us," Dragging Canoe said. "They have to come through the pass over Lookout Mountain. They're fools. Tell all the people from the new towns across the mountain to leave their towns and come here with us. Tell them to hurry. Then we'll wait for the Americans up along the pass."

From Ustanali and the other new towns, the former Overhills people flocked across the Lookout Mountain trail watched over by Dragging Canoe, John Watts, and others. Other Chickamaugans scouted, bringing back reports on the progress of the large militia force. While awaiting the arrival of the American force, Dragging Canoe and John Watts deployed their men. About halfway up the trail was a wide flat, towered over on each side by nearly sheer cliffs. At the base of the cliffs, on either side of the flat, were large boulders. From behind the boulders the Chickamaugans could command a view not only of the flat but of the trail below. There they waited.

Young Canoe slipped through the rocks to his father's side. "The Americans are in the town below," he said. "It looks like most of them will stay there, but some are coming up the trail—about a hundred, I guess. They're all mounted."

"Good," said Dragging Canoe.

They waited a while. Then as the first of the mounted one hundred rode onto the flat, the Chickamaugans fired. Several militiamen in the front rank fell from their horses. Right behind them, men turned their mounts in sudden desperation. In their undisciplined flight, they ran into their companions just behind them. Horses reared and neighed and men fell out of their saddles onto the trail. There were shouts and curses. Soon all the American militiamen who hadn't been killed had fled in disarray back down the mountain.

No more movement came from the deserted town below Lookout Mountain all that day. The militiamen had set up camp for the night there, it seemed. John Watts posted lookouts to watch the town, but the night too was quiet. The bold attackers apparently had had enough for the time being.

The Americans sent another small force with first morning light, but at the base of the mountain a larger force lay in wait. When the advance troop reached the flat, the Chickamaugans fired on them as they had the evening before. The results were much the same, except that the larger troop waiting at the base of the mountain, hearing the gunfire, started moving up. They ran into their own fleeing men about halfway up. In the meantime, up on the flat, the Chickamaugans fell back and took up a new position.

The Americans dismounted then and moved onto the flat more cautiously, one of the men who had previously fled being up front. "This is the spot," he whispered to his commander. "Steady, men," the commander said. Each militiaman had a gun in hand ready for the expected attack. All was quiet. There was nothing. They kept moving, slowly, kept watching the rocks on either side. Nothing happened. At last they stopped there on the flat. "They're gone," said the commander.

"We've scared them off," said another, and his boastful announcement was followed by a round of cheers. At last the commander managed to restore some order in his ranks. "Mount up," he said. "We're going to pursue the devils." The men all climbed back into their saddles, and the commander shouted, "Forward," motioning with his right arm, and they moved forward at a gallop, confident that the frightened and running Chickamaugans would be easily cut down. Shortly, however, the way grew steep and narrow, and they were forced to slow their pace. They were still riding between steep rocks on either side of the mountain road. All of a sudden, the air was split by the sound of a male turkey, and rifle shots followed immediately. Militiamen fell from their horses. Some, running on foot, tripped and rolled. Total confusion reigned in the ranks. The flight back down the mountain was both inglorious and undisciplined.

### October 1787

John Watts rode at the head of a large party of Cherokee and Creek Chickamaugans. Dragging Canoe had sent out several detachments in different directions. The relatively small group of Americans at the garrison at Gillespie's Station was surprised and quickly overpowered. A few prisoners were taken, and a few more escaped into the woods. Twenty-seven lay dead in and around the cabin. While some in his band searched the garrison for booty and some took the scalps of the dead, John Watts surveyed the situation.

He looked over the dead and saw that women and children were among them. It saddened him that war could not be made cleanly between grown, fighting men. Looking around the room inside the garrison cabin, he saw a desk, and on the desk, paper and ink and quill. He moved over to the desk, pulled out the chair and sat down. He spread a clean sheet of paper out on the desk, picked up the quill and dipped it into the ink. Then he wrote.

*To Whoever It May Consern;*

*We, who you know as Chickamoggies, have this day attacked and destroied this Gallespys Station. I deeply regret that in the prosess wimmen and children were killed. However, remember that we are at war, and your own peepel have treacheruosly killed our chiefs under a white flag. We do not want this war anymore than you, and when you move off of our land, then we will all have peace.*

*John Watts*

Watts took the letter outside and stabbed it to the door with a knife taken from one of the bodies. A man was coming at the cabin with a torch. "Don't burn this cabin," Watts said. "I want them to find this letter."

Once again Sevier called together his militia, moving so swiftly that he took the Chickamauga town of Coosawatie completely by surprise. They killed some Chickamaugans, including some women and children, but they did exercise a bit of restraint. Sevier had insisted that they obtain a sufficient number of prisoners to exchange for American prisoners held by the Chickamaugans. The prisoners were rudely shoved into a bunch, rifles and swords pointed at them. They expected to be slaughtered at any moment. Sevier rode his horse through the ranks of his own men and looked down on the Indian prisoners. "Who among you can speak English?" he demanded.

There was a long pause. Then a man stepped forward, a young man who appeared to be of mixed blood. "I speak English," he said.

"Do you know where to find John Watts?" Sevier asked.

"You can kill me," the man said. "I won't tell you."

"I didn't ask you to tell me," Sevier said. "I asked if you know where to find him."

"I know," the man said.

"I want you to take a message to him," said Sevier. "You'll not be followed."

The messenger found John Watts visiting with Dragging Canoe. "Sevier is in Coosawatie," he said. "He's wiped out the town. He has a large army there. He did not kill everyone. He took many captive. Then he told me to come to you with a message."

The man was addressing Watts, so Dragging Canoe sat back and studied the situation in silence. "What was the message?" said Watts.

"He wants to trade prisoners," the man said. "He said if we make the trade, he won't attack again. He'll just ride out."

Watts looked at Dragging Canoe.

"What do you think?" he asked.

"We have to try to save our people," Dragging Canoe said. "But I don't trust Sevier."

"What should we do, then?" Watts asked.

"You take my brother and Benge and get all of our American prisoners together," said Dragging Canoe. "Get ready to take them to Sevier. I'll get our young men together. We'll go to the mountains overlooking Coosawatie. If Sevier tries to break his word, we'll be ready to fight him."

Watts and Benge, accompanied by another eighteen men, walked into the ruins of Coosawatie with a group of American prisoners. Joseph Brown was one of the prisoners, as were his two oldest sisters. As prisoners were exchanged, Joseph was shoved toward Sevier. "Where's my little sister?" he said. Sevier looked at Watts. "Well?" he said.

"Leach, the man who has the little girl, refused to give her up," Watts said.

"I won't go without her," Joseph said.

"We must have her," Sevier said. "Without her, we have no deal."

"I'll fetch her here," Benge said. "Or I'll bring back Leach's head."

Benge found a horse and rode away fast. The final count of prisoners on both sides was made, and Sevier, taking note of the large number of Chickamaugans on the nearby ridge, agreed that once the little Brown girl was returned, their business would be satisfactorily concluded. He was noticeably nervous.

Watts took out a short-stemmed pipe, loaded its bowl with tobacco, and stepped over to a still-smoldering house. He found a burning stick with a cold end, picked it up and lit his pipe, looking the while at Sevier. "So, Little John," he said, "what will you do if the little girl cannot be brought?" He glanced up at the ridge. "Will we fight?"

"We shall see," said Sevier. "When the time comes, we shall see."

In a short while Benge came riding back up, holding in his arms in front of him Joseph Brown's little sister. Joseph ran to her, and Benge let her down into her brother's arms. The exchange ended peacefully, and Sevier and his army, taking the freed captives, rode back out the way they had come.

Franklinites continued to move onto Cherokee land under the blessing of John Sevier in his posture as Governer of the state of Franklin, and the Chickamaugans continued to raid the illegal settlements. Americans were killed, scalps were taken, more prisoners were taken. Sevier's militia retaliated, and Cherokee towns and fields were destroyed. Cherokees were killed. It still did not seem to matter to Sevier whether or not they were Chickamaugans.

"The American government, it seems," McDonald was saying, "has laid all the troubles along the frontier at the feet of John Sevier. His state of Franklin is declared to be illegal, and he himself has been declared an outlaw. The government wants to make a new treaty with the Cherokees. They want you to be there. Will you go?"

"I'll go," said Dragging Canoe, "to hear what they have to say. They can arrest Sevier for what he's done. That's all right. But will they get the white men off my land? That's what I want to know. But

McDonald, we know that the English are in Canada. I don't believe that they've really given up the fight. And I'll never make peace with the Americans as long as the English are still on this soil."

### July 2, 1791

Twelve hundred Cherokees gathered there at Holston. Among them were forty chiefs. Little Turkey was there as Principal Chief of the Cherokee Nation, and many were surprised that the Chickamaugans were well represented. Bloody Fellow, Double-head, Lying Fawn, John Watts, and Dragging Canoe himself showed up. Dragging Canoe was skeptical, but he listened.

The treaty, when concluded, made the same declaration of perpetual peace and friendship as had the previous one. It included the same promises to keep whites off Cherokee land. It reasserted the exclusive right of the United States to regulate trade with the Cherokees. And it reestablished the boundaries of the Cherokee Nation. The United States also promised to furnish the Cherokees with instruments of husbandry to turn them from hunters into farmers.

"Whose fields and orchards do they think they've been destroying all these years?" Dragging Canoe asked his son. "So now they will teach us how to farm."

He listened with keen interest when the boundaries were described. By signing this document, the Cherokees would be giving up more land, for the boundaries had been changed again. In the end, however, they signed the treaty. John Watts even signed it, as did Bloody Fellow, Middle Striker, Otter Lifter, and Double-head. Auquotague, the son of Little Turkey, signed. But neither signatures nor marks were on the paper for Little Turkey himself or for Dragging Canoe.

"I don't consider that paper to be worth anything," Dragging Canoe said to McDonald back in Running Water. "I didn't sign it and neither did Little Turkey. The Americans keep grabbing more and more of our land, and I mean to drive them back or kill them.

I'm getting old now, and the younger men will have to take over when I'm gone. John Watts, Bob Benge, my son Young Canoe, Bowl, Doublehead, and Bloody Fellow. These men will have to lead the way. But while I still have energy, I mean to visit all the nations of red men and seek again to establish the alliance we attempted before."

It had been a long and tiring trip, but Dragging Canoe felt good about it. He was certain that he had gained the hearts of many of the people he visited. It would be a strong alliance. Among the Shawnees, Tecumseh especially had been pleased to see him again and to hear what he had to say. Tecumseh had sworn to do everything in his power to support the cause, and he had grown into a very capable young man, influential among his own people. Dragging Canoe was now fifty-five years old, and he had been fighting almost all his life. He was tired, but he felt good. The alliance was the only way to hold the greedy Americans back, and he had made a good start on it. He asked for an Eagle Dance to be held at Running Water to celebrate the success of his mission and the peace he had established among the various tribes.

The dancers lined up on the dance ground, the women in one line and the men in another. They faced each other across the ground. Each man carried a gourd rattle in his left hand. Men and women held eagle feather wands, each made of a sourwood rod with an arched piece near the end. To the arch were attached five feathers from the tail of a bald eagle. The lead woman wore shackles of turtle-shell rattles strapped to her calves.

In a preliminary movement, in response to a call by the dance leader, the dancers all took a step in and then another back out. Then they circled the dance ground going from east to north to west to south and back again to the east. They were ready for the first period of the dance. As the leader sang the words, they circled the fire, shaking the wands, the men shaking their rattles, the lead woman dancer stomping rhythmically to shake the rattles on the shackles tied to her calves. They continued until the song came to an end. For the second period of the dance, they crouched and jumped, men and women circling the fire in opposite directions.

The third period was a pipe dance, and the men and women again lined up facing one another. To the beat of a drum, they stepped toward one another, waved the wands over their partners' heads, and stepped back again. Then they changed positions and repeated the entire dance again. For the second movement, they again stepped toward one another, then back, but this time they stepped back a distance of ten paces, then circled the dance ground in opposite directions, changing places as they finished the circle. For the third movement, the men and women turned their backs on one another. Except for that, their movements were the same as the previous movement of the dance.

Finally, the men and women formed a single line, men first and women following carrying baskets to symbolize the feeding of the eagle to pay for his feathers. When the dance at last ended, the leader collected the wands. The people continued to dance, however, with only their rattles. Dragging Canoe had danced all night long with the others, all through the eagle dance. He was tired, but exhilarated. He continued to dance the social dances with the others.

When the dancing at last broke up, and the Sun was crawling out from under the eastern edge of the Sky Vault, slowly lighting up the eastern horizon with bloody reds, Dragging Canoe, exhausted, panting, walked alone to his house. Approaching the door, he felt a sudden sharp pain in his chest. He sucked air, but he stepped inside out of anyone's view before he clutched at his chest and nearly doubled over with the pain. He staggered the few steps to his bed and collapsed heavily on it. He lay there a moment trying to catch his breath, and the pain continued to shoot through his weary body. He had felt pain before, many times, but this was a different kind of pain. This was something else.

There was something talking to him, and he knew that it was his time to go away. He wished for a brief moment that he could stay around just long enough to see the end result of all his hard work, but he told himself that the alliance had been formed. He told himself that Young Canoe, Benge, Watts, Bowl, and the others would carry on in his place. He thought of all the fights he had been in, and he knew that he had fought and killed for a just cause. Apparently he was not meant to see the finish. His work was done. He considered briefly the things he had heard about the white man's heaven, but his mind quickly threw away those thoughts. He knew that he would be going west to the Darkening Land on the other side of the Great Sky Vault. He thought of his father, Ada-gal'kala. He thought of his mother. He thought of his young wife and his more recent lover. He would see them all once again. He knew that they were all up there already just waiting for him to arrive. Suddenly and unexpectedly, he was anxious to go. And then, gradually and calmly, he drifted away into darkness. The last thing he saw was the eagle circling high in the sky, soaring peacefully above the high, high clouds.

PART FIVE

# The Falling Apart

# 16

John Watts and many of the other Chickamaugans had traveled to Echota for a council with the other Cherokees there, the main body of the Cherokee Nation. Watts hoped to unite all the Cherokees once again. They gathered in the townhouse where the benches all were quickly filled, and people stood around the walls and sat on the floor. When there was no more room inside, others huddled at the doorway. Those who could not get close enough to hear waited anxiously, stretching their necks in the back of the crowd outside, hoping for someone near the doorway to pass the news along to them through the crowd. Inside, Watts was addressing the huge gathering.

"We met with the Spanish governor at Pensacola," he said, "I, Young Canoe, Ata-lunti-ski, my brother Whitekiller, and others. The governor reminded us that the Spanish have never coveted our land, and that the treacherous Americans murdered our chiefs, Old Tassel and Hanging Maw, even as they flew a white flag and sued for peace. He urged us to continue to make war on the cowardly Americans, and to that end, he gave us several pack loads of good ammunition and arms. He assured us that the supplies will continue in sufficient numbers to fill our needs."

"John Watts is talking for war," someone outside said in a whisper.

"Guhna-geski?" someone asked.

"Yes," said the other. "He wants all Cherokees to join him in this. He wants us to declare war on the Americans."

The crowd murmured until one near the door said in a harsh whisper, "Hush, Bloody Fellow is going to speak." Then they grew silent again. Inside the townhouse, Watts took a seat as Bloody Fellow moved to the speaker's spot.

The man at the doorway listened closely, then whispered to the others outside. "Bloody Fellow is talking for peace," he said. "He thinks there has been too much fighting, and he doesn't like the Spaniards. He thinks that we should all make friends with the Americans."

They listened until Bloody Fellow had said everything he wanted to say and stepped down. Then the Shawnee Warrior stood to speak.

"The five Chickamauga towns," he said, "under the leadership of John Watts, Guhna-geski, have just determined to make war on the Americans. Although I am a Shawnee, formerly your enemy, I am now a part of the Chickamaugans, I and my three hundred men, drawn to join in this cause by the great Dragging Canoe. How can you Cherokees sit back and do nothing when even we Shawnees are joining with your own brothers in this war?" He paused, stretched out his arms, and opened his hands wide. "With these two bloody hands," he continued, "I have killed three hundred Americans, and I will kill three hundred more, drink my fill of blood and sit down and be happy."

Outside, lurking in the shadows at a safe distance behind the crowd, a trader from Tennessee stood listening. Hearing at last that war had been declared, though he could not tell by whom exactly, he fell back farther, then hurried to his horse to mount up and ride all night to carry the dreadful news.

John Watts stepped into the circular dance station about two hundred yards from the main dance ground at the Chickamauga town of Dakwai, on the north bank of the Tennessee River. He stood, rifle in hand, facing the east, and raising his rifle high over his head, he called out in Cherokee for the other male dancers to join him in the dance they called *aga-hoði*, meaning "big foreheads in motion." It was the dance that celebrated the appearance of the green corn, known to those white people who knew anything at all as the Green Corn Dance. Twenty men, also carrying rifles, whooped and ran into the circle in a single file, ready to follow Watts.

Watts, looking at the ground in front of him, began to walk around the circle. He moved from east to north to west to south and back to the place from which he had begun. The other twenty all followed him. Watts began to sing and to dance with a shuffling step. He moved in the same circle as before, and the others followed him as before. A man outside the circle shook a gourd rattle. Watt's timing was perfect, for as he finished his song, he stopped dancing at just the point where he had started, and then he fired his rifle into the air. Then the man behind him fired, and the next and the next until all twenty men had fired their rifles, the sounds of the shots signifying thunder. The dance paused while the men reloaded their rifles.

While the men were dancing, back on the main dance ground the women danced *aða-hona*, or "make wood." The women had lined up shoulder to shoulder. Out in front of them, facing them, stood the female dance leader, wearing shackles on her calves with turtle-shell rattles. The sound the rattles made as she danced, accompanied by the drumming of a man between their group and the men's group, gave them their rhythm. The women in line shuffled toward the leader as she sang, then back. They stopped with the "thunder" of the men's group.

The men reformed, still in a circle but now dancing two abreast. John Watts stood alone in front of the line. The women lined up behind their leader. This time the leader of the women began the song and the man with the rattle and the man with the drum joined in with their rhythm. Watts led the men in a circle again, in the same direction, but when he arrived at the west he left the circle and moved toward the main dance ground. At the same time, the women circled in their space, going in the same direction as had the men. From time to time, the lead woman paused in her song to allow time for a response from Watts and the men.

As the women finished their circle they stretched their formation out into a line, standing once again shoulder to shoulder, their leader once again facing them. At the same time Watts reached the main dance ground, and the men danced in a straight line across it, north of the women, leaving on the east side, then curving to head back to their own dance station. While they were doing this, the women circled once again.

The men danced back again to the main dance ground and surrounded the women, dancing around them and slowly closing the circle, pressing the women close together. Then they moved into the women's line, a man behind each woman, and once more they circled around the dance ground. The morning dancing was over, and the dancers all stopped to join in the feast with everyone else. Whitekiller sat down beside his brother.

"You're dancing well today," he said. "Your voice is strong, too."

"I hope my voice is strong after the dance," Watts said. "I have some important things to talk about."

"The people always listen to you," Whitekiller said.

"Not always," said Watts. "I'm no Dragging Canoe. And the times are desperate."

"The women prepared a good feast," Whitekiller said, changing the subject.

"I don't know how they did it," said Watts. "Our fields and orchards have been destroyed so many times."

"Our hunters still do good work," said Whitekiller, "and our women know where to gather wild food that the white man is too stupid to know is food, and so does not destroy."

Watts smiled. "Yes," he said. "That's true." Then his smile faded again, and his brother could see that his mind was on something else, something very different from the dancing and feasting.

The men moved back into the circle of their dance station, and the women gathered again on the main dance ground. The man with the rattle stood just outside the main ground, near to the women. He began with his rattle, then started singing. The drummer was silent. When the women's leader began to dance, the sound of her rattles joined with that of the man. Watts and the other men had shouldered arms. They danced in a circle as before, then moved out of their space and down into the main dance ground. As before, they encircled the women and closed in, eventually joining them, a man behind each woman, and they danced in a large circle. As they circled and zigzagged, the singer with the rattle moved into the circle and took the lead. This was called *ganona*, or "on the trail," and it lasted until sundown.

The rest of the night, those who wanted to continue danced various animal dances: the bear dance, the beaver dance, the buffalo dance, the pigeon dance, the partridge dance, the groundhog dance, and the pissant dance. They danced the friendship dance, too, and just before sunup, they danced the corn dance and finished with the running dance. Then it was over. People went to their houses and put out their fires. Then they went to the townhouse and got new fire to take home from the fire that burned there.

John Watts knew that they were not keeping the ceremony quite as the people had done years before. Even he could tell that it had changed in his lifetime. He wondered what further changes were coming to the Cherokee people. And he knew that his own mind had not been on the ceremony, certainly had not been on its purpose. He was even glad to have it over with and done. He felt a little guilty about that. He would not say that out loud to anyone, but he did admit the fact to himself, and in making that admission, perhaps, he thought, he was also admitting that he was at least a part of the reason for the changes. But he excused himself by saying that he had more important things on his mind. They were fighting for their lives. He remembered when Dragging Canoe had said that they must fight to keep from being wiped out as a people. He felt as if he were still following that great man.

Having danced all night, most of the men slept much of the next day away. Watts, although he too had stayed awake all night, was frustrated. He had serious business to talk over with the people, especially the fighting men. It was evening, though, before he could get many of them together. He looked over the small crowd and was disappointed that he did not see his own brother there. He wondered where Whitekiller might be, but decided not to wait any longer, and so began the meeting without him.

He talked about the declaration of war that had been made in Echota and how Echota had been ambiguous on that issue, not agreeing or adding their voices, and yet not condemning or openly arguing against the Chickamauga decision. "Some of the people there may later join with us," he said, "but the chief said nothing." He told them that they should strike the Americans soon and on several different fronts at the same time. That way, an American force raised in retaliation would not know where to look for them. He thought that they should leave the next morning, but then Whitekiller came back, and he brought with him a keg of whiskey.

"Let's celebrate," he called out. "Let's have some fun."

The young men grabbed up what they could find at nearby houses to drink from as Whitekiller bashed in the lid of the keg. He dipped in his own cup, and the men without cups or gourds or bowls dipped in their cupped hands. They whooped and hollered. They laughed. One man started to dance again by himself. Another began to sing for him. A few of the women and some old men came to join in the festivities.

Whitekiller noticed his brother sitting alone, a serious look on his face. He went to a nearby house to borrow a cup. Then back at his barrel, he dipped his own and the borrowed cup into the barrel and filled them. He walked over to join John Watts and held a cup of whiskey out for him. Watts looked at it with disapproval.

"Come on, Brother," Whitekiller said, "Have some."

"I meant for all of us to ride out of here in the morning to strike the Americans," Watts said. "You've spoiled that."

"The Americans will wait another day," Whitekiller said. "And since it's spoiled, you might as well drink. Here. Take it."

Watts took the cup, and Whitekiller sat down beside him.

"I'm trying to mold an army here," Watts said. "There's no discipline among us."

"You have enough discipline for us all," Whitekiller said. "You never relax. You need to have some fun now and then. Come on. What's wrong with an army having a little fun before they fight?"

Watts sipped the burning liquid in the cup. "Ha," he said, shaking his head. Whitekiller laughed.

"Brother," Watts said, "if Dragging Canoe had been here instead of me, and you had brought this whiskey and spoiled his plans, what do you think he would have done?"

Whitekiller suddenly got a serious look on his face and he stared at his brother almost long enough to be rude. Then he looked away again. "He'd have killed me," he said. "Come on. Let's get drunk."

The drinking and feasting lasted for seven more days, and it was three more days before anyone felt like riding.

Ata-lunti-ski rode out at the head of a party of Chickamaugans to the Cumberland Road. They came across no travelers, no settlers, no bands of militia. They burned two cabins that had been evacuated. Frustrated, they rode over to the Kentucky Road. Still they encountered no travelers. They came across no camps. They found a cabin, but no one was at home, so they looted it and burned it. They found some more empty cabins and did the same. "Someone has warned all these people," one of them said. Then they saw a lone rider approaching. They waited until they could see that he was a white man. Then the man standing beside Ata-lunti-ski raised his rifle to his shoulder and fired. The white man fell in the road and several Chickamaugans raced toward the body. The one who reached it first took the scalp. Ata-lunti-ski turned his horse around, and the rest followed him back home.

Middlestriker and fifty-five men, Cherokee, Creek, and Shawnee, all Chickamauga, knew that reinforcements were headed for the Cumberland settlement. They laid a careful ambush near a place called Crab Orchard and waited. Their intelligence had been correct, for it wasn't long before they heard the approach of a group of horses. Soon after that they could see the small militia force riding toward them. They huddled in silence in the brush and behind the trees beside the road.

As the riders rode in between them, Middlestriker gave the signal, and the Chickamaugans burst out onto the road in a fierce attack, dragging militiamen from their horses' backs, hacking, stabbing. Some fired from cover, knocking riders off their mounts. The brunt of their attack had separated the leader of the militia from the rest of his men. He turned and fired into the crowd, then, realizing that there was nothing he could do except sacrifice himself foolishly, he spurred his horse ahead.

Behind him the fighting continued. Some militiamen in the rear ranks turned to retreat. A Chickamauga saw the militia leader racing away, raised his rifle and fired. The horse went down hard and the white man landed on his belly in the dirt. Middlestricker saw him fall, pulled loose his war ax, and ran for him. As the man rolled over on his back, Middlestricker dropped down on his knees astraddle the man's chest. He raised his ax. The man held a hand up and said, "Canaly."

Middlestricker hesitated. It was a peculiar thing under the circumstances for this man, in imperfect Cherokee, to call him friend. He stood up and lowered his ax. "All right, *'ginali*," he said. "Throw your weapons aside." He watched, alert, as the man on the ground slipped a knife out of his belt and tossed it away, then an ax, and finally a pistol. Middlestricker extended his left hand, and the man took it. Middlestricker pulled him to his feet.

"What's your name?" he asked.

"I'm Captain Sam Handley," the man said.

"You're my prisoner, Handley," Middlestriker said. "Come on — friend."

George Fields and John Walker both looked like white men, and they were dressed in the manner of frontier white Americans. John Watts had sent them on a spy mission to find out what they could about the number and the movement of American troops. Riding the road toward Nashville, they saw two men at a fire beside the road. They stopped their mounts.

"Hello there," said Fields.

One of the two men stood up beside the campfire. The other remained seated.

"Hello," he said. "You been riding far?"

"From Georgia," said Fields.

"Going far?" the other man said.

"Nashville," said Fields.

"We got some fresh coffee here," said the man. "Want to step down and join us?"

"Thank you," said Fields. "That's neighborly." He swung down out of his saddle, and Walker did the same. They moved over to take their spots beside the fire.

"I'm named Fields," Fields said, "and this here is Walker."

"Jones," said the man who had first spoken, extending his hand. Walker and Fields each took it. Then Jones nodded toward the other man. "This is Burkett." They shook hands with Burkett as Jones poured coffee into cups for them. Fields took a tentative sip of his. "Good," he said. "Thanks."

"You, uh, you men got business in Nashville?" Burkett asked.

"No," Fields said. "Well, not exactly. We been down in Georgia, and it's just too hot down there. Chickamoggie raids and all. We thought we'd try Nashville. We heard there was more whites up there. It might be a bit safer. You know Nashville?"

"Yeah," said Jones. "We know it. It's pretty secure."

"Well," Walker said, "what brings you down this way? You're riding right down into Chickamoggie country."

"To tell you the truth, friend," Jones said, "we're on government work for Tennessee. We're riding into Chickamoggie country to find out what we can about their strength and their intentions. You all know anything that can help us?"

"Don't know much," Walker said. "They got five towns along Chickamoggie Creek."

"We know that," Jones said.

"Their leader is a man named John Watts," Fields said. "He's half white, but he's all Chickamoggie."

"What about the Tory McDonald?" Jones asked. "Is it true that he's in contact with the Spaniards? We heard that he was made a captain or something by the Spaniards."

"I wouldn't know about that," said Fields. "But I hear he's slowing down. He's getting close to fifty years, and from what I hear, he stays pretty close to home these days. Say, can I have a little more of that coffee?"

"Sure," said Jones, reaching for the pot on the fire. Walker slipped a pistol out from under his jacket, thumbed back the hammer, pointed it at Jones's chest and fired. Jones's eyes opened wide. His hand went limp and dropped the pot into the fire. Then he slumped forward, falling into the flames.

At the same instant as Walker fired his pistol, Fields produced a steel knife and, reaching quickly across the fire, drove it into the neck of Burkett. Burkett's hands went toward the blade. He gurgled, staring at Fields, then slumped over on his side. Walker and Fields took the scalps of their two victims. Then Walker looked at Fields. "Damned spies," he said.

### September 30, 1792
### Buchanan's Station

It was near midnight when John Watts and a force of two hundred and eighty Chickamaugans moved in quietly to surround the small garrison a few miles south of Nashville. Thirty of the number were Shawness led by the Shawnee Warrior. The rest were Cherokees and Creeks. Having been warned of the impending danger, several families of white Americans had gathered inside the walls of the small fort. Even so, there were among them only about twenty fighting men.

Watts gave the signal, and the Chickamaugans raced to the stockade walls. Some carried lengths of log that they then threw up against the wall at an angle and used to climb to the top and go over. Others found niches or portholes in the wall, poked their rifle barrels through and fired. Watts was one of the first to reach the top of the wall. He swung his right leg over, and a rifle ball drove straight through both thighs. He managed to hold to the top of the wall, get his right leg back across the wall, and lower himself back down the log with his arms. Then he collapsed on the ground.

The Shawnee Warrior climbed another log, swung over and dropped to the ground on the other side. As he was straightening himself up, a settler fired a long rifle, and the ball tore into the Shawnee Warrior's chest. He fell to the ground dead. Young Tom Tunbridge, carrying a torch, came over at a different point, got safely to the ground, and ran toward the house. He climbed the log wall of the house and was setting fire to the roof when a man on the ground shot him. He dropped, then rolled off the roof. He was dead before he hit the ground.

Some of the defenders of the fort managed to get themselves up to their defensive positions on the inside of the wall. From there they fired down on the attacking Indians. The wall was in flames at several different places, as was the roof of the house. It looked as if the garrison would fall at any time. Then Watts, in pain and bleeding on the ground, saw a large body of riders coming from the direction of Nashville.

"Retreat. Retreat," he shouted. "There's an army coming at us."

It took a while for him to get the attention of all the Chickamaugans, and all the while the army was getting closer. Some dragged Watts and the bodies of the dead and the other wounded with them, and they raced back into the woods. Because of the darkness, there was no pursuit. Seven of the Chickamaugans were wounded. Four had been killed. Inside the blockhouse, there was not one casualty.

As they carried him through the woods, both legs hurt and bleeding, John Watts felt his face burning with humilation. He had actually wanted to attack Nashville, but others had talked him into attacking the smaller fort. They had not even been able to accomplish that mission. He thought that, no matter how large a force he managed to put together, it remained an unruly, undisciplined band of warriors. He desperately needed to find a way to mold them into an army. Dragging Canoe had done it. Why could he not do the same thing?

Waiting for his wounds to heal, Watts thought about the need for more discipline in the Chickamauga forces. He tried to recall exactly what Dragging Canoe had done, what he had said. How had he managed to hold them together? How had he managed to stay in control? Watts realized that without anyone ever actually saying so, Dragging Canoe had been in command. It had been the force of his personality, the power and persuasiveness of his words, and it had been something else. Something that Watts could not put into words.

The attack on Buchanan's Station had been a total disaster. To Watts, it was a personal embarrassment. But it was more than that. If it was an accurate indication of the current military abilities of the Chickamaugan forces, then it was a preliminary signal for their coming final defeat. Watts did not want to think that, but he could not drive the haunting thought away. Images of the Buchanan Station episode kept coming into his mind, and the ugly thought came with them.

But he was determined to continue the fight. Dragging Canoe had conceived a great vision, a vision of the unification of all Native Peoples to hold the line against the further western intrusion of the Americans. And just before his death, he had made great strides toward that end. Northern Indians were allied and fighting. In the south it was almost entirely the Chickamaugans who continued to fight for the cause. Watts could not falter. Dragging Canoe had given his life to this great cause. The Northern Indians were still holding together the alliance. Watts vowed that he would not be the weak link.

He was lying there, these thoughts and others floating through his brain, when Whitekiller stuck his head in at the door. "Brother," Whitekiller said, "how are your legs?"

"They're healing, Brother," Watts said. "Come in. I'm glad to see you. How goes the war?"

"Doublehead, Bloody Fellow, Ata-lunti-ski, Benge, and others, me too, have been raiding with small groups," Whitekiller said. "We're killing Americans. A few hundred, at least."

"Has anyone attacked Nashville?" Watts asked. "Or Knoxville? Has anyone met an American army?"

Whitekiller thought a moment, shook his head. "No."

"When will our people learn to fight like an army?" Watts said. "We're fighting for our lives, for the lives of our wives and children, for our land, what little land we have left, and for our entire way of life. In order to survive and to win this war, we have to fight armies and win. Killing a few lone settlers is not the way to do it. When will you, my brother, learn these things?"

Whitekiller ruffled a little at that. He stood up, a scowl on his face. "We're Indian people," he said. "Cherokees, Creeks, Shawnees. There are white people among us, yes. But they came to live with us and to live like us. We fight the way we have always fought. The way our fathers and grandfathers fought." He turned away, heaved a sigh, and turned back again. "Brother, I didn't come here to fight with you. I came to bring you something and to give you some news."

Watts was silent a moment. He sighed and nodded his head. "All right," he said.

Whitekiller stepped outside and was back again in an instant, holding a pair of handmade crutches. "Benge made these for you," he said. He held them toward Watts, who took them, struggled to a sitting position, then pulled himself up and stood with the help of the new crutches. Watts smiled. "They're good," he said. "All right. What's the news?"

"There was a meeting at Echota," Whitekiller said. "Some of the President's men came from Philadelphia to meet with Little Turkey and other chiefs of the Cherokee Nation. A party of white men rode in with no warning and started shooting. Right in the middle of the meeting. They killed fifteen Cherokees, including the wife of Little Turkey and some other women. Little Turkey was wounded. Two hundred Cherokees wanted to ride for revenge, but the President's men convinced them that they knew nothing about this attack. They said the men that did it were outlaws."

"They always say it was outlaws," Watts said, "yet they don't punish those outlaws. They don't even arrest them and go through the motions of a trial. Maybe this latest treachery will convince those other Cherokees to join forces with us once again."

It wasn't long after that when an army of two hundred American militiamen rode into the Middle Towns of the Cherokee Nation. They rode in shooting, and when their guns were empty they rode their horses through the town hacking with swords and axes at anyone they could get close to. Children screamed and cried in terror. Mothers ran desperately, looking for their children. Some men tried valiantly to hold back the attackers, only to fall victim to the sharp blades. The people who could manage it fled into the woods and into the mountains. Soon the town and the fields and the orchards were in flames. The militiamen rode on. Before they were done they had destroyed six towns. They had killed fifteen Cherokees and rode home with fifteen Cherokee prisoners. The rest of the inhabitants of the six towns were homeless in the mountains.

The Cherokee Nation still made no move to join forces with the Chickamaugans, and Little Turkey continued to protest the innocence of the Cherokee Nation and to proclaim to the agents of the United States that the Cherokee Nation was at peace. "I want the Americans to stop killing my people," he said. "I want them to kill only Chickamaugans and the Spanish who are urging them to fight. Those are the ones who have been doing bad things. Not my people."

### September 1793
### Cavett's Station

John Watts, his year-old wounds fully healed, led a force of one thousand men toward Knoxville. Doublehead rode alongside him as second in command. Whitekiller, Bob Benge, James Vann, half-breed son of the trader and interpreter Joseph Vann, Doublehead's brother Pumpkin Boy, and the Ridge were among the rest. Watt's idea was to fight the way the white men fight, attacking with a large army. This method was still new to most of the Chickamaugans, although some of them had participated in the battle to rescue Augusta, and Watts had been doing his best for over a year to pound the idea into their heads. And while there had been a large number in the force that had been led to Augusta under the leadership of Dragging Canoe and John McDonald, they had ridden in a bunch. Watts was doing his best to lead his men in military formation.

Watt's army had ridden all night, and they had passed several small settlements and lone cabins. Doublehead had wanted to take them, but Watts had said no. "Someone might get away and run to Knoxville with the alarm," he had said. "We want to take Knoxville by surprise."

But it was morning, and the long night ride had put Doublehead and some of the others in short temper. Speaking in Cherokee, Doublehead said to Watts as they rode side by side, "Cavett's Station is just ahead. Let's take it."

"I told you," Watts said, "we need to take Knoxville by surprise. Cavett's Station and any other place along the way will have to wait."

Doublehead signaled for a halt and then turned on Watts. "I'm tired of waiting," he said. "I'm tired of passing by all those whites and letting them live. I mean to take Cavett's Station."

"Doublehead," Watts said, "I'm in command of this expedition. And I say that we ride straight to Knoxville."

Doublehead turned his horse and raised his voice. "I'm not a white soldier or a slave. I'm going to attack Cavett's Station," he said. "It's just up ahead of us now. How many will ride with me?"

"I will," someone shouted.

"And I," several others called out.

Watts thought deeply. If he insisted on his position, his force would be divided. Doublehead is a fool, he thought, but then he decided that he would have to go along. He would have to take a chance that the attack at Cavett's Station would not sound the alarm for Knoxville. The only other option was riding on with only a part of his force, while the others attacked Cavett's Station with Doublehead. Of the two choices, that was the least desirable.

"All right," he said. "We'll hit Cavett's Station."

It was a short ride. Cavett's Station was a blockhouse. Alexander Cavett and his large family lived there. They were three women and ten men and boys. One of the boys saw the large Cherokee army approaching and ran back inside to give the alarm. One of the Cherokees jerked off a quick shot at him, but the shot thudded into the thick wall of the blockhouse. The boy shut the heavy door. Cherokees raced toward the blockhouse, firing as they rode. Rifle barrels poked out of the ports in the blockhouse, and soon five Cherokees lay dead in the field. One of the fallen was Pumpkin Boy.

Watts called for them to dismount and take cover. Bob Benge joined Watts behind some brush around a large tree. "This is foolish," Watts said. "A thousand men held up in this manner."

"Nine hundred and ninety-five," Benge said. "Doublehead's thirsting for scalps, especially now that his brother's been killed."

"If only he had been willing to wait a little," Watts said, "he could have had plenty. Well, we're into this now. We'll have to find a way to finish it."

"Let me talk to them," Benge said. "If I can assure their safety, maybe I can get them to surrender."

"All right," Watts said. "That's a good idea."

They quickly fashioned a white flag and tied it onto the muzzle of Benge's long rifle. Benge, poking the rifle barrel ahead of him, stood up and stepped out in the open. "Hold your fire," Watts called out in Cherokee, then again in English. "Hold your fire. Benge is going in for a parley."

It was quiet as Benge walked across the open space toward the blockhouse. About halfway, he stopped. "Hello," he called out. "Cavett. Let's talk."

"I'm Cavett," came an answer from inside. "Come on over."

Benge walked to the door, and someone opened it from inside. A tall white man stood there in the opening. "Captain Benge?" he said.

"I'm Bob Benge," Benge answered. "Are you Cavett?"

"I am," Cavett said. "Lean your rifle against the wall there and come on in."

Benge put down the rifle and stepped into the house. "I've come to offer you terms," he said, "if you'll surrender."

"Ha," Cavett said, "we've dropped five of yours, and all of us in here are unscratched."

"That's true enough," said Benge, "but how many of you are there?" He glanced quickly around the room. "I see three women and some boys. How many fighting men? We have a thousand outside. It's only a matter of time. Surrender. We'll spare your lives. Hell, man, likely you'll all be traded before long for some Cherokee captives."

"Let me talk to my family," Cavett said.

"I'll wait just outside the door," said Benge. He pulled open the door, stepped outside and shut it again behind himself. He leaned back against the wall, beside his rifle, to wait. Across the field in the woods, Doublehead found his way to Watts. "What's he doing?" he demanded.

"He's trying to get them to surrender," said Watts. "We'll take them along as prisoners and use them to exchange for Cherokees who've been captured by the Americans."

"I want no prisoners," said Doublehead. "Why was I not consulted on this matter?"

The door opened at the house, and Alexander Cavett came outside, followed by the rest of his family. They were all unarmed. In the woods, Doublehead ran to his horse and jumped into the saddle. He gave a wild shriek, kicked the horse in the sides, and bolted out of the trees, followed by several other mounted men. Benge's eyes opened wide in surprise. The Cavett women screamed in fright. Watts, seeing what was about to happen, ran for his own horse, as did Vann and the Ridge.

Doublehead and his followers were on the Cavetts in almost no time, and from the backs of their horses they delivered chopping and bashing blows to the heads of their victims. Doublehead dismounted to finish a hurt and fallen Cavett. Desperately, James

Vann reached down from his horse and scooped up a young boy to save him from the frenzied attack. Doublehead looked up from his bloody work and saw what Vann had done. In a rage, he sprang at Vann, swinging his hatchet at the boy. It struck its mark, and the boy hung limp and dead in Vann's arms.

Doublehead aimed another blow at Vann, but Vann swung his horse around to avoid it. At about that same time, Watts grabbed up another Cavett boy and rode away fast with him, out of reach of Doublehead and the others. There were some men still back in the woods, and Watts found four Creek Chickamaugans. He knew them, and he trusted them. "Take this boy to safety," he said. "Doublehead has gone crazy."

By the time he got back to the blockhouse, it was all over. Twelve Cavetts lay dead and scalped, and some of Doublehead's followers had set fire to the blockhouse. They were whooping and singing about their victory. Watts rode over to where Benge stood, stunned, beside James Vann. "I swore to them that they'd be safe," said Benge.

"The white people call us bloodthirsty savages," said Watts, himself half white. "Doublehead wants to prove them right."

"He wants to be a Mankiller," said Vann. "To my mind, the only title he's earned is Babykiller."

"They'll be giving the alarm in Knoxville soon," said Watts. "We're close enough for them to have heard the shots from here. My plan's been ruined. I suggest we turn around and go home."

Most of the army rode with Watts, but Doublehead and his followers went their own way. Watts rode mostly in silence. He was upset because he had failed to maintain order with his "army." His entire campaign, meant to be a major assault on Knoxville, had been a failure. And he was upset at the cruel and treacherous behavior of Doublehead and his followers back at Cavett's Station. There was no excuse for such treachery, all it accomplished was convincing the whites who called them savage that they were right. Watts himself could think of nothing to call it but savage.

Never mind that Sevier and others like him had behaved as savagely toward the Cherokees. They did not get called savage, even when their behavior merited the label. Watts did not hesitate to kill in war. But there were rules of war, and he meant to do all he could to abide by them. He was afraid too that because he had organized and led this army, the atrocity committed by Doublehead would be laid at his feet. He, Watts, would be called savage, and perhaps he deserved the label.

They had made it as far back as the Etowah River not far from the Chickamauga towns, when a scout came riding hard back to Watts. "Americans are coming," he said. "I think it's Little John Sevier."

"How many, do you think?" Watts said.

"Maybe eight hundred," the scout said.

The road they were on led down to a ford in the river, then on up the other side. Sevier would be coming along the same road. Watts quickly ordered his men to line up along the riverbank and take cover. His intent was to ambush Sevier's troop as it approached the ford. Then someone shouted, "Look. They're downriver." Watts looked and saw some riders coming from that direction. Before he had time to consider the situation, many of the Cherokees had come out of their hiding places and rushed to meet the coming attack from downriver. Watts, too late, saw that the force was not a large one. And then the main body, led by Sevier himself, came charging down the road into the ford.

Watt's force, divided, was no match for Sevier. Cherokees fell in the river and in the woods. Watts and others saw men on both sides of them dropped by the heavy fire from the Americans. Watts felt the wind and heard the zip of a rifle ball as it sped by close to his right ear. "Fall back," he called out. "Fall back." The Cherokees retreated, each man on his own. They scattered through the woods in different directions, leaving behind most of their supplies.

Sevier marched on into the Cherokee towns, destroying several along with their cornfields and orchards, a chore at which he had much experience. The campaign that Watts had begun with such high hopes had turned out to be not only a disappointment, but a complete disaster. Watts made his way home, and there he inquired about the one surviving member of the Cavett family. "The Creeks that brought him back here," someone finally said, "killed him and took his scalp." That was the final straw for John Watts, Guhna-geski. He was not afraid to fight, not even to die, but now it seemed to him that further fighting was futile. The Cherokees would not be able to defeat the Americans. Any further attempts, he thought, would accomplish nothing. They would only produce additional acts of cruelty on both sides. It was time to quit.

Bob Benge had other ideas. Like Watts, he was disgusted by the behavior of Doublehead. And like Watts, he was, to say the least, disappointed at the failure of the Cherokee army to maintain military discipline. But he blamed Watts for that. In his mind, Watts had failed to enforce discipline. He, again like Watts, could see the end of their struggle. At last, he admitted to himself that the Cherokee fight against the Americans could not be won. There were just too many Americans, and their supply of arms and ammunition was much greater than that of the Cherokees.

But Benge knew that he would not be able to surrender to the hated American forces. If the end was near, he would face it in his own way. He went to find his brother Martin, and he told Martin what he had been thinking. Together, they recruited a few other men, and they headed for Virginia. Benge carried a long rifle and a sharp steel war ax. Benge and the rest of his party knew the road to Virginia well. They moved quickly.

Once inside the Virginia territory, they came across a lone house. Two white men were outside. When they saw the Cherokees coming, they ran into the woods. Benge led his small band on toward the house. The two white men were not worth pursuing. Then a shot came from the house, but its ball went wild. The Cherokees ran on up to the house, and Martin Benge kindled a flame and set fire to the walls of the house in several different places. They waited, weapons ready, for the flames to grow.

Soon a white flag on a stick was poked out one of the windows.

"They're surrendering," Benge said. "We'll accept their surrender. Don't harm anyone." He raised his voice. "Come on out," he said. "If you come unarmed, no one will be hurt." The door opened from the inside, and the inhabitants of the house came out. There were white women and children and black slaves. The only men were two of the slaves. Benge could not help but think with contempt of the two cowardly white men who had run away, leaving these people to their fate.

Benge looked the captives over, had them all grouped in a bunch, and then started his small patrol moving again. He sent most of his men ahead, told the captives to follow them, and he and his brother took up the rear. One of the white women was carrying a baby. Benge saw her hand the baby to a girl. He guessed that the girl was about ten years old. He saw the woman speak to the child. Then all at once the girl with the baby and three other children ran into the woods at the edge of the path. Martin made a move, but Benge put a hand on his brother's arm. "Let them go," he said. "We won't make war on children."

That night they camped. They cooked fresh venison and fed the captives as well as themselves. Benge moved over to where the woman who had sent the children away was sitting. He sat down beside her. "I'm Bob Benge," he said. "What is your name?"

"I'm Mrs. Livingston," she said. "I want to thank you for not following the children. You could have, I know."

"I don't make war on children," Benge said. "And I want to assure you that none of you will be hurt. We're taking you back to our towns, but I feel certain that you'll all be used to exchange for Cherokee prisoners. Probably soon. Between now and then, I want you to know that you won't be mistreated."

"Thank you," she said.

The next morning they prepared to resume their trip. Benge called Martin over to him. "Martin," he said, "take two men with you and race ahead of us to hunt. Leave some meat along the way for us. We'll travel faster that way. I think we're far enough away from the Livingston house so that no one is chasing us anymore."

Martin picked two men, and the three of them ran ahead. Soon they were out of sight. It was midday when Benge called two more men to him. "Run ahead," he said. "Catch up with Martin and tell him to wait for us. I don't think we have to hurry so much now. We need to make it easier on the women."

Soon the two runners were gone. Benge then told the others that they would rest a while. When the female captives were ready, they would move on. It was a few hours later when Benge and his small party moved down into a deep valley with steep, rocky mountain walls on either side. He walked ahead alongside Mrs. Livingston. They could feel the temperature drop as the sky became darker, the sunlight blocked by the mountains that towered above them. They were well down into the valley when shots rang out. The first shot tore into Benge's chest. He fell dead instantly. The battle was over in almost an instant. The ambush had been well laid, and Benge's party was a small one. With all the Cherokees killed, the white men came down from their ambush. One raced to embrace Mrs. Livingston.

"I hated to run away and leave you like that," he said, "but I knew we'd need help. Are you all right?"

"Yes," she said. "Are the children safe?"

"They're safe," he said. He looked at the body of the red-haired Indian lying there in the road. "Who was he?" he asked. "Do you know?"

Mrs. Livingston looked over at the body. She looked a little sad. "Yes," she said. "He was Captain Benge."

"The Bench," Livingston shouted. "We've killed the Bench."

# 17

John Watts was heartsick. It was not just the loss of his good friend Benge. He had lost friends before. That happened during times of war. But the losses these days seemed to be for nothing. The Chickamaugans were the terror of the frontier. That much was true. But they were terrorizing lone travelers and families in far-flung homes. They had failed to attack Nashville or Knoxville or any other significant military objective. As much as he had tried, Watts had been unable to instill any sense of military discipline in the Chickamauga warriors. He did not think that anyone would ever be able to take the place of Dragging Canoe, but he had intended to do his best. In spite of that, what Watts had believed to be a patriotic war, a war to preserve Cherokee lands and the Cherokee way of life, had degenerated into a war against women and children. It had degenerated into a war of a thousand men against twenty. He was on the verge of believing that it was over. He went to see John McDonald.

"My friend," Watts said, sitting on the porch of McDonald's fine home on Lookout Mountain, "I know that Dragging Canoe relied much on your advice. I don't know what to do. Dragging Canoe would never have stopped fighting. I know that. But I also know that I am no Dragging Canoe, and I look around, and I see no one else. Things seem to be falling apart all around us. I have never yet said this out loud to any man, but I'm thinking that maybe we should seek peace with the Americans. And I feel like a traitor to my people having said it. Have you heard? Bloody Fellow went to Philadelphia on his own and talked to the President there. They say that the President gave him a new name. Iskagua, the Clear Sky. The former Bloody Fellow is courting the Americans and is now hailed as a great peacemaker."

"Guhna-geski," said McDonald, speaking in Cherokee, "times change, and we must be ready and willing to change with them. If we are not, we'll die or be left behind. Dragging Canoe was a great man, but both he and his times are gone. I too had thought that I would never make peace with America, but England is no longer with us. The Cherokee Nation is not with us. Perhaps we should speak to the rest of our people about this matter."

A little one toddled out onto the porch just then, and McDonald smiled and held out his hands. "Come to me, Tsan-usdi," he said. "Come on." The little one waddled over to McDonald and scampered up onto his lap. "This is my daughter's son," McDonald said to Watts. "He's named John, for me. He's John Ross. We call him Little John. He's very bright for a three-year-old. I look for great things from him."

"We need peace for the little ones to grow up in," Watts said. "I'll talk to the people."


### June 1794

William Scott had a large flatboat loaded with merchandise and twenty black slaves headed for Natchez. Scott was a merchant of goods and flesh. He intended to return to Knoxville a rich man. He knew of the dangers in descending the Tennessee River, knew that he would pass right through some Chickamauga towns, but Scott was bold. He had five other white men with him, and they were all well armed. They had all fought Indians before and were not afraid. They had heard that the "Chickamoggies" were a ragtag bunch anyway. They were bold enough even to have brought along three women and four children with them. "Ain't nothing to be afeard of," Scott had said to his wife.

They passed by Dakwai without incident. Up on the bank, in a melancholy mood, John Watts watched them go by. They drifted briskly by Settico and Tuskegee and successfully negotiated the Suck. Scott was feeling smug. "What did I tell you?" he shouted. "The goddamned Chickamoggies want no part of us." As they moved past Running Water Town, going swiftly with the current, someone on the bank fired a long rifle. The ball went into the water a safe distance away from the boat. There were no more shots. "Ah, just showing off," Scott said.

A short distance downriver in Nickajack, Whitekiller, Bowles, and others were lounging on the bank smoking and drinking whiskey. They had their rifles beside them. They had heard the shot from Running Water and were curious, but no other shots had followed. Still they remained alert. Then, "Look," said Bowles. He pointed upriver at a large large flatboat coming in their direction. "White men," he said. All the men stood up and picked up their rifles. They did not know who had fired the shot at Running Water, or why it had been fired, but here were white men coming. They would be ready.

On the boat, Scott looked toward Nickajack and saw the group of armed Chickamaugans. Just upriver he had been fired on. This looked ominous. He raised his rifle to his shoulder, took careful aim, and fired. A man standing just beside Bowles howled and grabbed his shoulder. It was bleeding from a ghastly hole. Another shot was fired from the boat, and a second Chickamauga man fell, wounded in his thigh. Whitekiller, Bowles, and the others all raised their rifles and fired. All missed.

"Let's go after them," Whitekiller said.

Hearing the shots, people came running out of their houses. Some started tending to the two wounded men. Some young men joined Whitekiller and Bowles. They ran to their long war canoes, put one into the water and climbed in. They took up their paddles and began racing after the flatboat. The war canoe was much faster than was the clumsy white man's boat, and they could soon see that they were gaining.

Scott and his companions, seeing the pursuit, prepared for the coming attack. The men who had fired their rifles reloaded. The women huddled down flat, doing their best to cover the children. The slaves all crouched low. At a place called Mussel Shoals, because they were watching the pursuit, their boat ran hard onto a sandbar, and the six men, who had been standing, all fell over at the impact. A woman screamed, and the children started to cry in terror. The men scrambled to their feet, and the Chickamauga canoe was nearly beside them. Quickly, the white men fired their rifles. In the canoe, one Chickamaugan slumped forward.

The war canoe turned just in time to bash itself broadside against the grounded flatboat, and as it did, some Chickamaugans reached for the white man's boat to grab hold, others reached for the white men, still others simply stood up and jumped aboard. Scott fired a pistol as one man stepped onto his boat, and the Indian fell back. Bowles got aboard and bashed a white man's skull. A boatman grabbed up a long boat pole and swung it wide, knocking an Indian off into the water, but Whitekiller ducked under it and came up driving a steel knife into the man's ribs.

Scott pulled a second pistol out of his belt and fired a shot into the chest of another Cherokee just before the man reached him, but at almost the same instant another came up behind him and bashed in his head with a stone-headed war club. The two remaining boatmen were attacked by Chickamaugans, and it was impossible to tell who killed them or how. Whitekiller suddenly rose up between the Chickamaugans and the women, children, and slaves in the back of the boat. He held his arms out to his sides. *"Eliqua,"* he said. "That's enough."

They scalped the bodies of the fallen white men before dumping them into the river, and they loaded the bodies of their own dead into the canoe. A couple of men helped the wounded man. Bowles and Whitekiller stood before the white women and children. "We won't hurt you," said Bowles.

"We won't even take you captive," Whitekiller said. "We'll get your boat back in the water and ride with you a ways. Far enough to make sure that you're safe."

Well past the Chickamauga towns and any Creek towns along the way, Whitekiller and Bowles told the women that they were safe. Before long they would be in Natchez. They waved their war canoe over, and as it pulled alongside the flatboat, Whitekiller stepped across, then Bowles. They waved good-bye as the flatboat moved ahead. Then they pulled their canoe to the shore and got out on the land. They sat down there to rest and to consider what they had just done.

"I've never killed white men and not stolen their goods," Bowles said.

"We let captives and goods go," said another.

"We did enough," Whitekiller said. "My brother's not going to like it. He's thinking of going with McDonald to the Americans to talk peace."

"If he does that," Bowles said, "the Americans will want him to give us to them for what we just did."

"Yes," Whitekiller said. "I think we should just go away."

"Where would we go?" someone asked.

"West," said Bowles. "Across the big river."

And they all agreed.


### June 26, 1794
### Philadelphia

Perhaps the white men meant well. Henry Knox, Secretary of War of the United States, was there in person. They intended to put an end to the long and bloody Cherokee war, and the treaty they drew up was a good one. It reaffirmed the previous treaty, promising to make all the payments that had been called for in that document. It promised to survey the boundary lines between the Cherokee country and the United States according to the lines established by the previous treaty, and it asked for no more land.

269

The previous treaty had promised to pay the Cherokee Nation fifteen hundred dollars annually, and this new one raised the figure to five thousand. But there were no official representatives of the Cherokee Nation present. The most prominent signature on the treaty on the Cherokee side was that of Doublehead. The only Cherokees present at the meeting were Chickamaugans.

The treaty having been signed, Doublehead and his followers loaded up all the presents and made their way back to their Chickamauga homes, where they divided up all the goods among themselves. Doublehead managed to keep the best and the most for himself.

John Ish, a Tennessee settler, was shot and killed while ploughing his field. His wife said that it was an Indian who fired the shot. A deputation from the Governor of Tennessee went to see Little Turkey, still Principal Chief of the Cherokee Nation, and Little Turkey promised to seek out the killer. A few days later, some Cherokees showed up at Tellico Blockhouse to deliver the killer to the agent there. He was a Creek. He proclaimed that his nation was at war with the Americans, and that if he should ever again be free, he would kill more. They hanged him there.

The officials of Tennessee, having heard that a large force of Creeks was moving toward the Tennessee settlements, went to Little Turkey for help. The old chief knew that it was a test of his friendly protestations toward the United States. He gathered together fifty-five Cherokee men to ride with the federal troops. They encountered the Creek force and drove them back with but few casualties on either side. Then word came by messenger that the northern Indian alliance had been broken. The northern Indians had been defeated. The Creeks withdrew further into their own territory.

Watts had a letter from the Spanish governor of Florida urging him to make peace with the Americans and telling him that there would be no more regular shipments of arms and ammunition. He had also heard about the recent defeat of the northern Indians. He was totally dejected. Dragging Canoe's work had been all for nothing. The great plan was lost. He also heard about the men from Cherokee Nation riding with Americans to fight the Creeks. He was feeling very much alone in the Chickamauga towns. He was feeling surrounded. He was feeling like what many had called him and the other Chickamaugans all along. He was feeling like an outlaw. Then he heard the shooting.

It came from Nickajack. He was sure. There were a great many shots. He could tell that it was a major attack. He called for help, ran to his horse with rifle in hand, and started at full gallop toward Nickajack. By the time he got there it was almost over. He could see the town in flames. He could see the Americans shooting down into the river at Chickamaugans who were trying to escape by canoe. Watts and his small force rode toward the Americans shooting, but soon they were driven back. They were badly outnumbered.

The American force rode on to Running Water and did the same thing there. When they finally left the area, they had killed at least fifty Chickamaugans and carried off a number of prisoners. John Watts stood silently surveying the damage. John McDonald walked over to stand beside him. He was holding Little John in his arms. "Did you see who it was that brought them here?" he asked.

"No," Watts said. "I did not."

"It was Joseph Brown," McDonald said. "Remember Joseph Brown?"

Watts stood silent for a long moment. "Joseph Brown," he said. "At last he got his revenge for the time he was captive here, I guess. McDonald?"

"Yes?"

"Can you find Sam Handley? The white man that Middlestriker captured?"

"Yes," McDonald said. "I know where he is."

"Let's have him brought to your house," Watts said. "Let's use him to send a message to the Governor of Tennessee. I want to meet with the governor and talk of peace."

McDonald sighed a heavy sigh. "It's all over now, isn't it?" he said.

Watts stood for a moment in deep thought before answering the Englishman turned Cherokee. "It has been over for a while," he said. "We just didn't know it. It was all over when we lost our great man. It was over with the death of Dragging Canoe."

# Afterword

Following the collapse of the Chickamauga confederacy, the Cherokees never again took up arms against the United States. However, Dragging Canoe's remarkable prediction of 1775 did, in fact, come about. In 1803, President Thomas Jefferson drew up a plan of removal, the intention of which was to relocate all eastern Indian tribes to new locations west of the Mississippi River. Following up on Jefferson's plan, President Andrew Jackson urged through Congress a Removal Bill in 1830.

The Cherokee Nation, under the leadership of Principal Chief John Ross (the grandson of John McDonald) held off, refusing to remove and insisting on their rights to the land. In 1835, Jackson's agents signed a fraudulent treaty with certain individual Cherokees, not legal representatives of the government of the Cherokee Nation. Major Ridge (once a young Chickamauga) was a signer of this treaty and a leader of the group that became known as the Treaty Party.

The Cherokees who had gone west in 1794 with Whitekiller and Bowles had settled in Missouri until the great 1811 earthquake caused them to move into what is now northwestern Arkansas, where they became known as the Western Cherokee Nation. Having signed the Treaty of New Echota (the Removal Treaty), Ridge and the Treaty Party moved to the Western Cherokee Nation.

Chief Ross and the majority population of the Cherokee Nation remained in their ancient homelands resisting removal. The Cherokee Nation took its case to the United States Supreme Court, which ruled that it could not legally be removed without its consent. Andrew Jackson defied the Supreme Court and ordered the U.S. Army to round up and forcibly remove the Cherokees.

In 1838, eighteen thousand Cherokees were rounded up and held in stockade prisons until the trek west could be started. They were moved in thirteen waves, across the long trail from what was left of their homelands to what is now the northeast portion of the state of Oklahoma. Four thousand died along the way. There they rebuilt their homes and their nation. (The Western Cherokee Nation was soon moved across the line to join them and be reabsorbed into the larger Cherokee Nation.)

A long civil war began, in which members of the Treaty Party were killed for their part in the removal, and members of the other faction, known as the Ross Party, those who had suffered the forced removal known as the Trail of Tears, were killed in retaliation. In spite of this terrible domestic strife, the Cherokee Nation grew and prospered. A capital city was established at Tahlequah. An institution of higher learning was founded there. Called the Cherokee Male Seminary, it was the first such institution west of the Mississippi River. A female seminary followed.

Making use of the syllabary put forth by the Cherokee Sequoyah, the Cherokee Nation published its own bilingual newspaper. The government, tripartite with a bicameral legislature, operated under a written constitution. Everything was going well until the Civil War broke out in the United States. Led by Stand Watie, a nephew of Major Ridge, members of the old Treaty Party and their families and friends, in an effort to seize control of the Cherokee Nation, joined the Confederacy.

Chief John Ross, acting under a provision of the Removal Treaty that promised that the United States would protect the Cherokee Nation both from invasion and from domestic strife, requested that federal troops be sent to the Cherokee Nation to protect its neutrality. Troops were not sent, and now Confederate General Stand Watie forced Ross to sign a treaty with the Confederate States of America. At his first opportunity, Ross fled the Cherokee Nation and repudiated the treaty he had signed with the Confederacy.

Cherokees, mostly traditional and mostly full-blood, organized to defend the Cherokee Nation from the Confederate Cherokees, and the Civil War in the Cherokee Nation became a microcosm of the larger war in the United States. At the war's end, the Cherokee Nation was almost completely destroyed. But that wasn't the worst of it.

The United States, citing as its excuse the fact that John Ross had signed a treaty with the Confederacy, forced a new treaty on the Cherokee Nation and the other four tribes in what is now eastern Oklahoma. This new treaty organized the land of the five tribes, known as the Five Civilized Tribes, into Indian Territory. It took away some powers of their courts and some of their police powers. A federal court was established in Van Buren, Arkansas (later moved to Fort Smith), and given jurisdiction over the entire Indian Territory. The Five Nations were denied any legal power over noncitizens in their nations. (In other words, Indian police and Indian courts had no jurisdiction over white people who might be in their countries.) A period of excessive lawlessness followed.

White outlaws found Indian Territory to be a haven. No one could touch them except the deputy U.S. marshals patrolling the vast territory out of the court at Fort Smith. The Five Nations in the territory were then accused of not being able to provide law and order within their own boundaries. By the eighteen nineties the movement to allot the lands of the Cherokee Nation in severalty to its citizens in order to pave the way for statehood was under way. In 1907, the territories of Indian Territory and Oklahoma Territory were combined to create the state of Oklahoma, and the Cherokees became private landowners and citizens of the state and of the United States. The allotment process created a vast amount of "surplus" land that was given over to white settlement. The Cherokee Nation, it seemed, had ceased to exist. Its properties were sold. The newspaper, *The Cherokee Advocate*, was sold and carried to Muskogee, thirty miles away, where it became the *Muskogee Phoenix*. It is still published today under that name. The Cherokee Female Seminary was turned over to the state. It evolved into Northeastern Oklahoma State University. The Seminary building still stands and is still used by the university.

The United States government had done everything it could to destroy the Cherokee Nation as a government and the Cherokees as a separate people. The Cherokee Nation went into a state of dormancy, but it was not destroyed. Complications in the transfer of land deeds made a semblance of legal Cherokee Nation government necessary to the United States, and so, beginning with Oklahoma statehood, the president of the United States began appointing the chief of the Cherokee Nation, usually just long enough to sign necessary documents. The appointees during this bleak period of Cherokee history have come to be known as the "chiefs for a day." It seemed as if Dragging Canoe's 1775 prediction had come true. Most people believed that the Cherokee Nation was a thing of the past.

But Cherokees are persistent. The Cherokee language continued to be spoken, and Cherokee traditions continued to be followed, sometimes in disguise, in remote communities in northeastern Oklahoma, and grassroots Cherokee political organizations continued to meet. In 1938, the Cherokee National Council, an outgrowth of these meetings, elected Bartley Milam Principal Chief of the Cherokee Nation, and to legalize the election in the eyes of the United States, President Franklin Roosevelt appointed Milam Chief. Milam served until his death in 1949. President Truman appointed W. W. Keeler the next Principal Chief, and Keeler was reappointed by every president after that, up to and including President Richard Nixon; he served as an appointed chief for a total of twenty-four years.

In 1973, the Cherokee Nation was allowed to have elections

again, and Keeler was elected chief. He served one four-year term as a chief elected by the people. The Principal Chiefs of the Cherokee Nation since then have been Ross Swimmer, Wilma Mankiller, Joe Byrd, and Chad Smith.

As in Dragging Canoe's prediction, the Cherokee Nation was driven west and nearly destroyed. But like the soaring eagles in his vision, the Cherokee Nation has come back rising almost from the dead, to grow and thrive once more.

# Glossary

*Ada*   wood.

*Ada-gal'kala*   "Leaning Wood." Ada-gal'kala was known to the English as the "Little Carpenter." In the histories, his name is most often spelled Attacullaculla. As a young man he was known as Uku Unega, and the British called him Owen Nakan. He was the father of Dragging Canoe. See *Uku-unega* below.

*Ada-hona*   "make wood," the name of the women's part in the Green Corn Dance.

*Aga-hodi*   "big foreheads in motion," the Cherokee designation for the Green Corn Dance. According to Speck (in *Cherokee Dance and Drama*), in ancient times a segment of the tribe (clan, society?) pressed their infants' heads, causing them to grow protruding foreheads. This particular group was very energetic at the Green Corn Dance, which takes its name from them.

*Amagayunyi*   Running Water Town, the Chickamauga town that was Dragging Canoe's Chickamauga headquarters, built after Shelby's destruction of the original Chickamauga towns.

*Ammouskossittee*   the name of the son and successor of 'Ma-edohi, as recorded by the English.

*Anetsodi*   the ball play, also called "the little brother of war." Players carry two ballsticks, approximately three feet long, each topped with an oval-shaped, webbed racquet about five inches long and two and a half inches wide. The ball is a little larger than a golf ball.

*Ani-Gusa*   Creek (or Muskogee) people.

*Ani-Sawahoni*   Shawnee people.

*Ani-Tʃikʃa*   Chickasaw people.

*Ani-waniʃki*   bugle weed. Literally, talkers.

*Ani-yonega*   white men, or white people.

*Ani-yunwi*   people. See below.

*Ani-yunwi-ya*   the Cherokees' own name for themselves. *Yunwi* is a person. *Ani* is a plural prefix. *Ya* is an intensive translated variously as "real" or "original." The word is most often translated as "the Real People."

*Ata-lunti-ʃki*   usually corrupted to Talonteskee, or some similar misspelling. Mooney translates it as "one who throws some living object from a place, as an enemy from a precipice." A Chickamaugan, he later moved to Arkansas and became a citizen of the newly formed Western Cherokee Nation.

*Atj'a*   contracted form of *Atʃaδa* speckled trout.

*Auquotague*   the name of the son of Little Turkey as recorded by the American drafters of the Treaty of Holston.

*Awi*   deer.

*Awi Uʃδi*   Little Deer, in Cherokee lore, the spirit chief of all the deer.

*Ayehli*   center, or middle. The Cherokee Nation, translated into Cherokee, becomes *Tʃalagi Ayehli*. The word can also mean half a cup or half a dollar. In the form *ayehli-δuh* it can also mean something like "so so."

*Bloody Fellow*   see *Iʃkagua* below.

*Bowleʃ John*   also called the Bowl, Chief Bowles, Cherokee name, Diwali. In 1794 he led a group of Chickamaugans west to settle in Missouri. Following the great earthquake of 1811, he and his group moved into what is now western Arkansas and founded the Western Cherokee Nation. Later, told by the U.S. government to move to the other side of the river, he angrily moved all the way into Texas. Thereafter, Bowles and his bunch were known as the Texas Cherokees. They helped Texas win its war of independence against Mexico and signed a treaty with the provisional government, which the Republic of Texas refused to honor. Bowles was killed on the battlefield by Texans in his eighties.

*Buʃhyheaδ*   see *John Stuart* below.

*Cameron, Alexander*   a Scot, British army officer and Deputy Superintendent under Stuart (see below). He was the adopted brother of Dragging Canoe and was called "Scotchie." Cameron died on December 29, 1781.

*Canaly*   English corruption of the Cherokee word for "friend." See *'ginali* below.

*Canasoratah*   one of the hostages murdered at Fort Prince George. The spelling is a corrupt English rendering of the name.

*Chalakee*   the Choctaw (and trade jargon) word for the people who called themselves *Ani-yunwi-ya* or *Ani-Kituwagi.* They eventually accepted the designation, using the Cherokee form, *Tsalagi.*

*Cheeseekau*   a Shawnee living with the Chickamaugans, brother of Tecumseh.

*Cherokee*   latest Anglicization of the Choctaw word *Chalakee,* adopted by the Cherokees as *Tsalagi.* See *Chalakee* above.

*Chilhowee*   a Cherokee town.

*Chickamauga*   a town built by Dragging Canoe on Chickamauga Creek. Also a name for a follower of Dragging Canoe.

*Chickamauga*   creek in northern Georgia.

*Chickamaugans*   followers of Dragging Canoe. Sometimes *Chickamaugas.*

*Chickamoggies*   American frontiersman's rendering of *Chickamaugas.*

*'Chooch'*   short for *achujah,* meaning "boy." A common designation for a young man or boy.

*Conasatchee*   one of the Cherokee Lower Towns, destroyed by Montgomery.

*Cotetoy*   Cherokee name, imperfectly recorded.

*Cowee*   one of the Cherokee Middle Towns.

*Crockett*   the Crockett whose death at the hands of Cherokees is mentioned in the text was the grandfather of the later famous Davy Crockett, who, in spite of the manner of his grandfather's death, defended Cherokee rights as a U.S. congressman from Tennessee during debates over the pending Removal Bill. The bill was passed into law, and Crockett's political career came to an end.

*Dak'siuweya*   contracted form of *Dakasiuweya,* usually shortened and anglicized as *Toxaway,* one of the Cherokee Lower Towns.

*Dakwai*   corrupted in English to *Toqua,* the name of one of the Chickamauga towns. According to Mooney (in *Myths of the Cherokee and Sacred Formulas of the Cherokee*), *dakwa* is the name of a mythic great fish. *Dakwa* plus the locative *yi,* with a little elli-

sion, produces *∂akwai,* the place of the great fish. *Dakwa* can also
mean "whale."

*Dawuhjila*   red or slippery elm.

*Distayuh*   goatsrue.

*Diwali*   (literally, mushroom) man known as the Bowl, sometimes
John Bowles. See *Bowles* above.

*Doublehead*   a Chickamaugan, brother of Pumpkin Boy. Always
fiercely independent, he seemed to go more and more his own
way following the death of Dragging Canoe. His brother was
one of those killed at Cavett's Station, and Doublehead was
responsible for the killing of the Cavett family after they had
surrendered. Doublehead was eventually assassinated by Ridge,
by that time called Major Ridge, for accepting bribes and selling
Cherokee land.

*Duh∂is∂i*   pheasant or ruffled grouse.

*Echoe*   one of the Cherokee Middle Towns.

*Echota*   ancient Cherokee town name, meaning lost. Echota, originally a sacred peace town, or sanctuary town, in historic times,
evolved into the capital of the nascent Cherokee Nation.

*El-i*   Dragging Canoe's Cherokee pronunciation of Ellie.

*Eliqua*   that's enough.

*Estatoe*   one of the Cherokee Lower Towns, destroyed by Montgomery.

*Gahl'jo∂i*   house.

*Ganona*   on the trail. A movement in the Green Corn Dance, or Aga-
hodi. See above.

*Ganuhgwa ∂liski*   common speedwell.

*Gatayusti*   an ancient gambling game, played with a spear and a
stone disc. More widely known by its Creek name, Chunky, the
game was once widespread and extremely popular among many
of the southeastern tribes. According to Cherokee myth, the
game was invented by a shape-changing creature known as
Brass, the gambler, in Cherokee, *Untsaiyi.*

*Gayahulo*   saddle.

*Ghigooie*   Cherokee woman's name. A full-blooded Cherokee, she
married the white trader William Shorey. Their daughter Annie
married John McDonald, British assistant superintendent for
southern Indian affairs. Their daughter Mollie married Daniel

Ross, a Scot, and became the mother of John Ross, later Principal Chief of the Cherokee Nation.

*Giðhla*   scalp lock.

*Giga-hyuh*   possibly short for *giga,* red (or blood), combined with *agenhyuh,* woman. Red Woman. It's usually spelled in texts as *Ghigau,* which has no meaning. Translated variously as War Woman, Pretty Woman, or Beloved Woman. Nancy Ward is said to have been the last Beloved Woman of the Cherokees. The position was one not only of honor but of some political power.

*Gist, Nathaniel*   a trader to the Cherokees from Virginia, he is thought to have been the father of Sequoyah.

*Gogi*   summer, the warm part of the year. The Cherokee year was divided into two parts. See *gola* below.

*Gola*   winter, or the cold part of the year.

*Green Corn Dance*   an English term for the dances done by many Native American tribes at the time for harvesting the green corn. The proper Cherokee designation for this ceremony is, according to Speck, *Aga-hoði.* See above.

*Guque*   quail or dove.

*Guhna-gaðoga*   Standing Turkey

*Guhna-geski*   man's name (*guhna,* turkey, + *geski*?)

*Ha*   an exclamation.

*Hart, Nathaniel*   partner with Richard Henderson, below, in the Transylvania Land Company.

*Henðerson, Juðge Richarð*   North Carolina settler and land speculator, partner with Hart, above, in the Transylvania Land Company.

*Higinali*   contracted to *'ginali,* friend. English corruption, *canaly.*

*Iði yunwi-ya*   we are the Real People. See *ani-yunwi-ya* above.

*Inaða iyusti*   snakelike, a dance.

*Iskagua*   clear sky. Name taken by Bloody Fellow, once a Chickamaugan, which was said to have been given him by President George Washington to indicate his change of heart.

*Kanati*   the first man, in Cherokee mythology. He's called the Great Hunter, and is the husband of Selu, or Corn. He may also be Thunder.

*Kanohena*   a sour hominy drink, traditionally served to guests.

*Kanuga*   "scratcher," surgical instrument used for scratching. Comblike, it is sometimes made of a turkey quill and seven sharp pieces of the leg bone of a turkey.

*Katactoi*   one of the hostages murdered at Fort Prince George. Corrupt spelling.

*Kealharufteke*   one of the hostages murdered at Fort Prince George, name imperfectly recorded.

*Keetoowah*   Chickamauga town, named for Overhills town destroyed by Rutherford.

*Keowee*   one of the Cherokee Lower Towns, destroyed by Rutherford.

*Killianka*   one of the hostages released from Fort Prince George with Agan'stat'. Corrupt spelling.

*Kittegunɔta*   man's name, imperfectly recorded.

*Kogayi*   Crow Town, sometimes spelled *Kagunyi,* one of the new Chickamauga towns built after the destruction of the original towns by Shelby (*koga,* crow + *yi,* locative suffix).

*Kuhli*   raccoon.

*Kuwahi*   mulberry place.

*McDonalᵭ, John*   like Cameron, above, a Scot and a deputy under Stuart. He married Annie Shorey, the daughter of William Shorey and Ghigooie. He and his Cherokee family stayed with the Chickamaugas even after British forces withdrew at the end of the American Revolution, and was the grandfather of later Principal Chief John Ross.

*'Ma'ᵭohi*   short for *Ama-eᵭohi* "water walker," recorded by the English as "Moytoy."

*Malaquo*   one of the Cherokee Overhills Towns, destroyed by Rutherford. Dragging Canoe was its war chief.

*Mankiller*   originally a rank, or a title—each town had a Mankiller— the word eventually evolved into a Cherokee surname. When James Vann called Doublehead "Babykiller," he was playing ironically on the Mankiller designation.

*Nanyehi*   possibly the name of the woman known as Nancy Ward. It's sometimes given as "Nani," which may be a short version of the same name. It may have been derived from *Nunnehi,* or *Nanehi,* the name of a race of invisible spirit people. Mooney translates the word, "I dwell habitually," and suggests the meaning, "dwellers anywhere . . . but implies having always been there." Their name is commonly and loosely translated "the Immortals."

*Ni*   look.

*Nicholehe*   one of the hostages murdered at Fort Prince George, name imperfectly recorded.

*Ni-on-e*   Cherokee woman's name, thought to be the name of the mother of Dragging Canoe.

*Nolichucky*   name of a river and of a town.

*Notsi*   pine.

*Nottley*   one of the Cherokee Valley Towns, destroyed by Rutherford.

*Nuhyunawi*   Stone Clad, according to Mooney, from *nunya*, rock, and *agwanuwu*, I am clothed or covered.

*Oasanoletah*   one of the hostages murdered at Fort Prince George, name imperfectly recorded.

*Ogan'sdo'*   contracted from *Ogana*, groundhog, and *asdoda*, I'm pounding it, commonly translated "Groundhog Sausage". The name is usually rendered in the histories as Oconostota.

*Osi*   a small, dome-shaped house traditionally outside the main house. Hothouse. Winter house.

*Ostenaco*   Cherokee name, imperfectly recorded.

*Ousonaletak*   one of the hostages murdered at Fort Prince George, name imperfectly recorded.

*Oustanatah*   one of the hostages murdered at Fort Prince George, name imperfectly recorded.

*Pearis, Richard*   a trader to the Cherokees from North Carolina. A Tory, Pearis fled to the Bahamas following the American Revolution. Among his Cherokee descendants, the spelling of the surname evolved into Parris. He was the author's sixth great-grandfather.

*Qualatchee*   one of the Cherokee Lower Towns, destroyed by Montgomery.

*Quarrasatahe*   one of the hostages murdered at Fort Prince George.

*Ridge*   short version of the name Kah-nung-da-cla-geh, or Gun-nun-da-legi, "One who follows the ridge." (The first spelling was recorded by John Ridge, Ridge's son. The second spelling is Mooney's.) Probably a more accurate rendition, given by Tom Belt, is Guh-na-da-tle-gi. Ridge became Major Ridge after having ridden with Andrew Jackson against the Creeks. Later he became the leader of the so-called Treaty Party, signing the Treaty of New Echota, or the Removal Treaty, which led to the Trail of Tears. For that action, he was killed following the Trail of Tears.

*Saloli*   squirrel.

*Sannaoeste*   one of the hostages murdered at Fort Prince George. Corrupt spelling.

*Savannah*   a treeless plain or flat open region.

*Sawanooga*   a man's name.

*Scotchie*   Cherokee nickname of *Alexander Cameron*. See above.

*Selu*   corn, or Corn, the first woman, wife of *Kanati.*

*Seneca*   one of the Cherokee Lower Towns, destroyed by Rutherford.

*Settico*   Chickamauga town, named for Overhills town destroyed by Rutherford.

*Sevier, John*   despite his career of outlawry, Cherokee-hater Sevier was forgiven and later elected to the Senate of the state of North Carolina in 1789.

*'Siyo*   Short for *osiyo,* a greeting.

*Sinawa*   a man's name.

*Skaleloske*   one of the hostages murdered at Fort Prince George.

*Soconee*   one of the Cherokee Lower Towns, destroyed by Rutherford.

*Sogwili*   horse.

*Stuart, John*   British superintendant of Southern Indian Affairs, a career army officer and an adopted Cherokee. Married a Cherokee woman. Known as Bushyhead to the Cherokees, his Cherokee descendants have Bushyhead as a surname.

*Tahlequah*   capital city of the Cherokee Nation following removal, now in Cherokee County, Oklahoma. There is a tale told that when the newly relocated Cherokee Nation was looking for a place to put its capital, some men were sent out to find a suitable location, one where three streams came together. They found a beautiful spot, but there were only two streams. One of the men at last said, *"Tahli eliqua,"* or *"Tahlequah,"* meaning "Two are enough." A slightly different version of the story is that three men were supposed to meet and make the decision. Two men met and waited some time, before one of them said, *"Tahlequah."* The truth is probably that neither tale represents anything that actually happened, and Tahlequah does not mean "Two are enough." It is probably the same word that still is used as a place name in the old Cherokee country: *"Tellico."* Its meaning has been lost, and its Western and more recent form has simply been anglicized and recorded differently.

*Tahli-tihi*   one of the hostages murdered at Fort Prince George. Literally, Two-killer.

*Talase*   Chickamauga town, named for Overhills town destroyed by Rutherford.

*Taliwa*   Cherokee town name.

*Tamatly*   Cherokee town name.

*Tanase*   Cherokee town name, origin of the name of the state of Tennessee.

*Tecumseh*   a Shawnee, he lived and fought for a time with the Chickamaugans. He later carved out his own place in history.

*Tellico*   ancient place name, meaning lost. Almost certainly the same name that has been rendered as *Tahlequah* in Oklahoma.

*Tenskwatawa,*   Tecumseh's brother, a Shawnee, later known as the Prophet or the Shawnee Prophet. His name has been translated as "the Open Door."

*Tomassee*   one of the Cherokee Lower Towns, destroyed by Rutherford.

*Totaiahoi*   one of the hostages murdered at Fort Prince George, name imperfectly recorded.

*Tsalagi*   the Cherokee pronunciation of the Choctaw and trade jargon word *Chalakee*. See *Chalakee* and *Cherokee* above.

*Tsan usdi*   "Little John," a nickname given to the hated enemy John Sevier, and later to the grandson of John McDonald, John Ross, who would become principal chief of the Cherokee Nation.

*Tsinohe*   one of the hostages murdered at Fort Prince George.

*Tsi suh na*   one of the hostages murdered at Fort Prince George.

*Tsisdu*   rabbit.

*Tsisdu*   one of the hostages murdered at Fort Prince George. See above.

*Tsisduh*   spoken contraction for *tsisduhna* a crayfish, or crawdad.

*Tsisqua*   bird.

*Tsisqua-ya*   real bird (the sparrow).

*Tsiyu*   dugout canoe.

*Tsiyu Gansini*   canoe, he is dragging it. This name has also been translated as "Otter Lifter" and "Ark Bearer." Dragging Canoe seems to be by far the best of the given choices.

*Tugaloo*   one of the Cherokee Lower Towns, destroyed by Rutherford.

*Tuskegee Island Town*   one of the Chickamauga towns built after Shelby's destruction of the original towns.

*Ujonati*   rattlesnake.

*Uk*   like the American English word *ass*, it can mean "buttocks" or "donkey."

*Ukah*   one of the hostages murdered at Fort Prince George.

*Ukah Ulah*   man's name *ukah*, owl + *ulah*, meaning "unknown."

*Ukitena*   abbreviated, *Uk'ten'*. (literally, keen-eyed). A mytholgical creature, like a giant rattlesnake with wings and antlers. He can look at a person and kill. His breath can kill, and he sometimes breaths fire. His has a crystal between his eyes which, if obtained by a gifted conjurer, is a valuable diving tool. See *uluhnsuti*.

*Uku-unega*   White Owl (*Uku* or *Ukah*, owl + *unega*, white).

*Uluhnsuti*   literally, transparent. A crystal, used for divining, said to have come from the forehead of an *Ukitena*, a giant anomolous creature from Cherokee mythology.

*Unoluhdani*   January.

*Usdi*   sometimes spelled *usti*, little, also an infant or small child.

*Ustally*   name of a town burned by Sevier and his Franklin militia.

*Ustanali*   a place name, denotes a natural rock dam across a creek.

*Vann, James*   half-breed son of *Joseph Vann* (see below), a Chickamaugan, he tried to prevent Doublehead from killing the Cavett family, and for Doublehead's actions there named Doublehead "Babykiller."

*Vann, Joseph*   white trader to the Cherokees, father of *James Vann* (see above).

*Wado*   thank you.

*Wahya*, sometimes *waya*   wolf.

*Walelu uh natsi luhgisdi*   spotted touch-me-not.

*Wanigisti*   "something is eating them," a childhood disease, possibly worms.

*Watauga*   from Watagi, ancient Cherokee town, meaning of word is lost.

*Watauga River*   river in Tennessee.

*Wataugans*   the white frontiersmen who settled, illegally at first, then with a lease from the Cherokees, the area known as Watauga or the Watauga Settlements, initially along the Watauga River.

*Whoa-tihi*   one of the hostages murdered at Fort Prince George. Spelling of the first part of the name is a corruption. *Tihi* is "killer."

*Willinawa*   a man's name, meaning unclear.

*Woði*   a red stone from which red paint is made, by extension, red paint, and paint.

*Woyi*   (literally, pigeon) one of the hostages released from Fort Prince George along with Agan'stat'.

*Ya*   real or original. Used as a suffix to a noun. See *tðiðqua-ya* and *Ani-yunwi-ya*.

*Yoneg*   short for *yonega*, a white person.

*Yu*   word with no translation, a formal closing to a song, prayer, etc.

*Yunwi*   a person.

CPSIA information can be obtained
at www.ICGtesting.com
Printed in the USA
LVHW031406280122
709441LV00001B/84